To David Lean

H. E. Bates

The Sleepless Moon

Penguin Books
in association with Michael Joseph

Penguin Books Ltd, Harmondsworth, Middlesex, England
Viking Penguin Inc., 40 West 23rd Street, New York, New York 10010, U.S.A.
Penguin Books Australia Ltd, Ringwood, Victoria, Australia
Penguin Books Canada Ltd, 2801 John Street, Markham, Ontario, Canada L3R 1B4
Penguin Books (N.Z.) Ltd, 182–190 Wairau Road, Auckland 10, New Zealand

First published by Michael Joseph 1956
Published in Penguin Books 1964
Reissued 1985

Copyright © H. E. Bates, 1956
All rights reserved

Printed and bound in Great Britain by
Cox & Wyman Ltd, Reading
Typeset in Linotype Granjon

PENGUIN BOOKS
The Sleepless Moon

H. E. Bates was born in 1905 at Rushden in Northampton-shire and was educated at Kettering Grammar School. He worked as a journalist and clerk on a local newspaper before publishing his first book, *The Two Sisters*, when he was twenty. In the next fifteen years he acquired a distinguished reputation for his stories about English country life. During the Second World War, he was a Squadron Leader in the R.A.F. and some of his stories of service life, *The Greatest People in the World* (1942), *How Sleep the Brave* (1943) and *The Face of England* (1953) were written under the pseudonym of 'Flying Officer X'. His subsequent novels of Burma, *The Purple Plain* and *The Jacaranda Tree*, and of India, *The Scarlet Sword*, stemmed directly or indirectly from his war experience in the Eastern theatre of war.

In 1958 his writing took a new direction with the appearance of *The Darling Buds of May*, the first of the popular Larkin family novels, which was followed by *A Breath of French Air*, *When the Green Woods Laugh* and *Oh! To Be in England* (1963). His autobiography appeared in three volumes, *The Vanished World* (1969), *The Blossoming World* (1971), and *The World in Ripeness* (1972). His last works included the novel, *The Triple Echo* (1971) and a collection of short stories, *The Song of the Wren* (1972). Perhaps one of the most famous works of fiction is the best-selling novel *Fair Stood the Wind for France* (1944). H. E. Bates also wrote miscellaneous works on gardening, essays on country life, several plays including *The Day of Glory* (1945); *The Modern Short Story* (1941) and a story for children, *The White Admiral* (1968). His works have been translated into sixteen languages and a posthumous collection of his stories, *The Yellow Meads of Asphodel*, appeared in 1976.

H. E. Bates was awarded the C.B.E. in 1973 and died in January 1974. He was married in 1931 and had four children.

Part 1

Chapter One

After all there were no carriages for her wedding. The distance between the church porch and the house on the corner of the square was so short, everyone said, that it was simply not worth while.

It was still possible, in the year 1922, to hire carriages in Orlingford: carriages with white horses carrying white-ribboned whips for weddings, the same carriages with black horses for the dead. She wanted very much to have carriages; but it was, as everyone said, quite unnecessary and silly for so short a distance and she was too shy to make a fuss.

And so in her quiet way she kept quiet about it. There were no carriages and she did not complain. She simply walked with Melford Turner across the churchyard, crunching loudly on sugary brown gravel, between long fat paunches of grave-mounds freshly mown and here and there already planted with scarlet geraniums for summer. In a far corner of the churchyard a double white cherry was still in flower and now and then the wind puffed from it dry buttons of blossom that drifted against the head-stones. It was the first warm wind of summer, coming straight from the south, and she felt it blowing the white silk of her dress against her long legs and then smoothly under the silk itself, rippling across her skin. The feeling of this gentle summer wind on her body was more exciting to her than anything she remembered that day. It made her feel astonishingly free and exalted. It was more exciting than the moment when the wind in a sudden gust snatched the veil from her head and she turned and caught it as it flew upward and in doing so thought she saw the steeple and its four battlements suddenly totter like ninepins across the sky.

'It was ordained as a remedy against sin,' she remembered a voice saying and then they were at the house. The old strong grey walls were pleasing to her with their sharp-masoned stone. The long upper windows were painted white, with black sills. The door had panels of white and black to match them. And then at the bottom the single horizontal window of the shop, painted black too, and above it the upright gold raised lettering: *Melford Turner, Provisions. Blender of Tea and Coffee. Finest Wines and Spirits.* The shop closed for the afternoon; the blinds still undrawn; the coffee roaster cold and cleaned in one corner; everything about it all immaculately fresh and painted; the two door-sills whitened over a second time since twelve o'clock in order to erase the footprints of the boy bringing telegrams; the brass knocker like an altar-piece in the sun. Confetti was dancing everywhere and among it a few pink and white florets of chestnut blossom blown gently down from the big trees at the side of the square.

There was only a single moment in which she could look at the square. The picture of it flashed past her like something she had seen for the first time and was to lose for ever: the stone quadrangle of houses, the market cross in the centre, the little stone town hall that was also the council chamber and the lock-up jail, the four shops, the line of chestnut-trees, the bank that opened only from noon to 2.45 on Wednesday and Friday afternoons. It floated from her horizontal view on a turn of air, lifted up, absorbed in sunlight, and was obliterated.

Presently she was in the house, the first person to cross the white threshold, the long dress trailing over the steps like a silk snake, her mind and her vision equally dazzled. She wondered suddenly why she was there. She wondered how it was that she had ever come to be there. The wife of Melford Turner, who would one day be mayor, could surely not be anything but an important person and she did not feel important. She had never felt important. A strong smell of linseed oil and wax candles and wine and brewing tea filled the house. Guests were laughing and talking everywhere and someone actually called her Mrs Turner by name.

'You were so quiet, Mrs Turner. You were the quietest, calmest person there.'

It was her nature to be quiet; she could not help it; she did not suppose she would ever be otherwise. She had always found it hard to demonstrate her feelings. She supposed she would always be shy. Perhaps that was why, with her large brown eyes, she looked so composed and dignified, too dignified for a girl of twenty-four, with a composure she did not feel, exactly as she had looked and felt when dancing with Melford Turner for the first time eighteen months before.

And then she remembered why she was there. She was there, stupid though it sounded now, by accident, because someone had dared her to be. She had been dared by her friend Norma Willis to dance with Melford Turner, at a mayoral New Year Dance, in a *Ladies' Excuse Me.* Norma Willis was a fat, shapeless, freckled girl of thirty who sat most of the evening licking a strawberry ice with the tip of her thick red tongue as if she were taunting it. The two girls, one so fat, the other so shy, spent most of the evening waiting for dances that never happened, until finally Norma Willis began giggling into a little blue and white cambric handkerchief folded triangular-wise like a sandwich and said:

'I dare you to ask him in the *Ladies' Excuse Me.* Go on, Constance – you daren't do it. You're scared. Will you do it if I do first?'

Constance was horrified. The two girls shared a room over Thompson and Phillips drapery, at the south end of High Street. In the shop Constance worked upstairs in the millinery department and Miss Willis on the ground floor, in materials and dresses. The girls worked from eight-thirty in the morning until seven at night, with an extra hour on Fridays and two extra hours on Saturdays. The position of assistant in a good shop like Thompson and Phillips, though badly paid, gave them a certain social standing above maid-servants and factory workers and they shared a prospect of saving perhaps ten pounds a year if they were very frugal, well-behaved, and lucky.

'You're frightened. I'll ask him first if you'll come later. Will you ask him if I do?'

Firmly she said she would not ask him; she could not be seen lowering herself in that way.

'It isn't lowering. That's what the dance is for. To get people together. To get the shy ones out of their shells. You're frightened.'

She was shy: that was true. But she was not frightened.

'You haven't got it in you. And what's more I've only had two dances all night. If I can ask him you can. I'm going to ask him.'

'But why him? – why him particularly?'

'Oh! he's so gentlemanly. He looks so nice in evening dress.'

Two minutes later Norma Willis was dancing with Melford Turner and Constance sat watching them, unbelievably shocked and now also frightened. She was frightened first that she would be stupid enough to ask him to dance; then that she would be stupid enough not to. She sat scoured by waves of uneasiness that made the palms of her white gloves wet with perspiration.

A few moments later she could bear it no longer and was on her feet, touching Miss Willis on the shoulder.

'Excuse me. May I please?'

The first few moments of dancing were most embarrassing because she was the same height as Melford Turner. There was no way of looking away from him. He kept his grey eyes on her and held her rigidly, almost at arm's length, and looked at her as if he were surprised or impressed or simply incredulous about the assurance and dignity of a girl whose name he did not know.

'I'm sorry the band is so awful.' He apologized twice about the band. He spoke as if in some way it were his own responsibility. 'I'm sorry they didn't get a decent band.'

Although she was fond of music she had not noticed the band. His voice was slow and dry: not an unpleasant voice. His face was long and thin-fleshed and dry too and she knew that he was several years older than she was: at least ten years older, perhaps even older than that. He was one of the few men wearing evening dress and the starched front of his shirt protruded stiffly and noticeably, like a hard white breast-bone.

'It'll be better when they get the new band.' His jaw was bluish with close-shaving; his manners were somehow pleasant without his smiling much. 'They tell me a chap named Palmer is starting one. Did you hear that?'

No: she had not heard that. She seemed to speak easily and calmly. It might have been thought that she was the calmest, serenest person on the floor.

'Would you have the next dance with me?'

Yes, she said: she would be glad to have the next dance with him. She spoke automatically, without thinking, without apparent surprise, and again there was nothing in his face to show that she was anything but full of serenity.

'Thank you.' He smiled thinly: a sort of partially repressed smile, a mere half-aristocratic stretch of the lips. He said he was glad about the dance. It would mean that he could be sure that no one would poach her.

The word made her smile a little too.

'Do you mind if I ask you something?' he said.

No, she said, what was it? She did not mind.

'You're not from this part of the world, are you?'

No, that was right, she said. She was not from that part of the world. She was, she said, from Godmanchester.

'I thought you didn't speak with our local accent,' he said.

Was she as bad as that? she said.

'It's not that,' he said. 'Don't think that. I meant it was nice to hear someone whose voice was different. And I take a bit of an interest in accents – in local words.'

She danced with him twice more that evening. She noticed that his hands were long and bony and white, with exceptionally fine cuticles. His dark hair was thinning very slightly at the temples and was meticulously brushed back, peppered very minutely with grey flecks about the ears. His voice was always thin, in a certain way rather deferential, but whenever he spoke to her, nearly always to ask questions, it was with kindness and the manner of an uninquisitive listener.

'And if you don't mind my asking: how do you come to be so far from home?'

In her own particular quiet way she told him very simply about that. Her father had been knocked down and killed in a street accident; her mother had got married again to someone she, the girl, did not care for. She thought it better to move away from home and she had heard from an aunt of the post – she did not call it a job – in Orlingford. There was no more to it than that.

Only that you could not spend all your life, could you, she said, in the one same little all-behind-hand town?

'That was a good expression,' he said. He laughed for the first time; his voice crackled like stiff crumpled paper. 'But what makes you think you won't find the all-behind-hand here? There isn't much difference between Orlingford and any other little country town.'

Oh, wasn't there? she said. She didn't know about that. You never knew what you would find.

'Well,' he said, 'I've lived here for forty years and there's been no sign of an earthquake yet.'

In that way she knew how old he was. Forty: a person, as she regarded it, another generation away from her. Almost a middle-aged man. A fixture. She noticed that he wore a heavy gold signet ring on the third finger of his right hand and that too helped to establish the impression of a personality fixed, settled, and consolidated.

During all this she was not excited. The sight of a ring on a man's finger always gave her an inexplicable feeling of disquiet. It always seemed in a curious way unnatural and she looked at the heavy ring several times in a half-bemused sort of way without really knowing it.

'I see you're looking at my ring,' he said. 'It was my father's. His father had it given to him by his mother when he married. It must be all of a hundred years old. It's become a kind of tradition now to pass it on from son to son.'

She began to be aware, then, for the first time, of a background of prosperity: evening clothes, gold ring, clean meticulous cuticles, ancestry.

'My father,' he told her, 'was Mayor here seventeen times.'

She supposed, she said, that that meant he could be Mayor quite often too?

'They've asked me three times already,' he said, 'and I've told them No. When I'm married I'll say Yes. Not until. I always say the job is a two-horse affair.'

That expression about horses was one, she afterwards discovered, that he used quite often.

'So now the Claridges are Mayors. Arthur is Mayor this year. Thomas will be Mayor next year. It alternates between the two families. There's only been one break in that in fifty years and that was when a man named Spencer stood.'

It was six months before he kissed her. She did not really mind this so much because, in her great shyness, she dreaded the moment even more than he did. And having dreaded it, she was carried away: not exultantly, not on the smallest breath of anything ethereal or tender, but in a surprising surge of pity. The simple act of kissing her made him shake all over. He might just as well have been terrified by the thought of having an aching and unanaesthetized tooth drawn.

'You see,' he said, 'you see,' and in brittle spasmodic bursts he revealed that this extraordinary thing was something that had never happened before. She was not amazed. She thought afterwards that she would have been amazed if, on the contrary, he had told her anything different. She kissed him back in a manner that had something consolatory in it. She did not mean it to be quite like that, not quite as a mother kissing away tears or pain or misunderstanding, but it was the best that she could do.

At the end of it all she felt him shudder. It was summer time. She was wearing a thin blue voile blouse with long sleeves through which her arms were visible. That too seemed to frighten him into inertia. He could not bring himself to take hold of her arms. He put his hands instead on her shoulders and then held her at arm's length, much as he had done when dancing. She knew that all about him a world was violently rocking while her own now remained in unexpected suspense, astonishingly stable and unshaken. Afterwards she used to ask herself what would have happened if she had been sensible and detached enough to resist two impulses of stupidity, the first when she had danced with him, the second when she suddenly put out her arms and embraced him and held him to her like a distressed and breathless dog that had been running in fear of being beaten.

That evening, when she went home to Norma, she sat on the edge of her bed and said, 'If he ever asks me to marry him I'll say no. I know I couldn't bring myself to do it. I know I never could.' Six weeks later he did ask her and she gave her acceptance exactly as she had given the acceptance of the first extraordinary kiss. It was consolatory; it was something to help soften his awkwardness. She did not experience a single sensory moment that excited her. She felt overwhelmingly shy and wondered instead if it was really herself and not some amorphous and separate creature who was saying 'Yes' to him by the gate that led into the orchard at the back of his own house, in

13

winter darkness, just out of reach of the path that went through the churchyard.

And now she was in the house. She had been into it many times before. She already knew every room of it. Physically it was familiar to her in detail, exactly as the stables behind it and the shop in front of it were familiar, and exactly as the orchard, with its trees of small sweet pears and golden gages, its apples and lines of red currant trees, was familiar. It was a very pleasant house. The orchard between its four high stone walls was untidy, its large trees unpruned and shady, its yellow August pears falling down and rolling wine-scented into uncut grass; a lost and mellow place at the end of which there were nightingales on June nights and even, in very hot summers, a few apricots on the walls.

She could hardly have asked for a pleasanter house in which to live. Above it, like a great stone pencil that threw morning shadow on the orchard, rose the spire of the church, with the hands of its clock sailing slowly like golden boats round a pond. That too seemed part of the house; it was impossible ever to separate spire and clock and shadow, together with the sound of bells, from the existence of the house and shop on the corner of the square. All that too was wonderfully pleasant: the white double cherry blossoming in spring, choir-boys like fluttering magpies hurrying across the green churchyard under the sound of bells, the round solid clock-chimes that, so often afterwards, kept her awake at night. She knew that she could not, and moreover ought not to, ask for more.

'Mrs Turner, I should like to drink your health. Mrs Turner, may we offer our congratulations? Constance, you looked wonderful. You were the quietest, calmest person there.'

There were port and sherry to drink, but she moved among the guests without a glass. The afternoon had grown very warm indoors. At the extreme upper edge of her cheeks were two bright spots no larger than birds' eggs where her blood had flushed up. For some reason they made her eyes seem larger and fuller than usual, just as the white oval of her headpiece made her hair seem a shade or two darker. The long white silk dress made her seem unusually tall and under the bodice of it her breasts curved out young and firm and in proportion.

Just before she ran upstairs to change the dress for her travelling things she heard someone begin calling:

'Where is Melford? Has anyone seen Melford? We want to take a photograph. We want a group in the garden. Where is Melford? Somebody find Melford please.'

There was some laughter, together with calls of 'Melford!' and then another voice:

'You might know where Melford is.'

'Where? Where is Melford?'

She found herself laughing too, as if this particular piece of the wedding was a foreshadowed joke with which she was already quite familiar.

'You might know,' someone said, and again there was laughter. 'Melford is saying good-bye to Pilfer.'

Melford Turner could not afford to keep more than two hunters; sometimes, as at the time of his marriage to Constance, he kept only one. He did not count the pony that drove his delivery cart. But each of the last of his three hunters, the first two chestnuts, the third a black, had been called Pilfer. He had no explanation for the name. It was an odd and endearing word that had dropped into his head one day when he was giving some lumps of sugar to the first of the two chestnuts. The horse began nuzzling at the pocket of his riding habit and suddenly he was saying: 'You'd pilfer, would you? You damned cheeky, knowing old Pilfer.' After that there seemed no reason to change the names of his subsequent horses and now he could think of no horse of his with another name. It was a soft and curious name. It ran off the tongue affectionately. At the same time he felt there was something rather cheeky about it, something a little spirited. It fitted the sort of horse he rather liked: a reasonably spirited horse, friendly, not too docile but with manners and character. The present Pilfer, the black, was exactly like that. But now he had plans for keeping two horses because of Constance, who he hoped would also ride. If she did not ride he hoped she would use a horse for driving out sometimes.

When he left the house on the afternoon of his wedding and crossed the yard at the back and entered the stables it was not quite true that he had gone merely to say good-bye to a horse. The horse was the only excuse he could think of that would allow him to get away by himself for a moment or two without appearing eccentric before his guests. He knew that no one would be surprised if he disappeared for a moment to say good-bye to Pilfer.

But when he reached the stables he did not bother to enter the box where the horse was standing. He unbolted the door of the empty box instead and went inside. In the stable, out of the sun, the dark air was almost cold. He breathed at it eagerly for a few moments, panting like a man taking a long-needed drink of water, and then he shut his eyes and pressed his back against the door.

Through the coolness of the dark stable air a recurrent impression of the agony of the marriage service kept coming back to him. It came as unreal, diffused and haunting as a nightmare. He had not slept the night before and at the moment when he was obliged to stand up for Constance's entry into the church his body rocked with sudden sickness and he knew that he was falling down.

Somehow he did not fall down. He gripped both hands against the edges of his cut-away coat and stared beyond the priest in front of him and at the high stained glass window behind. He looked once, and only once, with the sideways wiry jerk of a ventriloquist's doll, at Constance. She smiled and he felt his belly, in terror, running to water.

He could not remember much after that. He did not want to remember. He still felt sick. The only relief he now felt was the relief of having got through the whole affair without falling down or otherwise making a fool of himself in front of the congregation. The other thing that had heightened his fear into nausea was the first sight of Constance in her long silk dress. Its peculiar substance, its smooth white shine and its way of fitting closely to her skin made him very sharply aware of her body. He had never really been aware of it like that before. He had continually conducted himself with her with a half-detached affectionate formality that concealed all adoration. He had hardly ever been able to do more than grasp her hands or hold her by the shoulders or walk with her arm in arm. His own shyness, fused with hers, had held their relationship, over and over again, in a vacuum.

A few moments later he heard people begin calling his name from the house. He slipped through the dividing door of the two boxes. His horse, hearing him come in, stamped a front hoof on the bricks and turned his head and gave a whisk of the stiff black tail. Melford wished that this single moment, in which the eye of the horse turned in the shadowy stable like a glistening oyster, could have been expanded into the whole afternoon, leaving him free and secluded and mercifully apart from everybody, but a moment later people were at the door and someone was saying:

'Ah! caught you, Melford. Didn't I say? Saying good-bye to Pilfer – as if we didn't know!'

Presently he was standing confusedly in the garden, in the centre of a group of guests. From under a black triangle of cloth a figure, in brilliant sunlight, put out a red rubber ball and squeezed it and said:

'One more please! And this time, Mr Turner, a little closer to Mrs Turner please – closer – a little more intimate please – '

He smiled and felt the silk of Constance's dress touching him and a wag called out:

'Go on, Melford, she won't bite you.'

He smiled again and caught, in the warm summer air, a sweet-sharp breath of Constance's perfume.

'Too late now!' a voice called. 'He's already bitten.'

The figure of the photographer, besmirched with a large yellow-toothed smile, came from under the black cloth and advanced on the centre of the group.

'Mr Turner, please – may I? More like this. The hand up a little – like so. Better, Mr Turner, better – the hand up a little more – that's it, splendid, keep it like that. And Mrs Turner – perhaps Mrs Turner could lean across a little, resting on Mr Turner? That's it, that's it! – Rest on Mr Turner – Hold that, please.'

He felt Constance's soft young arm against his own. He stared ahead of him with an inert smile on his face, beyond the black cloth of the camera, to where young pears were already forming on trees in the orchard. Inconsequently he thought of the oyster-eye of Pilfer and then he wished his mother were there.

'If this doesn't break it,' someone said, 'nothing will.'

A tear came into his eye. He heard Norma Willis's giggle. Then Agnes Twelvetree, the middle-aged daughter of his solicitor, Charles Edward Twelvetree, said in her brusque way:

'For goodness gracious everybody quiet in the bear-garden please. The train goes in three-quarters of an hour.'

Always, long afterwards, Constance vividly remembered the train. It was one long unurgent essay in kindness, in pleasant moments that were created softly like the soundless stitches in a piece of knitting. 'Are you all right, dear? Is there something you want? Would you rather sit here?' Half-way through it she and Melford walked through the corridor to the dining-car to have tea. And there was some delay about the order because Melford insisted on having real fresh cream, and not milk, with the tea.

'There wasn't any need to ask for cream,' she said. 'It doesn't really matter.'

'This is our wedding day,' he said, 'we want the best, don't we?'

Then she said, as in fact she had already said once or twice previously:

'You know, it seems awfully silly, but I've never seen the sea before.'

'You will like it at Eastbourne,' he said. 'It's very select. If we get the room I've asked for you'll be able to look all the way up the gardens to the cliffs. The coast is wonderful there.'

In the way he tipped the waiter a shilling, taking the coin from his right-hand pocket of his grey waistcoat, holding it between thumb and forefinger, there was no hint of nervousness, still less of distraction. Nor, back in the compartment, did he look anything but composed as he took a cigar from his inside jacket pocket and said:

'Shall I smoke it now? George Makins gave it to me just as we were coming away.'

'Yes,' she said, 'smoke it now, dear. That would be nice for you.'

'No,' he said, 'I don't think I will. I'll save it for tonight. We've only half an hour to go now and tonight there'll be more time.'

And at the hotel it was the room he wanted. He remembered

it, and had asked for it, because of a series of visits with his parents as a boy. The big windows were rounded at the top, with thick mahogany divisions and scalloped yellow blinds with lace fringes and long silk tassels. The wallpaper repeated itself in big warm red patterns of fleur-dy-lys. Constance had brought her bridal bouquet of gardenia and carnations with her and a maid came up with a vase to arrange the flowers, which shone sharply, like china, against the thick crimson paper.

'And the sea,' she said, 'I didn't think it would be so near. You can even see it reflecting on the ceiling, Melford.'

After dinner they sat over coffee for a long time and then they danced for an hour. He held her, as he had always done, at arm's length. He said once or twice: 'Not too tired? You must say if you're tired.'

She said she was not tired. And then, at the fourth or fifth time of asking, she suddenly said:

'Yes, I think I am after all. It's been a long day. It was a long way in the train.'

It was then, after they had climbed to the head of the first flight of stairs, that he said he thought it would be as good a moment as any to try George Makin's cigar. 'It'll give you a chance to finish your unpacking and that sort of thing. I'll be up in five minutes or so.'

He went downstairs. She went alone into the bedroom. She switched on the light. In the ceiling a big ugly green chandelier with brass limbs and inverted opaque glass cups had been converted from gas to electricity and the room was filled with the white light of half a dozen bulbs. She stood uncertainly in the centre of the room, the harsh light pouring down on her. On the bed, the sheets of which had been turned down at the corners like two opposite pages of a book somebody had wished to mark, her nightdress, a pale blue one with ribbon threaded through the neck, was laid out next to Melford's night-shirt. The night-shirt, also laid out, looked remarkably like a surplice. She stood uncertainly looking at it for a few moments and then she switched off the light. Even when the light had been switched off the room was not quite dark. From the esplanade below the hotel the light of street lamps shining upward came through the thin fabric of the blinds and diffused itself throughout the room.

After a time she let up one of the blinds a little and sat by the window. It was open at the top. She could hear the sound of the sea. It made a series of regular hissing sighs as it flowed and receded over the pebbles of the shore. Below, on the esplanade, people were still walking to and fro, and it was clearly true, as Melford had said, that you could see far along the gardens to the cliffs beyond. In fact she could see that the march of lamps, as it continued along the esplanade, climbed half-way up to the sky.

After she had waited for more than half an hour she drew the blind again and then began to undress. She was a tall girl – it was something Melford had liked about her from the very first – with long slim thighs and sloping shoulders. Her body had still not developed fully. It looked like a cream-white pencil with a black charcoal head as she stood by the bedside wondering whether or not she should put on her nightgown.

She finally decided not to put it on. She lay down instead as she was, pulling the sheets up to her shoulders. It was quiet and she listened to the continued sound of the sea. The repeated sigh, the hiss, the sucking back of sand and shingle down the slope of beach made a single hypnotic rhythm in the summer night air.

Over and beyond it she lay listening for the sound of Melford coming back. The act of undressing had excited her. She trembled once or twice as she lay there but because of the darkness she was no longer shy. There was, she thought, no need now to be shy. She was married; she was a wife and she must not be shy. This was not the train where only cream was good enough for tea, or the dance-floor, or the orchard, or the churchyard where even the dancing white florets of white cherry and blowing confetti killed all sense of secrecy. Everything was secret now. She was married now. It was very different now.

She lay there by herself for a long time, listening, partly hyno-tized, to the sound of the sea. At midnight half the lamps on the esplanade went out and most of the rest an hour later.

Somewhere between the extinguishing of the first lamps and the last she fell asleep and woke again. She felt chilly and she put on her nightgown. By the time Melford came in at half past one she was asleep again. And then he was so quiet, padding his way about the dark room like a cautious and purblind cat, that he did not wake her.

Chapter Two

When she came back from her honeymoon at the beginning of July there appeared to be no change in her except a certain stiffness in her bearing. She might still have been a single woman. She still seemed very shy and serene, but now there was a certain coolness in her face. The experience of going a hundred and fifty miles southward had given her the chance, for the first time, of seeing the sea, of eating her food in a good hotel, of having cream in her tea not merely one day on a train but every day, of parading a different dress along the lawns of an esplanade every Sunday and of hearing, above all, the sound of the sea.

She felt she would never forget the sound of the sea. The slightly haunted expression of coolness in her face was partly a reflection of the fact that she was really still listening to it. She felt she would go on listening to it for the rest of her life: to the almost tired, lonely but mocking hiss of it that had at first so fascinated her and had ended, after three weeks, in haunting and taunting her like an unpleasant tune she could not get out of her head.

She had grown so used to it during this time that one result of her coming home was that she found she could not sleep well. The sea had gone; now the church clock, chiming and striking four times an hour, forty times a night, less than fifty yards away across the churchyard, took its place. So much farther north the full summer nights were also shorter and whiter. On stark moonlight nights in July it was hardly dark at all.

She and Melford shared a room, and in it two new brass beds draped at the head with thin transparent white material threaded through with pink ribbon, overlooking the square. But they undressed, each night, in separate dressing-rooms across the corridor. Melford, from long bachelor habit, always took a long time to get ready for bed. He spent considerable time doing things like clipping superfluous hair growth out of his ears and nostrils, attending to his nails and cuticles and then brushing his teeth and hair. It was sometimes nearly an hour before he came into the bedroom, smelling slightly antiseptic, wearing a light woollen dressing-gown and carrying a book or more often than not the local evening paper.

'Here's an extraordinary thing, Constance. Listen to this. A sexton at a churchyard down in Warwickshire found sixty pounds of honey in one of the church bells. Sixty pounds – that's over half a hundredweight. It seems they wondered why the bell hadn't rung properly for years – oh! really, I find that a bit hard to swallow, don't you? That's a bit of a fairy tale. By the way, I'm going over to Weston tomorrow to see a mare I thought might do for you. You'll come over, won't you?'

'Why couldn't the honey be in the church bell?'

'Oh! my dear.' His reproaches, as his mother had always instructed, were never unkindly. His voice gave the impression of being gloved. 'It just isn't practical, is it? I mean the honey hanging upside down? It's another of these newspaper tales. They've got to fill the papers.'

She said she supposed they had.

'But I remember learning at school,' she said, 'that the hexagonal design of honey-comb was the strongest shape there is in nature.'

'Oh! did you?' He brushed a particle of clipped hair from his nostril. 'Well, I don't know about that. In any case I think you'll find it octagonal, dear.'

'Perhaps it is.'

Honey in a church bell – she seemed to see it hanging there, sealed in its golden comb. A strange thing, she thought, if it were true – bees flying so high, multiplying behind the dark belfry stone, building their own waxy private cloisters.

She lay thinking of it for a long time. And then the pleasant golden idea drifted away and she was alone and starkly awake in a July night that still had a reflection of pale yellow across the sky. The church clock, which she had stopped noticing for the hour while Melford was doing his toilet and reading his paper, began to boom and mock with its regular quarters across the sky. Between the four quarters chiming the hour and the actual strike of the hour there was an interval of what seemed like half a minute: a gap of tension and a death of sound that made her feel the strike would never come. Each time it made her uneasy or unnerved her. And then when the strike eventually boomed out she felt her nerves contract again, fusing like the sharp and jagged edges of a severed wire. All her body began to feel bleached and dry and without softness. Her mind raced about and picked up the same jerky spasmodic thoughts over and over again until there was no way, all night, of soothing it down.

In the mornings she came downstairs to a routine that had gone on so long that Melford never noticed it.

The shop opened at eight o'clock and by a quarter past, when she was dressing, there was a smell of watered dust from the pavement outside. In the house there were three other people besides themselves: Mrs Butterworth, a heavy, placid woman with a large grey bun of hair who kept house, Edna, a general maid, who wore an ordinary white cap and apron in the mornings and changed into cream ones in the afternoon, and Britton, a tall gangling man with clothes-peg legs who cleaned the stables, dug the garden and groomed and exercised Pilfer.

At nine o'clock Constance and Melford breakfasted in the dining-room at a thick oblong mahogany dining-table with pie-crust edges. Mrs Butterworth, wearing a fresh starched apron, brought in eggs, bacon and sausages in plated entrée dishes and plenty of dry toast in large silver racks.

'And how is Mrs Butterworth this morning? Sleep well? No cheese dreams?'

Mrs Butterworth ate frequent suppers of cocoa and toasted cheese. She slept restlessly and there were constant jokes, the whole year through, but especially in winter, about her cheese dreams.

Between eight-thirty and nine o'clock Melford walked about the yard, smoked a mild Virginia cigarette in an amber holder and talked to Britton about Pilfer and then to Pilfer, for a few minutes, alone. It was pleasant to put his hands against the thick underlip of the horse and work his way down, caressing

23

and patting, to the deep pouch of the throat and the hard column of the neck. 'How's my old boy? How's old Pilfer rascal, you rascal you? You're a cheat, that's what you are, you're a cheating old rascal of a Pilfer.' In the air was a sharp, fleshy, ammoniac smell of horses, with a lighter corn fragrance of fresh straw floating about it. It was a wonderful smell. He liked that smell. He always filled his lungs with it, giving deep, hearty, eagerly snapping bites at it, in the warm summer morning air.

At nine-thirty he was in the shop. He wore a black coat and striped grey-and-black trousers and a black cravat with a butterfly collar. The shop had two long counters, the one for butter and ham and bacon and lard on the left side as you came in from the door, the other for tea and biscuits and coffee and porridge oats and things of that kind on the other. Big black and green canisters of tea labelled with golden Chinese lettering stood about the shadows and a pale young man named Flaky worked at the bacon-cutter.

'I must tell you how he came to be known as Flaky.' In two months Melford repeated the explanation several times. 'When he first came here as a boy he was terribly nervous and one day he fainted. I picked him up and when he came round I asked him how he was feeling. "All air, Mr Melford," he said. "All light and air. Just like a piece of flaky pastry." '

At the far end of the shop a young woman with soft red hair and almost hairless eyes named Miss Mackness worked in a glass and mahogany box, taking cash. With her pale red hair and an almost albino pinkness under her lower lids she looked frail and sickly, and Melford poked mild fun at her behind her back and called her 'Our Miss Weakness'.

'Ah! but that's naughty of me. She's really a very capable girl, our Miss Mackness. She may look weak, but there's nothing weak about her head.'

Among the groceries moved the white-aproned, bald, unsmiling figure of a middle-aged man named Hyde. His presence was stiff and rather soldierly. His manner was to remain aloof from people, especially from Melford, coldly, not speaking except when spoken to. His eyes were flinty and contemptuous. He was drawn with a pitying sort of affection towards Miss Mackness, imprisoned in her cash-box, and was aware that Melford called her 'Our Miss Weakness' behind her back.

'Very well, Mr Melford, if you say so. I will see to it, Mr Melford, if that's the way you feel.'

There was a certain touch of exclusiveness about Melford's trade. Above and beyond things like butter and rice and cheese and barrels of common vinegar that were kept in the cellar downstairs he had a constant call for more unusual things. From country houses outside the town there were not only demands for things like Roquefort cheese, anchovies, the best Lapsang Soochong tea and olives, but real green turtle, Strasbourg *pâté de foie* and even bombay duck. He kept a regular stock of Hymettus honey and palm hearts and pumpernickel. His more modest clientèle in the town was made up mostly of small businessmen, other shopkeepers, doctors and solicitors and retired persons, who could not afford these things. But out in the country big houses held parties, mostly in summer or during the hunting season, and frequently gave balls and dances, so that Melford was never without a regular supply of best wine vinegars, Indian chutneys, Chinese ginger and cumquats and could even get, at less than twenty-four hours' notice, by telegram, such things as caviare and sharks' fins. One or two of his friends in the Hunt were retired military men who had seen service in India or Hong Kong and retained a taste for things they had learned to like there. There was a Colonel Fawcett who was fond of roll-mops and salami. Melford himself was very fond of crystallized ginger and he liked to help himself to a piece of it from a jar on the counter as he came into the shop after lunch, afterwards standing looking across the square, slowly chewing and licking sugar from his fingers.

His delivery van, driven by an ex-yeomanry man named Jennings, was a kind of coach-built trap in bottle-green and brown, highly varnished, with a big black leather hood that could be folded down. Sometimes on a particularly fine afternoon, for a particular customer, he would drive it himself, trotting the horse slowly out to a house in the country. Close to the town the countryside was flat upland, with few woods, the fields mostly of wheat and potatoes and grass, with big hedgerows of hawthorn and bony ash-trees. To the north-east it gradually richened and four miles away a river came in on a series of long curves over which bridges went with low thumb-and-forefinger spans of stone.

In this park-like valley of big beeches and oaks and occasional gigantic limes, drowsily sweet in summer above acres of meadow hay, he preferred to do what hunting he did. He knew that the barer, flatter hedgerow countryside was really better for hunting but it always seemed to him cold and unexciting and without surprise. He liked the richer hollows about the river, the swampy copses of alder and osier that were such impossible places in wet weather, and the brown leaf-deep oak-woods on higher ground. In the heart of this country was a long wood, mostly oak, but with occasional thin hornbeam, where you could ride for nearly a mile down the central riding, dead straight, and see the other end all the way like the far eye of a telescope. He supposed that wood was full of foxes, but it did not bother him that he had hardly ever seen one there. It was full of nightingales too, but then he was never there in summer.

His chief pleasure in that wood was the long telescopic drive between the yellowing, browning, dripping leaves. On autumn days, before the air began to have its first clenching cold, the wood was full of that tan-sharp smell of oak leaf dying. You never got that smell on the barer, ash-and-hawthorn land. It always struck into him a fine exhilaration. Physically he was not only tall but angular, with surprisingly big shoulders that were not very obvious because of his height. As he smelled the first deep dying oak-smell he always felt the excitement of it flick down, like the lick of a snake, through his limbs. His muscles seemed to turn pleasantly warm as he sat on the horse and then the warmth, darting, shot through the centre of his body.

Until he met Constance he had never experienced anything like these same sensations except once. That was at his confirmation in church. The bishop had touched him with his hands and in a second the darting lick of warmth was running down through him like water.

When you came out at the end of the wood the village of Ascott St Mary lay in the hollow below. The village seemed to have been pinned on the green landscape by a short stone steeple. Among the patchy roofs of thatch and stone was a pub called

The George and Crown, kept by a Mrs Duncan and her daughter Effie. Mrs Duncan prepared wonderful lunches for shooting parties and hunts, Melford supplying much of the grocery, and if ever you called back late in the afternoon after a run there would still be a plate of hot Irish stew left or a ham sandwich or a porty Stilton cheese. The pub itself was thatched. The tables and chairs in the public bars were boned white by scrubbing. At the Ascott St Mary meet, in January, Melford always spent a night there. The place, clean and warm and full of malty odours and old tobacco smoke that spread up into the two storeys of bedrooms, seemed almost better than home.

Towards the end of July he drove out here one afternoon with Constance, just the two of them in the delivery van with its hood thrown back, to choose her mare.

'We'll go to Weston to see the animal first and then on the way back, if you like, we'll have tea at Mrs Duncan's.'

'Don't talk about tea,' she said. 'It's so hot now.'

'Well, anything you like, dear. I'm sure Mrs Duncan can fetch up something cold from the cellar.'

Heat blazed on the landscape in curious horizontal bars that trembled at the rim of sky. Harvest had already begun in a few fields and Constance heard sometimes the dry hustle of oat-straw as men set up the sheaves.

'I hope you'll like this mare. I sent Britton over to see and he says she's pretty fair.'

'You mustn't ask me. I don't know about horses.'

'I know that, I know,' he said. 'But you can learn.'

Across the hot valley the river unwound like a roll of flat bright zinc. On the first of the hump-backed bridges Melford drew up the horse and from the high trap seats he and Constance looked down on the stream. A roach jumped from the water and she actually saw the flash of its scales, clean silver, in the sun. Water-lilies were blooming, pure white, further upstream, little wax bowls, motionless on dead still water.

Over the bridge and the road hung big white poplars and shorter dark clumps of alder, keeping out the sun. She felt the air as cool as water on her face after the heat of the road and suddenly she said:

27

'Tie the trap up a few moments and let's sit down by the river. It's so cool – just for a minute or two.'

'I think we ought to push on to this place,' he said. 'I said we'd be there by three and you know how I am. I hate being late for things.'

He took out his watch. It was small and gold, with an enclosed face. He clicked it open with a nail that was beautifully trimmed.

'It's a quarter-past now.'

As with the question of carriages at the wedding, she did not protest. She did not make a fuss.

'Perhaps when we come back,' she said.

'If you like. But I thought of taking you back another way.'

The roach jumped again, in exactly the same place, like a signal which Melford immediately obeyed by slapping the reins across the back of the horse. A moment later he and Constance were driving out again in the heat of the sun.

Half an hour later she was watching a groom trotting a mare up and down a hot stone-flagged stable yard. The mare was all black, with a smallish head and rather a dainty way of walking, proud but not finicky at all.

Melford approached her critically, looking into teeth, lifting one of her front legs, walking round her, not speaking much. Constance stood aside, folding her hands, and as heat glared up into her face from the flagstones she could not tell whether the mare was young or old or pretty or stupid or worth buying at all.

'I tell you one thing,' Melford said. 'She looks to me for all the world like a Lady Pilfer. Don't you think so?'

She said she didn't really know. She supposed she did look something like that.

'Would the lady like to try the saddle for a moment or two, sir?'

'Yes, I think so,' Melford said. 'You'd like that, wouldn't you?'

She had never been in a saddle in her life. She was suddenly shy and terrified of making a fool of herself by missing a stirrup or slipping or behaving wrongly in some way. She did not know how to act. She felt suddenly like a child trying to climb a wall that was too high for her.

'Let the hands go. That's it. Just up and down the yard a couple of times.'

Melford stood back, watching the groom lead the horse up and down the hot yard. Constance, quiet and tall, did not cut so bad a figure, he thought. A summer dress was not the right thing, of course, and she would look much better in a habit.

Then as the mare turned at the end of the yard, under the shadow of the big stable roof, a sudden odd turn of air whipped along the wall and lifted her skirt. He saw one of her fine long legs as far up as the thigh, pale against the black flank of the mare. In a second she held the dress down with one hand, but it was too late: a shocked feeling of embarrassment went through him. He might have been seeing her, or part of her, for the first time.

He was still standing there, heat stabbing down on him, when he realized that the groom was already helping her down. And as she slid from the mare, a little awkwardly, raising the dress again, he saw the groom look quickly at her body and then immediately away.

A second later he made some excuse to inspect the opposite flank of the mare. He smoothed the black skin for a moment or two with the flat of his hand and then felt better.

'Well: what do you say? Shall we take her?'

'It's for you to say.'

His embarrassment had gone now; a stab of annoyance, defensive as well as aggressive, replaced it.

'Well, if you're going to ride her – ' He broke off short, turning to the groom. 'What do you call the animal anyway?'

'Sugar-loaf, sir.'

'Sugar-loaf?' He felt annoyed. 'That's a damn fine name for a black mare, I must say.' He turned tightly to Constance. 'Don't you think so?'

'Well, I suppose for a black – '

'I think if we took her we'd call her Lady Pilfer,' he said. And then: 'Well, what shall we say?'

'It's for you to say.'

His angular face was quite fiery when flushed. The veins about the cheek-bones would go purple in later life, but now they merely spurted vermilion tendrils in the sun.

'Well, we'll leave it. Tell Mr Pomfret I will let him know.' That was another thing. It was pretty discourteous of Pomfret, a man he knew and hunted with, not to be there. 'I'm sorry he wasn't here.'

'I'll tell him, sir. I knew he was sorry to have missed you, sir.'

He gave the groom five shillings and the groom touched his cap.

As he and Constance drove away in silence she felt the burning heat even more than when they had driven out and she thought several times of the river, the big poplar trees, the white water-lilies and how cool it was by the stream.

He said at last: 'I suppose you'd like some tea at Mrs Duncan's? She'll do us very well.'

Yes, she said, she would like some tea at Mrs Duncan's.

It was cool in the parlour of the public-house where the windows were open. Mrs Duncan was a pleasant woman of fifty with greying hair parted down the middle and a big metal steel-like brooch at the throat of her high dress. She sent her daughter Effie in with tea and the girl, who was pleasant too in a fresh guileless sort of way, brought in three kinds of bread and butter and two of jam.

'I'll bring some honey too, sir,' she said. 'We just got the first comb in today. They tell me comb-honey's scarce this year – I don't know why.'

Constance helped herself to honey slowly and absently, watching it run like spun golden toffee from the spoon, making pools on her bread.

'You're very quiet all of a sudden,' he said.

He liked to think that perhaps, as he was, she was thinking of the mare.

'I was thinking of that honey in the church bell,' she said.

'Oh, that,' he said.

Rather sharply he picked up his cup. He suddenly felt that the only way of dealing with Constance was to bully her. Then his sudden motion with the cup made her drop her spoon, its handle in the running honey.

'Look there!' he said. 'Now look what you've done.'

She sat like a child. She wondered whether to pick the spoon from the honey and lick it or simply let it lie.

She let it lie. In the same moment some automatic distant record of maternal reproof played itself through his mind and he remembered he ought not to speak to people like that.

'Constance' – when he spoke appealingly his voice was like ointment – 'didn't you care for the mare?'

'It isn't that.'

'I thought you'd like her. She's a beautiful little thing.'

'It isn't that,' she said. 'I don't know about horses, that's all.'

'Well, shall we take her? or would you like to look at something else? It would be rather nice, though, wouldn't it, to call her Lady Pilfer?'

'Very well,' she said. 'If you'd like to take her.'

He smiled. At that moment he could not have been happier. He was delighted she wanted the mare. Generously he helped himself to black currant jam and said in an unctuous voice: 'It's good here, isn't it? It's always been good. Like home. We could stay here for the night sometimes after the hunts are over.' He spread jam to the thickness of a finger on his bread. 'Something else you'd like now?'

'Yes,' she said. 'I'd like to stop by the river when we go back again.'

'Of course,' he said. 'Of course.'

An hour later, lying on the river bank, listening to the sound of turning poplar leaves and the chink of the pony's bridle as it grazed in thick shade, she began slowly to be aware of a strange thing. A small wind had sprung up and now and then it swept minute fish-scale waves across the stream. She heard once the flap of a water-lily lifted up and shut flat again, like a box-lid, and then the run of wind along the bank, threading in reeds and then leaping out, like a scurrying animal, through the grasses.

The sensory impression she began to experience from the sound and run and touch of wind on her body was like the one she had experienced as she walked across the churchyard, in her silk dress, on her wedding day. The wind running through the thin stuff of her dress explored her skin, exciting her. Her skin was soft and supple and almost hairless but now it was exactly as if small hairs were beginning to grow from all the pores. She felt herself quiver involuntarily several times and then in a curious way the thread of wind seemed to blow itself into her mouth and

31

go down through her throat and centrally down through her body until it finally pulsated free. She turned restlessly in the grasses and suddenly put out her hand.

'Melford, where are you?' She turned and saw him walking away to the bridge. 'Where are you going, Melford?'

'I thought the pony seemed restless, that's all.'

'Come and lie down. The pony's all right. It's heavenly by the water. Come and lie down.'

'I'll just go look at him, I think. The flies are bad this afternoon.'

She lay down again, shutting her eyes. Under the closed lids a world of bright sun-diffusion, in all colours, swam with molten restlessness. She felt her eye-balls melting, and then her legs melting, wind-smoothed, in the sun. A squeak, almost a squeal, of a kingfisher piercing its way down-river made her start suddenly, not knowing what it was.

Some moments later she opened her eyes and Melford was there, saying something about giving the pony a little longer rein and how bad the flies were and how he thought they ought to be pushing on very soon. She actually saw him take out his watch. Then she lifted a hand towards him and said:

'Come and lie here a minute. Feel this wind on you. It's so lovely and fresh after the sun.'

He sat down. He was still wearing his cap. It was of a check material, black and white, with a shallow peak. The cap reminded her sometimes of a piece of armour. It was like a correct and upraised vizor that a single movement would pull down, encaging the face.

Suddenly and clumsily she pulled it off. The face of Melford, reddish on the cheeks, whiter against the hair, looked remarkably naked. She put her arms round him and in the clumsiest way he fell backwards, her body against him. As with the business of mounting the horse she did not know how to act and she could not have been more awkward as she tried to fold her legs against his and at the same time to touch him with her hands.

For some seconds he lay completely rigid, as if she had stunned him. His eyes were bright and enlarged. Then he suddenly struggled up and said in a constricted voice:

'People can see. People can see.'

All sensory life ebbed suddenly out of her on a quickly cooling wave. The kingfisher, returning with a still longer shriek than the first time, made a flash of blue and copper fire, partly in fright, as it twisted over the opposite meadow. As it disappeared Constance felt quite cold and said:

'I'm sorry. I don't know what got into me.'

'Better go, I think,' he said.

He searched for his cap, found it and drew it vizor-like down his forehead. She got to her feet rigidly. In the hot sun she felt that her mouth was parched. Then in an embittered moment she did not know whether to pity herself more than Melford or to hate herself more for an act of clumsy stupidity. Then she discovered that she had lost a hair-pin or two and she said:

'You go on. I want to comb my hair.'

She stood on the river bank, holding two or three hair-pins in her mouth, combing her hair with long deep strokes that hurt her. Deliberately she dug the teeth of the comb against the scalp so that it scoured the skin and the exquisite pain of hurting herself did something, for a moment, to calm her.

Then she could not bear the recollection of her awkward fatuity any longer. She felt the sun beating fiercely on her eyes.

'You're just a fool.' She remembered with bitterness the original and greater fatuity of dancing with Melford Turner because someone had dared her. 'You always have been. You always will be. A born, idiotic fool – '

She let her hands fall to her sides, no longer able to prevent herself from crying. As her tears started to come the hair-pins fell out of her mouth and presently she was on her hands and knees, groping for them in the summer grasses.

Chapter Three

By the middle of October most of the leaves of the chestnuts in the square had fallen, curled like brandy-snaps, dry and shrivelled, to be followed presently by softer yellower shoals from limes in streets leading out of the square. In the orchard the pear leaves turned a peculiar fine bright crimson, hanging on still days like breathless fire, and then suddenly flickering and pattering down in quick turns of autumn wind.

About this time Melford began to think pleasantly of the hunting season. He did not hunt much, or regularly. He would have been happy to have hunted as little as twice or three or four times in a season, missing most of the more distant meets, but the fact that he had a good sound horse and could hunt if and when he chose gave him the same satisfied feeling as having the church near at hand. He brought nothing particularly devout to either parson or fox. But the fact that the hunt was there meant the same to him as the fact that the church was there. Life would have been much poorer, in fact inconceivable, without them. He loved them both without ever being fanatical.

By this time he had decided not to buy a horse for Constance. It was clearly not sensible to press the matter of the horse. Obviously that was the reason, he thought, for her outburst on the river bank, when she had suddenly knocked his cap off and unaccountably lost control. He had thought over that incident a great deal, coming to no other explanation for it than she was upset by the mere notion of doing something, such as the riding of a horse, that she had not been used to.

About this time he became aware too that she did not sleep well. He did not ask himself why, but he was disturbed when he woke on a night in October and saw her sitting by the window, with the curtain back, looking out on the square.

It was a sharp stark night, with an almost full moon and a

touch of frost in the air. Presently he got out of bed and went over to her and asked her with pained surprise what on earth she was doing there.

'Get back into bed. You'll catch your death. You haven't even a dressing-gown on. What on earth's the matter?'

'I don't sleep well just lately, that's all.'

'Since how long?'

'Oh! on and off.' She crept back into bed and lay on her back, her hands and feet cold against the sheets. 'It's rather worse with the moon.'

'If I were you I should see Dr Davison.'

She did not say anything. Shuddering under the bed-clothes she simply thought how pleasant and nice, how comforting and assuring it would be, to have someone hold and warm her hands.

'Davison will give you something. I'll tell him to come and see you tomorrow. He used to give my mother things.'

'I'd rather he didn't come here.'

'Why?'

'I'd just rather not. I'll go over to see him.'

'Oh! very well. You know best,' he said.

A few moments later the church gonged its quarters, ready for striking four.

For the rest of the night Melford did not sleep well himself. He felt disturbed by what she had told him and in the morning he found himself oppressed by something else. After nearly thirty-five years of bachelor life he had become a man of several fixed habits he could not think of breaking. One of these was to walk across the square before breakfast, at a quarter to nine, to buy his morning papers.

Coming back with his papers that morning, across the empty square, he was suddenly struck by the size of the house above the shop. In all there were fourteen rooms there. At some stage in its history two upper windows overlooking the square and three overlooking the street had been bricked up and plastered over. Now the spaces were painted black. And it was largely because of them that the house, in a way he had not noticed before, seemed gaunt and melancholy.

Then he became aware of another reason. The gilt words of

35

his name above the shop were distinguished and large and shining, but today he was acutely aware that the word 'son' did not follow them. He not only wanted a son. It had been the chief of his reasons for marrying Constance. Then his paralysing impotence and fear and inability to touch her on the first night of their marriage had sent him walking for over two hours along the esplanade, by the sea, until all his emotions about her were grotesquely distorted and he felt almost that he could run away and not go back.

It was by a series of mischances that the word 'son' had never been added to that of 'Melford' over the shop. All through his youth his father had got into the habit of amusing himself at the blacksmith's forge a hundred yards down the street, devising clever and useful objects in steel and iron for the house, and at the age of nineteen he had come very near to inventing a new kind of patent safety-catch for a shot-gun. The idea was not quite fool-proof and not entirely practical, but a gun-smith who saw it gave his opinion that its inventor would be wasted as anything but an engineer. Six months later he went to Birmingham to begin an apprenticeship, his back turned on rice and sugar, as he supposed, for ever. A year later his father died and within a week he had once again put on his grocer's apron.

Melford had no desire or ambition to do anything but follow him into the shop. From the age of fifteen he served an apprenticeship like an ordinary boy, climbing slowly from the stage of unpacking goods in the yard at the back and sweeping up straw and rice to the moment when he would be twenty-one and could be taken into partnership. Six weeks before his twenty-first birthday his father struck his left hand a small blow with a file at the forge down the street. It was a trivial blow that merely sliced through the skin of the index finger but the septicaemia that set in took only ten days to kill.

After that his mother sat a great deal in the window of the sitting-room and stared out at the square. Like him she was bony and rather tall. And gradually she took to putting more and more powder on her face, an odd bluish-pink powder that gave the impression, with more rouge, of her being embalmed. Her slightly tinted hair had a dry flaxen look, like a doll's, and she invariably wore long pearl-drop ear-rings and a pair of gold pince-nez on a chain. Both made her seem longer, thinner, chillier than ever.

His mother, after his father's death, did not seem any more affectedly possessive than she had done before it. She merely seemed more watchful and reproachful. It amounted to very much the same thing in the end, except that he was never conscious of it. When he grew excited or on the verge of emotion or irritation or anger about something it was she who held him back: 'I wouldn't do that, Melford dear. That won't make a very good impression on people, will it? Try to control yourself. We don't want people to think we're like that, do we?' It was she, in consequence, although he did not know it, who gave him, or helped to give him, his air of genteel uprightness, the thin nice kindliness of manner expressed in the unexcitable, well-kept, starchy hands. The idea of her husband being a grocer, in a shop, behind a counter, was something she had never really grown used to, but if Melford had to be a grocer too she was determined from the first that he should be a superior grocer, a gentleman grocer, a grocer who could meet anybody, even the most exclusive of the hunting people, on equal terms.

And so now, in a sense, his mother was a greater presence in death than she had been alive. In certain phases of his life it was difficult for him to believe that she was not still there, aloof and powdered and forbidding. At church on Sunday mornings it was hard sometimes to believe it was Constance and not his mother, stiff in proud and severe embalmment, who walked across the churchyard and sat beside him in the pew.

He did not go to church to worship; he never stopped to ask himself why he went there at all. He had no ear for music and no voice. He took only a mechanical part in the responses. Most of the time he spent staring at the big window beyond the altar. In the upper part of it the glass, in crimson and blue and yellow, radiated in a kind of star; in the lower part there were ten scriptural pictures. The only one he knew for certain was that of the Angel appearing to Zacharias and he knew that it was a picture of Zacharias because, as a boy, his father had told him so.

He also knew the height of the tower and the steeple because his father had told him so. The height of the tower to the battlements was exactly seventy-one feet; the hexagonal spire above it went up to another ninety-nine feet – not a hundred, as his father in his precise engineering fashion would beg him to remember – making a total of one hundred and seventy feet. In the tower were six bells.

Below the bells was the clock. He knew all about the clock too not only because his father had told him so but because, for many years, his father had wound it up. With rigid zeal for punctuality he had wound it up at precisely ten o'clock every Saturday morning. If it lost or gained time, varying for more than a few minutes in the year, his engineering pride was greatly troubled, and whenever the clock went wrong he devoted days and nights to it until it was put right again, sometimes working alone by hurricane lamp in the dark tower.

But Melford's greatest thrill about the tower, perhaps the greatest thrill of his life, did not belong to the occasions when his father had taken him, as he often had done, to see the inner workings of the clock. It came from a clear bristling December afternoon when he was six. He remembered his father unaccountably seizing him and running with him across the churchyard. His father had powerful muscular hands and very thick forearms that hardly tapered at all. The boy found himself carried, half-afraid, into the church and then up the stone spiral steps and then up the series of straight wooden steps that led to the clock. His father was not often so excited. In the walls flanking the clock were open slits about nine or ten inches wide that were protected by iron grilles. His father held him close up to the most easterly of these grilles and said breathlessly :

'Look, Melford, look. Look over there. Over there by Duchy Farm – this side of it. That's something you might not ever see again, Melford. There's a prince there – a prince riding with the hounds, that's what that is.'

The boy hooked his fingers against the grille and quivered with excitement. Over the bright wintry fields at the back of the town the hunt was dashing like a herd of little red and black animals chasing another herd of smaller creatures, the hounds, with a crowd of wormy, waving tails. He heard the uplifting whining distressful voices of the hounds in full cry. It excited him too. It excited him even more than the fact that somewhere among it all a prince was riding. And together his excitement and the wind driving through the grilles brought tears to his eyes, so that horses and dogs and men were dissolved in a weeping stream of colour across the familiar fields and his father had to lift him down, saying:

That was a fine way to see hounds running, wasn't it? Perhaps you'll live to be a hundred and never see them like that again. And a prince there – that's something perhaps you'll never see again, Melford, in all your born days.'

That was nearly thirty years ago and it was always exactly as if it were yesterday. He would never forget the great thrill of that sight from the tower.

Apart from that single exciting memory what he chiefly inherited from his father was a habit of punctuality and precision without himself having anything very important to be punctual or precise about. This made him fussy. He began to be fussy if Constance could not find her gloves at three minutes to eleven on Sunday mornings; he began to be restless if the sermon lasted for more than a minute after twelve-fifteen.

Every Sunday morning, at twelve-twenty, he continued to be the slave of yet another bachelor habit by walking three doors down the street and going into The Prince of Orange. He always entered the private bar. The Prince of Orange was kept by two sisters named Waters, Miss Em Waters and Miss Carrie Waters, two minute-faced, circumspect, spare little ladies, the younger of whom could play skittles very well in the public bar.

Melford liked to refer to the two bright little sisters as Dot and Carrie. He also referred to his habit of taking a drink with them on Sunday mornings after church as 'taking the waters'.

Miss Carrie Waters served in the private bar. When Melford entered she reached under the bar counter, took out his own private silver tankard and filled it with draught ale. Melford was convinced that ale tasted better out of a silver tankard than out of a glass and also that it tasted even better out of his own. Before drinking he said to Miss Waters, 'And now Carrie my dear, what will you have?' Miss Waters would thank him politely and say that if he did not mind she would have one with him later. He knew perfectly well that she never had one with him later but he did not think any the less of her for that and he would have been surprised, and perhaps even hurt, if she told him otherwise.

Melford then paid for the two drinks and stood away from the bar, holding the tankard in one hand and somehow, out of long habit, tucking the little finger of his left hand in a corner of his upper waistcoat pocket. At about twenty minutes to one he found that his tankard was empty. As if it were a circumstance of great surprise he stared at the bottom of it for a moment and then said, 'Well, I suppose there's just time for another.' He then put the tankard on the counter and Miss Carrie filled it up again.

Between the private bar and the public bar was a stone passage, once the driveway for coaches. One Sunday morning, before marrying Constance, he had stayed in the bar until long past one o'clock. Then at the same moment as he came out of the private bar a figure in a bowler hat came out of the public bar across the passage. It was only by the flinty and contemptuous eyes under the hat that he recognized his counter-hand, Hyde. He said, 'Good morning, Hyde,' but Hyde did nothing but nod in answer. The meeting gave him the curious feeling of having met a ghost: an unpleasant and sneering ghost, a stranger who, unnecessarily and unaccountably, hated him. The look on the face was mean and spiteful.

If he had been married to Constance at this time he would have gone home to her and said, 'I ran into Hyde coming out of The Prince just now. And do you know that man didn't speak to me? How do you account for that? That man has been with us now for twenty years and by the way he looked you'd think we didn't pay him enough or something. He gets thirty shillings a week and all sorts of bits and pieces from the shop and I give him a sovereign at Christmas and a box of stuff. I tell you that was a class distinction look if ever I saw one. It hurt, that look did – but that's the way the wind is blowing now.' He did not remember that only the previous day in Hyde's presence he had called Miss Mackness 'our Miss Weakness' while she had gone into the back of the shop to wash her hands, but the result of the meeting was to teach him once again the value of punctuality, so that now he made sure of never leaving The Prince of Orange later than one o'clock exactly.

A day or two after he had found Constance sitting at the bed-room window at four o'clock in the morning he was standing with his tankard at the bar when Miss Carrie Waters, in her polite circumspect way, asked him how Constance was keeping.

'As a matter of fact it's funny you should ask that,' he said, 'because she's not sleeping very well.'

Miss Waters said there was one thing you couldn't do without and that was sleep, and Melford said:

'That's true. Anyway I'm sending her over to see Davison tomorrow. He'll fit her up with some tablets.'

A glass of port, Miss Waters said, was better than all your tablets. She advised him strongly to tell Constance to take a glass of port last thing. Tablets could get to become a habit. You never knew where you were when you left them off again.

'Well, we'll try that,' Melford said. 'A glass of port last thing.'

'That will do the trick all right,' Miss Waters said and then paused significantly. 'Is everything all right otherwise?'

He said that everything was all right otherwise. It was simply that she did not sleep well.

'I was talking to Dot and Carrie about you,' he said, over his roast beef and baked potatoes, 'and they say if you can't sleep you should take a glass of port last thing.'

'I don't care very much for port.'

'Yes, but if it's a cure I should have thought it worth trying. Of course see Davison if you like, but we've got the port in the shop.'

'I think I'll see Davison,' she said. 'As a matter of fact Miss Mackness telephoned yesterday and made an appointment for me tomorrow evening.'

'Our Miss Weakness is quite useful sometimes.'

'I don't think she's quite so weak as we' – she would have liked to say 'you' but once again, as so often, she was too shy – 'imagine she is.'

'Oh! no, no, no,' he said. 'I know that. It's just my way.'

The following evening, going to see Dr Davison, she felt shyer and more uncertain than ever. She would not have been so diffident and unsure about herself, she thought, if Dr Davison had been there to meet her when she arrived. Instead he had been delayed at a pneumonia case, so that she sat for more than forty minutes in the private consulting-room, alone, waiting for him to come back. By the end of this time her hands were shaking.

Davison was a short dark middle-aged man with unusually broad muscular hands covered with crisp black hair. Other hair grew abundantly out of his nose and ears. His eyebrows were very like thick black caterpillars under which the eyes were held in a deep unsympathetic glare.

'And how long have you not been sleeping?'

'Some weeks,' she said. Shy and nervous, she stumbled over her words. 'Three or four weeks,' she said. Then out of sheer fright, coupled with shyness, she changed it again. 'A month or two, some months,' she said.

'Do you go to bed very late? What time do you go to bed?'

'Ten o'clock,' she said. 'Not late. Half past ten.'

'Do you remember anything it might have started with?'

Stupidly she remembered the sound of the sea; it seemed unthinkably foolish to refer to it and then she remembered the clock. She thought perhaps they were a little near the church clock, she said.

His caterpillar-shrouded eyes held her in a positive glare of interest that made her shyer than ever.

'Nothing else?' he said. 'Anything you could possibly think of?'

No: nothing she could possibly think of. All the time her hands were shaking in her lap. She was gripping her black leather gloves tightly together, too tightly, so that now and then her hands gave a shudder.

'Be as frank as you like with me.'

Immediately a glass shutter seemed to slide down across the front of her mind. She was suddenly incapable of thinking. She could not even think of the sea or the clock. She could only sit there mutely and stupidly staring, gripping her involuntarily shuddering hands.

He asked her another question or two. She really did not hear them properly. There was something about whether or not she took exercise or if she had any recreations. She heard the word headache and then that was all.

She gave her answers so quietly that he had to lean forward

several times, turning towards her a big bushy ear and glaring at her from under the big caterpillar brows. And then suddenly, as if she irritated him by her whispering or as if he had come to the conclusion that she was too simple a case to bother with, he seemed to give her up.

'I see,' he said. The voice was not unsympathetic. Nor was it neutral. Nor did it convey anything of what he might be thinking. Presently he went out of the room, coming back five minutes later carrying a plain red circular pill-box with a label stuck on the lid.

'Take two of these at night. Three if you find that two are not enough. Try a glass of hot milk at the same time and then in about a week – '

Again she was not really listening. Shyly, in a barely audible voice, she said, 'Thank you, doctor,' and a few moments later she was out in the street.

It was quite dark by that time. She stood for a few minutes under the street lamp outside, trembling and breathing hard. She knew that it was childish and foolish not to have had more control of herself in the consulting-room but she knew too that she could not help it. Then she began to walk away and it was only after she had been walking for some time that she realized she was walking away from the square.

She turned back and walked home through the churchyard. A slight breeze was blowing; now and then a crowd of dry leaves sprang up and pattered about the paths. She stood still for a few minutes, smelling the leaves and the dank autumn clay-smell of late October.

Then suddenly she clenched her right hand and crushed the pill-box like an empty egg, throwing it into the churchyard, hearing it rattle into the steely leaves of a bush of holly.

'No, he didn't give me anything,' she said to Melford. 'I told him about the port and he said he had heard it was a good thing too.'

'Good,' he said. 'Good for Dot and Carrie. Shrewd little things.' He seemed pleased about it all and made another of his customary jokes about the two sharp little sisters at The Prince of Orange. 'Consult Dot and Carrie and save the doctor's bills.'

That night as she sat in bed, waiting for him to finish his usual

43

long and tedious toilet, she was surprised to see him come into the bedroom carrying a bottle of port and a glass on a tray.

'It's Cockburns,' he said. 'It ought to be good.' He touched the bottle with the back of his hand and said he thought it was warm enough. 'It was one I got in for Christmas last year.'

As he uncorked the bottle and poured out the wine she suddenly could not help wishing that there were two glasses. Then almost as if he were reading her thoughts he said:

'I'm going to have mine downstairs. I won't come up yet. I've got the Montagu account to check.' Colonel Montagu was a man of coarse and ebullient temperament who entertained heavily and shot and hunted a great deal in the country beyond the river, beyond Ascott St Mary, six miles away. 'He'll only come in and make a scene if I charge him for half a biscuit too much.'

Coming over to the bed, carefully carrying the glass of port, which he had filled up too much, so that the wine lipped at the brim, he said:

'Perhaps you'd better sip a drop out of it, so that it doesn't spill on the bedclothes.'

He stopped by the bed. Over her nightdress she was wearing a new green woollen bed-jacket that she had knitted herself that autumn. It hung loosely over her shoulders, the ribbons not tied up. She was taken slightly unawares by Melford's gesture of bringing the port and then by the idea of sipping at the glass as he held it for her. The result was that she leaned forward, holding the glass with both hands, forgetting to hold the open front of her jacket, not realizing until afterwards that the front of her nightdress was open too.

Then as she took the glass and licked the drops of port from her lips she was surprised by another thing. Melford was sitting on the edge of the bed. It surprised her so much that she forgot once more about her nightdress and simply sat there staring at him, the glass cupped in her two hands, the front of her nightdress open, showing the plunge of her breasts.

Suddenly she saw that he was not looking at her. He did not often come so close to her and sometimes his eyes, when he did, seemed to lose focus and distend. A curious glaze started to cover them, breaking occasionally into painful wateriness.

Presently she realized that he was not looking at her now

because the front of her body was uncovered. For a few seconds longer she let her bed-jacket and her nightdress remain open, showing her body. For a mere fraction of a second she was conscious of deliberately wanting to remain like that. It was the only way she knew of offering herself or attracting him.

Then she got the third of her surprises that evening. She became aware of why he had sat down on the bed. It was not merely to see that she drank her glass of port in comfort. It was not with the object of staring at her body. It was simply to say:

'I've been wanting to ask you something. I wondered if you'd like a gramophone?'

In amazement she did not know whether to laugh or cry. A gramophone? Why a gramophone? A gramophone? What should she do with a gramophone?

'I saw a very nice one in Schofields' today.'

'A gramophone?'

'Yes.' He went on to say something about her liking music. It was true that she liked music and that downstairs, in the sitting-room, was an old rose-wood upright piano with silk and fretted front that she sometimes played. But she did not play well enough to enjoy the pieces she liked most. She had never thought of music as a serious part of her life and now he was saying:

'I know you're keen on it and thought it might help a bit. I thought – you know – ' He was becoming as hesitant and nervous about it as if he were a small boy trying to convince a mother of the necessity of buying a new toy. 'You could have it up here.'

'A gramophone in the bedroom? What about you?'

His eyes had become noticeably watery. He sat scratching one cheek, afraid to look at her.

'I was thinking – I thought,' he said, 'well, if you like – I was thinking I could go back to the old room.'

The room in which he had slept as a boy and a single man was at the far end of the landing, almost at the other side of the house. Above the bed in it was a badger head mounted on a fumed oak plaque. The badger was the first animal he had ever shot as a boy. On another wall hung a cloth in which the coat of arms of the borough was embroidered in white and cocoa-coloured wool. Nine burghers' heads were depicted on it, with a hand stretching horizontally in blessing above. He had embroidered it himself one year because his father became mayor and consequently, as the boy thought, the leader of the world.

'I see,' she said.

She felt cold inside. Not angry or even irritated. Not even pushed aside. Not in any way frustrated. But cold: negatively and neutrally cold, with a frozen, stony finality that kept her locked in a stare.

'I'd see about having a gas-fire put in here,' he said, 'and then you treat it as your own.'

The gas-fire or the room? she wondered. Deep under her shyness something like a metallic little spring, hard and tightened, gave a startling jerk and by the smallest fraction released its tension. The spring releasing itself at that moment had nothing to do with feeling. It seemed like a mere accidental quiver far down inside herself. It was possible that one day the entire spring would uncoil itself and fly wildly and shatter her with feeling, but now all she felt was a jerk, a punctuation that pricked and startled her and was not repeated.

Curiously, from that moment, as she sipped her port, she did not feel so shy.

'The gas-fire would keep it pretty warm up here and you'd have the gramophone and you could do as you liked,' he said.

Yes: she supposed it would be warm. She supposed she could do as she liked up there. She set her glass on the bedside table and then sat coldly tying the ribbon of her bed-jacket. She supposed it would be warm and exciting for her, alone with a new gramophone, listening to records. What make was the gramophone?

'A Columbia I think Schofield said it was,' he said. 'It's rather special. He got it in for someone who couldn't take delivery after all. Anyway go and see it. See how you feel. Schofield was unpacking a lot of new records too. I think there were one or two by that man you said you liked – that German fellow.'

'Schubert?'

'I forget now. Something like that. One of those fellows,' he said.

He seemed immensely relieved. He got up from the bed. It

was on the tip of her tongue to say something to him – not anything particular, just a word, and to deliver it in a shout. She did not say anything. Instead she picked up her glass. Then she drank and sat staring at the oil in the wine as it slipped, slowly and thickly, down the sides of the glass.

'See what you think about it tomorrow,' he said, 'will you?'

'I'll go,' she said.

'Good.' He was so relieved, so pleased with himself at that moment that he did not notice how the tone of her voice had reduced itself to a mere thin scratch.

'I'm pretty sure you'll like it,' he said. 'It's in a walnut cabinet – it's one of the new sort, without a horn. Shall I take the port away? Or would you like some more?'

'Leave the bottle,' she said. 'I think I'd like some more.'

He stooped and kissed her forehead. The kiss was a mere brush of dry lips and she did nothing in reply. It was an undemonstrative, customary, nightly salutation. She did not hate him for it. And afterwards, whenever she was driven to examine her feelings more closely, she found that she did not hate him for anything. There was nothing in him to hate, just as there was nothing inside herself that was remotely capable of hating.

All she felt was coldness. It was exactly as if a great draught of wintry air had solidified inside her, gripping her heart in a freezing neutral shroud: the sort of coldness, she sometimes thought afterwards, that could not be dispelled by a gramophone in a walnut cabinet, a glass of port or the honey of bees in belfry towers.

Chapter Four

Fields came so close to the town behind the church that sometimes as she lay awake at night she could hear the cough of a sheep or the note of an owl or in the distance a fox barking. She did not lie awake every night. After a time she actually found that the playing of gramophone records made her sleepy. She would lie for a time with the gas-light turned low, or sometimes merely by the light of a candle, and play over a few pieces of Schubert, her favourite composer, or a few of Brahms. They were mostly for piano. The gramophone itself was of the type with a spring-winding motor. Occasionally after a time she got too tired to wind it or did not wind it enough. Often this happened when she was dropping off to sleep and then the descending whine of the motor roused her again and soon the old stark white insomnia was back.

The shop where she bought her records was kept by a man named Schofield; a rather undersized short-sighted man with a drooping blond Teutonic moustache stained bright yellowish ginger in the centre from too much smoking. He wore spectacles with heavy lenses and thin gold rims. Besides sheet music and hymn books and parts for oratorio he sold pianos and stringed instruments and occasional clarinets, mostly second-hand. There was always a strong smell of french polish in the shop. From a room at the back, reached by a short flight of stairs and a muslin-curtained door, there was a continual sound of several babies crying or laughing or sometimes shrieking, with a woman's voice among them.

Schofield was very forgetful. The shop was always in a mess. It was lit only by a plain unshaded gas-mantle that in draughty weather flared or plopped or sometimes went out altogether. Under this gas-light Schofield would stand scratching his smoke-stained moustache, saying to Constance:

'I know I ordered it, Mrs Turner. I remember ordering it as plain as I see you standing there. It's here somewhere. It must be here.'

Then he would begin searching among piles of dusty sheet music or on piano tops and among music-canterburys for the record she had ordered. Sometimes he knocked over large and untidy piles of music and let them lie where they fell on the floor. Then sometimes as he searched she would actually see the new record lying in front of him on the counter.

When she pointed things like this out to him he would pull at his moustache, swear softly and say something about getting his glasses changed.

'I'll get myself a pair of treble-magnifiers when I can afford it. Whenever that might be.'

Sometimes she stood in the shop for a long time and Schofield never appeared. Or he came suddenly in from the street, pushing a bicycle, carrying a black bag of piano-tuning tools. Then he pushed the bicycle behind a piano and glared short-sightedly about him and snapped, but without unkindliness:

'Shop's closed. Shop's closed. Can't you read the notice on the door? It says closed there, see? – plain as a pike-staff.'

Then he would lift one corner of his glasses, realize who she was, and say:

'How did you get in here, Mrs Turner?' realizing at the same time that he had come in himself. 'I don't know. I don't know. Kids again. Kids again – nothing safe here.'

One evening she stood in the shop for ten minutes or more under the low gas-mantle, waiting for Schofield to answer the bell. From the back of the shop she could hear the noise of children's voices. Over the door was a big brass spring bell. Finally she opened the door and swung it backwards and forwards several times, ringing the bell loudly and then a voice said:

'Good evening. I am so sorry, but Mr Schofield is not here.'

The voice was soft and pleasantly modified. She turned to see on the steps leading from the back of the shop a young woman not much older than herself: in the gas-light her hair, loosely done up at the back, shone very smooth and almost white.

'It's Mrs Turner, isn't it? Is there something I can do for you,

Mrs Turner, or would you care to come in and wait while he comes back?'

'I just called about a record.'

It was the first time she had seen Mrs Schofield. She had expected, because Schofield himself was fifty-three or four, a much older woman. She had somehow formed a picture of a sloppy middle-aged woman in a perpetual sack-apron, hair in curling pins. She was surprised to see how pretty Mrs Schofield was. She was small featured, with ivory skin, and astonishingly young fresh blue eyes.

'Why don't you come in and wait, Mrs Turner? It's warmer in here. He shouldn't be long now – he's gone to tune the Liberal Club piano. They've a concert there.'

She said it was really not important at all, but Mrs Schofield laughed and said: 'Do come in. He would be quite upset if he knew you'd been and he wasn't here.'

As she went up the stairs and into the crowded little room at the back she was struck again by another thing about Mrs Schofield: her voice. It reminded her of something Melford had said to her at their own first meeting. Mrs Schofield did not speak, as Melford had remarked, 'with our local accent'. It was not merely a totally different accent from the accent of the town. It was a fluent and cultivated accent. Constance did not like the word 'class' and whenever Melford used the word, as he often did, she found it grated on her; but she felt at once that Mrs Schofield was a girl of class who had somehow got herself married to an untidy piano-tuner with yellow moustaches and weak eyes who often did not remember what day it was.

She was so interested in the four Schofield children eating bread and jam in the room at the back of the shop that she did not remember how long she stayed there. Washing hung airing and drying under the mantelshelf and on the oven doors of the stove. It hung too on lines across the ceiling. The centre table was a crowded mass of crockery, bread and jam-pots, with cruets left over from lunch-time.

Somehow among all this there was still space for another piano. And presently the four children, three girls and a boy, the youngest of the girls only three, stood round the piano and sang in high voices *Now I lay me down to sleep*. Mrs Schofield sat on a circular revolving piano stool out of which horse-hair was frothing and played the accompaniment, looking like the mother of four bright-haired dolls.

After the singing the children laughed and shouted at Constance. 'Do you play?' they said. 'Do you play?'

'I play a little.'

'You play to us! You play to us!' they said. 'Play *Three Blind Mice*. Play *Every Week Day Mary Jane* – '

She smiled, hesitating, plucking at the fingers of her gloves.

'I think she's shy!' the boy said. 'I think Mrs Turner's too shy to play to us – '

'Now that will do,' Mrs Schofield said. 'Mrs Turner has her gloves on and it's an awful bother to take off her gloves just to play for you. But if you're nice to her perhaps she will play next time – '

'We'll be nice to her,' they said. 'Play next time. Will you play next time?'

'Perhaps,' she said and she plucked again at the fingers of her gloves.

Schofield did not come back that evening and in a pleasant mood of recollections about the four fair children singing round the piano and afterwards washing their hands and feet in a bowl on the uncleared tea-table she walked slowly home. A surprised and slightly irritated Melford met her in the hall and said:

'Where on earth have you been? We'd given you up. We thought we'd lost you.'

She said she was sorry. 'I stayed,' she said, 'talking to Mrs Schofield.'

He laughed with a sort of quiet scoff.

'Oh! that girl,' he said.

'Yes,' she said. 'Is there something wrong with her?'

'I don't know,' he said, 'but I never feel easy with her. She's too nice. False somehow.'

She remembered Mrs Schofield's ivory skin, the remarkable pale blue eyes, the beautiful soft bleached hair.

'She seemed very nice to me – '

'Oh! She's nice enough. I'm not saying – Of course she's not Orlingford. I suppose she's a Londoner – I don't know.'

Nothing could have been more derogatory to Melford than the

word Londoner, which he used as a term of contempt. He supposed Schofield was a Londoner too. You could generally tell them. It was a pity there wasn't another music shop in the town. It was a bit of a nuisance having to do trade with a shop like that, but there it was, Schofield traded with him and he, out of decency and recognized custom, had to trade with Schofield.

Suddenly he was cheerful.

'Anyway, no use bothering about people like that,' he said. 'Come into the warm and let's have supper. I've got something to tell you.'

The dining-room, like its three-tier mahogany sideboard and its pie-crust mahogany table, was much too big for the two of them. It was warmed by a big coal-fire at one end. In very cold weather Melford and Constance sat at the fire-place end of the table; when it was warmer Mrs Butterworth laid two places at the other. These places were never close to each other. They were always on opposite sides the table, so that Melford and Constance were separated by perhaps four feet of polished mahogany.

Melford was fond of lamb chops and rice-pudding. He liked to tell Mrs Butterworth that she made the best rice puddings in the world. Constance was not particularly fond of rice pudding, with the result that his own special pudding, slow-cooked, with burnished nutmegged skin, was set before him every night with a little show of ceremony by Mrs Butterworth.

'Mrs Butterworth, Mrs Butterworth,' he would say, 'Mrs Butterworth, I think you get better and better and better.'

Later, raising his spoon with a piece of skin clinging to it like thin brown leather, he would say:

'Look at that – that's the best part. The skin. I always save the skin till last – because it's the best part.'

That evening he had reached the stage of holding up the specimen of skin before Constance had courage to say:

'You said you were going to tell me something.'

Spoon still poised, he leaned forward and said between closed teeth:

'Not in front of Mrs Butterworth.'

'Oh! I see.'

'I don't want it all over the town.'

She felt she had been reprimanded. Like a child, in silence, she waited for him to finish his pudding. The last vestiges of pudding had to be scraped from the sides of the dish with a spoon. Like brown rinds of sugary peel they curled off and then Melford ate them, slowly crunching with pleasure.

After this was all over she rang the bell for Mrs Butterworth, who came in and cleared the dishes, to receive, also, a little joke from Melford:

'Not so good as last night, Mrs Butterworth.'

'No, sir?' Gloom seemed to spread over Mrs Butterworth's already pale face like still paler skin. 'I'm sorry, sir –'

'Not so good, Mrs Butterworth.' He paused significantly. 'Better! Better, Mrs Butterworth, better!'

The same joke was not made every night. Melford made it on only two or three nights of the week, as if he thought it might get stale if too often repeated.

After Mrs Butterworth had cleared the dishes and left the cheese and biscuits and celery and mustard on the table Constance waited for what Melford had to tell her.

He did not tell her for some time. Another of Melford's habits was to eat mustard with cheese.

'A little piece of mustard on cheese makes the same difference as salt to celery. Try it,' he would say. 'You'll be astonished. It makes all the difference in the world.'

She had never been able to bring herself to try mustard with cheese, even though he would impress on her that it was a tip he had first taken from Lord Chelston when hunting. And now, as she did every night, she sat waiting quietly for him as he made bright little pagodas of food consisting of biscuit, cheese, celery, and yellow mustard on top. He made three or four of these neat saffron-topped pagodas, ate them and then said:

'This is what I've got to tell you. But I don't want it all over the town.'

'Of course not.'

He leaned back and adopted the attitude of putting a little finger in his top waistcoat pocket.

'They're going to ask me to be mayor.'

Without thinking she said:

'But they've just asked Spencer again.'

'I know they've just asked Spencer,' he said. 'But that's

this year. I'm talking about *next* year. They're going to ask me next year.'

'I see.'

'By this time next year,' he said, 'you'll be mayoress.'

'Oh! no.'

For the first time since their marriage she knew that he was angry. The extreme tips of his angular cheek-bones flared with little sprouts of purplish fire.

'Why "Oh! no"? You mean you wouldn't want to be?'

'Oh! no, it's not that.' She knew that it was not that. She did not know, either, what else it was. Confusedly she said: 'It's just that – you know – I wouldn't be much good at that sort of thing – processions. But of course if I have to be – '

'Well, naturally, you have to be. You don't expect me to ask Mrs Butterworth, do you?'

There was no more she had to say. He began to make another pagoda, staring at the biscuit, the cheese, the celery, and the mustard with concentration, like a boy building something with toy bricks.

When it was finished he held it for a few seconds longer in front of his face. The edges of the face were still fiery. His eyes bulged with grey damp anger. She had never aroused in him any emotion like that before and suddenly she felt that he might get up and shout at her what a fool she was and how he hated her and what nonsense she talked and how he was sick to death of it, and she would start sobbing and throw her serviette at him and run upstairs.

Instead he put the pagoda in his mouth. He chewed for a few moments with rumination, mouth quite closed, jaws champing steadily down, like a cow.

Then he swallowed and poured himself a glass of water. As if remembering his mother he gazed for some time at the water and then said:

'That wasn't quite the thing, was it? Sorry about that. Shouldn't have said a thing like that to you.'

The fieriness in his face had become damp, actually damp, from moisture in his eyes.

'But you see my father was mayor. And his father was mayor. And you know how it is, naturally – '

She realized suddenly how fast her heart was beating. She did not realize, at that moment, though perhaps she was at the beginning of realization, how much she had wanted anger to burst from him in a flash of physical explosion. She was still too deeply wrapped in her own shyness to know, consciously, that she would have been glad of it and even more glad of her own anger in reply.

Presently, when she began to fold her serviette, she felt an unusual hot and stabbing sensation in her finger-tips as she pressed the linen. Then gradually the sensation ran away. She was her own cool, quiet self again. She put her serviette in its silver ring. Then she noticed that the ring had not been properly cleaned that day. A bluish mark, like a bruise, had come off on the tips of her fingers. She would have to tell Mrs Butterworth about it and Mrs Butterworth would have to tell the maid. Then she laid the serviette neatly by the side of her plate and said:

'I see they're meeting at Evensford tomorrow. What time do you go?'

'Never go to the Evensford meet nowadays. Since the big house closed down there's nowhere really decent to meet and it's such dull country.'

Her change of subject had made the atmosphere quite friendly. He took another drink of cold water and said:

'No. Ascott St Mary – that's the meet I like. The second week in January. Wonderful country.'

For some reason she suddenly remembered the record Schofield had been going to get for her. She remembered Schofield's wife, the children with the bread and jam, the piano under the lines of washing and the songs at the piano. It had all been very pleasant there, unexpectedly and inexplicably pleasant, and she knew she looked forward to going back.

A moment later he said, folding his own serviette:

'Oh! I meant to say. You don't want to be seen with that Schofield tribe too much. Schofield's all right. I don't mind Schofield. But I never really liked that girl. I don't know what it is – but you know how things are. You'll be mayoress next year.'

'They seem quite happy.'

'Oh! I know. I grant you,' he said. 'So are pigs in their dirt.'

And then added quickly: 'Well, perhaps not quite so bad as that, but you know – '

The following quiet windless November afternoon a strange thing happened. Rain had fallen heavily in the night on a westerly wind and all through the morning; after the wind had dropped it clung in brilliant drops to the bare twigs of the street trees and in the grass in the churchyard. A few trees of late apples in the orchard at the back of the house had still been laden, the day before, with squarish brown-russet fruit. Now wind and rain had stripped them down.

When sun broke through about two o'clock, she decided to spend the afternoon in the orchard, picking up skips of apples. Ivy, still in blossom in thick honey-coloured clusters on the walls of the garden, began to steam with clouds of bees as sun warmed the November air. The afternoon grew gradually golden: the grass lit with fallen apples, the sunlight deep yellow, the bees about the ivy vaporous and golden themselves.

As she picked up the apples she remembered the Schofield children. It would be nice, she thought, to take apples to the Schofield children. She would take a basket when she went to the shop next time to inquire about her record.

Then she heard, in the distance, across the field behind the church, the thin baying cry of hounds in the air. It always seemed to her a mournful sound. Above it the sound of a horn was like the tooting of a toy that a child would not put down.

By the middle of the afternoon she had grown so used to the sounds that she did not realize they were coming much closer until she saw Melford suddenly running from the back of the house.

'That must be hounds over by Duchy Farm. They must be coming down by the spinneys. We can see them if they get clear by Foskett's meadow – '

She suddenly saw a peculiar look on his face. His lips were hanging open. She realized with surprise how weak they were. And then he laughed, excited. It was a kind of high-pitched gurgle pressing its way up through the wind-pipe. He could not control it properly and it sprang out, finally, like the whoop of a boy.

'Come on! – we don't want to miss them – we don't want to miss them – !'

Then he was running. She did not know quite how it came about, but she was running with him. They went together through the wooden gate at the bottom of the orchard. Beyond the gate was a stone footpath, then beyond it the churchyard.

In the churchyard he suddenly stopped. He seemed to remember something. He looked up. For a second time his excitement came gurgling up through his wind-pipe in a peculiar whoop. Then he turned to her, gripping her hand excitedly, and said:

'Come on. I'll show you something. I'll show you something you'll never forget – '

Less than a minute later she was climbing behind him up the spiral steps inside the church tower. The sound of hounds and horn was cut off from her by the thickness of the walls. All she could hear was Melford, panting and scraping up the spiral flight above her.

If there was anything stupid about this panting rush up the half-dark steps she did not realize it until afterwards. She did not stop until she reached the stone platform just below the clock. Then she could hear the crying of hounds again and she came to a first conscious realization of why Melford had brought her there.

'I thought I'd never see this again. I saw it once with my father. There was a prince with the meet that day. Prince Edward I think – God above, there they are! There they go! There they are!'

With his mention of princes, she did not know quite what he was talking about. He was standing at one of the iron grilles, gripping it with his fingers, as he had done when a boy.

'Look, Constance, look at them – there they go! Between the Spinney and Duchy Farm. God above, God Almighty, it's as near as anything the place where I saw them before – !'

Then she was looking out. Across damp sunny fields she stared for two minutes, perhaps three, at the entire strung line of the hunt, black and scarlet and white, as it stretched across the soft, half-wintry afternoon. She heard him panting. Again the chuckling constricted sound came up through his wind-pipe.

Then the hunt began to disappear behind the spinneys, hidden by a screen of ash and oak that was still part yellow and tan with dying leaves, and finally he gave an enormous sigh of relaxation and said:

'Wasn't that a sight?' His face, previously red, seemed to go a shade yellowish in reaction. 'Goodness gracious, I just remembered. This door isn't always unlocked. That's a bit of luck! – we might have missed it all.'

It was only after the hunt had disappeared behind the spinney that she found herself, for the first time, looking down to the churchyard. A great nauseating chill of vertigo seemed to scrape, with terrible cold, the skin off her back. For two or three seconds she had a vision of bright rain-soaked grass, the fore-shortened grey headstones of graves, a mass of winking apples still lying under half-bare trees in the orchard beyond. She could not bear it and she looked away. Then the chill relaxed and she was drawn back, in spite of herself, to the same perpendicular, magnetizing view as before: the churchyard, the orchard, the house, and the corner of the square.

This time she saw two more things, one of which was not there and one of which she was not quite sure was there. She thought she saw the bees, in a flash of golden smoke, streaming out from the dark ivy on the crest of the orchard wall.

The other thing she seemed to see was herself. She was walking down below. It was her wedding day. The light summer wind was blowing her, too free and too entranced, across the churchyard. She could feel the wind rippling through and under the silk of her dress, pressing the silk, tingling against her legs and thighs.

'Amazing how you just get these things by half a second. If I hadn't just stepped out to check a box of cheese in the yard. Just a chance like that and there you are.'

She turned and found that he was sweating. He had let his mouth fall open again and he was sucking his breath in sharp-drawn sighs.

'How about going up to the battlements?' he said. 'We might still catch another look at them – '

'I think I'll have to go down,' she said. 'I feel quite strange up here.'

'Ah! it's high,' he said. 'It's high up here. It's a hundred and seventy feet to the top.'

That day she had been married for a little less than six months. She had grown used to the fact that she did not sleep well. She had also grown used to Melford building little evening pagodas of biscuit and cheese, celery and mustard. She had also stopped asking herself how long these things, and everything else about her, might go on, or if anything would happen to change them at all.

Afterwards she used to think that they might have gone on for ever if she had not, six weeks later, almost by chance, gone out one evening to post a letter and buy another record.

Chapter Five

She might have become simply a reclusive person growing more and more attached to inanimate objects or to dogs and cats or even birds and horses. Instead she walked a great deal. Every afternoon after lunch, about two o'clock, she put on a thick winter coat or a tweed costume, with a scarf and good walking shoes and gloves, and set off for the country.

By this time she had acquired the habit of walking with her head down and also slightly cast to one side, as if afraid to look at people. This gained her a reputation, in the town, of being a person of aloofness, cold and standoffish. There were even people who called her 'the Untouchable Mrs T'. This habit of walking with her head down began also to give her the appearance of being round-shouldered, slightly bowed down. It also helped to increase the disturbing effect, when she looked up, of her large brown eyes. By that winter they seemed to have grown too large. They were almost too wide and still and staring, with sometimes an arrested look of being startled.

She made few friends, but once Miss Willis came to tea. The big shapeless girl, once her friend in the shop, looked at the house, the linen, the silver, the wedding presents and the bedroom in which she slept, or tried to sleep, with her gramophone and her records. She seemed nervous and overawed by these things. She stuck out the little finger of the hand holding her tea-cup and said:

'Is it right you'll be Mayoress this year? That's what they say. Aren't you lucky? I can't forget it. I never thought you had a house like this. Do you like married life?' She giggled, letting tea drip from her suspended cup to her saucer. 'I'm sure you must do. I know I should – if I was ever that lucky.'

Constance did not talk much. Afterwards Miss Willis, talking of it to the girls at the drapery, said:

'It was funny – she didn't say much. I don't know how it was, but I got a funny feeling she didn't want me. I don't wonder they call her "the Untouchable Mrs T".'

When Constance went out to buy a record on a dry fresh evening in January, ten days after Christmas, she had also a letter to post. Coming out of the house, drawing on her gloves, turning up her coat collar, she tucked the letter into her pocket and did not remember it again until she was well beyond the square. By that time she was almost equidistant between the post-box by the town hall and the next one that stood on the street corner of Schofield's music shop. She decided then to post the letter at the second box but by the time she got there she had forgotten it again.

The letter was to her mother. In it she had said:

I ought to have written before to thank you for the present you sent me at Christmas, but you know how it is – there is such a lot to do at Christmas and the days go by and before you know where you are another week has gone. It was very nice to have a cheque because now I can buy a record that I have been wanting – perhaps two. Christmas was very quiet with us. We had Mr and Mrs Tom Spencer in for Christmas Day dinner. Mr Spencer is Mayor this year. Then we had Charles Edward Twelvetree and his daughter Agnes and the Rev. and Mrs Orme-Burgess to supper. Mr Twelvetree is a retired solicitor and his daughter keeps house for him. She's rather tart and can take people off rather well, so she kept us amused. For Christmas Day we had a turkey but luckily Melford had been shooting the previous Saturday and got four pheasants, so we had those in the evening, cold. We also had a tree. Melford says it isn't Christmas without a tree.

Although it was ten days after Christmas the ceiling of the Schofield shop was still hung with festoons and chains of green and crimson paper. When she opened the door the chains swung about, rustling in the draught from the street, and the single gas mantle gave its usual pop and spurt, winking shadow.

She waited some time, as she nearly always did, for an answer to the bell. From behind the glass door she could hear the sound of children laughing. Then she opened the street door again and pulled it backwards and forwards once or twice, ringing the bell, and after a few minutes Mrs Schofield appeared.

'Mrs Turner, you should come in, you know, you shouldn't

stand there. You know how we are – you can always come in. Leo is in Leicester today. Was there something you wanted?'

'Just a record.'

At this moment she remembered her letter. It was terribly silly to have forgotten to post it a second time. She took it out of her pocket. For a moment she thought of running as far as the corner with it before she forgot it again and then nervously she put it back in her pocket and said:

'That's my letter. I must try not to forget it again. I've forgotten it twice already.'

'What was the record?' Mrs Schofield said. 'I don't suppose we have it in stock but we can write for it tomorrow.'

Suddenly shyness and confusion about her stupidity in forgetting the letter twice made her also forget the name of the record. She said she knew that it was by Brahms. It was a piece for piano. She knew as well as anything how it went. It had been running through her head all day.

Her large brown eyes were shy and troubled in the narrow face. And as she stood there, trying first to remember the name of the piece and then the first few notes of it, she again pulled uncertainly at the black fingers of her gloves. The gas mantle plopped again above her face and in the greenish dart of light she seemed to have the appearance of jumping because she was startled.

And then Mrs Schofield suddenly turned and called into the back of the shop.

'Frankie. Come into the shop a minute will you, Frankie?'

A young man with thick fair hair came and stood in the doorway at the top of the steps. He was in his shirt-sleeves. His grey trousers were kept up by a light brown leather belt and it was the belt, more than his height, that made him seem extraordinarily slim and supple.

'Mrs Turner, this is my brother, Frankie Johnson,' Mrs Schofield said. 'Frankie, this is Mrs Melford Turner.' The name sounded formal and stiff and perhaps for this reason the young man smiled and gave a slightly formal bow. 'Frankie, Mrs Turner wants to order a record. It's Brahms, isn't it, Mrs Turner? Frankie, you help her. I've got the children to do. You know all about these things.'

Mrs Schofield went up the steps. Her brother stood aside to let her pass and she patted him on the face, affectionately. Then she stood on the top of the steps, smiling with bright fresh blue eyes that were so exactly like her brother's, and said:

'He's a newcomer to the town, Mrs Turner. He starts on Monday at the Rialto. In the orchestra. Playing the piano.'

'Oh! yes,' she said.

Constance had never been to the Rialto. In her shyness she could think of nothing else to say. The Rialto was a former Baptist chapel converted into a cinema that ran films with vaudeville acts between, a place so outside the life of Melford and herself that until that moment she had never given it a single thought. And now Mrs Schofield said:

'You ought to come, Mrs Turner. We're all going to hear him play for the first time, aren't we, Frankie?' He smiled almost exactly as his sister smiled and she said: 'Frankie can play anything. If you can just hum that tune, Mrs Turner, Frankie will play it for you.'

It did not occur to Constance until long afterwards how often, that evening, Mrs Schofield called her brother Frankie or how often Frankie smiled. She was too confused to notice that over-affectionate touch of demonstration. She saw only two people looking very like each other, with their thick fair hair, fresh blue eyes, ivory complexion, and a certain habit of smiling, perhaps, too readily and too frequently.

Some time afterwards, not that night, but later, she realized why the smile seemed to her, at first, too ready and too repeated. It was because, she thought, Melford never smiled in that way. Melford smiled through his teeth. His smile, though not unkindly, was mostly a little elastic muscular exercise. Sometimes it was even less than that. From behind the lean bluish jaws an invisible string was pulled and the lips jerked a brief sharp grimace in reply.

'Well, let's see if we can get this thing, Mrs Turner. Can't you really remember what it's called?'

He smiled again. She began pulling again at the fingers of her gloves, lowering her eyes, trying to think of something to say.

'Couldn't you hum a few bars of it? Just a couple of dozen notes or so?'

Her head felt bleak and empty. The tune that had flowed so pleasantly through her mind for several days past was no longer there.

He sat down at the piano, put his fingers on the keys and smiled.

'Is this it?'

She heard him play a few bars of a piece of Brahms that she did not know. She shook her head and he looked up, smiling again, and said:

'It's a song, isn't it? Not a piece for piano?'

'Oh no, not a song.'

She stood still, watching him under the gaslight. She had hardly moved except for the intermittent pulling of one gloved hand against another. Then he said:

'There's a very beautiful song by Brahms that goes like this.' He played over a few bars of a second piece by Brahms that she did not know. 'But you say it's not a song?'

'No, not a song.'

He smiled again, perhaps for the fifth or sixth time, in as many minutes, and said:

'Well, I'll give a guess what it is. Shall I?'

'You think you could?'

She actually found herself, in that moment, smiling too. The smile came involuntarily, though not into her eyes, and for a moment she stopped pulling at the fingers of her gloves.

'It's this,' he said. 'At least I think it is.'

A moment later he was playing the piece she wanted: an intermezzo, as she then knew quite well. As she stood listening some of her shyness receded. On her face was a look of great surprise. She did not feel quite such a speechless and uncertain fool now that the difficulty of identifying the piece was over. She actually walked a step or two nearer the piano and then he looked up and said:

'Well, was I right? Is that it?'

'That's it,' she said.

He stopped playing. For the first time it was actually she who opened the conversation:

'How did you guess?'

'Intuition. You look terribly surprised.'

It was at that moment that she noticed another thing about his smile. His mouth twisted itself slightly at one corner, quick, a little nonchalant, very slightly mocking. The movement was not unlike a wink. And suddenly she completely astonished herself by saying:

'And what do you know about intuition?'

'What does anybody?'

The shock of her own remark made her suddenly speechless once more. Above her she heard the gas-lamp give a hollow plop and the sound might have been that of her own mouth falling open in astonishment.

'Well, that's *Intermezzo No. 3*. It's a very beautiful one. I've always liked it too.'

She was going to say, in her usual echoing unthinking repetitive way, that yes, it was a very beautiful one, when the gas-mantle above her head gave a series of louder, greener plops and almost went out. He watched it for a second and then went to the stairs and called in to the back of the shop:

'Lois, this mantle seems to be going. I'll fix it if you've got another.'

Almost at once Lois Schofield came to the door at the head of the stairs, carrying the youngest of the children against her hip and said:

'It's always going. This is the second one this week. You'll have to go out and get another, Frankie, if you wouldn't mind. Did you find your record, Mrs Turner?'

'Yes, we found it. At least your brother did.'

'I told you Frankie would,' she said.

The gas gave a series of big expiring flops, with orange-green flame curling at the edges of the white mantle fabric, and she said: 'You'd better put it out altogether, Frankie, and get another as soon as you can.'

'Where can I get one?'

'Oh, Mrs Turner will show you, Frankie,' she said. 'And you can see her as far as the square at the same time.'

He stood on a chair to turn out the gas. Mrs Schofield said 'Good night, Mrs Turner, you really should come on Monday,' and suddenly the shop was dark, with Constance and the young man feeling their way to the door and the street beyond.

It was only long afterwards that she was struck by the importance of a triviality like the breaking of a gas-mantle. She was still too shy that evening to be anything more than half-conscious of what was happening. She remembered walking up the broad, almost empty High Street between its high causeways, in the direction of the square, not speaking much, aware of street-trees naked under gas-light and a watery half-moon above the church.

Nothing of this was important. The one important thing that she did notice was so obvious that it escaped her completely until they reached the square. Then it surprised her so much that she stopped in the middle of the pavement, horrified.

'I've only just noticed it. You haven't got your jacket on!'

He laughed and plucked at his shirt-sleeves.

'Oh! I'm never cold. I never notice it.'

'But you should have a jacket. It's January, it's cold tonight. You'll catch your death. You must be frozen.'

The look of polite horror on her face was so great that he laughed again and said:

'All right. Feel.' He put out one hand. 'No. You've got your glove on.'

Suddenly he laid his hand against the side of her face. It lay there for a second or two; it was not cold. Afterwards she knew that the fingers were comparatively short and thick, but the only impression she got that evening was one of lightness. The fingers brushed her lightly and were taken away.

'Always warm,' he said. 'Good circulation.'

'Yes, but that's no excuse for the jacket. It's treacherous up here. The wind can be damp and dreadfully cold in these valleys. You need a good warm coat – and you haven't even a jacket on.'

He laughed again.

'Well, if you must know Lois is mending it,' he said. 'I tore one of the pockets on the door-handle of the train.'

'That's all very well,' she said, 'but you need it all the same.'

Then she was aware that she was speaking to him as she never spoke to other people. She was amazed to find herself speaking peremptorily, a little annoyed, but whether with him for being so stupid as to come out without a jacket or with Lois Schofield for not mending it she was not quite sure.

'Anyway you'd better get your gas-mantle quickly and make haste back home,' she said, 'and get by the fire.'

Like many shy people who do not trust themselves she sometimes spoke rather quickly, almost tersely. It was really her way of getting her words out before total shyness blanked them out altogether, but sometimes it had the effect of giving her voice a certain shortness. That too had given many people the impression that she was a person who was aloof and cool.

'Oh! well,' he said and he laughed again, almost gaily. 'If you want to get rid of me – '

'Oh! I didn't mean it like that.' She was horrified now by her own clumsy presumption. 'I didn't mean it that way.'

'Come with me to get the gas-mantle,' he said.

'You don't think I meant it that way, do you?' she said and again, through sheer nervousness, she was speaking rather quickly. 'I should feel awful if you felt I meant it like that.'

'Come on,' he said. 'Come with me to get the gas-mantle. Where is this shop?'

She stood on the pavement at the edge of the square, embarrassed by her own clumsiness, almost bewildered, and said:

'I think Smithson's have them. This way – down here.'

Gas-globes of all sizes and colours filled the window of the shop outside which she stood waiting two minutes later. Inside, on a wooden counter, a man was cutting a length of lead-piping fixed in a vice. She watched him unscrew the vice, swivelling the handle. Then he reached up to a shelf behind the counter and took down a little square cardboard box and put it in front of the young man in his shirt-sleeves.

A moment later an unexpected thing happened. She saw the young man begin to feel in his pockets. He even made a gesture as if to feel in the inside pocket of the jacket that was not there.

Then he turned to her, shrugged his shoulders and lifted his hands. A moment later he was outside the shop again, saying:

'I'm terribly sorry, Mrs Turner, but my note-case is in my jacket – '

'Oh! I have money. Don't worry about that. A few coppers for a gas-mantle – '

She came close under the light of the window to open her purse.

'You take it,' she said. 'I've got my gloves on. Take half a crown.'

He took the coin from her purse, thanked her and went back into the shop. After shutting her purse she looked up and saw Smithson, a man with steel-rimmed spectacles, peering uncertainly towards her through the gas-globes: as if perhaps wondering if it were really Mrs Melford Turner outside there, unaccountably lending money to a strange young man who, on a cool fresh winter evening, had forgotten both his jacket and his money.

When Frankie Johnson came out of the shop he had the gas-mantle in one hand and the change in the other. He held out the change to her and said, smiling:

'Perhaps that'll teach me to come out with my jacket next time. I was going to ask you to have a drink with me too – but now that will have to wait until next time.'

'Oh! I really don't drink,' she said.

She knew that what she really meant was that she did not drink in public places. But the mere idea of saying so seemed unthinkably prim, strait-laced and old-fashioned. It was impossible in any way to convey the idea that it could have been in some degree not nice for her to have taken a drink in a bar. But because she wanted to efface any impression of narrow and stupid convention she said:

'But that doesn't prevent you from having one. Yes, that's a good idea. You call in at The George or somewhere on your way back and buy yourself a drink and get yourself warm. Buy yourself a good big sherry.'

He said something else about having no money. She told him not to bother about a thing like that and he put the money in his pocket. At the street corner a sudden wind coming out of the square lifted the entire mass of his thick fair hair, tossing it about his face. He looked at that moment, in his shirt-sleeves, brushing his hair into place, athletic and easy-limbed and confident and very young. All the time she had forgotten, as in fact she had been slowly forgetting for the past six months, how young she was herself. She had never given a single thought, except when she had undressed herself and lain waiting for Melford on the night of her marriage, to the notion of how young she was. That was the only night in which she had felt her youth, the awkwardness, the expectation and the uncertainty of it, either consciously or acutely, and that was why she said now, in a way quite beyond her years and with a touch of kindliness that might have been learned from Melford:

'Now you hurry back and get that drink and warm yourself up – '

'There's a good boy.'

'No, I didn't mean it like that. You know I didn't mean it like that. But I know how treacherous these valleys are.'

'I know,' he said. He gave once again the small, mouth-winking, partly nonchalant smile. 'It's very nice of you.'

'And it's very nice of you,' she said, 'to have found my record. You won't forget it will you?'

He promised not to forget it.

'Mr Schofield is dreadfully forgetful,' she said. 'Sometimes I order a record and he forgets it and then I'm – ' she was on the verge of saying lonely and then she checked herself and said, 'lost without it.'

'I won't forget it,' he said. 'It's a beautiful thing, the Brahms.'

At the last moment, as she said good-bye, she forced herself to lift her face. Her large brown eyes stared at him with the first fully deliberate glance she had given him all evening. It did not last more than a second or two but even then she felt herself holding her face in a vice in order to complete it. Then he smiled for the last time, said 'Good night' and a moment later was walking out of the square.

It was not until she was actually standing in front of the house again that she remembered her letter. She walked slowly back across the square. Lights burning in the upstairs chambers of the town hall threw long bars of yellow on the bare line of chestnut trees below. She walked under and past the chestnut trees, into shadow beyond them and then out of the square, not really thinking.

When she stopped to post her letter she got as far as holding it against the mouth of the box before she drew it back again. Then she began to walk down the street, for the second time that evening, towards the Schofield shop. She was still not really thinking. All she was aware of was a feeling of trying to prolong, in suspense, an inexplicable sensation that was slipping away. The air that evening was fresh and dry but sometimes, in a sudden lull of wind, it was perfectly still and without a sound. She felt she could reach out and grasp it like a tangible fabric and hold it in her hands.

That was precisely the sensation she was trying to hold inside herself. It was like a sensation of great quietness that she was afraid something might shatter. It was neither a feeling for anybody nor about anything. It had nothing to do at that moment with music, a gas-mantle, a smile or a sensation of a hand touching the side of her face. It was more as if she herself were suspended in an inexact and curious state of wonder.

She posted her letter at last at the corner by the shop. Then she walked up and down on the opposite side of the street outside the shop. The shop was dark and shut. There was no sound of voices.

It was only when she began to walk home again that the stream of all her self-consciousness came flooding back.

'What did I say?' she thought. 'I was talking all the time. I never stopped talking. I was saying the most idiotic things.'

Crushed by a greater pall of shyness than ever she began to hurry home. She turned up the collar of her coat and hid her face in it. Afraid of meeting him again she branched off hurriedly into back streets, going home through the churchyard, half running the last few yards under the one gas-light, between the graves.

'You fool,' she kept saying to herself. 'You poor, idiotic, talkative fool. Whatever in the name of all that's holy will he think of you?'

It was some weeks before she could bring herself to go down to the shop again, even for her record. It did not occur to her during this time that her reluctance was abnormal or stupid. She was incapable of realizing that although what she called her idiotic and talkative phrases had never stopped repeating themselves in her own head they might well have been forgotten by someone else in ten minutes or so.

It is possible that she might never have gone to the shop again if she had not accidentally run into Schofield one February afternoon in the square.

'I've got your record, Mrs Turner,' he said. 'The one you ordered. It's been in some time. You've never been down for it, have you?'

No: she had never been down for it. She had always been meaning to come down for it, she said.

'The children have asked after you several times. They haven't forgotten that day you came down.'

She was glad about the children, she said. She hoped they were well. She would come down some time in the week for the record. She was sorry she hadn't collected it before.

'Come early one evening before the children go to bed,' he said. 'They would like to see you. About five – that's a good time.'

In her quiet way, face averted and slightly looking down, she promised she would do so.

'Well,' he said, 'I must get on.' He looked from under the sparkling rims of his spectacles at the February sky. Big, deep-folded clouds were running in from the north-east and the wind was dry and cold. 'I don't like where the wind sits,' he said. 'Sunday it was like spring and today when I woke up I said to Lois I could smell the snow.'

'Yes, it was like spring,' she said. 'We've got snowdrops in the garden. Even a few crocuses.'

'I don't fancy their chances,' he said and looked again at the cold, big-clouded sky.

When she got home again she remembered what he had said about snow and snowdrops and she went down into the orchard to gather a bunch or two of the flowers. They grew everywhere in the grass at the feet of the apple-trees. By this time the clouds were rough and grey underneath, with white-clawed upper edges. The wind made her hands reddish-blue with cold as she bunched the snowdrops together and she was glad to get back into the house again.

'Just a few snowdrops for you, Miss Mackness. I thought you'd like them.'

One of the few friends she had made was Miss Mackness, 'our

Miss Weakness' of the shop. Sometimes on afternoons when the shop was not very busy she went in and whispered into the pigeon-hole behind which the anaemic face of Miss Mackness sniffed wetly:

'Mrs Butterworth has a cup of tea in the kitchen, Miss Mackness, if you'd like to go through.'

She was sorry for Miss Mackness. Without ever saying so or really feeling it very consciously she resented Melford's 'our Miss Weakness'. There was something touching and affectionate about the pale red-lidded girl that reminded her of a partly starved and timid cat. In her enclosed glass trap, busy with her ledgers and carbons and bills impaled on hooks, Miss Mackness seemed to purr delicately about her with tiny lips and albino-looking eyes, scratching at papers with thin arms covered with palest freckles.

Constance not only took bunches of flowers to Miss Mackness. Sometimes she gave her a hat or a dress that she did not want any longer. In turn Miss Mackness rewarded her with half-finished confidences in which there was a touch of mystery:

'Well, we shall some day. If we live and have good luck and things come out right and we get a house of our own.' Constance took sentences like this to refer to coming marriage, but to whom or at what time Miss Mackness, shy in her own way, never disclosed. Miss Mackness did not even wear an engagement ring. 'We sometimes see you when we're out of an evening. We saw you one day last week, but you were too far away to see us.'

From this and other half-resolved remarks she gathered an impression of youth in love. 'I love the fields,' Miss Mackness said. 'I love to get out of the town in summer and walk in the fields.' Miss Mackness was possibly twenty-five or -six and from behind the reddish hairless eyes Constance was given glimpses of thrifty romance, secret tendernesses and even hints of passion in summer fields.

'I don't know how you feel sometimes,' Miss Mackness said, 'but some flowers have a queer effect on you. Not snowdrops. Not on me. But cowslips – I can hardly bear to go into a field of cowslips. There's something about the way the flowers feel when you touch them. Did you ever get that feeling with flowers?'

'No, I never felt that with flowers,' Constance said.

About five o'clock that evening she put on her big coat and gloves and walked across the square to collect her record. At the last moment before leaving the house something made her pin a large bunch of the snowdrops on her coat. She pinned them upside down.

As she got nearer to the shop, holding her head down and turning up the collar of her coat against the wind, a few flakes of snow began to drive in from the north-east. They were so hard that they bounced without breaking along the gutters, gathering dust as they rolled.

By the time she had reached the shop they were falling quite thickly. They were skimming like blown white seeds along the pavements, spiralling up in bitter dusty whirlwinds.

As she went into the shop she hoped that Mrs Schofield's brother would not be there. She hoped that Schofield himself would answer the bell. She had already decided not to stay for more than a few moments in the shop, but simply to pick up her record, pay for it and go. Already the evenings were growing lighter and this time there would be no gas-mantle, she thought, to make her stay and talk too much and end by making herself a fool.

To her great relief it was Schofield himself who answered the bell.

'All ready and wrapped up for you, Mrs Turner,' he said.

'I'm so glad,' she said, 'because I think I ought to get back as quickly as I can before the snow sets in.'

'Didn't I tell you?' he said. 'I could smell it in the air. You gathered your snowdrops just in time.'

While he was peering into an under-the-counter cash-box, trying to find a last odd sixpence for her change, she stood staring through the shop-window at the snow. It was falling now in thicker, larger flakes that floated round and round on whorls of wind.

Suddenly he startled her completely by putting her change on the counter and saying:

'I've just remembered, Mrs Turner. Frankie wants to speak to you.'

'To me? To me?' she said. Shyness, coming back in one

73

suffocating and enveloping wave, gave her voice something like a stammer. 'To me?'

'Frankie!' he called.

Less than half a minute later the young man stood on the steps at the back of the shop. He was wearing a jacket this time.

'It's Mrs Turner, Frankie,' Schofield said. 'Did you say you wanted to speak to her?'

The young man came down the steps, smiling with the corner of his mouth, looking straight at her.

'Yes. I wanted to apologize.'

'Apologize?'

She could not think of any possible reason for apology. It all seemed suddenly very silly and she said, rather shortly:

'I can't think what about.'

'It wasn't No. 3,' he said. 'It was No. 4.' She stared at him as if he could only be suffering from some enormous illusion. 'The intermezzo.'

'Oh, that.' The sudden relief that followed her shyness made her speak quickly without her realizing it. 'I couldn't think what on earth you were talking about. It couldn't possibly make any difference as long as it was the right piece, could it?'

'Could to me,' he said. 'Bit of pride attached to it. I didn't want you to think when you opened the record and found No. 4 – '

He stopped and smiled again.

'Think what?' she said.

'I didn't want you to think I'd fooled you,' he said.

'Oh! I wouldn't think that. I would never think that.'

'It was just damned stupid,' he said. 'I knew all the time it was No. 4 and there I was like a fool telling you No. 3 – '

'Well, the only thing I can do is to go home now and play it,' she said, 'and see if it sounds like I thought it would.'

He smiled again, twisting the corners of his mouth rather more sharply than usual.

'One to you. I suppose I deserved that,' he said.

By this time Schofield had gone back into the room behind the shop. The quickness of speech that had embarrassed her before had already come back without her noticing it. But now for a moment or two she simply stood with open mouth, looking at him with large brown eyes.

Then she said: 'Deserved? I can't think what you mean by deserved.'

'Teach me to show off,' he said. His smile this time was charming and less quick. 'Teach me to try to impress you with my musical knowledge and all that. You know – when all I do is hack away at a piano.'

She did not know what to say. She resumed for a few seconds her habit of pulling at the fingers of her gloves. Then he said:

'That reminds me. I'd better get down there.' He began to go up the stairs. 'Hang on a minute. I'll be good and get my overcoat this time and then I can walk part of the way back with you.'

It was snowing very fast, with big whipping flakes, as they walked up through the town. The air was sharp and bitter. Snow had driven most people indoors and except for a late postman wheeling a bicycle against the wind the streets were deserted. Most of the pavements were already thinly covered, smooth and without tracks, but at street corners wind lifted the snow into furious and dusty drifts, leaving naked stone.

'Isn't this your turning?' she said. They were two hundred yards from the empty snow-swept square. 'Isn't this the way you go?'

'I'll come the rest of the way,' he said.

'Won't that make you late?' she said. 'I hope not. We'd better go this way.'

She very often took the short-cut that went behind the church-yard. The streets were narrow. There were fewer people that way. The walls of a few big houses enclosed the streets and were hung with branches of big lilacs, copper-beech and evergreens. Already now snow was settling quietly on the branches, along the sheltered walls, out of the wind.

'I often come this way,' she said. 'I like it this way. It's pretty with the big gardens and there aren't so many people.'

'Don't you like people?'

'Oh, yes, I like people.'

They walked on for perhaps another thirty or forty yards.

Suddenly he stopped by a wooden gate that led into one of the gardens and asked her what time it was.

She always wore a small blue-enamelled watch pinned to the front of her dress, just under her left shoulder. Now she opened the collar and front of her coat so that she could find the watch. By this time, under snow and snow-cloud, the evening was almost dark. She could not see the hands of her watch clearly and now she lifted the watch towards him and said:

'I can't quite see it. Can you see?'

'Looks like a quarter to six,' he said. 'I think I ought to go back.'

'Perhaps you should,' she said.

He stood watching while she buttoned up her coat. Snow had covered the entire crown of her hat. A few flakes had attached themselves like little feathers to the tips of her dark hair. He seemed to be looking at these dark and white fringes of hair instead of fully at her face when he said:

'Why do you wear them upside down?'

'Wear what upside down?'

'The snowdrops.'

She laughed. Suddenly, without knowing why, she felt happy and excited.

'Fancy your noticing that.'

He touched the snowdrops with one hand. 'I noticed them when you came in.' He lifted the heads of the snowdrops slightly and let them fall again. Then, a moment later, he was holding her lightly by both shoulders.

'I've been wondering about you,' he said.

'Wondering? – About me?'

The next moment he was holding her by the wall. She tried to say something. At the same moment she realized, amazedly, that he was taking off her hat. She turned her face sharply up to him to say something else and then felt a flake or two of snow fall on her cold bare skin.

A moment later he kissed her. She did not say a word. She simply made a quick darting sideways movement of her face and said:

'You shouldn't do that. You shouldn't kiss me.'

'When can I see you?' he said. 'I wanted to see you and you never came down – '

'See me?'

'Tomorrow,' he said, 'how about tomorrow?'

'It's snowing,' she said. A strange amorphous creature who was not herself was speaking for her. The snow was big and cold as it fell on her face and her mouth was trembling. 'There'll be snow tomorrow.'

'I get the afternoons free,' he said. 'Every afternoon except Thursday and Saturday. I could come tomorrow.'

'Even in the snow?'

'Even in the snow,' he said, and without protest she let him kiss her again.

As he kissed her she heard the branch of a tree crack somewhere above her in the freezing wind. It cracked only once. Then all about her there was nothing but dead stillness, the streets soft under snow, the air and the darkness thickened and cushioned by snow into an enormous silence, in the centre of which was herself, amazed and half-distracted, wondering what she had done.

Chapter Six

She went home to the usual sort of supper in which Melford brought adoration to rice-pudding and built little pagodas of cheese and biscuits crowned with mustard. Although there was now, in February, no more celery, he was able to build the pagodas just as high and carefully without it, and he was able to make the usual joke to Mrs Butterworth about the pudding not being so good as the night before.

'There was a fellow in the shop this afternoon at four o'clock who said it began snowing in Leicester at two,' he said. 'But then that's farther north. I never like late snows. If this keeps on it will upset the point-to-points.'

It had been a good season for hunting. Not too much frost. He had struck a really good fine day every time he had gone out and he had enjoyed it very much.

'Pass the salt will you please?' he said. 'You're on the quiet side tonight.'

'Am I? I was just thinking. I might take up music again.'

He poured a little pillar of salt on to the edge of his cheese plate and stuck a piece of cheddar into it.

'Music?' he said. 'Piano?'

'That's what I was thinking,' she said. 'Is there anyone here who teaches?'

'There used to be a Miss Tompkins down by the station,' he said, 'but whether she's still there I couldn't say. Wait a minute – didn't our Miss Weakness used to go there at one time? I rather think she did. Ask Miss Weakness.'

He did not think of her taking up the piano as either a very good idea or a very bad idea. If he had been asked he would have said, most likely, that he was sorry she had not changed her mind about taking up horses. He still hoped she would do. Apart from anything else he thought it would do her good physically. She looked droopy. Her eyes, apart from their natural deep brownness, were heavy underneath, with bruise-coloured shadows, and there was never much colour in her cheeks, so that sometimes he thought she did not look healthy.

'I forgot to tell you,' he said, 'but they still have that mare, the one we saw. I always felt we made a boob there, not having her.'

One of his less frequent but favourite expressions was 'making a boob'. The parson sometimes made a boob on Sunday morning by giving out the wrong hymn. Miss Weakness sometimes made a boob with her ledgers.

'Perhaps we will have it one day,' she said.

'You've only got to say and I'll go over and fix it up,' he said. 'I honestly think you ought to get more exercise. There's nothing like fresh air.' He stopped suddenly and looked up from one of his little pagodas. 'What are you doing?'

She was at the window, holding back a corner of the curtains, looking out.

'Looking at the square,' she said. 'At the snow.'

The square, deserted, all white under its street lamps, had the appearance of a small hushed desert in which the market cross made a pyramid in the centre. There was no longer any wind. Snow was still falling in large dreamy flakes. Already it hung thick, like big blown flowers, on the branches of the chestnut trees. From time to time one of these too heavy flowers of snow fell without a sound, an enormous bursting flake exploding under the street lights. And as she saw it she remembered the flake or two of snow that had fallen sharp and cold on her bare face in the moment before she had let herself be kissed by Frankie Johnson. It seemed a great while ago, that moment, but its expansion into full experience was still not complete. It was still much more like one deep and prolonged hush of suspense than an incident. Like the big flowers of snow hanging on the chestnut boughs, strained to breaking point until they fell and exploded, she felt herself still waiting for this single moment to break into fragments and take her with its fall.

'How is it now?' he said.

She could not describe how it was now. Her breath condensing on the window, had put between herself and the snowy deserted square a diffused white bloom. The houses were dreamy and insubstantially white cubes, floating in a dead white world.

'I said how is it now? Letting up at all?'

She rubbed with her sleeve on the glass. Across the square a great flower, pulling down another and then a third and a fourth, fell in a slow shower of snow-blossom from the branches of a chestnut.

'Still snowing,' she said. 'Faster than ever.'

'Nuisance,' he said. 'You get these late snows sometimes and they hang on for weeks. After all it's nearly March. We don't want snow in March.'

'What did they want for the mare?'

She had no conscious or special reason for asking about the mare. She really had neither use nor interest for the animal. The question was evolved and spoken without thought, before she could stop it.

'To tell you the honest truth I can't remember,' he said. 'I'm not even certain we got as far as that. But it's easy to find out. I could easily go over.'

Someone was walking across the square, a solitary black figure in a white desert, heavy-footed, trudging in white space. When it had disappeared the transfiguration of everything was restored again, pure and lovely.

'Were you really thinking of – you know honestly I think it would do you a power of good. With spring coming on and all that. Once you started riding I think you'd get no end of fun out of it.'

'I wish I could skate,' she said.

What made her talk suddenly about skating? he thought, although her second inconsequential remark that evening did not strike him as unusual. He was used to her wrapping herself up in a day-dream, behind the big brown meditative eyes, and then suddenly saying something that did not belong to any previous conversation. Guests at the house sometimes found this habit disconcerting, but he was growing quite used to it now.

It simply made him say:

'Well, I'm going to skate into the sitting-room for a glass of port. What about you?'

'No thanks. I think I'll go up to bed.'

'I've a good mind to smoke the last of those cigars Tom Spencer gave me at Christmas,' he said. 'It's the sort of night for a cigar. Somehow snow on the ground makes you think of cigars.'

'Does it?' she said and without saying anything more she let the curtain fall, shutting out the square and the snow. And then, just before she went out of the room and up to bed, he said:

'Think about the mare. Give it a thought. It might be a thing for the summer.'

When she had gone to bed he went into the sitting-room, found the last of the cigars Tom Spencer had given him at Christmas and poked the fire. When the fire woke into flame he lit the cigar with a piece of coal held in a pair of steel tongs and then poured himself a glass of port and sat down.

The easy chairs were upholstered in smooth brown leather. A dado of dark brown wallpaper, grained like old oak, ran completely round the room. Round the fire stood an upraised oak kerb on which he could put his feet. The masculine air of the room continued on the upper walls with pictures of hunt-meets, point-to-point winners and several coloured prints of lean stretched horses running in Victorian or even earlier steeple-chases. Over the fireplace hung three riding crops, a brush and a hunting horn. On the black wooden mantelshelf stood a big stone tobacco-jar and a rack of pipes and a vase of paper spills.

In the snowy air the fire burned brightly, with little springing leaves of fierce blue flame. He sat directly in front of it, legs outstretched, and without realizing it, because he was thinking of Constance, drank his port rather quickly. He had almost given up as irretrievable her decision not to ride. Now she suddenly brought it up again and he felt something more than pleased. It would be a fine thing, he could not help thinking, if he could persuade her finally into it, if they could ride together and if he could gradually introduce her to that world where, as he said, he thought she would get so much fun.

Suddenly the full recollection of the afternoon when he had taken her to see the mare came back to him. He remembered not only the mare and her lack of interest in it but the way she had slipped from it, clumsily, ruffling her skirt.

The recollection brought him to a conflicting and miserable

state of emotion. Once, as a boy at school, he had fallen in a sudden faint at morning prayers. The next morning, in white terror, he waited for his blood to recede, his legs to loose their strength and the blackness to smother him again. After he had fallen down in a second faint he felt that never again could he go to morning prayers. Each morning afterwards he hid himself in cloakrooms or behind staircases or in empty classrooms, shaking and strengthless, unable to face it. It was six months or more before he could fight through his impotent agonies and bring himself to go back.

His experience with Constance had been very much the same. Two attempts to make love to her had been such a failure that he could not bear to think of them; and as with his fainting he could not make a third. Neither of them had changed her status as a single woman except to give her a new kind of surprise about male behaviour that she had never expected. She had never known that after the second of them, as after the second of his fainting fits, he had shut himself up in an empty cloakroom downstairs and broken into weeping.

All the time, behind it all, lay his constant and mocking idea of a son. She did not know that very often as she lay awake at night, listening starkly to the maddening repetition of clock chimes, he was lying awake too, feeling as arid, though never so frenzied or deeply, as she did. He had many bitter thoughts about himself. His brain could never sort them out. Like intensely ravelled knots they were simply too much for him. He lacked the ingenuity and resource, and finally the sheer impatience in his blood, to tear them into solution.

His failure to be able to go to her, to express elementary affection, to be able to have a son, did not simply mock him. It seemed to drive him more and more into masculine habits that outwardly made him seem insensitive, genial and hearty. It could not possibly have occurred to anyone, watching him ride, seeing him coming home with face blue-savaged by winter wind after a day of shooting, that there was a black worm inside himself, crawling insidiously round and round, eating at him, filling him sometimes with miserable self-hatred.

His third glass of port renewed the image of Constance slipping from the mare. He did not often drink three glasses of port in an evening, even though they were small. But now, as the port warmed and soothed him, he felt himself slowly being drawn into a state of mind when he could bring himself to think of going up to Constance, bending over her bed and actually touching her. Several times he saw again the image of her long legs against the firm black skin of the mare. And in a curious way it was not only Constance that excited him. There was something uneasily compelling about the black gleaming naked- ness of the mare.

As he went upstairs he kept wishing that he could bring him- self to touch his wife as easily as he could run his hand over the skin of a horse. By the time he reached the head of the stairs he was breathing hard and trembling. He always went in to say good night to her, mostly with deliberately perfunctory phrases, generally about something he had read in the evening paper, which he always carried in his hand, but tonight he could hardly bring himself to touch the door.

Then he stiffened up, making himself go in. He had not been reading the evening paper. He felt curiously lost without it. His hands were free. He did not know what to do with them and he began to rub them to and fro against each other, stiffly, as if they were cold.

Then he was standing against the bed. The gas-fire was burn- ing. The gramophone was playing her record. Constance herself was lying half on her side, deep in the pillow, with the overhead light still on, her dark hair long and her face half-hidden in it and tucked down, in much the same way as she walked with her face tucked into her collar.

Perhaps because of the sound of the record or simply because she was lost in listening to it she did not hear him at first and she gave a sudden start as he came to the bed.

'Constance,' he said. He spoke inquiringly. 'Constance –'

With almost a stutter he found himself searching for some sort of endearing phrase which would explain why he was stand- ing there. He could not find it; nor could he explain; instead he reached down and touched her bare neck, through the open nightdress.

'What on earth do you want?' she said. She jerked her head and looked up at him with vast brown eyes broken out of a dream-glaze. 'What do you think you're doing? What's the matter?'

He managed to gather together a phrase or two about coming to say good night. Then he stood away. His jaw, falling open, gave him once again a look of weakness. All the time the gramophone played on and the gas-fire hissed in the fireplace.

'Don't come in here like that!' she said. Her voice was cold and neutral. 'I don't want you in here. I was listening to something. I don't want you in here.'

He had never seen her eyes narrow before as they now narrowed, under the gaslight, until the pupils seemed clenched and black.

'And don't touch me,' she said. 'Don't touch me. Don't try to touch me.'

Snow continued to fall for three days from a thick packed grey sky. It blew in from the east, horizontally, on a wind that drove it into curled and crusted drifts about the square. When it finally ceased the wind still drove it up in dense white powder, so that sometimes beyond the entrance to the square almost nothing was visible except the vague black forks of crooked telegraph poles hung with drooping ropes of snow.

At lunch-time on the third day Melford tapped the glass of the barometer in the hall for a fifth time that morning and then came in to the dining-room and said that he thought it was getting warmer. Icicles hung from the windows like narrow candles without sparkle in the grey air. Snow had frozen to the panes in thick salt-like crusts. If it was coming warmer, Melford said, then you could be sure that there would be fog too. And that was a fine prospect, he said, fog on top of snow.

'And everybody's got colds,' he said. 'Everybody's sniffing. Hyde and Flaky started it and now Miss Weakness has got it. She sniffs like some old goat – every three seconds.'

Once again she felt sorry for Miss Mackness. She felt a sense of companionship between herself, imprisoned in the house by snow, and the pale red-eyed girl imprisoned in the cubicle of her cash-desk.

'You should make her take a few days off,' she said. 'She would be better in bed.'

84

'Miss Weakness off?' he said. 'And who in the world is going to run the cash if Miss Weakness is off?'

'I could run it.'

'I don't want my wife working in the shop, thank you,' he said. His voice crackled like starch. 'We haven't quite come to that yet, thank you.'

'I used to handle the cash at – '

'Whatever you used to do has nothing to do with it,' he said.

She was quiet and did not answer. Everywhere the snow, the icicles and the thick-crusted windows created a sense of imprisonment. She could not go out. Several times that week she had remarked how she loved the snow, how beautiful it was and how much she would love to walk in it, and each time Melford had said:

'All I can say is you're welcome to it. I've seen enough this week to last me for ever. There's been nothing like it since that year the Nene froze.'

That afternoon when she went down into the shop to tell Miss Weakness that there was a cup of tea in the kitchen the girl was breathing with short snatching strokes. She struggled with her mouth open, trying to get her breath, bringing tears to her eyes.

In the kitchen the tea continually made her cough. Her coughing rasped from her thin chest with a harsh sound of scraping. The cold had settled right down in her system, she said.

'You should never be here,' Constance said. 'You should wrap yourself up in bed with hot bottles and stay at home.'

'You think I should? That's what Mr Hyde said yesterday.'

'Mr Hyde is right,' Constance said. The entire face of Miss Mackness seemed to stream with moisture and now and then she snuffled. 'Stay at home tomorrow.'

'I think I will,' Miss Mackness said, 'if I feel no better.'

The following morning Melford stamped into the house in outrage.

'Neither Hyde nor Weakness have turned up,' he said. 'How do you like that? Both of them. I could understand one – but both of them. It wouldn't surprise me if they put their heads together.'

She was quiet again and he went on:

'Flaky and I have to do the entire shop. And now the snow has stopped people are drifting in again. By afternoon we'll both need forty pairs of hands.'

Over the snow, which had stopped in the night, a light raw fog had formed. It lay on streets and square like low damp smoke. In the windless air the snow had lost its crispness. At the windows icicles were beginning to thaw very slowly, greyly dripping moisture.

All the morning the thin lifeless fog increased her sense of imprisonment. By midday the fog had thickened and darkened so much that underneath it the snow seemed dead and crushed and she could not see the distant sides of the square.

'Chaotic,' Melford said at lunch-time. 'Chaotic. Yesterday we had exactly three people in. This morning we had nearer fifty.'

'Let me come and work in the cash-desk.'

'No,' he said. 'I've told you no and I mean no. What do you think people would say if they saw you there?'

'They would say,' she said in her quiet way, 'that Miss Mackness was ill and I was helping you.'

By afternoon she was working in the cash-desk. It was strange, at first, to be sitting in the too-small, too-enclosed cubicle, with its three glass sides, its central shaded electric bulb and its tiny pigeon-hole through which she took the bills. Much of her shyness came back as she sat there. Under the glass of the overhead electric light, in the foggy darkening afternoon, she felt like someone painfully held there by a shaft of limelight, almost nakedly exposed.

At the same time she felt a sense of isolation. The afternoon gradually dissolved, beyond the light of the shop, into a strange wintry blueness that had less and less reality. Somewhere beyond it, in the silent fog, the entire town had melted away. And with the town, dissolving into its mass of fog and snow, the young man from the music shop, Frankie Johnson, had vanished too. It was impossible to believe he had ever existed. She had never spoken to him. She had never lifted her face, and let it be kissed, unexpectedly and without protest, in a single astonishing moment under the first fresh fall of snow.

It must have been about four o'clock that afternoon when she looked up from rubbing out a pencilled mistake in the cash-book to hear Flaky, the youth on the bacon counter, say-ing:

'Yes, sir, it's rare weather. It cuts right through you. It seems to get right down to your bones.'

Then in the act of blowing away the dust of her pencilled mistake she sat suddenly stiff and trapped in her cubicle. The mechanical bacon-cutter made a series of skidding slices at the air and Flaky said:

'A pound of best back, sir, and what else will there be? Would there be anything else, sir?'

'Eggs.' It was Frankie Johnson speaking. 'A dozen please.'

She could not move. She simply sat staring at him standing by the counter. The collar of his coat was turned up. The edges of his fair light hair were touched with the beaded vapour of fog. She felt a great quiver of surprise and excitement cut through her and then Flaky said:

'Eggs are always sold by the score here, sir. Will you have half a score?'

'I was told to get a dozen.'

'Well, you could have a dozen if you wished, sir,' Flaky said. 'But we generally sell them by the score.'

She sat staring from the cash-desk, shy and stiffened. From the opposite counter Melford pulled at an overhead reel of string. The reel whirled, the white string hung in the air as in a sort of rope-trick and Melford said across the shop:

'Of course the gentleman can have a dozen. It's just that they're always sold here by the score, sir, I don't know why.'

Half blindly she wrote something in the the cash-book and then rubbed it out again, eyes held down.

'Wicked weather,' Melford said. 'The last we had like this was eight years ago. That started in February too and there were still drifts under the hedgerows in May.'

He stared with chilly pallid eyes at the windows of the shop and at the strange blue snow-fog beyond them and then shud-dered.

'Give me the spring days,' he said, 'and anybody can have the snow.'

'I rather like it,' Frankie Johnson said. 'I don't mind it at all. Yesterday it looked beautiful.'

Melford finished tying a parcel, cutting the string with a sharp snip, and said:

'You ought to talk to my wife. She's a snow-lover.' He looked across the shop and in rather a louder voice addressed her in the cash-desk. 'You're a bit of a snow-lover, aren't you, Constance?' he said.

In her shy way she said, 'Yes,' but her voice was so low that Melford, as if not hearing her, said:

'I don't think she's quite so convinced about it today though. Not since the fog came.'

She wrote again in the cash-book, eyes held down. In suspense she twisted one foot against another. Then, after several moments of agony because she dared not look up and because she feared that Melford would speak again and make her look up, the door of the shop opened and she looked up involuntarily, startled.

Then in the same moment as she saw a woman customer shaking a wet umbrella by the door she saw Frankie Johnson waiting beyond the pigeon-hole.

He put his bill, together with a ten-shilling note, on the cash-desk. She picked it up. She looked quickly at its figures and began searching nervously in the cash-drawer for change. She was once again painfully aware of being imprisoned, and at the same time exposed, under the bare electric light bulb. She fumbled with change and then finally she pushed it across to him, acutely aware at the same time of his rather short small hands waiting to pick it up.

Then she remembered she had not stamped the bill. For some seconds she could not find the rubber stamp and in confusion she started trembling. Then she could not find the indelible ink-pad and while she was still searching for it he said:

'I think you gave me too much.'

She looked up. Her eyes were swimming with nervousness. She saw him smile. She managed to smile too and he said:

'Isn't that right? Three-and-eight from ten – that's six-and-four, isn't it? Not seven.'

'I'm sorry. Yes.'

She put out her hand to take the shilling he pushed back to her. At the last moment he held the coin there with one finger.

Then he lifted the finger and touched her hand. For a second or two she felt as if her hand had been nailed to the cash-desk. Then she drew it away and somehow found the indelible ink-pad and stamped 'Paid with Thanks' on the bill.

'I think the snow's going,' he said.

'Is it?'

Her natural low quiet voice had fallen to a whisper. Across at the other counter Melford set a reel of string whirling again. She looked up, startled for the third time, with large still eyes.

'I think it will have gone by Saturday.' For a few moments longer he held her with a smile and she felt herself responding with a timid reflection of it. 'Perhaps before.'

'I hope so.'

'I hope so too,' he said. 'Saturday?'

A moment later he was walking out of the shop. She did not move for some moments. She sat staring instead at her hands stained with violet smears of indelible ink. Then the bright stains on her fingers seemed to wake her up. She went out of the cash-desk and ran upstairs, calling to Melford as she went something about getting her hands in a mess and going to wash them.

In her bedroom she stood looking down on the square. The afternoon was still not quite dark. The fog was closing thickly and steadily down above the snow. In the gloom she stared for several minutes across the empty square. There was nothing to be seen and then suddenly the street lamps came on. Vague moons of orange shone in the fog, and the church clock struck three hollow quarters of five.

Somehow, between the drowned lights of the street lamps and the sound of the clock drowning itself too into limitless fog, she felt the first of several waves of loneliness. She did not realize until that moment how lonely she had been. There had been no way of knowing it. There had been no way of making comparisons. This, her life in the square, was the life she had chosen and until now there had seemed no way of changing it. She had never seriously thought of changing it. Somehow she had to resign herself to it and, without fussing too much, make it acceptable.

Now as she stared out into the dead, fog-bound square she

knew that it was not acceptable. She was not so much excited as amazed by the discovery, exactly as she had been amazed rather than excited by allowing herself to be kissed three days before. She was aware too of a strange rising sense of tension. There was a growing fear, a tightening up inside herself, a questioning. What was going to happen? What was she going to do? What happened now?

Outside, in spite of fog, the air had begun to freeze again. On the window her breath froze in iridescent patterns. Her sense of imprisonment, heightened by tension, sharpened by another wave of loneliness, made her rub her hand across the glass. For a second or two, through a cleared circle, she caught a glimpse of the fog-bound square, buried in snow, with the market cross looking like part of an abandoned wreck in the centre of it, and then it was gone again, frozen away.

It was only when she got downstairs again, five minutes later, that she realized she had not washed her hands. They were still violet with ink stains. And for the rest of the afternoon and evening, until the shop closed, she folded them as much as possible under the desk, trying to keep them out of sight from Melford.

All through the following day she sat in the cash-desk. Frost and fog held the air clenched above masses of sullen snow. Cold blew bitterly into the shop whenever the door was opened, funnelling sharply through the cash-desk pigeon-hole.

Throughout the day she looked at the door. Customers came in shaking wet umbrellas, stamping boots and goloshes, blowing chilly clouds of breath. Unbearably the tension inside herself heightened each time she saw a figure frame itself behind the frozen foggy glass.

Towards four o'clock the shop became empty and she took the opportunity of slipping out into the kitchen to have a cup of tea. When she came back again Melford was standing inside the cash-desk saying:

'Well, and how does it strike you today? Not much beautiful about it today.'

Frankie Johnson was standing at the pigeon-hole. Today he was wearing a thick dark blue scarf round his neck. His breath had condensed in spidery threads on the wool of the scarf.

When Melford saw her coming he made one of his customary attempts at a joke and said:

'Ah! here comes our other snow-lover. She'll attend to you now. Let me make way.'

He stepped outside the cash-desk, automatically slipping a finger into his top waistcoat pocket. He laughed and said: 'We shall have to call you the snow-maiden, shan't we? That would fit you,' and then laughed again in his crackling way as he turned to his counter.

This time it was she who spoke first. Frankie Johnson's bill was already on the desk. After she had looked at it she glanced up and stared at him tensely and said:

'I'll try to get it right this time.'

He pushed several coins through the pigeon-hole and said:

'I think you'll find that exactly right,' and smiled.

She felt deeply touched; she was touched because she knew somehow that it was an attempt to forestall her nervousness and ease it. She made some attempt at counting the coins, hardly seeing them, and then as she was searching for the rubber-stamp he said:

'It's very cold today.'

'Yes, it's cold,' she said. 'You look cold.'

'I'm not cold.'

'You look cold,' she said. 'Don't get cold.' She stamped 'Paid with Thanks' across the bill. 'It's very treacherous. It's easy to catch cold.'

'I'm all right,' he said. He smiled again. His fingers remained for a moment attached to the bill. Then he drew them away. His voice fell completely to a whisper. 'Good-bye,' he said. 'I'll be in again tomorrow.'

She nodded very slightly, smiled a little and then watched him go. It struck her that there was something very ordinary about a young man carrying a parcel of groceries, wearing a big blue scarf and no hat on his head. A young man who thumped a piano in a cheap cinema six nights a week. It was all, like their conversation, very ordinary: so ordinary that again she was amazed. She could not believe in its unreality. And again, as the strange blue world of fog swallowed him up, she had the impression of an existence melting away.

The following morning the fog lifted slightly. Frost covered everything with pencillings of delicate white hoar, like icy feathers: a world of intricate laciness spinning out of wintry gloom, transfiguring iron railings, roof-tops and the bare black chestnut boughs above the square.

At the same time the world underneath it remained dark and gripped. The gutters were hard and bitter. The steeple of the church was an iron bar buried to half its depth in an iron-coloured sky.

'It's settled in,' Melford said. 'You mark my words. It might be April before we shift it now.'

In continuing tension and isolation she waited all day in the cash-desk. Whenever the fog lifted a little more the stencillings and pencillings of hoar-frost seemed to stiffen and grow thicker. 'I could do with a mite of hot ginger,' a woman said. 'I can feel my bones grating together.'

At the mention of hot ginger Melford helped himself to several pieces of his favourite sweet. In deference to the customers he always retired to the back of the shop to eat it and then came back boyishly licking his fingers. Once as he came back he paused at the cash-desk, wiped his fingers on his handkerchief and then blew his nose heavily and said:

'I'm not at all sure I haven't got Miss Weakness's cold. Take care you don't get it. If you feel tired you can go – you've only to say.'

'I'm not tired,' she said. 'I'm not at all tired. I like it –'

'Well, anyway, I've just heard that Hyde and Weakness are coming back on Monday,' he said. 'Hyde and Seek would be more like it' – he laughed without pleasure, crisply. 'Hyde especially. Hyde by name and Hyde by nature.'

It was after five o'clock before she looked up, perhaps for the hundredth time that day, and saw Frankie Johnson standing for the third time by the counter. Once again it was the perfect ordinariness of it all that struck her. Unbelievably and tensely she waited in the cash-desk, under the piercing light, until he had bought butter, a tin of sardines, a pound of biscuits and some cheese.

Then he was again at the pigeon-hole. Again with all her tightened nervousness she was trying to read the bill, give change, stamp 'Paid with Thanks' on it and speak as if he were simply another customer. She did her best to hide the fact that her hands were quivering by holding them as much as possible under the desk. He did not speak much. He seemed content to stare quietly at her face, smiling occasionally, and wait for her to lift her eyes.

'I'll be in tomorrow again,' he said.

'Tomorrow's Sunday.'

'Oh! my God,' he said. For a few seconds he stared at her unhappily. She stared back helplessly and without a word. 'Monday then.'

'The cash-girl comes back on Monday.'

'When then?' he said. 'When?'

She shook her head. She didn't know when; she was incapable of thinking; there was nothing to say. She fumbled helplessly with the indelible ink-pad, staining her fingers. Behind his face, with the big blue scarf again wrapped round it, the face of a woman customer appeared and a voice said:

'Would you mind, Mrs Turner please? I want to get across to the chemist before he closes,' and in another moment Frankie Johnson disappeared.

She did not sleep much that night. Frost seemed to have enlarged and refined the spaces of air above the town, so that all night the strokes of the clock seemed more than usually clear and sharp and prolonged. The sense of tension and imprisonment inside herself, beginning as a small ache, seemed to enlarge too with the slow clock strokes. Presently the stark white insomnia was back. She lay for hour after hour thinking of Frankie Johnson: the smile, the ordinariness, the way she didn't want him to get cold, the unhappiness, the helplessness of the face at the pigeon-hole. She experienced once again the sensation of his melting away into fog. Then without him the waves of loneliness came pouring back, darker than ever, then receding, leaving her desolate and dry.

Towards morning she dozed off and then woke to what she thought was the sound of rain. She lay for some moments listening. Then she got out of bed. She went over to the window and pulled back one of the curtains and looked down at the square.

She saw that the fog had lifted. Rain was falling straight and soft on the snow. Gutters were running noisily like brooks and already the cross in the centre of the square was washed almost clean of snow.

She opened the window and put out her hands. For a few moments she let the rain fall on them, feeling the warm western air no longer treacherous in the rising wind. A few hours before her breath had frozen with bitterness on the windows. Now the panes were running with drops that were green-silver in the light of the one remaining lamp in the square.

'Perhaps it will all be gone tomorrow,' she thought, 'and then we shall see the grass again.'

Part 2

Chapter One

As spring came on she began to meet him four or five afternoons each week, sometimes more. At first they met almost formally, always in the same place, at the same time. Every afternoon too she pinned a buttonhole of flowers on her coat or her dress, primroses or violets or anemones or other spring flowers as they came, always pinning them upside down. This habit of hers of pinning her buttonhole upside down continually amused him, so that he never failed to tease her about it:

'One of these days you'll forget and come with the flowers right side up and then I shan't know you.'

Whenever he said this she felt half-afraid. The day when he would no longer know her was an idea she pushed hastily into the background, an unpleasant thought, a problem she did not want to solve.

At first they met in the public gardens, at the other end of the town from the square. They met there at half past two, always at a place where two paths forked, one going off towards formal beds of tulips, the other downhill past clumps of birch-trees and rhododendron towards a stream. The gardens were not large. On the first windy cold spring days there were few people about. There was a sense of secrecy among and beyond the rhododendron bushes, under the light, quick-bursting buds of willows. Then as the days grew warmer the gardens began to attract more people. Old men and young mothers with children and perambulators filled seats in the sun and on the grass children made daisy-chains.

All this time she was sharply conscious of holding a great part of herself back. She was still so quiet that occasionally he would even accuse her of not listening.

'I am listening. I'm always listening. I listen to every word you say.'

'You were far away,' he said. 'You were miles away again with those big brown eyes, weren't you?'

Then she knew, after a time, that a great part of herself was afraid. She was not afraid of meeting him in daylight, of being seen with him or of Melford knowing that these things went on. She did not care about Melford; she had even adopted, in her own quiet way, an attitude of contempt for Melford. What she was afraid of was not easy to explain. It was not even remotely tangible. Later it was to be altogether too easily explicable and too terrifyingly tangible to ignore, but now, in the spring, in the already too-crowded gardens, it simply expressed itself vaguely as a fear of people.

'Frankie, I don't think we should meet here any more.'

'Why?' He merely seemed to tease her gently with the question.

'I don't know, there are so many – it's getting so –'

'You're shy!' he said. 'That's why. You're afraid of being seen.'

'Perhaps I am,' she said, 'but that's my way and I can't help it.'

'Are you really frightened we'll be seen?'

'Perhaps I am. But you see,' she said, 'I can't really be near you here and say all the things I want to say.'

Towards the end of May they began to meet at a place outside the town. The stream that came down through Orlingford could hardly be called a river; but a mile and a half beyond the town it widened and split, running into a backwater hemmed in by poplar and marshy clumps of willow. Here, at some time, a family named Pollard had worked a water-mill. Two years later a cycle of three dry summers left the stream no more than a trickle and a year later the Pollards abandoned the place and never went back. Since that time, more than fifty years before, no one else had ever been back. The sturdy stone house had become lost in a tangled oasis where elderberry flourished in doorways, coarse grass grew out of roof-tiles and blackberry flowered from window-sills. Moorhen and wild duck and occasional heron inhabited the deep mill-pond and in summer there was a hot thick smell of water-weed drying on abandoned sluices.

It was Miss Mackness who had told her of all this. 'It's beautiful up there,' she said, 'at Pollards' Mill. You go some time. No one ever goes there. Except us. Me and my friend go sometimes.'

On the first day they walked to Pollards' Mill she did not talk much. The weather was warm and breathless. At first she was not quite certain of the way and gradually the path lost itself, overgrown with elder and hawthorn and big savage wands of dog-rose coming into flower.

Then suddenly there was no path. Only, beyond a broken gate, the oasis of the mill: the windowless stone house with elder foaming at door-gaps, sluice-gates rotten, mill-pond ringed with high dark reeds, and over everything the hot baked smell of marsh-earth drying in sun.

She stopped and looked at it. 'This is the place,' she said.

Most of that afternoon, their first visit, they lay above the sluice, watching the water. A few small fish were basking in the sun. A dull skin stretched across the pool, with only occasional small water-beetles rowing paths across it.

She turned to say something and saw him lying with his face to the sky. Across the pool a sudden scuttle of light wind travelled like a shoal of rising fish. She saw it lift his hair. Then it rose and blew into her face, lifting her own hair and brushing down her body.

As she felt the wind blowing softly on her the needs and feelings of her body began waking. It was like an artery that had been tied and suddenly released again. Blood began pouring and racing back, with sensations of sharper, brighter pain.

After a moment he turned his face too and they were looking at each other. The vivid pale blue eyes were transparent, almost colourless, in the sun. She looked at them for almost a minute, completely transfixed, in wonder.

Then he was touching her. He held her quietly and lightly with his fingers, on her bare upper arms. She could not move. She felt the wind quiver from the pond again, disturbing her skirt. For some moments she let it blow on her legs and body and then her skirt lifted again and she moved her hands, trying to smooth it down.

Suddenly they lay against each other in an agony of kissing. She found herself holding his mouth in pure bright pain. In

97

the hot silence she could hear nothing but the occasional dreamy croak of the moorhens lost in reeds and a sudden quiver of wind in willow-leaves above the pond.

For a long time, in mystified excitement, she had nothing to say. She brushed his hair once or twice with her hands. When she did speak it was in a whisper.

'I want to ask you something.'

'Don't look so serious.'

He smiled, readily, as he always did, his mouth twitching at one corner.

'I am serious. It is serious. For me.'

For a few moments longer she stared into the light pure blue eyes.

'You won't stop loving me will you?' she said. 'I couldn't bear it now if you stopped loving me.'

He smiled again. A moorhen croaked across the pond. Another splashed water and Frankie Johnson said:

'Stop loving you? How could I if I haven't loved you yet?'

She did not say a word. The bright excited pain in her veins ran cold. He smiled again and said:

'I said I haven't loved you yet. It's hardly begun.'

She still could not speak. Embarrassed and stupid, caught up again in the trap of shyness, she could only listen to him say:

'What's the matter? What's troubling you? You can talk to me, can't you?'

Her eyes were shy and troubled and she turned them away from him.

'Tell me. You know you can tell me anything you like,' he said.

'I know,' she said. 'I know that. But not yet. Not today. But I will try to tell you. You're the only one I can talk to.'

After that, smiling, teasing a little, he would sometimes tell her she was frightened. Then she remembered how he had also teased her, in the gardens, about being frightened and she said at last, a day or two later:

'Perhaps I am frightened. Perhaps I am afraid. But not in the way you think. It's just that I'm afraid of explaining it wrongly – so that it sounds stupid and silly, that's all.'

'You know I wouldn't think that.'

'I know,' she said, 'but in a way it is silly. It is stupid. It's hard to explain.'

Finally she found it so difficult to explain that she said:

'I'll tell you, but don't look at me, will you? Don't look at me, will you? Promise you won't look at me.'

She turned her face away. She stared across the pool to where moorhens moved invisibly among high reeds, making the tips tremble as they swam there.

'It's just this,' she said. She began to try to explain, slowly and shyly, how it had been with herself and Melford. Her voice stumbled. She said several times how hard it was to explain and how badly she was putting it. All the time he listened in silence and at last she said: 'Supposing I put it like this – I'm really not married, that's all.'

He still listened in silence but she suddenly turned, facing him.

'Oh! I've got a ring and all that. There was a wedding in the church – I don't mean that. I just mean there's been no marriage. No love. Nothing at all.'

She began to cry quietly, with embarrassment. Then she was crying, presently, with anger: anger at her herself, at Melford, at the monstrous situation of her incompleteness.

'I had to tell you. You're the only one I could tell,' she said. 'Now you can think what you like of me.'

With her face lowered she said several times what a fool she was and how she wouldn't blame him either if he thought too that she was a poor idiotic fool. Then finally she lifted her face and she thought she saw him smile.

'You wouldn't laugh at me, would you?' she said. 'Not because of that?'

He smiled again, kissing her face.

'Don't ever laugh at me,' she said. She drew him against her suddenly with distracted tenderness, almost violently. 'Because it's a terrible thing.'

All he said was: 'I was just smiling at something. You know I think this pool would be deep enough for swimming. Don't you think we could come swimming here some time?'

The summer became a close and stormy one. A few days of heat would gather oppressively and then develop into strange yellow evenings of groping thunder. When the storms had broken and the sun came out again heat seemed to smoulder damply about the town and the fields, sucking at air, leaving the afternoons breathless.

By July the mill-pond was partly covered with white water-lilies, over the pads of which small blue dragonflies hovered and young moorhens walked with slow daintiness, heads down, as if fascinated by the reflection of themselves in dark waters.

In the mill-house were several rooms where floors had not decayed. Above them the hard stone roof was still good and at the back of the house was an iron staircase that was still as sound as ever.

She first allowed him to make love to her in a room overlooking the pond, at the top of the house. She remembered, as she took off her clothes, how once before she had taken them off and then lain waiting, alone, listening to the sound of the sea. It seemed a very great way back in her life, the night of her wedding at the seaside, and now it was the sound of summer rain, drilling softly and steadily down on the pond, that possessed her mind, in the way the sound of the sea had done, and consumed it completely. She thought afterwards that if love had come to her normally she might even have been disappointed by it, as she had sometimes heard people were disappointed, or even afraid of it or afraid of its being repeated. But that afternoon the sound of rain streaming down from a summer sky drowned every thought in her mind, leaving her body glowing and fluid with tenderness. For the last time loneliness flooded out of her, leaving her quivering and sobbing to be held and taken again, her mouth wet and imploring as she took the long kisses and gave them back.

After that, every morning, all summer, she woke with the same thought in her head: she would go to the mill and Frankie would be waiting. All she wanted was a bare room, a pond with water-lilies, fish rising with startling explosions in dark water under summer rain, blue dragonflies suspended exquisitely between banks of quivering reed.

The world outside all this gradually seemed more and more unreal and empty. One Sunday afternoon she ran into Miss Willis in the square. Miss Willis had never repeated the tea-time visit that had awed her so much and now it was all she could do to bring herself to speak to the elevated Mrs Melford Turner, once her friend.

She too had begun to call her 'the Untouchable Mrs T', and with soft politeness and fat loose lips she inquired:

'And are you keeping well?'

'Very well. Wonderfully well. And you?'

'Oh! the same as ever,' Miss Willis said. She blushed and giggled. 'Only I need another *Ladies' Excuse Me* – nobody asked yet. We can't all be as lucky as you are.'

She had not thought of herself as lucky. But now as she looked at the virginal fat Miss Willis, still hoping for love, she knew that she was lucky. She felt that she looked down on Miss Willis, so fatuous and so hopeful, from a rare and wonderful height. 'Poor Norma. Poor Miss Willis,' she thought.

At the same time the existence of Melford, the square, the church, the house and the shop continued as before. Because of her habit of always walking a good deal, and always alone, it excited no one for a time that she left the house every afternoon and did not come back until five or even later. People were not only calling her, at that time, 'the Untouchable Mrs T'. To them she was not merely aloof and stand-offish; she even seemed, with her way of cutting herself off from people, walking with her head down, avoiding glances and taking long walks by herself into the countryside, a little queer. She was, they said, a strange girl, a bit of an oddity, an outsider who did not conform. 'Of course,' it was commonly said of her, 'she isn't Orlingford born and bred', as if this explanation disposed of any and every oddity. Other women attended sewing classes, church teas, cinemas, whist drives, chapel bazaars; had babies, did useful work and took tea with rectors. She did none of these things. 'But just wait,' people said, 'she won't be much of a catch as mayoress when the time comes.'

Once only, that summer, she had an argument with Melford about her walking. 'I can't think what fun you get out of it day after day,' he said. 'You'd be so much better with a horse.'

'I don't want a horse,' she said. 'I like walking better.'

'You get the finest exercise in the world on horseback,' he said.

'I don't want the finest exercise in the world,' she said and her contempt of him was deeper and more biting because she expressed it, as she always did, so quietly. 'I like my own way better.'

Then on a day in early August, as she and Melford sat down to lunch, there were sudden cracks of thunder. Rapidly the square became a dusky yellow under a strange sulphur sky.

'There are two of them,' Melford said. He turned his face southward over the square and then north-westward over the valley. 'If they meet we'll be in for a packet.' In the oppressive air his reddish jowls were already sweating. 'I don't like these two-horse affairs.'

Apprehensively she sat through lunch, hardly touching the food. In the heat Melford drank glass after glass of water and kept saying that when two storms got stuck in the valley like this you could never be sure what would happen.

'I remember the steeple got struck with a packet like this when I was a boy,' he said. 'Aren't you going to eat anything?'

'It's too hot,' she said. 'I never have much appetite in thundery weather.'

'I wish it would come and get it over with,' Melford said. He looked up at the ceiling, his skin curiously aglow in the darkening air. 'Send it down, David.'

She picked a little longer at her food and then left it. Then she saw that Melford had finished too and she rang the bell for Mrs Butterworth.

To her surprise there was no answer. From a distance she heard two long separate peals of thunder. She rang the bell again and for a second time there was no answer.

'That's odd, isn't it?' she said. 'She always answers so quickly.'

'My guess,' Melford said, 'is that she's putting the cutlery away.'

A sudden irritation at the childish notion of a grown woman putting away cutlery at the approach of a thunderstorm made her get up and leave the room and go into the kitchen. Palely Mrs Butterworth was sitting at the bare central kitchen table, clenching her hands. Every vestige of steel had been hidden out of sight. Even the saucepans had been draped with cloths and dusters and the blinds drawn half down the windows as if for the dead.

'Mrs Butterworth, this is silly. Why don't you or Edna answer the bell?'

Trembling convulsively, the big, normally placid woman could hardly frame her words.

'It puts me in mind of the day the steeple was struck,' she managed to say. 'I shall never forget that. I shall never forget it as long as I live. It was like a fire-ball coming down on the square. That was a day like this – twenty-three years ago come this September.'

'Come and clear the table,' Constance said. 'The thunder's still miles away.'

'Don't ask me to do that,' Mrs Butterworth said. 'It's more than I dare do to pick up a knife in my hands till it's blowed over.'

'You're meeting trouble half-way,' Constance said. 'That's the silliest thing you can do.'

'I can't help it,' Mrs Butterworth said. 'I can't help it. There's some things you can't help – you know they're silly and you can't help them. You're driv on by something and you can't help it for love nor money. That's how I am with thunder – '

'And where's Edna?'

'She's down in the cellar, madam,' Mrs Butterworth said. 'I told her to come but – '

'I'll clear the table myself,' Constance said.

To the sound of Mrs Butterworth gasping for frightened breath in the humid air Constance went back into the dining-room to clear the table. A smell of onion sauce, a favourite dish of Melford's with leg of mutton, filled the hot oppressive air in a way she had not noticed before. The odour of onions had grown stale and sickly. The empty plates were greasy.

In renewed irritation she packed the plates on the sideboard and said:

'The woman sits there paralysed. I don't know what she'd planned for your second course. There's some cheese here – will you have cheese?'

'It's understandable she's frightened of thunder,' Melford said. 'A lot of people are. My mother was. She always covered the mirrors up.'

A violent double crack of thunder split the air from the south. Almost immediately another rolled across the valley. 'By Jove, that was a whole lot closer,' Melford said. A moment later she put the big flowered triangular cheese-dish on the table in front of him and found herself speaking with extraordinary boldness:

'Then your mother must have been a lot sillier than I gave her credit for. What's the use of being frightened of thunder? What harm can *thunder* do?'

'I know, I know,' he said, 'but I can't say I care for it all that much myself – '

'It is *lightning* that strikes,' she said. '*The lightning* –'

She did not realize how much, at that moment, she was over-emphasizing her words, or why. He looked up, about to say something like 'I grant you, oh! I grant it's the lightning,' when he saw her eyes, larger and darker than usual in the thickening thundery air, flash emphatically, burning strangely.

It was the first time he had ever seen her look like that. Suddenly he lifted the lid of the cheese-dish and peered hastily inside.

'Look at that,' he said. 'That'll show you what the weather's like. They talk about milk turning with thunder – but look at the cheese.'

Bluish mould, already whiskered, had begun to grow on the big cream triangle of Cheddar in its almost airtight dish. With the point of a knife he nicked off a little of the mould and looked at it fastidiously. An odd undertone of thunder, somehow separated from the two main storms, gave a low warning stutter from the clouds directly above the square and he said:

'I can't say I fancy that. I'll hop down to the shop and fetch myself a piece of fresh.' Then civilly he added: 'Can I bring you some biscuits or something? A sponge finger?'

'I'm going for my walk now,' she said. 'I don't want anything, thank you.'

He stood amazed. In the strange light the whiskered cheese-mould seemed to him like blue phosphorus on the point of the knife, which he still held in his hand.

'You're never going out?' he said. 'Not in this? Not until this has blown over?'

'I'm going for my walk,' she said. 'I'm not frightened of thunder – or lightning – or rain for that matter.'

Again she was unaware of the emphasis in her voice. Her way of speaking, as always, was very quiet. The emphasis came from the rapidity of the words, which seemed stifled and congested.

'But it's raining now,' he told her. 'Look at that – look at it. Teeming down.'

Rain, in a white flash, had abruptly exploded from the curdled black-sulphur sky. The square was suddenly half obliterated in steamy torrents. A figure with a jacket shrouded over its head rushed gropingly across the centre of it and a second later the two storms struck each other with stunning impact overhead.

By this time the room was almost dark. Melford, as if in involuntary sympathy with Mrs Butterworth, dropped the cheese-knife. It fell on a plate with a clatter and he said:

'You can't possibly go out in this.' He picked up the cheese-knife and seemed to be about to shake it at her. 'Anybody would be quite mad to go out while this was on.'

She did not answer. She looked at the marble clock that stood on the mantelpiece in front of a copper mirror, something like a dwarf grey model of St Paul's Cathedral, and saw that it was already two o'clock. The clock was faced with a gold-leaf inscription marking its presentation to Melford's father on first being elected mayor of the town. In due course she and Melford, she did not doubt, would be presented with a similar clock with a similar inscription on a similar occasion. In the thundery gloom the two gold-rimmed holes for winding keys stared out like two eyes compressed into a pair of dwarf spectacles. The copper of the mirror-frame glinted with a strange rose-yellow flash, reflecting another flash of lightning.

Melford poured himself another glass of water. For some moments she had been busy clearing part of the table, leaving Melford with cruet, biscuits, butter and cutlery. Now she rolled her serviette and slipped it into its ring. The ring was of bone – silver ones were used only at night, for dinner – with the initial C affixed in silver.

As she put away the serviette into the sideboard she scratched the tip of a finger on a loosened edge of the initial. A few drops of blood spurted from the cut. She hardly noticed it and as she shut the sideboard drawer another violent flash of lightning seemed suddenly to drive clean down the long triangle of the church spire, making a great crack of thunder and even heavier torrents of rain.

'Don't you want your cheese?'

'By God, that was near,' he said. 'No, I don't think I do. I don't think I'll bother after all.'

'All right,' she said, 'if you're finished I'll get ready to go.'

Again he stood amazed. Her voice was still so quiet that, against the huge hiss of rain, it might have been that he had not heard it.

'What?' he said. 'What?'

'I'm going for my walk,' she said. 'I told you.'

'You must be quite mad.'

'I'm not mad,' she said, 'but I might well be if I didn't get outside sometimes.'

'All I can say is that anyone who goes out in this must be raving mad.'

'Very well then,' she said, 'I'm raving mad.'

He stood astounded, not knowing what to say. For a single moment longer the peculiar over-emphasis of her manner made her eyes seem larger and darker than usual. In the thundery air the pupils seemed much too white and staring.

For the second time in their marriage he thought that perhaps the only way of dealing with Constance was to bully her. He was saved from doing anything about this by a sharp knock on the door, which Constance answered.

'Yes, Britton, what is it?'

In agitation Britton almost ignored her and called into the room:

'Are you there, Mr Melford, sir? Could you come, sir? It's Pilfer – I don't think I can hold him much longer.'

Melford, suddenly and completely oblivious of her, pushed past her and followed Britton down the passage outside. He was still carrying the cheese-knife. In an instant the fear that anything might possibly happen to Pilfer drove out of his mind the fear that Constance would get soaked, perhaps even struck by lightning, by a ridiculous excursion into the rain.

Running out of the torrential rain, into an almost dark stable, he found Hyde, flinty and almost expressionless in the gloom, trying to hold his horse. The big black head kept flaring up out of his hands, which were soaped with slobber. As Melford came into the stable a double crack of thunder split the sky above the church. The horse gave a terrible surging spasm of fright, rearing upwards, lashing back at the stall. A great muscular quivering ran up the throat, breaking cruelly into a cry. The power of the neck was so great that Hyde could not hold it and suddenly the horse lashed free, crashing back at the dark shadows, the white eyes helpless and demoniac, the head flaring wildly upwards and giving its terrible whimpering cry.

As he saw Britton reaching out for the horse he heard himself calling in a queer constrained voice: 'Pilfer, Pilfer boy. Steady there now, Pilfer. It's all right boy.' Then he heard Hyde begin saying something that he only partially heard against another roll of thunder and the hiss of rain on the stable-roof and the yard outside.

'I just come in to put my bike out of the rain. I just come in and he started.'

Then as Britton grasped the head again, trying to hold it down, Melford saw a halter on the wall and snatched it. He began to rush forward with it when Britton called:

'Stand back, sir. I don't want to crowd him, sir. Give me the halter.'

Melford gave up the halter. Then, a second later, standing back, he realized exactly what Hyde had said.

'You don't always put your bike in here, do you, Hyde? What the hell made you put your bike in here?'

'I had to dive somewhere out of the rain, didn't I?' Hyde said. 'I don't want to get struck by lightning. I don't fancy holding bicycles in a thunderstorm. I had to get in somewhere quick, didn't I – '

'So you got in here, you damn fool, and now look!'

'I had to get in – '

'You started him!' Melford said. 'You started him!'

'Don't say that to me,' Hyde said. 'I never started him.

The storm started him. He was raving mad with thunder.'

'You started him! – Pilfer – !'

He felt all his antagonism against Hyde fuse with his desperate fear for the horse. 'We had him like this once before, sir,' he heard Britton say. 'You were away at the time.' The big black neck flared up again, the teeth exposed like a rake. The inner red of the mouth ran wet and piteous. The eyes gave a great white swirl and all the power of the body forged itself upwards, bringing the forelegs up like a dancing bear.

'You'd better get across the road and find Draper,' he yelled to Hyde. 'Go on – get Draper.'

'We don't need a vet, sir,' Britton said. 'I can handle him –'

'Get Draper!' he yelled to Hyde.

Hyde stood still. The normal expression of his face was flat except for the mouth, which dropped sharply in. It gave the impression that he had lost his teeth, so that the mouth was simply a single bitten contemptuous line.

Suddenly Melford knew that Hyde was not going for Draper. Stunned for a moment, quite speechless, he came suddenly as near to hating Hyde as he had ever hated anyone in his life. Another crack of thunder burst and rolled across the town and he shouted above it:

'If you won't go I must go. Somebody's got to go.'

He almost struck Hyde as he rushed out across the yard. As he plunged into the rain he heard from the stable another piteous, sucking cry from the horse and it made him break into running.

Coming into the square he missed by a few yards the figure of Constance leaving the house. He was vaguely aware of a half-familiar shape, head down in the streaming-rain, crossing the corner of the square towards the churchyard. He gave it no recognition. It meant no more to him than the gutters running with sheets of rain. And with loping desperately awkward strides he squelched through the flood of rain to the far side of the square.

As Constance went through the churchyard, sheltering under an old black umbrella she had grabbed in passing from the brass stand in the hall of the house, the rain seemed to drive everything out of perspective. At the edge of the town the fields, most of them yellow with corn, dissolved under strange light into thunder mist. With the storm a wind had sprung up and now it lashed through the corn in twisting waves.

The path through the fields was sodden. She walked with her head down, staring at her feet as they slopped through pools. She had no thought for either Melford or the horse. She was unaware that the horse had been terrified by thunder or that Melford had missed her by a few yards in the square.

She was thinking simply of Frankie. She was afraid of missing Frankie. She was afraid the storm had delayed Frankie or put him off altogether. Sometimes he put sandwiches in his pocket and started early and was waiting at the mill when she got there. She began to pray that this was one of those days.

During the entire summer they had never missed each other; neither of them had ever failed to turn up. When she looked back on the winter, recalling the days of snow and fog when she sat in the cash-desk and spoke with him at the pigeon-hole, she was astonished at the patient docility of herself. With amazement she wondered at the distant and wooden creature who could have sat there undemonstratively waiting.

Apart from moorhens walking daintily and dreamily across islands of lily-pads nothing moved about the mill when she got there. She went into the mill and straight upstairs. A big room on the south side, formerly a bedroom, still had glass in one of its windows. The ceiling was good and a few widths of wall-paper, the pattern completely colourless, still hung on the walls.

'Frankie,' she called. 'Frankie. Are you there, Frankie?'

She sat there all afternoon. Gradually the sky cleared a little. The storms swept out of the valley. Rain settled into a steady summer downpour, straight and without wind. She stood most of the time at the window, staring across the pond to the sluice, the sodden copses and the path beyond.

After a time she took off her shoes and stockings and put them on the window-sill to dry. She had left the house so quickly that she had forgotten her handbag and now she had nothing with her for tidying her hair. She ran her fingers through it several times, combing it out. It was wet from blown rain and it hung down in dark and separated strands.

By four o'clock the rain had stopped. In a few moments the sun came out. The world below her began to steam. For some time she sat on the floor and tried to put on her stockings. They were soaked and she could not pull them on. Then she tried to put on her shoes. They had shrunk in the rain and were too small for her bare feet and now she could not wear them. As she tried to pull on her shoes she opened again the scratch she had made on her finger with the serviette ring and blood spurted down her hand. She did not notice it. In her bare feet she went downstairs and out of the mill and stood in the stormy sunshine. Moorhens walked in their slow preoccupied fashion from island to island of lily leaves, almost the only things, except for a few blue suspended dragonflies, moving in the oppressive afternoon.

She waited until half-past five. With the strain of waiting her face seemed to have tightened up. A curious sort of muscular contraction had drawn the mouth in, throwing the eyes into wider and larger relief. In the sunlight the whites of them were bluish and moist and large.

Towards six o'clock she began to walk back. In one hand she carried her umbrella, still wet and unrolled, and in the other her shoes and stockings. She walked without thinking. She stared down at her bare feet and legs splashed now with summer mud and at the skirt of her dress soaked almost to the waist from brushing through summer grasses.

At the point where the path joined the road a farmer named Wheeler was sitting on a stile staring at a crop of oats, ripe for cutting, that rain and storm had beaten down into a flat and sodden mattress of straw.

He stepped down from the stile to let her pass. He recognized her and touched his cap to her.

'Good afternoon, Mrs Turner. Rare weather, madam,' he said. 'Quite a storm.'

She got over the stile. She walked past him, out into the road, without answering. Her head hung down. She did not bother to lift it up.

Later that evening Wheeler went home to his wife and told of how he had seen Melford Turner's wife slommacking along in her bare feet, without a hat, her hair soaked and in rats' tails, her skirt soaked and her legs plastered with sludder, carrying her shoes and stockings in her hand, and how there was blood on one of her hands and how she had not spoken to him.

'She looked,' he said, 'as if she'd been a-layin' in it. She looked more like a mare as is bin a-layin' out all winter.'

When she came to the square she was checked for a moment by an incident she had not expected. Even then the sight of a knacker's cart driving away from the back gates of the house, two exposed horse-shoes glittering in the sun and two hooves clocking stiffly on the backboard, did nothing to surprise or distress her.

It was not until she was half-way upstairs that she came to herself and realized that the house was full of a curious sound. She had also forgotten to leave the umbrella in its stand in the hall. And as she went back downstairs to replace it she stopped for a moment at the door of the sitting-room.

Inside, leaning his head on his hands against the mantelpiece, Melford was weeping like a boy.

Chapter Two

Melford's grief at the death of his horse expressed itself in three different ways. It temporarily distracted him from the oddities of Constance, from her frigid refusal even to be touched by him and her moody and inexplicable habit of walking long distances by herself, even on days of violent rain. It also left him lonely: not lonely in her own agonizing insomniatic way, but lonely as a child is lonely: helplessly, without companionship. It also aroused his emotions in a totally unexpected direction. He found himself caught up in a feud of hatred with Hyde.

He became convinced that Hyde had been responsible for the death of Pilfer. Hyde on his side knew quite well that he was not responsible; he had heard the vet, Draper, say that the storm was merely an aggravation of a brain condition that meant, sooner or later, a violent end. But he had not forgotten Melford's uncontrollable shout of 'You started him! You started him!' and its hinted accusation. He was not a man to forget things. He had not forgotten, either, Melford's old, well-mannered, unthinking sneer at Miss Mackness.

Melford had never quite understood whether the inscrutable and stony look of contempt on the face of his counter-hand was habitual or somehow directed at him. He had never been able to make up his mind. He had always treated Hyde with civility. He had always shown, as he viewed it, the generosity of a good employer. He gave Hyde thirty shillings a week, paid him for time off and sickness, let him have groceries at discount and saw that he did not want at Christmas-time. In return Hyde was punctual, adept and conscientious. Yet the look never changed. The face seemed continually bloodless and chilled. The lips were folded hard into their toothless line that never smiled. And the eyes were always, it seemed to Melford, contemptuously veiled and without gratitude.

The two men had never spoken with ease or freedom to each other. Now they stiffened sharply whenever they met in the shop. As the weeks of early autumn went by Melford refrained from buying another horse. This was partly because he did not really need another before the hunting season began, partly because he did not know of a hunter that might suit him. Nevertheless when Britton said one day, 'Have you lit on anything yet as'll suit you, Mr Melford?' he snapped back in the same uncivil voice his mother had so often condemned:

'No, and why should I? Get a horse? And have the damn thing terrified to death by some blamed fool or other? Not likely.'

He knew that presently and quite naturally he would get a horse; he knew too that the fact of his not having bought one had nothing to do with Hyde. Yet the tension of his feelings, the grief that he could not and did not want to show, was released if he said so.

Hyde's feelings towards Melford were based also on a need for an object of hatred. Hyde had not only long felt that he hated Melford but moreover that the reason for his hatred was a reasonable and just one.

He had worked in the shop since the age of fourteen. Things had gone very well at first. He had worked conscientiously and steadily under Melford's father and perhaps even more conscientiously and steadily under Melford himself. Melford in fact had promoted him to be chief counter-hand. In his undemonstrative way he was very satisfied. Then after seventeen years, when he was a man of thirty-one, married and with a house to keep up, the first war with Germany began.

In eight months Hyde was one of a great army of soldiers who did not particularly want to be soldiers. But it was not this so much that he resented. What first aroused him to resentment, then bitterness, was that Melford, four years younger than himself, a free, healthy and single man, somehow avoided the call to the colours. The fact that Melford suffered from mild varicose veins and had failed to pass a series of medical boards did not impress Hyde. Some people had varicose veins and were able to dodge the column; some people had varicose veins and ended up, as he did, at Passchendaele.

He never forgot Passchendaele. Before the war he had been a steady Methodist of ultra-temperate habits and great rectitude who worshipped twice on Sundays. After Passchendaele he was spiritually dead. He went through the hell of its mud and rats and bloated dead and sheer foul senselessness with a twisted and seething notion that there was one law for the rich, like Melford, and another for the poor, like himself. The fact that Melford was not rich did not matter. Nobody could ever talk him out of that. The things he had done and seen and suffered and seen others suffer at Passchendaele were spiritual death, and somehow, from his twisted viewpoint, he felt that Melford, the column-dodger, was in part responsible.

Then when he came home, more with an air of defeat than a mere illusion of victory, it was to find that in his absence something more important than Melford's defection had been going on. His wife had been seeing a great deal of a sergeant in the Welch Regiment. She was a pretty fair-haired woman who had sung contralto a good deal in the chapel choir. The sergeant, in the Welsh way, had a taste for music too. The sergeant had not been at Passchendaele either but for some reason had remained at a southern headquarters where red-tabs gathered. After a month as a civilian Hyde came home from the shop one evening to find a letter propped up on the kitchen table between the bread-board and the teapot. It told him starkly that Mrs Hyde, preferring the love of the former sergeant who now worked in a steel mill, had gone to Wales.

And again, by a process of twisted logic, it seemed that Melford was responsible. Melford, the younger, single man, ought to have been at Passchendaele. And perhaps in that case Hyde would have avoided Passchendaele. Perhaps in that case Mrs Hyde would not have fallen for the attentions of the sergeant from the Welch Regiment. Perhaps in that case – comfortlessly and with cynicism Hyde felt himself to be old, wronged, destroyed and unwanted.

Then, one evening the following winter, he found himself, for the first time since the double hell of Passchendaele and his wife, the object of an unexpected touch of comfort. It was customary for the three assistants, Miss Mackness, Flaky and himself to leave the shop every evening together. Flaky the boy, went his own way at the far corner of the square. After that Miss Mackness and Hyde walked on together as far as the post office, where Hyde touched his cap and said good night to her.

That evening it was cold and blustering and something made him say, beyond his more formal good night:

'Well, I must get home now and get my fire lit and my ironing out of the way.'

'Ironing?'

Miss Mackness was surprised and shocked.

'You do your own ironing?'

'Ah,' he said. 'And mending. And cooking. That's one thing the army does to you.'

From under her nervous red lids Miss Mackness found herself looking at Hyde with great pity.

'Why didn't you tell me?' she said. 'I could have done a few little things like that for you if you'd told me.'

Presently she was doing these few little things. In the evenings, after the shop had closed, she washed his shirt and socks, ironed for him and sewed on buttons. She would cook a kipper for him, bake pastry and cakes and call at the butcher's for a chop.

Before long she was calling for two chops. She was frying two kippers and hoping, without ever saying it, that presently Hyde would be able to arrange a divorce and marry her. But the divorce, Hyde said, cost money. What with the years of army pay and one thing and another it was more, in fact, than he could yet afford. And so gradually they drifted into an arrangement, quietly domestic, in which they did not live together and in which Miss Mackness managed to conceal, behind her pale, lashless, seemingly passionless eyes, all the charitable and protective passion she felt for him.

In summer they walked out a good deal into lanes and fields: he, much older than herself, wearing a rather out-dated starched collar and front, a bowler hat and, on Saturdays and Sundays, a buttonhole; she wearing rather light-coloured clothes and pale straw hats and white gloves that accentuated all her cotton-plain looks and her frailty. They were each very fond of the fields: that was what Miss Mackness meant when she spoke to Constance of 'my friend and me, we love the fields', though she was too shy and scared to add that her friend was Hyde.

Under all this Hyde's hostility to Melford became pacific. The effect of Miss Mackness's charitable affection was to take away its venom. It receded and settled down into the habitual look of unhappy and stone-eyed contempt that Melford knew. He in turn did not know that Miss Mackness washed socks and shirts for Hyde, playing a part not unlike that of daughter-mother to him in his smoky little terrace house, with its back-garden buttonhole roses and rows of onions and potatoes, by the railway station. If Hyde and Miss Mackness had demonstrated affection for each other in the shop it would have been very different. Then he would never have called her 'our Miss Weakness' and Hyde would never have heard the adolescent often-repeated joke that grated in an ugly way on the still raw edges of his Passchendaele hates and nerves.

Nor did Constance know. It was impossible that the thin taciturn mouth of Hyde should ever relax enough to speak of his arrangement with Miss Mackness. It was equally impossible for Miss Mackness to speak of it, except in veiled hints of fields and flowers and vaguely shared communions in primrose copses. They kept that part of their lives to themselves, carefully guarded, in secret, cherished apart. It was their business and they extracted from it perhaps more happiness than they might have got from more formal, open love.

It was early October before Melford bought himself another hunter. Already, by this time, he was becoming more and more aware of another circumstance that would, in due course, make the autumn eventful. In November he would be mayor.

The two things, that autumn and early winter, distracted his attention still further from Constance, with her oddities of solitary walking and what he thought were her chill rejections. He found himself becoming gradually captivated by circumstances that would give him, like a boy, two special treats to enjoy. It was as if he had been given chocolate-cream and ice-cream to eat at the same time. A horse and a mayoralty – either one would have been compensatory for a year that had not gone very well. The two together promised to take him out of the final fringes of loneliness, his enmity of Hyde and his groping confusions about Constance and her lack of love.

The horse he finally chose was a medium chestnut. It stood rather more than a hand less than the black, Pilfer, and it was rather shorter in the head. But the head was held well up, with confidence, giving the animal a look, sometimes, of being on parade.

He had the horse for nearly three weeks before deciding what to call it. The problem was almost like that of naming a baby. He considered it with care. He never liked other people's names for horses, and his own animals, on the last three occasions, had presented no difficulty because he had called each of them Pilfer.

Now he felt that a fourth Pilfer was quite impossible. It was out of the question. He needed a clean break, something entirely new. He did not like names like Beauty and Prince and Flasher and so on. He had once called a horse Flasher, only to see it turn out to be a mean animal of untrustworthy habits with less flash or verve in it than a cow.

One morning in late October he served a customer, his friend the solicitor, Charles Edward Twelvetree, with a bottle of brandy. Before wrapping up the bottle he held it, for a moment or two, up to the light. The morning was fine, with air distilled so purely through delicate October sunlight that it seemed to draw from the chestnut trees a brown candescent glow. An even purer distillation of light seemed to penetrate the neck of the brandy bottle as he held it up to the sun.

And then he knew that he had found his horse's name. Brandy – perhaps, in moments of affection, old Brandy. Perhaps Brandy Ball? No: just Brandy. It was very good, Brandy. It was almost, he thought, as good as Pilfer.

Presently he felt so pleased about it that as soon as possible he went out of the shop, across the yard and into the stable to look at the horse. Light falling through the narrow stall windows, with the same purity of distillation as he had noted when holding the bottle of brandy up to the sun, gave to the horse's coat a wonderful oil-brushed glow. He ran his hands up and down the flanks of the animal, feeling happy. A great sense of communion seemed suddenly to develop between himself and the horse. He felt the final miseries and past hatreds of the loss of Pilfer drain away. It was not in him to be vindictive for very long. He liked to be amiable with people if he could. And suddenly he pressed his head against the throat of the horse and said:

'Well, old boy, that's you then. Brandy. Are you listening? How do you like it? Brandy. How's that, old boy? Brandy? How do you feel about that?'

He went out into the yard and found Britton strawing a potato clamp at the corner of the garden. The fresh straw gleamed bright with sun and he said:

'Well, found it at last, Britton,' as if the morning had been blessed with a miracle. 'Brandy – I don't think we could have found anything better than that if we'd' – he was going to say 'prayed for it' and then altered it and said 'offered a prize.'

'Yes, sir, that's him, sir,' Britton said. 'Brandy – that's him all right, sir.'

'Yes, I think so. I like it,' he said. 'Brandy – now I think of it we could have had Sherry. I don't know though – no it's not the same. Brandy's the one. Where is Mrs Turner, Britton, do you know?'

Britton said he thought that the madam was down in the orchard, picking up apples. Melford left him and walked down the garden path towards the trees. The same mild pure glow of autumn lay on the orchard as on the square, the potato clamp and the flanks of the horse. A touch of winey fire was running through the leaves of the pears.

Soon it would be November. There would be that touch of frost white like thick dew on morning grasses. The oaks would turn their gold-tan colour, with their deep tan-smell of decay. The late afternoons when he came in from hunting would be blue – not exactly blue, not quite grey, but a mysterious half-colour of great softness. The days at the end of November, as they nearly always did, would grow completely tranquil and without wind and the sound of hounds crying over great distances would be the first sharp herald of winter-time.

'Decided to call him Brandy,' he said. 'Are you there?'

She was wearing a dark green dress that made her difficult to pick out, at first, among the old thick apple trees. 'Oh! there you are.'

She was picking up apples, big squarish yellow ones, Lord

Derbys, in a skip. She looked up, fixing him with a stare that might have been indifferent or puzzled or simply one of remoteness. She held an apple in one hand and rubbed it against the skirt of her dress until it too glowed with the golden air of the day.

'Call who Brandy?'

'The horse. I was serving Charles Edward Twelvetree with a bottle – '

He saw by her eyes that she was not interested. He broke off. He was cut away from her. He was outside, further away than ever. She dropped the partly polished apple into the skip and in the same moment something made him look up at the church-spire.

He took out his watch. The clock, with its hands and figures that also seemed autumn-coloured and in a glow, said sixteen minutes to twelve. His watch said fourteen. He could not decide which was right. He only knew perfectly well that in his father's day the clock would have been right.

He decided to put the blame on the clock.

'I don't know,' he said, 'they never seem to be able to make up their minds about this clock nowadays. One day it's fast. Next day it's slow.'

He snapped his watch-face shut and put the watch back in his pocket. He saw that she had turned her back on him and he walked suddenly away, the pleasure of the morning broken by gnawing ridiculous irritations.

Twelve days later he was inaugurated Mayor. A mist came down on the morning of the ceremony, with a raw touch of frost in the air, and he tucked his hands in his cloak as he walked behind his mace-bearer. He had often seen the mace, enormous and brassy, flashing brilliantly at the head of mayoral processions as they crossed the square on the day of inauguration, and as a boy he had thought of it as a colossal stick of crusty golden rock. But today there was no light in the air. His bones felt cold. Bits of fur kept coming off the edge of his cape. The mayoral chain rattled like a string of counterfeit coins and because he was rather tall the edges of his ordinary pin-stripe trousers kept appearing from underneath his cloak skirt. He felt chilled and self-conscious, like some ancient and over-solemn medieval bur-gess dressed up in a play.

But on the following Sunday, in church, at the service of dedication for his office, he felt better. He felt dignified. When the time came to pray he knelt with solemnity, with a sense of dedication and a humble promise to do his best about things. Repeatedly throughout the service he looked at the window depicting the angel appearing to Zacharias and he thought of his father. He felt keenly, and yet with humility, the responsibility of his being, like a monarch, in a line of succession. At the same time he knew perfectly well that it was really all a question of his forking out pretty heavily for a year. He would be expected to put his hand deep in his pocket. He would have to be a man of charity and benefaction. He would also be a magistrate. In the little police court, above the jail, he would preside at a monthly court and fine drunks ten shillings or send others to prison for fourteen days for clouting their wives. He would preside at the meetings of the council, open many bazaars, make speeches and be called 'His Worship'. He would be doing things, ceremoniously and personally, and trying to do them with decency and dignity, that had been done by other mayors in the same place and in something of the same way for seven hundred years.

He did not know what Constance would make of this. She too would be expected to open bazaars. She too would have to make speeches and preside at functions. He felt uneasy and discouraged whenever he thought of it. Not merely, he thought, had she grown more and more aloof. She seemed to have developed a distant contempt for the town and its people that kept his friends away. Early in their marriage they had given occasional dinner-parties. The Spencers came; Charles Edward Twelvetree, a widowed and retired solicitor who amused himself with archaeology, came once or twice with his daughter, Agnes; two or three younger couples, men and their wives whom he had known since boyhood, also came. But, as one of them said, the going was hard. It was difficult to know what to make of her. Her great shyness gave everyone a feeling of inferiority, of having somehow inexplicably affronted her.

And now, he asked himself, what was going to happen? Was she going to break herself of that? It was difficult to see how she could let him run through a year of office without some sort of token cooperation. He hoped she would pull herself together. It

120

was important to be mayor. He wanted his term of office to be popular, smooth, and successful.

And then, as he came out of church on Sunday morning and waited for a few minutes at the head of the mayoral procession in an air that again had about it a wonderfully fresh autumnal glow, he caught sight of her standing in the churchyard. She was wearing a rather long pale green coat and a hat of the same colour with bright yellow trimmings. The length of the coat made her look unusually tall. In some way that was difficult to define she also looked more erect, more sure of herself and more – personable was probably the word – as she stood there in the autumn sunshine.

He saw that she was talking to the wife of the man from the music-shop, the girl he did not like very much, Mrs Schofield. A young man he recognized vaguely as having been in the shop once or twice was also there and Constance was laughing.

You did not often see her laugh like that, he thought. Her face became softer and more open when she laughed. She threw back her head a little. The intensely dark brown hair caught at its thick rippled edges a touch of light. She did not pluck nervously at her gloves, either, but held her hands firmly and surely together.

In a way difficult to explain he thought he saw a great change in her. He could not help thinking too that it was perhaps a reform undertaken out of consideration for himself, his position, and his office. He hoped that it was. It would relieve him of a lot of anxiety. It would be so much better for himself, for his friends and even for her own sake if, for a change, she behaved like a normal person.

There was also another thing that struck him on that early November day. In the sunlight, and perhaps because of the sunlight and again perhaps not, she had a look of something radiant about her. She had lost her look of anxious diffidence and seemed surprisingly free and happy.

Women were strange creatures, he could not help thinking. Gloomy one day and radiant the next, wanting one thing one day and the opposite another, they changed more often than the weather – and for the most part a man never knew why.

Chapter Three

He did not know that day, and was not to know until two months later, of the existence of something that had shaken the lives of Miss Mackness and Hyde.

As autumn went on and he grew used to his horse and accustomed to the routine of his office he suppressed his antagonism against Hyde and presently half-forgot it. Perhaps after all it was better to let bygones be bygones; nothing could be gained from feuds. In much the same way, pleased with the horse and kept busy and energetic by the calls of office, both of which he enjoyed with the eagerness of a boy given two treats instead of one, he put the anxieties of Constance aside.

If women were explicable, he thought, it would have to be by better men than him. He had given up trying to explain why they were radiant and amiable one day and withdrawn and untouchable the next. It was true that Constance, rarely radiant, was mostly withdrawn and untouchable but now he was too busy any longer to determine why. His life was full. His office demanded him five or six evenings a week. Sometimes until midnight the light in the council chambers burned out across the square. The days were full too and it was December before he could even spare a day for hunting.

There was also, in her own behaviour, not much to which he could take exception. If she was an aloof, shy, uncomfortable creature perhaps it was better to let it go at that. A woman who preferred lonely walks to riding on horseback wasn't, he thought, making the best of life; but there it was. There was nothing wrong in walking. If she liked walking so much he could not stop her.

With the shortening days he was glad to see also that she did more and more, as mayoress, to help him. She became chairman of the ladies' committees. She opened a bazaar or two. At one of these she did not simply say, 'It gives me great pleasure to declare this bazaar open'. She made a short speech, quite a good speech, without a note, succinctly. He felt quite proud of her and afterwards he heard several people congratulating her.

He was glad too that she did a good deal of sick-visiting. That took her out several afternoons a week and kept her most times until after darkness. She seemed to work hard at this. He heard that people liked her quiet way with the sick. Invalids do not as a rule care for visitors who stay too long and chatter too much and Constance was liked and welcomed because she did not overstay her welcome or gossip tiresomely.

He did not know, at that time, that her sick-visiting was another excuse for seeing Frankie Johnson. Or that her way of making her visit short gave her more time with him in the early evenings, when the streets were dark. He had, until some time later, no way of knowing. He did not know either that sometimes when she went out late at night, between ten and half past ten, it was not merely to take a jar of chicken essence or a pot of calves' jelly or a bottle of invalid wine to a sick person on the far side of the town. It was also to be waiting for Frankie Johnson, in an alley by the station, when the cinema closed.

The people who really knew of these things were Miss Mackness and Hyde.

In the back garden of his house by the station Hyde kept half a dozen white Leghorn chickens and a boxer dog. The chickens gave enough eggs for his breakfast and for Miss Mackness and himself at tea most evenings, after the shop had closed. The dog was company after Hyde had seen Miss Mackness home to her family every night. Most nights he and Miss Mackness took the dog with them, walking arm-in-arm, with the dog on a lead.

Every autumn it was something of a ritual to give up their one half-day of the week, a Thursday, to go into the country to glean corn for the hens. That was one of those things about which Miss Mackness spoke so fondly to Constance: the long days after harvest, tea in a vacuum flask and bread and butter in a basket, the stubble cleared, four or five hours in the fresh good air of the fields, and then home tired and contented, the basket full of corn ears, and Hyde with a sack of gleanings on his shoulder.

That year there were good fields of corn on the high brow of land beyond the stream outside the town. And late on a hot September afternoon when Hyde and Miss Mackness came home from gleaning Hyde thought the girl looked tired with the heat and suggested the short cut by Pollards' Mill to get them home. They could save themselves twenty minutes or more that way.

As they came down the narrow path by the mill-pond Miss Mackness was walking some yards in front of him. Suddenly she stopped. She seemed upset and turned and said quickly, in a low voice: 'Let's go back. Jim, turn round and let's go back!' but by the time she had finished her sentence she knew by the startled look in his eyes that he had also seen what she had seen.

Frankie Johnson was swimming in the mill-pond. On the far bank, in the hot sun, Constance stood combing her wet hair. She was fully dressed except for her shoes and stockings, which lay on a towel. One of the few things she did well in a physical way was swimming and now with her bare legs and feet and wet dark hair she looked exhilarated and happy, young and excited. Her face was flushed with exertion and sun and water and she was laughing as she called:

'You'd better hurry, my sweet. I make it half past five. You'll never get there.'

At that moment Hyde and Miss Mackness hurried past the far corner of the mill-pond. Hyde, who was able to screen part of his face with the sack he was carrying, was never sure if she saw them passing. The path was very narrow. The boughs of the willow trees were thick and low and still in the full leaf of summer. The pond was thirty or forty yards across and the sun was behind them, putting the path in shade.

Hyde ducked his head, screening it still more with the sack, and hurried on. It was Miss Mackness who could not take her eyes away from what was happening.

She saw Constance sit down on the bank by the pond and begin to put on her stockings. As she bared her legs and then pulled on her first stocking and fastened the suspender at her thigh Frankie Johnson swam into the bank. As he pulled himself out of the water he half-lay, half-crawled across the bank and then leaned forward and pressed his mouth quickly against the soft inner flesh of her one bare thigh.

'Oh, sweetheart, don't,' Constance said. 'You'll make me all wet again. I was so warm and dry. Oh! not again!' and once more she was laughing.

Miss Mackness and Hyde walked on rapidly, in silence, down the path. As if he were trespassing and did not want to be caught Hyde scurried along, doubled-up, keeping his head down in a fashion he had learned at Passchendaele, the sack almost horizontal on his shoulders.

Two hundred yards away Melford's thin pallid cash-girl stopped suddenly and put her head on the top bar of a stile.

'I shall have to wait a minute. I feel bad,' she said. 'My stomach keeps turning over.'

Hyde put down the sack and straightened up, sweating. Miss Mackness sat down on the step of the stile and stared up at him, shocked.

'I saw him kiss her leg. Did you see that? Kissing her bare leg when he came out of the water?'

'No I never see that.' Hyde's face was inscrutably flat as he wondered about Melford. 'I kept my head down.'

'Oh! Mrs Turner, what have you been up to?' Miss Mackness said. 'I knew you were the quiet one but whatever have you been up to?'

Hyde was still wondering about Melford. He wiped sweat from his face, wondering a little longer, and then said:

'You think he knows? Melford?'

Miss Mackness stood up. The red rims of her eyes were burning.

'No, and he's not going to know. Never. Not if we can help it. She's been very good to me and I'll never say a word.'

'Well, there must be two sides,' Hyde said. 'There's always two sides – '

'Never mind about that. Two sides or one side – I don't care. Nobody'll ever know if we can help it.'

Hyde continued to wipe sweat from his face. His thoughts were stunted. He did not know what to make of it all. He wanted to feel that Melford, perhaps, had deserved it. He felt half-inclined to believe that Melford must have asked for it somehow. There were always two sides.

'There must be some reason for it,' Hyde said. 'She wouldn't do a thing like that without some reason. I'd say Melford's to blame – '

'Never mind who's to blame,' Miss Mackness said. 'We'll never say anything. We never saw anything. It's not our business.'

'No, but I'll bet there's a reason. I wouldn't put it past that fellow to – '

She seemed to read his thoughts. Her normally frail and uncertain appearance had changed to one of stiff determination. Her throat was painfully flushed.

'I know you hate him but you ever say a word about it and I'll never speak to you again,' she said. 'I'll have nothing to do with you again as long as I live. She's been nice to me. I like her. You think she'd do a thing like that if she was happy? Women don't do things like that if they're happy.'

'The only thing I hope is that she never saw us,' Hyde said.

And then the frail Miss Mackness, who had hair of a carroty shade that she hated and who hoped that somehow Hyde would one day save enough money to divorce his wife and marry her so that she could make legal the business of ironing and mending and darning for him and not have to sleep by herself at nights, said vehemently, bravely, and with surprising passion :

'I want to forget this day. And you better forget it too. I know what this town is like. All those horse-faced church-people and chapel-people peeping out of curtains and pointing – they love to point if you give them half a chance. I know. They point at me.'

So they kept quiet about it. They kept to themselves something that, in perspective, seemed sometimes never to have happened, and they never went by the path to Pollards' Mill again.

But gradually, as winter came on, they became aware of another thing: or rather a series of regular repetitions of the same thing. And again it made them unsure, surprised, and troubled.

Walking home alone one December night, leading his boxer dog, Hyde was the first to become aware of it. He was coming through narrow streets between the cinema and the station when he felt his shoe-lace come untied. He stooped down to re-tie the lace, letting the dog-lead loose. The dog sniffed for some moments under the light of a lamp-post, went trailing its lead along the wet pavement and disappeared into the darkness of an alleyway.

Suddenly the dog was barking. Hyde finished tying his shoe-lace, began running after the dog and shouted:

'Come here, you noisy brute. Come back. Come here – come back here, I tell you.'

He liked obedience in dogs. He heard the clip of the dog-lead trailing in the alley. Rain had been falling earlier in the evening and now the streets were greasy with winter slime. He knew the dog-lead would be filthy now and with annoyance he blundered into the alleyway, shouting.

Ten yards down the alleyway he almost knocked over a man and a woman embracing against the brick buttress of a wall. He saw the woman quickly turn her face away. Then he ran the full length of the alleyway, another twenty yards or so, and caught up with the dog. The lead was filthy, as he expected, and he gave the dog a clout or two on the neck before turning back again.

By the time he was half-way back he saw the man and the woman walking away. Perhaps even then he would never have known who they were if the woman, at the entrance to the alley-way, had not dropped a glove. It was because she stopped to pick up her glove and turned her face in the street-light that he saw that she was Constance. It was more easy to recognize her too because her dark head was bare and she was carrying her hat in her hand.

He did not speak of this to Miss Mackness. If Miss Mackness had two outstanding qualities behind the frail substance of her pallid eyes and her hated carroty hair they were affection and loyalty. She was brave. Men did not like her unseductive ginger appearance and the only man she had ever been able to attract at all was Hyde, fifteen years her senior, taciturn, moody, already married and as he thought, ill-used.

Hyde knew, in turn, that he was lucky to be attracted. Not many young girls wanted to sew and iron and cook and darn for a married man still legally tied to a wife who had left him. Miss Mackness was not obliged to cook and wait for him, but she did. She knew that people pointed. She knew that people said she was a fool, that she was wasting her life and that she ought to have had the sense to know better. They always did. But then they did not see, as she did, beyond the shell of Hyde's flintiness, a loyalty not unlike her own. Hyde would have sacrificed most things for his peculiar hatred of Melford, but not Miss Mackness.

So, as Constance herself had done about the carriages for her wedding, he kept quiet about it. Soon afterwards the New Year came in and at the end of the first week there was a light thin fall of snow. About this time of the year there were many dances and parties. Hyde belonged to a working men's club where he could go to play an occasional game of draughts or cribbage and have a glass of beer. Every New Year the club gave a dinner to its members with a smoking concert afterwards.

At two o'clock in the morning Hyde and Miss Mackness were walking home from the concert. The streets were empty and the lamps were out. Thin snow, frozen hard, glittering under very brilliant, brittle stars, made the surface of the asphalt pavement treacherous, and Hyde and Miss Mackness walked in the roads.

Soon they were hearing gay voices from a man in a dinner jacket and a tall hatless woman in a long balldress. The colour of the dress was difficult to see under her black coat, above the snow. But there was no mistaking the gaiety of the voices. The man and the woman were laughing and running. In the brilliant winter starlight it was possible to see, as Hyde and Miss Mackness came closer, that the woman's coat was undone and flowing out behind.

She was running with a snowball in her hands. She was trying to press snow into and down the collar of the man's neck. Her voice was panting with the excitement and exertion of running and suddenly she was saying:

'People? Who cares about people? Who minds about people?'

'Promise then,' the man said. 'Promise no more down my neck.'

'Promise,' she said, 'on my honour, no more down your neck.'

Then the man gave a gasping shout as snow slipped cold under his collar and again the street was full of the sound of

Constance's voice laughing gaily and happily in the crisp snow-bound air, under the brilliant winter sky.

'Oh! it was wonderful,' she said. 'It was the most wonderful evening ever. Oh! Frankie, look at all the stars!'

Melford knew that she was dancing that night. He knew that the dance was some small unimportant affair that did not call for his presence – it was nothing like the Hockey Club, the Tuberculosis After Care or the Liberal Association – and he knew that she had been quite open and frank about it and had asked his permission to go.

'The Schofields have asked me to join their party,' she said. 'It's Mrs Schofield's birthday. With all those children she doesn't get much fun.'

That night the Rating and Lighting Committee kept him at the Town Hall until eleven o'clock. He had been asleep for three hours when Constance came home. There had been a great deal of unpleasant and weary discussion at the committee as to whether the twenty-three gas lamps in the High Street were adequate or not. A fellow named Parsons, one of these Bolshie demobbed soldiers, had brought it up. He had been very arrogant about it. He had thumped on the table and said he *demanded* that the streets be better lit before another winter. He *demanded* at least thirty lamps. He *demanded* that the matter be placed before the general council without delay. In the end it remained for Charles Edward Twelvetree, in his icy legal fashion, to choke the fellow off so that everybody could go home.

In spite of all his sympathies Melford was getting a little tired, he sometimes thought, of ex-soldiers. They were in and out of the shop every day, trying to hawk things, cadging. They came in with suitcases filled with cards of elastic, pins, stockings, boot-laces, buttons and that sort of thing. There was a fellow with one arm who came round with pencils and envelopes and notepaper. He granted it was pretty bad about the one arm but at the same time you could cut his whisky breath with a knife. Another chap made purses, wallets, and leather bags. He had been gassed very badly at Ypres. He had difficult spells of breathing when his face went blue. He had a wife and three children but Melford had personally seen him dive out of his own shop into The Prince of Orange, where he had no doubt he didn't drink water.

It was all very well, he thought, but there were limits. The war was over. At first you were sympathetic with these people. You tried to be polite and understanding. But when it came to somebody yelling across a committee-table about streets being made light enough for heroes to walk in it made you rather tired. It was time to get things into proper perspective. The war had been damned difficult for everybody, not only soldiers. The peace was pretty sticky too and the money had to come from somewhere.

It was not only that. He was beginning to find the constant committees, the incessant demands on his time, irritating and exhausting. He hardly ever got an evening at home. So much of it was pretty too – the sort of thing a businessman like himself would have disposed of in five minutes – and he could not help thinking there were aldermen and others who looked on committees simply as an evening out, a pastime or a chance to escape from their wives.

He had not been hunting since three weeks before Christmas. He had missed the part of the year he liked best: the blue-grey afternoons, the woods deep in oak leaves. Now there was snow on the ground. Hard frost bound it to everything like a thin tough white skin that never thawed in the raw sunless air. That irritated him too. It was bad weather for hunting. If it did not change within another week he would miss the meet at Ascott St Mary, his favourite meet of the year.

After a few days the wind turned to the west. The air was suddenly warmer and the snow cleared. His spirits lifted. On an afternoon of miraculous opal light he could even see the buds of the chestnuts shining like brown melted sugar across the square. He got a sudden false impression that spring was near.

Two days later the wind rose and stiffened. Suddenly out of the west came a cold soggy snow falling in huge wet flakes that hit the pavement like watery bird-droppings. The snow began at lunch-time, catching people as they hurried back to work, and towards four o'clock there were peals of thunder.

The phenomenon of snow on a westerly wind and thunder in winter-time not only irritated Melford that day. It revived unpleasant memories of Pilfer. By half past four the square was deep in watery snow. All the roofs were thawing waterfalls. Another peal or two of thunder rolled across the town and again he remembered Pilfer.

More out of curiosity than any anxiety he left the shop and went across to the stable yard. Everywhere snow was turning to slush. The air was wet and raw. But inside the stable a docile and almost sleepy Brandy was staring peacefully into a gloom strongly sweetened with hay.

He smoothed his hands once or twice down the animal's flank and said, 'Good old Brandy. Good boy,' and then tucked his fingers under the pouch of the throat and said, 'Well, Ascott next week. Keep your fingers crossed, Brandy boy,' and then turned to go back to the shop.

In that moment he saw Hyde's bicycle standing inside the stable, against the adjacent empty stall. He was so angry that he picked up the bicycle and threw it against the wall outside. He felt all his irritations of the past few weeks boil up like a fester.

He started striding furiously towards the shop. Then the pacific part of himself, the reproachful white wing of his mother, suddenly held him back.

'Later,' he said to himself, 'later. This can be dealt with later. We'll have this out when the shop has closed.'

By the time the shop was ready to close his anger had been smothered. Nothing remained but the old pure hatred he had felt for Hyde on the day Pilfer had been shot.

At five minutes past seven Hyde shut the bolts of the shop door and then took off his apron. Miss Mackness was locking up drawers in the cash-desk. Melford watched Hyde draw his apron over his head. Flaky had already turned out the window lights and pulled down the blue-grey street blinds.

'You can go, Flaky,' Melford said.

Hyde rolled up his apron, putting it neatly into a drawer underneath the counter. Flaky went out of the shop. Hyde, taking a pencil from behind his ear and putting it into his waistcoat pocket, prepared to follow him.

'Just a moment, Hyde.'

The voice seemed neutral, choked back. Hyde did not speak. Miss Mackness, cut off in the cash-desk, rattled her keys.

'I thought I told you not to put your bicycle in the stable, Hyde.'

Miss Mackness, about to turn out the gas-light above her desk, lifted her face. Under the light her thin throat was whitish-green. She did not turn out the light and Melford said:

'Well, Hyde? Well?'

'It was snowing,' Hyde said.

'And so the first thing you thought of was to bring it in the stable. Why didn't you put it in the store-shed?'

'It was full of stuff,' Hyde said. 'The drayman had just been.'

'Drayman, drayman,' Melford said. 'Good grief, man, what are your hands for? Things are moveable, aren't they?'

'I meant to go back,' Hyde said. 'I was going to move it later.'

In the cash-desk, under the gas-light, Miss Mackness jumped as Melford brought his hand crashing down on the counter. The purplish veins of his neck were growing livid. Miss Mackness bent over her desk, pretending to unlock a drawer, and her hands began trembling as Melford said icily, accentuating all the syllables:

'Unadulterated rubbish. You put it there and you meant to leave it there. You put it there on purpose.'

Hyde came out from behind his counter. His eyes were fixed. His lips were folded so thinly into each other that he looked toothless.

'I won't have that.'

'I don't care whether you'll have it or whether you won't have it,' Melford said. 'The bike was there and you put it there. You were distinctly ordered never to put it there and you deliberately did so.'

'Ordered?'

'I said ordered.'

'I don't like being ordered,' Hyde said. 'I been ordered enough. For five years. Orders you wouldn't understand. Out there. In France. Some were giving orders and some were taking orders, but I didn't see you there.'

'Don't try to change the subject,' Melford said. 'Let's keep to the bike, shall we? You put the bike there, didn't you? That's plain enough, isn't it? Do you think I want another damned horse killed?'

In the cash-desk Miss Mackness was at the end of her pretence with keys. She remembered she had to give the keys to Melford. She was trembling, clutching the keys in one hand and her handkerchief in the other, when she came out of the cash-desk to hear Hyde say:

'That horse would have died anyway. You know that. You heard the vet say so.'

'I heard no such thing,' Melford said, 'and moreover I don't want your advice about horses, thank you. You stick to bikes. I'm perfectly capable of managing my own affairs.'

'Oh?' For the first time Hyde gave something like a laugh. It was cracked and bitter. 'Oh? You are, are you? You think so?'

'The keys, Mr Melford,' Miss Mackness said.

Bravely and wretchedly she had some sort of hope that if she gave the keys to Melford everything would be straightened out. Melford took the keys and hurled them on the counter.

'You can go, Miss Mackness, thank you.'

'Yes, Mr Melford – '

She did not go. She stood ineffectually and nervously watching the two men facing each other in the centre of the shop. She heard Melford say:

'And what exactly did you mean by that last remark?'

'What I said, that's all – just what I said.'

'Very well,' Melford said. 'Come on. We've started this – out with it. Let's have it out.'

Suddenly the cold phlegmatic face of Hyde was sneering.

'You think you're capable?' Hyde said. 'Capable of what? You don't know what's going on – you never have done – here, there, anywhere else. Me – Miss Mackness – anybody – your wife – !'

'Wife?'

Miss Mackness, suddenly alarmed, began pleading with Hyde.

'Jim,' she said, 'Jim, you go home now. You put your coat on and go home.'

'Yes,' Hyde said. 'Wife.'

'Jim, you go home,' she said. 'I'll get your coat and you go home.'

She walked over to Hyde. She began to pull at one of his shirt sleeves. He did not notice it.

'Oh! no,' Melford said. 'Don't go home, Hyde. We've started this. Let's have it out now, man to man – let's have it all out and get it over. Now – my wife, did you say?'

'Yes,' Hyde said. 'Wife –'

'Jim!' Miss Mackness said. 'You know what I told you. You say a word about anything and I'll never speak to you again.'

Hyde, white-faced, staring straight at Melford, the close-bitten line of his lips dark, did not seem to hear her. Fatefully, in a cold oblivious trance, he kept his eyes on Melford.

'Well, I'm waiting,' Melford said.

'All right,' Hyde said. 'You know everything. You're boss. You're the one who gives the orders. You're the one who's so capable. You know everything. Now I'll tell you a few things you don't know –'

'Jim!' Miss Mackness said. 'I'm going. Jim, I warn you – I'm going and I won't be waiting. I won't be waiting I'll tell you, Jim –'

As she turned and went out of the shop she heard Hyde let loose, half-shouting, a long sentence about war and mud and orders and people not knowing what went on under their noses. It was simply an incoherent jumble of the accusations, grievances, and stored-up agonies of a man misused. Whatever there was in it of Constance and the things Miss Mackness and Hyde had heard and seen she did not wait to hear. She grabbed her hat and coat from the passage and went out into the evening of raw, thawing snow.

She had reached the far side of the square before she heard Hyde running after her. She did not stop. His feet flapped sloppily in wet snow as he caught up with her. She walked on and did not look at him.

'Wait a minute,' he said. 'Wait – I want to talk to you.'

'I don't want you to talk to me. I'm going home.'

'Don't go home yet,' he said. 'Look.' He called her by her Christian name. 'Ada,' he said. As she turned at a street corner he stumbled at the pavement edge, slipping into a gutter of running snow. 'Ada – stand and talk a minute. Ada,' he said.

'I'm not standing to talk to you,' she said. 'Ever. I told you. I told you if you said anything about her, I'd never speak to you again.'

'I never said anything – '

She stopped. Her face, normally so withdrawn and diffident, flared in the light of street lamps in the raw wet air.

'You liar,' she said. 'I stood there and heard you. You act like a fool and now you start telling lies on top of it. I heard you. Why couldn't you keep your mouth shut?'

'He give me the sack,' Hyde said. 'I never got as far as telling him. He sacked me. That was what I meant.'

'Serves you right. It was what you deserved,' she said. 'I'm glad. Now I won't have to be bothered with you any more.'

She turned suddenly and ran across the street and out of it into another. He stood for a few moments shaken, trying to recover some sort of calmness, and then he walked on. He did not try to follow her. During the first part of the argument with Melford he had felt extraordinarily calm, icily calm, without excitement. He had known exactly what he was going to say because, over and over again, he had rehearsed it in his mind. It was about officers and orders and men falling over rat-rotten bodies in mud and other men living out unexposed and cushy wars far from the sound of gunfire. It was about trench-feet, hand-grenades bursting in his face, lice on his body and the eternal stunning mind-murder of barrage guns.

He had been quite clear about it all. Then suddenly he was not so clear. Strange noises had started marching at the back of his mind. He was not really thinking. The noises were sometimes like those of a treadmill, utterly repetitious, monotonously beaten out, driving him. He remembered shouting his long final furious sentence at Melford but it was not the sentence he had meant to shout. It had gone wrong somewhere.

He walked home, staring at his feet slopping through snow. The noises in his head showed no sign of stopping. At times they increased and were like the sound of a distant locomotive rushing forward out of great distances. His mind was like a tunnel in its path. If the locomotive could force its way through the tunnel the noise would clear. That sometimes happened, and after that his head did not ache any more.

He had grown so used to Miss Mackness coming home with him in the evenings, to cook his tea-time eggs, his kippers or his sausages, that now, in the small back kitchen of his house, he hardly knew where to find simple things like cups and saucers. For some time he wandered aimlessly about the kitchen, searching for things, trying to arrange some sort of meal. He filled a kettle and put it on to boil on the gas stove. He made tea and then poured it and sat staring at the cup. He cut himself a slice or two of bread and butter, but suddenly he was sick in his throat and did not want to eat it. Throughout all of this the noises in his head showed no sign of dying and he could hear the voices of Miss Mackness rising among them too:

'I won't be there. I won't be waiting. I'm glad. Now I won't have to be bothered with you any more.'

About seven o'clock he put on his cap and coat and, unable to bear it any longer, went out to find her. By that time the sky was clearing. The wind was quietening down. Already there were black prints of frost on cleared patches of pavement and in other places snow was treacherous and crackling.

He did not notice these things. He walked rather as Constance had once done, head partly down, tucked into the collar of his coat, not thinking. The idea of Melford sacking him made no impression on his mind.

At twenty minutes past seven he made his way among the water-barrels, coal-sheds, and back-garden fences of the terrace where Miss Mackness lived with a married sister and her mother. The window of the back living-room was in darkness. A laurel bush by the back door had thick frozen snow on its leaves. He rapped several times on the door and finally a woman opened the door of the house across the yard and put her head out and said:

'Ain't no use you hammering. They bin gone out hour or more.'

Depressed, head down, crunching through islands of frozen snow, he walked back. He lit the gas in the kitchen, sat at the table and tried to read the paper. A cold draught came whistling through the keyhole. After a time he remembered the fire in the kitchen range. He went out to the coal-shed and brought back a bucket of coal and made up the fire, forgetting at the same time to open the damper.

Gradually the fire, smothered by new coal, blackened and died down. He did not notice it. Completely thoughtless, he remained staring at the paper. Words jumped blackly about the pages and at the back of his head the accumulated noises thumped with increasing pain.

He put his head into his hands. He wanted to cry for Miss Mackness. There was no way of crying and in staring loneliness he could only express himself in gasps of dry and tearless sobbing.

When they stopped at last, about nine o'clock, it was the sudden pressure of noises at the back of his mind that suffocated them. Suddenly his mind was overrun and overpowered by a rushing blackness. It poured through him, obliterating his sobbing, the last of his confidence and even the words of Miss Mackness:

'I won't be there. I won't be waiting. I'm finished. Now I won't have to bother with you any more.'

A few moments later he opened the door of the gas-stove. Almost reverently he turned on the gas and then knelt down.

Miss Mackness had gone with her mother and her married sister to watch a film featuring an artist named Clara Bow. As she sat watching the film, listening at the same time to the four-piece orchestra of one violin, one double-bass, one clarinet, and Frankie Johnson, she felt more and more troubled by thoughts of Hyde. She felt a queer rising anger about it all: anger no longer against Hyde or against Melford or, as it had first been, against herself. She was angry that a string of disjointed circumstances that had really nothing to do with her should suddenly have come together and caught her, at last, in a trap.

Presently, in desolation, she was feeling sorry about Hyde. She was sorry for the way she had flaunted off and left him. She was sorry for things she had said to him and desperately sorry, above all, at the thought of his being sacked. She knew that it was terribly easy to do and say things that you did not mean in the heat of the moment and perhaps, after all, Hyde had not mentioned Mrs Turner. She did not know. Perhaps he had after all told the truth to her and she, in the way of people in anger, had not wanted to hear.

About half past nine she could bear it no longer. She got up and excused herself and went out of the cinema into the streets of partly frozen snow. It was normally pleasant to come out of the cinema with Hyde and breathe, after the close stale tobacco air rising like a fog in front of the screen, the fresh sharp night air. Then to walk home arm in arm, slowly, not talking too much, and at last, by the water-butts at the back of her mother's house, under the screen of laurel bushes, be kissed good night by Hyde.

But this evening she did not feel like that. She actually wondered, as she hurried through snowy streets towards the station, whether Hyde would ever want her again. She could not bear it, she thought, if Hyde should never want her again. She could not do without Hyde. Even the reputation of Mrs Melford Turner was not worth that.

In the kitchen of Hyde's house she found him lying with his head on a cushion inside the stove. In terror she lifted him up and dragged him as far as the step outside. His hands were still warm and his breath, as she moved him, came dryly rattling up his throat with something of the same sound as his dry tearless sobbing.

'All suicides are mental cases,' Melford said to Constance five days later. 'Still, I'm glad they've been lenient with him. He'll be better off up there.' By 'up there' he meant an asylum, but there was something indelicate and painful that he did not like about the word. 'I think he's been mental some time. The way he looked sometimes. Bottling something up, terrible grievances. And all that raving – that mad stuff about trenches and officers and orders and you going to that dance the other day.'

Haggard and tired and dispirited about it all, he found a final moment of solace in a sudden added thought.

'You know,' he said, 'I tell you what. It sounds crazy I know, but here's a crazy person. I almost wonder sometimes if he wasn't jealous of you.'

The following week, at the end of January, came his break for hunting.

Chapter Four

Every winter Melford looked forward to the meet at Ascott St Mary as a child looks forward to Christmas. For many years the expectation, the ritual, and the experience of that meeting had been the same.

It was his habit to send over his hunter by Britton the previous day. He himself followed by trap in the late afternoon. By spending that night at The George and Crown, well looked after by Mrs Duncan, eating a good dinner, sharing a bottle of wine with one or two other gentlemen there who adopted the same procedure, sleeping well and breakfasting well, he could be fresh and in good fettle for the following day. He could not remember the time when he had not known The George and Crown. He supposed his father had first taken him there. He was too young to remember. His earliest experience there was of being served by a much younger Mrs Duncan with what she called a 'dip-in egg'. It was a boiled egg, softly done, into which he dipped thin fingers of bread and butter. He remembered too that it was a young Mrs Duncan who had first cut an orange for him, still unpeeled, into four equal quarters, afterwards making piglets of the empty skins. For ever afterwards he preferred his oranges 'Mrs Duncan's way'.

But this year he found himself driving over in a chilled, uneasy mood. He had not recovered from the affair of Hyde. It had upset not only himself but the entire workings of the shop. He could not get anyone to replace Hyde: he was managing temporarily with Miss Mackness's married sister. Then there was the police inquiry. That in itself was bad enough; but for a man in his position, mayor and magistrate, it was painfully difficult and embarrassing. It was lucky Hyde had recovered and there had been no inquest. He shuddered when he thought of that nightmare. He was relieved to be away from it all.

He arrived at The George and Crown as darkness was falling, about half past five. He took the trap to the stables, spoke with Britton for a few moments, patted Brandy on the neck and then went into the house with his bag.

In the entrance hall, at the foot of the dark oak stairs, a strange woman came forward to greet him. She was a woman of fifty, large and fair-complexioned. She wore big pearl-drop ear-rings and several rings on the fingers of her left hand.

'Good evening, sir. Something I can do for you?'

'Mrs Duncan, please,' he said. 'Isn't Mrs Duncan here?'

Her pearl ear-rings quivered, as her shoulders did, when she laughed.

'Mrs Duncan? Mrs Duncan has been left since Christmas, sir.'

'Mrs Duncan left?' He could not believe it. He was more than astounded; he felt that an unfair advantage had been taken of him. He was stunned. 'Mrs Duncan left for where?'

'Mrs Duncan has gone to keep a public near Worcester, sir. The White Hart.'

He could not speak. Mrs Duncan left? No Mrs Duncan? No Effie? People he had known since childhood. He looked querulously and provocatively at the woman with big ear-rings.

'And do you – are you the new landlady?'

'I am, sir. Yes. Mrs Corcoran.'

'Not the Corcorans from Bedford?'

'No, sir,' she said. 'My daughter and I are Londoners.'

Inevitably he was affronted. He had a deep-rooted and unconditional dislike of Londoners. He even disliked the word.

'I·think you'll be just as comfortable and welcome as you were before, sir.'

Possibly, he thought, but that was not the point. He liked Mrs Duncan; he disliked Londoners. That was the point. He had grown up with Mrs Duncan. Things would not be the same any more.

'What name would it be, sir?'

'Mr Melford Turner.'

'Oh! yes, sir. Your room is ready,' she said. 'The one you always have. We knew you were coming. I'll get Brown to take your bag.'

Well, that was something. Brown, the boots-handyman who

had been there, to his knowledge, for twenty-five years – Brown had not gone. At least there was a link with Brown.

'And we've got a very nice dinner on, sir. Roast saddle of lamb with red-currant jelly. I know you like that.'

He felt a little less cheerless after that.

'And plenty of other nice things, sir. I'm sure you'll be comfortable.'

'What dessert?'

He hoped she would say hot apple-pie with cream for dessert. Mrs Duncan made a very special apple-pie in which there were raisins and cloves.

'For afters, sir?' she said and he recoiled at once from the cheap objectionable London word.

'That's what I meant.'

She smiled. 'There'll be hot apple-pie and cream, sir,' she said.

Upstairs he was glad to find a fire in his room. There was always something wonderful about a fire in a bedroom. Mrs Duncan had always given him a fire. Then when Brown brought up his bag he said:

'Well, Brown, I see there have been some changes since I last saw you. How do you find things? How are the new people?'

'Very nice people, Mr Turner sir,' Brown said. 'Mrs Corcoran and Phoebe. Very nice, friendly people.'

'Well, I shall miss Mrs Duncan.'

'Don't doubt it, sir,' Brown said. 'But I think you'll find the old place much the same as ever.'

'I hope so,' he said. He put his hand in his pocket and gave Brown two shillings. 'And bring me up a whisky, will you, Brown?'

As the evening went on he did in fact find the old place much the same as ever. He changed his clothes and sat for some time in his shirt-sleeves, drinking his whisky before the bedroom fire. Soon he began to get hungry. He could detect the smell of roast lamb coming up the stairs.

About seven o'clock he finished dressing, lit a cigarette and went down to the bar. Two or three gentlemen he knew were already there. They too were for the hunt tomorrow. They hailed him like schoolboys at a reunion party and one, a big raw-faced man named Captain Whitling, struck him, in a gesture of brotherhood, on the back. A big fire of coal and oak logs burned in the open fireplace and most of the time Captain Whitling, who was still wearing breeches and brown leggings, kept kicking it heavily into flame.

Another man, a wiry dark-haired fellow with slightly bent shoulders and deep side-linings, wearing a long grey hacking-jacket and a yellow check waistcoat, hailed him with coughing drawls. His name was Rampling. He smoked thin cheroots and said:

'Ah! if it isn't the old Turner. The veritable Turner. The old comestible. Welcome, Turner. Well met. So she let you loose after all?'

'We were just laying the odds you wouldn't come this year,' Captain Whitling said. 'Not since the change of status.'

'Well devised, Turner,' Rampling said.

'Drink up,' Captain Whitling said. 'Everybody drink up. Turner, what will it be? Bill, where the hell is the Major?'

From outside came a Major Beeton, obese and red, with a head completely hairless except for small wisps of smart iron-grey curls about the ears. Several buttons of his waistcoat were undone. 'The wind is cold on the blasted heath,' he said.

'Well phrased, Beety,' Rampling said. 'Jolly well phrased. From whence comes this wind?'

'Out of the bloody north,' Major Beeton said.

Everybody roared with laughter. Captain Whitling kicked the fire, making that roar too. A great air of jolly comfort hung about the bar and Melford himself laughed when Rampling said:

'Observe our surprise visitor, Beety. None other than the old comestible. Out of the marriage bed into the fire.'

'Good for you, Turner,' Beety Beeton said. 'Well fought, sir.'

Later they went into dinner together, joining in the saddle of lamb. The meat was excellent. The red-currant jelly was also excellent and Melford ate large quantities of it, boyishly, not thinking, so that presently Captain Whitling found himself being passed an empty pot and rang the bell for more.

'Speaking of empty pots,' he said, 'I must tell you a little thing I heard.'

He was still telling a story of a man afflicted with some congenital disorder of the bladder when Phoebe, Mrs Corcoran's daughter, came in to answer the bell.

Holding the pot up to her: 'Empty pot,' Captain Whitling said. He spoke with fine significance. 'Can't have an empty pot. Never know.'

The girl took the pot coldly, not speaking. She was a girl of medium height, with dark hair that grew abundantly about her neck and ears, and a skin that was thick and deep-coloured. As she took the pot from Captain Whitling she flung up her head, held it stiffly and then floated out of the room.

'Oh! oh! oh dear!' Captain Whitling said. 'What have we said? Have we said something we shouldn't have said? Have we or have we not? Gentlemen, what did I say?'

'A few well-chosen words.'

'Ill-chosen, ill-chosen,' Rampling said. 'Captain, I warn you to mind your p's and q's.'

'Pees and chambers more likely!' Beety Beeton said. 'Pees and chambers I would say.'

They were still laughing at this remark when the girl came back. In her same floating way, head held up, dark skin flushed, she came to the table and put the pot of fresh red-currant jelly among the dishes. To Melford, suddenly, the laughter seemed too pointed. He could not help feeling that it was ungentlemanly, a little unfair. Some of the jokes had been a little ripe too. He stopped laughing, helped himself circumspectly to brussel sprouts, and then peppered them thoughtfully.

She was quick to notice his lack of laughter; and suddenly she stared coldly at Captain Whitling, Bill Rampling, and Major Beety Beeton and said:

'It's nice to know we have one gentleman here.'

After that he felt curiously uneasy whenever she came into the room. He could not join in the laughter behind her back. Nor could he look at her. Each time he carefully helped himself to something from the dishes, poured a little wine, or stared at a heap of sugar in a spoon.

By the end of the meal Captain Whitling, who had drunk a bottle of claret following an hour or more of whisky, was drunk enough to mistake a sifter of salt for sugar. With torpid, juice-eyed care he sprinkled salt on apple-pie, poured cream on it and ate it fumblingly. This mistake was seen by Rampling and Beety Beeton, who kept it to themselves, heavily declining to tell Captain Whitling what the joke was.

'The fact is,' Rampling said. 'We must not tell jokes. Telling jokes is not nice. Phoebe would hear. Eh, Turner, my old comestible, Phoebe would hear?'

Not having drunk so much as Captain Whitling or being as tipsy as Rampling and Beety Beeton, he soberly resented Rampling's remark about 'the old comestible'. He suddenly knew they were pulling his leg. They were joking at him for being a grocer. They wanted to get him on the raw. It was not the first time, but he liked to think that he was a sport and did not mind. But now they were also gibing at him, for some reason, about the girl and he found himself resenting it quietly and uneasily.

'Blast!' Captain Whitling said. 'You swobs! I've been eating bloody salt for sugar! And you knew, you bastards, didn't you? – you knew!'

'Steady,' Rampling said. 'No language. Ladies about. No jokes. Sackcloth on, Whitling, sackcloth. Mourn your mistakes, old man. Phoebe is here – our pure Phoebe –'

'Oh! Phoebe pure,' Beety Beeton sang. 'Oh, Phoebe pure, the days may come, the days may go –'

A moment later Captain Whitling was sick on the carpet and Melford, hearing the slop of it, felt sickened too.

Some time later, after taking a turn in the yard, he came in to go to bed. At the foot of the stairs he was met by Mrs Corcoran's daughter, who said:

'I don't like that wind, do you, sir? It's bitter. Going up to get some sleep, sir?'

Yes, he said, he thought of going up to bed. He didn't like the wind either. It was too much in the north for his liking.

'Something you'd like before you go up, sir?'

He thanked her and said no, he thought there was nothing he wanted. Then she said:

'You're Mr Turner from Orlingford, aren't you, sir?' Her voice was friendly. The fact that she kept her thick soft lips almost closed when she spoke was responsible, perhaps, for the effect of its being intimate and low. 'Of course we've heard about you.'

'Heard about me?'

'You're the Mayor, aren't you?'

'Yes, I'm the Mayor.' It was pleasant that she knew about that. He was glad and he tried to belittle it. 'For my pains.'

'Oh! I'm sure it's a great honour,' she said. 'Mayor of a town – I should call that an honour.'

'Well, I don't know about honour,' he said. 'It's mostly a question of putting your hand in your pocket.'

She said, 'Well, like most things,' slightly shrugging her shoulders. They were plump firm shoulders and the bare skin of her arms was deep olive in the country lamp-light as she folded her arms and smoothed them with her hands.

'Still,' he said, 'we're used to that. My father had to do it. And his father before that. So I suppose I must do it, as long as they ask me.'

'I'm sure they'll ask you for a very long time.'

At the last moment, just before going up to bed, he felt uneasy about what had happened at dinner-time.

'I'm afraid it got a little out of hand at dinner.'

'Oh! in a public you've got to get used to that,' she said. 'Perhaps it was a bit coarse – but, well, I think I know a gentleman when I see one.'

As she said this she looked him full in the face. Her dark eyes roamed about him without haste, warm, and friendly. He was more than ever glad he had not been too much a part of the ribaldry at dinner and he said:

'Well, good night, Miss Corcoran. Thank your mother for the dinner. Tell her I said it couldn't have been better.'

'I will, sir. Good night. Sleep well, sir,' she said.

Up in his bedroom, as he went to draw back the curtains before getting into bed, the light of the fire, still with a yellow flame or two about the coals, sprang up afresh and reflected itself in the dark panes of the window.

The window was the northerly one and as he watched the reflection of fire leaping up in it he remembered another occasion when he had stood at a bedroom window in The George and Crown and looked out, in darkness, at a wintry sky.

It was a year or two before his father's death; he was eighteen at the time. He was tall for his years, but in all other ways he was rather young for them. That January he was staying overnight, as he always did, for the hunt next day, and his father was staying with him. After his father had gone to bed Melford took a turn in the yard and suddenly, as he stood looking at the stars, a woman's voice said out of the darkness:

'They tell me you can see the Northern lights.'

She was a Mrs Marchmont, a biggish woman of fifty with broad hips and a large piled bunch of reddish hair. He remembered speaking to her for a moment or two at dinner-time. He did not know anything about Northern lights and she said:

'But everybody's talking about them. It was in all the papers. It's the best display for years. The point is I don't know which way to look. Which is the north?'

He found the Pole Star for her and pointed it out, clear in its dark space beyond The Plough. She said he was very clever to be able to know things like that, but where were the lights that everyone said were there?

'We're probably too low down,' he said. 'We're in a hollow here.'

He searched the sky for some moments, seeing nothing in the winter blackness, and then said again:

'Yes, that must be it. We're too low here. The fields are too high on that side.'

'Perhaps we could see them from upstairs,' she said. 'Let's have a look from my bedroom. That's on the north side.'

Then they were in her bedroom, dark except for its glow of fire. They stood for some time peering into blackness through the window. She laid her hand on his shoulder. There were, as he knew quite well later, no Northern lights to be seen. In the small alcove her broad body pressed against him and suddenly she turned and put both hands on his shoulders and said:

'I looked at you all through dinner. I was watching you.'

Her dress, open to reveal a deep creased chest, was heavy with perfume. Her mouth had an old corrupt breath of whisky in it. She took his face in her hands and said:

'Let's you and I do nice things together, shall we? Nice things tonight and then tomorrow forget it all?'

He loathed her face, big and blotched and excited, in the light of the fire. She tried to kiss him. She actually put her thick sucking lips on his and he loathed that too. Then she was breathing heavily, telling him not to be shy, not to mind, there was no one coming, no one who could possibly come, and before he could stop her she had turned the key of the door.

He loathed her too, lying on the bed, urging him to come to her. He caught sight of her enormous white pouchy limbs in the light of the fire. She tore down her dress, showing the great plain white bay of her chest encased in a camisole before it suddenly burst free. Then she was holding up her fat naked arms and saying, almost whimpering:

'Melford, come on, Mel – you see, I know what your name is. Melford, come here. Please,' she said and the whimpering grew to a sobbing murmur as she asked him over and over again to come to her. 'If not for you, Melford, for me – for me. Come on, be a good boy, Melford, for me.'

All his ineffectual feeble terrors with Constance sprang from that moment of being trapped with Mrs Marchmont in the bedroom. His retreat from her on the night of his wedding had been, in effect, a retreat from Mrs Marchmont. He had never forgotten her breath of corruption. It had been like being asked to make love to a sow. After it he had been in retreat from women so often and so much and in such terror that it was only the unaggressive shyness of Constance herself that had finally won him over.

But the loathing, the difficulty, remained. It had been the one blemish on his visits, ever since, to Ascott St Mary. He could never come into his bedroom at night, in the light of the fire, without remembering Mrs Marchmont, her pouchy white limbs, her idea of fun, and his loathing.

That was why it was nice to have a well-mannered, pleasant, friendly girl like Phoebe Corcoran about the place. She clearly had pride and knew where her place was. She was the kind of girl who did not upset him and perhaps it was not so bad after all. She had done much to lessen his chilled and anxious mood.

The morning broke grey and bitter: not the day he had hoped for. A brutish wind went driving through the oak-woods, rattling at dead leaves. Out across exposed fields it whined over naked hedgerows, cutting like glass at the balls of his eyes. It was a day without light, and by afternoon the chill was clenched and sullen in his bones.

Hounds found only twice that day, once in the morning at a wood on a hill called Shelton Spinneys, and again about three o'clock at a place called Butcher's Farm. There was too much cover in the spinneys and the coarse hard wind was hampering the hounds. From the woods behind the farm a vixen, a big old yellowish-rusty animal, actually struck out into open country and then made for ground in a stone pit grown over with elder and blackberry and clumps of blackthorn. It was cold work waiting for hounds to pick up scent again. The air, just above freezing point, seemed colder than frost itself and he felt as if he was sitting on a concrete animal as the vixen finally broke out and went loping away up a field of quivering corn to the long oak-woods he knew so well.

It was not long before she found cover again and the ridings down the woods were echoing with the fretting noises of baying hounds. By that time he was so cold that he felt one jolt would have unhorsed him like a log. He was glad to ride into the shelter of the wood and take a tot of brandy from his flask. As he uncorked the flask Rampling and Beety Beeton came cantering down the riding and Rampling called:

'Secret drinker, eh? Come on, Turner old fruit, I think they've found again!'

Far down the riding there was a sudden agitation of blowing horns and hounds crying and whippers-in and huntsmen yelling. With chilled hands he fumbled to put the brandy flask back in his pocket and then dropped it on the ground. By the time he had dismounted and picked it up most riders had disappeared. The few that he could see were simply red flickers darting beyond an undergrowth of hazel boughs.

Then – and he did not know quite how it happened except that it was perhaps his clumsiness and delay with the brandy-flask – he was in the centre of a riding down which hounds were crying back. He actually saw the vixen, like a curl of dirty yellow smoke caught by wind, veering from side to side down the riding before suddenly she seemed to catch sight of him and turned away.

A moment later she was lost among hazel undergrowth;

horses and hounds were crowding through and a savage voice was yelling:

'Get back, you bloody fool! Back there – Get behind, you idiot, damn you!'

He had never liked Montagu, the new master of hounds. In the years before he had taken over as master he had always been more like some coarse, squat purple-mouthed bulldog than a man. Now he was even grosser. He brought a snarling domineering note to things. And now suddenly he was shouting, not to Melford, but to a rider behind him:

'Who was it? That bloody grocer? Frigging about there like an old woman in a daydream – By God – !'

He was glad when the day was over. He rode back alone, cold to his inner bones, in a premature twilight through which were driving the first tiny stinging bullets of snow. At the foot of the hill it occurred to him that Brandy was slightly lame in the left fore-foot. He dismounted and with stiffening hands gouged out a long thin flint from the hoof. By the time he had finished snow was sweeping in a hard horizontal cloud across the hillside.

But again, in The George and Crown, it was warm and comfortable. He went up to his room, washed, changed his clothes, put on his slippers and sat for an hour with a big fierce neat whisky before the fire. His body thawed and blood began to run again. Only his mind remained chilled: coldly haunted and depressed by Montagu's savage public remark about himself. He granted, perhaps, that he had been a trifle on the stupid side in not keeping his eyes open a little more in that riding, but did it call for a gross ill-mannered public tick-off like that? Perhaps he had deserved a rebuke of sorts, but that coarse yell about a grocer –

His depression about Montagu renewed and redoubled his depression about Hyde. He felt increasingly badly about Hyde. He knew he had not acted rightly. He could hear the aloof and distant reproaches of his mother, keen and searching for all their gentleness. No: he had been at fault, badly and meanly at fault, about Hyde.

He was purposely late in going down to dinner. He did not want to be caught up too much again with the Rampling, Whitling, Beety Beeton crowd. He dreaded to be taunted. But to his relief the bar was quiet. The three men, apparently uneasy about snow, which was falling now in a sweeping half-blizzard, had called for an early taxi home.

In the dining-room only a man named Sartoris, a corn-merchant from Evensford, and his son Roger, were eating. Again the food, hot thick jugged hare, was very good. Again there was red-currant jelly, with plenty of brussel sprouts and chestnuts and light creamed potatoes.

'Not a pleasant day, Melford,' Sartoris said. He was fair-moustached, with an open honest blue-eyed face and abundant stiff hair that sprouted from his ears like barley bristles. 'I don't think you know my son, Roger. Eighteen. Just finished his last term at school.'

'No,' Melford said. 'How do you do, Roger,' and leaned across the table and shook hands.

Not merely was the boy, tall and fresh-eyed, a replica of his father. In his leanness and simplicity and his very fair English-ness he reminded Melford of himself. He must have looked very much like that at the time of his experience with Mrs March-mont. No wonder he had loathed it. Small wonder he had turned and fled.

Throughout dinner he looked at Sartoris and the boy with envy. He felt a curious aching hollowness in his heart every time he looked at the boy. The eyes were so candid and glinting in their young blue-whiteness. The clean well-cut mouth, not quite nervous, was so sensitive with its untouchable youthful diffi-dence, quivering like a young animal's and as fine as a girl's. He envied Sartoris. With something like pain he felt a recrudescence of his longing for a son.

Then he was aware of a strange unaccustomed flavour in the potatoes.

'That's odd,' he said. 'That touch of something in the potatoes, Sartoris. Did you notice it?'

'I did, but I thought it was my mouth,' Sartoris said.

For some minutes he went on trying to detect and put a name to that elusive touch of something in the potatoes and then Phoebe Corcoran came in.

'Tell us,' Melford said. 'What is this odd flavour about the potatoes? We can't quite make it out.'

'Ah,' she said. She smiled in her polite warm way as she put down, on the side table, a dish of lightly sugared mince-pies. 'I had an idea you might ask that, sir.'

'Well, what is it?'

'Nutmeg, sir,' she said.

'Nutmeg?' he said. 'In *potatoes*?'

'Yes, sir. Don't look so shocked. It's a touch of my mother's. She was told of it by a Swiss friend.'

Something about all this, the company of Sartoris and the boy, the friendliness, and the strange taste of nutmeg in the potatoes, did a good deal to assuage his recollection of the gnawing insult by Montagu. The sugared mince-pies were very good too and tasted even better with a glass of port. He invited Sartoris and his son to join him in a glass of port but Sartoris said:

'No, thank you, Melford. I think we're for bed. We must be up betimes.'

So he sat in the smoke-room alone, putting on his pipe, sipping another glass of port and nursing the last of his hurt about Montagu. All the time, in spite of everything, there was a chilled and stony touch far down inside him: an echo left from the grey, bitter day, the insult by Montagu and the wretched affair of Hyde.

Soon after ten o'clock Phoebe Corcoran came into the smoke-room.

'Just to see if you'd like anything else, sir,' she said. 'A night-cap, sir? Another glass of port? Or some hot milk in the bed-room?'

'Well, that's a considerate thought.'

He paused. The fire in the smoke-room had fallen low. The clinging cold of the day seemed to come back with a draught from the open door.

'Have some hot milk, sir,' she said. 'Mother's been gone to bed with hers an hour or more. Chilled to the bone.'

'You know,' he said, 'I think hot milk is not a bad idea.'

'I'll bring it up, sir.'

Twenty minutes later he was sitting before the fire in his bed-room. The milk had still not come. He was just beginning to wish he had never ordered it when there was a knock at the door.

Phoebe Corcoran came in with a steaming cup of hot milk and a plate of thick round ginger biscuits on a tray. She was wearing a red dressing-gown. Her hair was partly down, falling outside her collar. He noticed again that her hair, thick and strong on the crown of her head, grew much more softly about her neck and ears.

'I'm sorry I've been so long,' she said. She set the tray on a table before the fire. 'But the milk almost had ice on it in the larder. Then like a loony I had to go and let it boil over while I was doing my hair.'

He thanked her for taking so much trouble.

'I brought you ginger biscuits as well,' she said. 'I hope you like them?'

'My favourite. Anything ginger.'

'Well,' she said, 'I think that was clever of me to know.'

She laughed in her pleasant way and he took the cup of milk and stirred it. She said, 'I put sugar in the saucer, sir. I didn't know if you liked it,' and he dropped two lumps of sugar in the cup and stirred a second time.

'You didn't kill today, sir, did you?'

He was nibbling, with pleasure, on a ginger biscuit.

'No,' he said, 'we didn't kill today. As a matter of fact we only found twice and we lost again both times.' The biscuit was very good; he sold the same make himself. 'But I didn't mind. It was really wretched. No day for hunting. I was glad to get back.'

'You know I'm rather glad to hear you say that,' she said, 'because I don't really care much for the killing part either. I'm not much for the killing part.'

Drinking the milk, munching the biscuit, he felt altogether warmer and better.

'Rather quieter tonight,' he said, 'at dinner.'

'Yes, sir. A bit more gentlemanly.'

'Very pleasant people, Sartoris and his boy,' he said. 'A very nice boy.'

'But oh! so young,' she said. 'He blushed crimson if you looked at him.'

'And did I really look shocked,' he said, 'about the nutmeg?'

'Really shocked.'

She laughed again. Her open mouth, with its good well-kept shining teeth, was soft and red in the light of the fire.

'Properly shocked,' she said. 'But honestly, didn't you like it? I think it's nice for a change.'

'Yes. I liked it. Not very English, though.'

'Oh! it does you good to try new things,' she said. 'New ways – that's good for you. You get bored and dull with the same old ways.'

She had given up calling him sir. She held out her hands to the fire. He looked at the nails, pink, semi-transparent at their edges, in the light of it. She seemed for a minute or more to lapse into thought, eyes glazed and deep on the heart of what remained of the fire.

'Thoughtful all of a sudden,' he said.

'Sorry,' she said. 'I was thinking. And do you know what?' She kept staring at the fire, her eyes glowing with small central rosy reflections. 'Do you ever get the feeling you've met someone somewhere before?'

'Sometimes.'

'That's how I feel with you,' she said. 'Strange – but the minute I first saw you I felt I'd met you before.'

She gave him a single unbroken glance, steady, and clear, before suddenly turning away again. A moment later she was saying something about his early morning tea and when would he like it?

'Oh! eightish,' he said. 'When it suits you.'

'I wouldn't stir too early,' she said. 'The snow's nearly a foot deep already. Have a lie in. If it keeps on like this all night I've got an idea you won't be going very far.'

He woke to great carvings of snow. The bedroom windows were feathered to the top and he could not see out of them.

When Phoebe Corcoran brought his early morning tea her face was stark white with snow reflection as she drew the curtains and stood gazing from the window. There were drifts, she said, ten feet deep and more. All the telephone wires were down. In some places drifts were higher than the hedgerows. The whole top road, she heard, was blocked with fallen trees. The top road was his way home.

'And they're still plucking the geese by the look of it,' she said.

'The sky's just full of snow.'

He breakfasted late on porridge, kipper, ham and eggs, bread, two pots of tea and plenty of toast and marmalade. That was another good thing about The George and Crown: they gave you proper breakfasts.

After breakfast he tried to telephone the shop. All the lines were down. It was impossible to telegraph either. No post had arrived and there were no morning papers. Snow continued to fall in a dense driving mist, on an almost horizontal wind that cracked through tree boughs with the melancholy and startling noises of breaking bones. Flocks of occasional rooks flew over, lost, swinging downwind helplessly. Cavernous drifts hid the hedgerows and the little river at the end of the front-garden was no more than a thick yellow trickle between curled and knuckled crusts of snow.

'Make yourself comfortable, Mr Turner,' Mrs Corcoran said. 'We've plenty to eat and drink. We'll look after you.'

He spent some part of the morning between breakfast and lunch-time with Brandy, who had already been fed and watered by Brown. He kept himself reasonably warm by cleaning and grooming the animal but it was hard to keep his hands warm and when he finally went back into the pub about noon his fingers began aching and tingling painfully.

'Hot-ache,' he said. 'Hot-ache.' He stood first on one foot and then the other in the bar. He hated hot-ache. Right from boyhood he'd not been able to bear that strange hot-ache agony of exposure. He pressed his hands painfully under his armpits and Phoebe Corcoran said:

'Have a good big whisky. That'll help. Here, let me rub them for you.'

She poured him a large whisky and rubbed his hands. He was too agonized to feel her much, but her face was screwed up in sympathetic pain for him and she said:

'Oh! I know how it feels. You don't know what to do with them. You don't know where to put them. You feel you could cut them off, don't you?'

After a time the pain receded from his hands. The whisky curled like a hot snake through his stomach. Soon he thought he could smell roast beef from the kitchen. He hoped it was roast beef and he naturally hoped there would be horseradish sauce with it and Yorkshire pudding too.

Then he felt that perhaps he had made rather too much fuss about his hands and he was glad when she said:

'I like that horse of yours. I like its colour. If I had my way I'm not sure I wouldn't like hair that colour.'

'Oh! he's all right,' he said. 'But I lost a better one.'

Then suddenly he was telling her about Pilfer: the thunderstorm, the excitement, the breaking of the leg, the inevitable shooting. He omitted all mention of the bicycle.

'He would have died anyway,' he said. That was the measure of his stupidity about the whole affair: the horse would have died anyway. It was all nonsense about the bicycle. 'Tumour on the lung. They're apt to get it at his age. The thing is you can't always detect it – you don't know about it till afterwards. Till it's all over.'

'That was sad,' she said. Queer: but he had never got round to discussing the matter with Constance. He had never even told her of the tumour.

'Yes, it was sad,' he said. 'In ten years you can get very fond of a horse.'

'I'm sure,' she said. 'But then you're probably a fond sort of person.'

Was he? He didn't know. He had to confess he had never looked at himself from the fond point of view. He had never thought of it.

'Do you like horses?' he said.

'I love them. I love that one of yours especially.'

Whether he was a fond sort of person or not he did not know; but all that day, imprisoned in the pub by snow, the only guest in a strange, transfigured world of whiteness that ought to have made him uneasy simply because he could not escape from it, he was increasingly aware of an element of fondness in her.

He could not quite explain that fondness. It was not aggressive or positive; it did nothing to excite him. On the contrary it calmed him down. It had something of the same soft and insulating effect as snow. Exactly as the harsh grisled landscape of yesterday had disappeared under snow, leaving everything pure and transfigured, so his life of the day before yesterday seemed to have vanished into some sort of embalmment.

He did not think of Constance all that day. His thoughts hardly turned again to Hyde and the shop. He ate a wonderful lunch of roast beef, Yorkshire pudding, horseradish sauce, roast potatoes, brussel sprouts, plum pudding, celery, mustard and Stilton cheese. He made his little pagodas with pleasure, undisturbed. Afterwards he had a glass of port and then dropped off to sleep before an enormous fire of coal and oak-logs in the lounge.

He woke to the sound of tea cups. Phoebe Corcoran had come in with tea, cheese-cakes, quince jelly and two kinds of bread and butter on a tray. She was wearing a dark green tweed skirt and a bright red woollen jumper. As she was setting out his tea Brown came in with fresh coal and logs for the fire. He broke up the coals with his foot. In the fresh light from the flames her figure shone round and glowing and Brown said:

'I fed and watered him, sir. No need for you to go out again. I covered him over well and put a bale of straw against the door to keep the wind out.'

He thanked Brown, who went out, and Phoebe Corcoran said:

'I went to have a look at him too. He's so affectionate. I love affectionate things.'

It was no longer snowing, she said. It was freezing hard and bitter. It was going to be an awful night and she would draw the curtains and shut it out. She asked then if the tea was enough for him? Would he like some toast? No, he said, and she began to draw the curtains.

'And how,' he said, 'did you know I liked quince jelly?'

'I didn't.'

'I'm beginning,' he said, 'to think you've got some sort of second sight about me. Ginger biscuits, quince jelly – it looks as if you can read my mind.'

'It sort of looks like that,' she said. 'But is the jelly all right? I don't care for it myself. It was made from the quinces here.'

'Perfect,' he said.

She finished drawing the curtains, and Brown brought in the lamp.

'I fancy they're quince trees at the bottom of the garden, by that little river,' she said. 'It must be nice there in summer-time.'

'I suppose there are fish in that river,' he said, 'but I've never tried.'

'You must come over and try in the summer,' she said. 'I think it'll be wonderful here when the summer comes.'

That night, as before, she brought hot milk to his bedroom. In the great silence of frost he could hear nothing, until she came in, except the crackling of the fire. This time she was not in her dressing-gown. Her hair did not fall over her shoulders. She had put on an extra red cardigan for warmth, with a green silk neck scarf that matched her skirt.

'Now I don't know if this is another piece of mind-reading or not,' she said. 'But I brought up the rum. Do you like rum in your milk or not?'

'No,' he said and began laughing.

She laughed too, showing her straight well-kept teeth again in the glow of the fire.

'Well, that's a relief,' she said. 'I'd begun to think I'd got to keep this thing going for ever. I'm not used to reading minds.'

With a sense of great placidity he stirred his milk. He was over forty. He liked a night-cap. He liked either whisky or port as a night-cap, but he was also fond of milk.

'But I'll tell you something that doesn't need any mind-reading,' she said.

'Yes?'

'You're not going to get away tomorrow, either. Unless there's a sudden change.'

He discovered that he did not care if he got away tomorrow; he was indifferent about it. The shop must look after itself; it didn't really matter.

'You are married, aren't you?' she said. 'Won't your wife be worrying about you?'

'I shouldn't think so.'

'Well, if I were her I should,' she said. 'No you coming home. Me all by my lonesome and not knowing where you were.'

He did not speak. Was it worth explaining? He did not know how to explain it if it was. He could not go into all those details. They were difficult. Some of them seemed absurd. At the same time he was aware, once again, of the element in her of calming, unaggressive fondness. She was waiting to give him, if he needed, some sort of soothing commiseration, and presently he said:

'Well, you know how it is sometimes.' Did she know? How could he put it? 'I'm quite a bit older than she is.'

'I don't see that that makes so much difference,' she said, 'except that a lot of girls like older men.'

'Do they? Why?'

The remark, innocent as far as he was concerned, quite naïve, made her look at him sharply.

'Well, you know,' she began to say, and then hesitated. 'Take that boy last night. Well, I don't know, but if I had to choose between a boy like that and someone like you I wouldn't hesitate.'

He nearly said 'Why?' for a second time.

The fire crackled. He stirred his milk. She gazed with rose-dark eyes at the fire. Perhaps she was waiting for him to say something; perhaps, on the other hand, she did not expect him to speak. She did not indicate one way or the other. She remained silent, quite unaggressive and undemanding about him, and he was glad.

'Well, this won't do,' she said. 'I'll really have to say good night,' and a moment later she left him alone with his milk, the crackling fire and the great embalming outside silence of snow and frost and winter stars.

It was three days before he could get home again. They were three days not merely of great comfort. He was infinitely soothed. He had wronged poor old Hyde, but now it seemed, somehow, an altogether less wretched business than it had been. Insanity in Hyde seemed not unlike the tumour; a catastrophe would have happened anyway.

He even felt a certain sadness as he drove off into a sloppy landscape of rain-pocked snow and ditches drowned in half-thawed ice and water, and he was glad when Phoebe Corcoran said, just before he drove away:

'Oh! I hope you won't mind my asking this. But it's my mother's birthday in ten days and I wanted to give her something she's very fond of. Do you keep those oblong chocolate biscuits – the ones with sugar on top – in fancy tins?'

'The Bourbons?' he said. 'Oh, yes.'

'I suppose you don't deliver out here? If not I'll have to come over and fetch them.'

'Don't bother to do that,' he said. 'I'd be glad to come over. As soon as the snow clears I'll come over one afternoon. Pound or half-pound? I'd be glad to.'

'Pound,' she said.

Riding away through the wet sludge of the roadside he turned round and looked back for a moment at The George and Crown. It fitted snugly into the cup of the hillside, among green and white islands of melting snow, and in front of it Phoebe Corcoran, bright in a scarlet jumper, was waving her hand.

Chapter Five

Throughout the late winter Miss Mackness suffered from continual colds and splitting headaches. She coughed harshly and slept with flannel on her throat, putting great faith in eucalyptus, goose-grease and blackberry vinegar. Imprisoned in her cash-box, counting change, stamping bills under gas-light that burned all day and gave a little warmth to her chapped hands, she grieved inexpressibly for Hyde. When Sunday came she would take a bus, ride for ten miles and visit a stranger in a large pleasant house with extensive grounds deep in the countryside. The stranger was Hyde and sometimes she sat and held his hands.

Behind the shop, in the sitting-room by day, in her bedroom at night, Constance lived an existence, that winter, that was in some ways like that of Miss Mackness. Imprisoned and impatient, she waited for the evenings in exactly the same way as Miss Mackness waited for Sunday. She hated the short sour days of January when smoke and fog sat over the town like a grey brooding bird. She hated the sudden tenacious spells of frost and snow. She wanted spring to come and spring was slow in coming.

It began to come eventually with delicate sowings of snowdrop in the apple-orchard, a flaring of orange crocus about the churchyard and with stars of blackthorn cold white on naked branches by the path to Pollards' Mill. Late snow fell in April, keeping the buds of daffodils tight and sheathed, or with short trembling tongues of half-opened yellow petal. The first buds of prunus were nipped and shredded by sharp and dusty winds.

It was nearly May before she and Frankie Johnson began to meet again at Pollards' Mill. There were still late violets in the copses but half the oaks were bare. The land seemed to quiver on the edge of winter, holding back, half green, half dark, and sometimes with stubborn banners of snow by woodsides. The young blades of corn would not lift themselves up and larks sang chilly breathless songs, ruffled and buffeted across skies of driving hail-cloud.

Then suddenly, at the end of May, all summer seemed to rush forward in a single sultry breath. With luxuriance the oaks flowered into thick curtains of dusty yellow. In a few days a darkening of leaf knotted copses into solid masses, unlightened except for tips of wild-cherry smoking white in the sun.

The days were so beautiful, thick with sappiness, choked to over-richness with blackbird song, breathless with too-sudden heat that woke the first crowds of May-fly across the glassy water of the millpond, that she could walk for the first time in a summer dress. It was a yellow dress, silk, with sprigs of green fern-frond repeated about it, and the day she first wore it she could feel the softness of May wind blowing about her skirt again, flowing excitedly across her limbs.

That day, lying on the edge of the millpond, hatless in hot sun, she picked a dandelion stalk, held it against the sky, blew on the ball of seed and felt that she was blowing the final cloud of winter away.

'Five o'clock.' She blew hard at a last fragment of seed. 'Half past.' Once or twice more she blew on the clinging tuft of seed. 'No : that one doesn't want to go.' She held the bare stalk against the blue May sky before throwing it away. 'Call it half past five.'

Frankie Johnson sat sharply up on the edge of the pool.

'Half past ? Already ? – good God, I'll have to fly.'

His eyes were so bemused and agitated that she did not think his mistake about the time of day was funny.

'Frankie, what's the matter with you ? It's only four. You've been on edge all afternoon.'

'I thought you said half past five.'

'That was dandelion time. Didn't you see me blowing at the seed ?' She looked hard at his face. 'Frankie, you weren't listening, were you ? What's the matter ?'

'I had another row with Leo, that's all.'

'You're always rowing with Leo,' she said. 'I can't think what you find to row about anyway.'

'Everything.'

'Well, what for instance?' she said. 'What did you row about today?'

'Apricot stones.'

'Oh! that's ridiculous. What a thing to quarrel about. Why apricot stones?'

He made several gestures of fretful annoyance with his hands. He ended by throwing earth into the pool.

'The kids had tinned apricots for lunch, whole ones. Stella wanted to save the stones and grow them in the backyard. I said they would grow and Leo said they wouldn't grow. He said the canning sterilized the stones.'

The vexation on his face, irritable and petulant, seemed almost childish.

'So you had a row about a thing like that.'

He threw more earth into the pool.

'Well, of course. I'm not going to be told by any old fool that something is wrong when I know it's right.'

'How do you know it's right?'

'Because I do,' he said. 'Because when we were kids Lois and I tried apricot stones like that and half of them grew.'

'Didn't Leo take notice of that?'

'Take notice?' he said. 'The man never takes notice. He hates it because Lois is on my side.'

He threw more earth into the pool. The plop disturbed a sprinkling of small fry among the reeds. From bushes of hazel on the far bank of the pond a blackbird, which had been singing madly all afternoon, broke cover, shrieking away over marshy ground beyond.

'Last Sunday it was Bach. We rowed all morning over Bach.'

She was still lying down. From across the marshy places beyond the pool, where islands of kingcups flamed golden in black mud, the blackbird began its singing again.

'Leo thinks Bach is God. Lois and I hate him.'

'Can't you agree to differ?' she said. 'Can't you all have your own opinions?'

'You don't live in that house,' he said. 'You wouldn't say that if you lived in that poky room behind the shop.'

All the thick sweetness of the day floated across the water in blackbird song. A breeze crept about her limbs, pressing the silk of her dress into the shape of her body. That winter she had written him several letters and in one of them she had said:

'I think I'll die if spring doesn't soon hurry up. Do you remember all the summer days we had at the mill? I don't know about you, but sometimes I feel they never happened. I've never known the winter to seem so long as this year.'

Now she realized that perhaps the winter had been long for him. She thought that perhaps the fretting and the tiffs with Leo Schofield were merely part of it and she said:

'I wonder if the water's warm? A few more days like this and we might go swimming.'

She sat up and leaned forward and put one hand in the pool. The water was still sharp and cold from winter.

She gave a little shudder and said: 'Not yet. We could sunbathe though. This summer I'm going to get all my body brown.'

Something about the chill of the water and the fact that he did not answer made her slightly uneasy. With disquiet she looked at him for a few moments before realizing what was changed in him that she had not noticed before. Then she said:

'You know, you haven't smiled all afternoon.'

'Haven't I?'

Once, she remembered, he was always smiling. That was almost the first thing she had noticed about him. It was, in a way, the thing that had first captivated her. Now there was something half-sullen in him; he was not with her in quite the old way.

'Just hark at that blackbird,' she said. 'Did you ever know a blackbird singing quite like that?'

Madly, with long thrilling repetitions, the blackbird poured its singing across the pool. Kingcups flared in the sun and a scent of may, clotted thickly, too sweet, was borne in waves of warm breeze from somewhere across meadows rich with buttercups.

She began to think of something else. She stared dreamily across the pool and said:

'Did you ever eat a blackbird's egg? I did once. A boy gave me one when I was a little girl. I took it home and my mother fried it. It was so little, just like a toy hen's egg on my plate.

Not much bigger than a button. I never listen to a blackbird singing without I remember it.'

If there was any sign of interest in his face about that childhood egg of hers she was too late to notice it. She was still speaking, saying, 'I cried when I'd eaten it. I started to think of the blackbird it might have been and all of a sudden I was broken-hearted,' when she noticed suddenly he was standing up.

'I just remembered. I ought to get back,' he said. 'I promised to try over a couple of new arrangements with Wingate at five.' Wingate played the violin in the four-piece cinema orchestra. 'I haven't seen the piece yet – '

'Oh! don't go,' she said. 'Don't go yet, my sweet. It's so early yet – it's only four.'

'Yes, but by the time – '

'Oh! who cares about time? As long as you're there at six you can make anything up. Who cares?'

'Well, I do,' he said. 'It's my living.'

Earlier in the afternoon she had taken off her shoes. Now, without speaking, with some of her old shyness and hesitation, she began to put them on again. As a little girl she had eaten a little egg that might have developed into a blackbird. She had been broken-hearted by that egg. But she had consoled herself, ever afterwards, that there were many other eggs, many more spring-times, many blackbirds.

With studied immaculate strokes he sat combing his thick fair hair. In the last moment before she got up she lost her shyness and seized his face in her hands and put her mouth against his, kissing him hungrily.

'Oh! mind my hair,' he said. 'Oh! do you mind? You've gone and ruined my hair.'

Frankie Johnson had come to live in Orlingford at his sister's invitation. 'You can live with us, Frankie dear, and it won't cost you much,' she wrote to him. 'You can save most of the money you make and then go on to something better.'

Lois and Frankie Johnson, the children of a retired army major, had been brought up with an aunt of faded cultured appearance who was interested in church work, music and animal welfare. The house at Brighton was full of cats. A curious stale fishy cat-smell hung about the rooms draped with heavy chenille curtains and furnished with ecclesiastical types of chair, big pier glasses and pictures in cruciform frames containing steel engravings of scenes from Greek mythology. Everywhere cats ailed, sickened, fattened, pined, slept and produced, in time, more cats. The sicker the cat the better Miss Johnson liked it. Cats were brought home from the street, rescued from accidents, from starvation on rubbish dumps and from the manifestations of cruel boys who tied bricks round their necks. The world was full of maltreated cats whom it was Miss Johnson's chosen duty to succour.

Miss Johnson also gave violin lessons to pupils who paid as they played. Cash with the lesson was so much easier, she said, than sending bills. Most of the money thus earned was spent on cats, cat-food and the general welfare of cats, and very little on Frankie and Lois Johnson. As a compensation she taught both of them music: Lois the violin and Frankie the piano. Lois did not like the violin but the promise of Frankie, her aunt said, was a wonder that all could see. Frankie improvised on the piano more easily than other boys improvised games with Red Indians, railway trains, kites and such things. One day Frankie, Miss Johnson said, would become a great pianist, and Lois believed so too.

Besides being cat-ridden the house was dirty. Meals were forgotten on tables; cats were sick in chairs; the stove was greasy and the sink continually clogged with tea-leaves. Miss Johnson forgot that cleanliness was next to godliness and neighbours sometimes complained of smells.

When she was twenty Lois met Leo Schofield. He was new to the town and came to tune her aunt's piano. Schofield was at once attracted to the pleasant, fair-haired girl with ivory skin, small features and bright blue eyes. He liked her seemingly cultured way of talking. He listened with sympathy and patience to her devoted belief that Frankie would one day be a great pianist and he noted the smell of cats' fish in the air.

It was not long before she was secretly meeting Leo Schofield in side-street cafés for a hurried meal or a cup of coffee. It was war-time; at night the streets were strange and dark. To be kissed by Schofield in darkness, sometimes in air-raids, among unnamed earth tremors and under the crossing forks of searchlights, was more like an adventure in truancy than a love affair. The fact that Schofield was a married man more than twenty years older than herself only added to the excitement. It was very flattering to be picked out by a married man and soon, also, it gave her a pleasant sense of comfort and stability.

And presently it was natural too that she should hear of Mrs Schofield: an addled, dyspeptic, querulous woman of spiritualist leanings who could not boil an egg. A mastoid had left her permanently deaf in one ear, so that she lived in a semi-silent world of spiritual gropings, listening for messages from other spheres.

And soon, naturally, from beyond Mrs Schofield, came the story of Schofield's dreams. As set out by Schofield they had a remarkable quality of coherence, sense and charm. He forgot to reveal that their fulfilment had muddled, eluded and defeated him for thirty years; or that, like many dreamers, he really preferred a state of unfulfilment to reality. All he asked for was a shop: a shop in which he could sell pianos, sheet music, gramophones, records, violin strings and things of that sort. He would also tune pianos and give piano lessons. And since the world of that time was, as he rightly maintained, full of passionately ambitious mothers who longed for their children to play the piano, it was almost unthinkable that anyone should fail in any proposition where pianos and piano teaching were concerned.

At twenty-one Lois came into a legacy of eight hundred pounds from her mother. Six months later Mrs Schofield died. A few weeks later Lois and Leo Schofield were married and were living in Orlingford, in the shop that Constance knew. And since like so often attracts like the girl of twenty-one and the man of over fifty were almost perfectly suited. Both liked music, both had been living too long in houses presided over by women tottering mildly on the fringes of lunacy; both were used to muddle, ill-cooked meals, uncleaned tablecloths and sinks blocked with tea-leaves.

And for a time both were happy; or, as Melford put it, happy in their dirt. It was also, in Orlingford, much as Schofield had predicted. Numbers of ambitious mothers longed for their children to play the piano; many people, after the war, were prosperous. Leo Schofield was constantly busy tuning pianos, selling sheet music and teaching five-finger exercises in cold front-rooms.

Then Lois, with fluent regularity, began to have babies. The table in the back living-room began to be messier than ever, covered with uncleared dishes, playthings, newspapers and the marks of jammy fingers. Napkins dried all day on the fire-guard and there was a pungent depressive odour in the air. Schofield could find nowhere to sit down and write his bills. Soon he got into the habit of making them out every two months instead of one and then, having sent them out, discovered that even Orlingford was filled with defaulters.

Then Frankie Johnson came. The job of pianist at the cinema fell vacant six months after Constance was married; and Wingate, the violinist, meeting Leo Schofield in the street one day, asked if he would take it. Schofield refused and told Lois, who said:

'That's just the job for a brilliant boy like Frankie.'

Bad food, cold front parlours, days of cycling in treacherous weather to tune pianos in distant houses, babies that did not sleep at night, a tendency to bolt his food and suffer from heartburn: Schofield, by the time Frankie Johnson reached Orlingford, was a man of fifty-five with moustaches stained yellow by too much smoking, increasingly bad sight and hopeless, embittering indigestion. He was not merely forgetful. Indigestion clamped on his life a greyness of pain that he tried vainly to assuage with cigarettes, bismuth, charcoal tablets and hot peppermint and water. Sometimes he got up at night and walked distractedly up and down the landing, beating his stomach with his hands.

At first he got on well with Frankie Johnson: a pleasant boy, always smiling, whose ivory kin, fair hair and smooth light voice reminded him of Lois. Frankie would even occasionally take a lesson for him, attend to a customer, as he had attended to Mrs Melford Turner, or look after the shop. He told himself too that the money Frankie paid Lois was very useful. Another thirty shillings a week helped a lot when there were so many infant mouths to feed. He was unaware that Lois said:

'Now you tuck it back into your pocket. Go on, tuck it back,

Frankie. We don't need it. You'll need that when you start to study.'

Every week Lois found an excuse to put back into her brother's pocket half, sometimes all, of the money he paid for board. She too had her store of dreams, most of them for Frankie. She dreamed, like her aunt, that Frankie would become a great pianist; but she knew, too, that pianists are not made without limitless practice, hard work and study. That was why she had seized so swiftly on the chance of a job where she could help to look after him. In that way, in two years, if he were careful, he could save a hundred and fifty pounds. With that he could go to London, take a room, attend courses at the Royal College and in time become the man she wanted.

'Frankie will be a great pianist. Don't argue,' she would say to Schofield. 'I know. I always have known. He's got the gift. He's got the temperament. Look how sensitive he is.'

With her seemingly cultured voice, a certain pride of manner and fluency of speech and a way of repeatedly referring to the childhood of Frankie and herself as something aristocratic that misfortune had blighted, Lois Johnson felt herself to be aloof from Orlingford.

'Of course I don't expect people in a hole like this to recognize it. There's no appreciation here. Nobody in a one-eyed town like this knows Brahms from a tin of baking powder.'

So she struggled for Frankie; she was ambitious for Frankie. With something more than sisterly affection she gave Frankie back his board each week and sought to press on him the encouragement, the impregnation, of all her dreams. But the piano in the back living-room was one that never got tuned; Schofield was too tired and too harassed to bother for nothing with a piano of his own; and Frankie did not practise much. And since he was always late coming home from the cinema each night she took his breakfast up to him in bed next morning and said:

'Now, don't bother to get up. Here's the paper. Have a lie-in while I try to get things straight downstairs.'

All that winter Schofield rode or pushed his bicycle about the town and the countryside. Struggling against rain and slush and snow he felt more and more clamped in the grey vice of indigestion. Front parlours without fires, long dragging hills up which he had to push the bicycle, rain that soaked through his dirty mackintosh and down through the soles of his boots and chilled his feet: all day he sucked peppermint lozenges, belched with the pain of flatulence and, as the winter went on, thought more and more grimly of Frankie Johnson.

One evening, towards the end of the winter, he came home at seven o'clock, worn out, his spectacles misted with rain, to find the living-room table a mass of plates and dishes still uncleared from lunch-time.

Rain had been falling coldly all day and as he hung up his wet mackintosh in the passage Lois called downstairs:

'Is that you, Leo? The kettle's on the trivet. Can you make yourself a cup of tea? Stella's made a mess of herself with paint and I'm trying to get her clean.'

In a fog of weariness and pain Schofield made a pot of tea, cleared a space for himself at the table among the wreckage of dishes and then swallowed a dose of bismuth. He was almost too tired to drink the tea. He simply sat bent over the cup, letting the hot fumes of it steam up through his scraggy moustache. His glasses were misty and it was too much trouble to wipe them. Then he lit a cigarette, drew at it a few times and afterwards let it burn away, dropping ash down his chest and into his cup and saucer.

He was still sitting like this when Lois came down.

'I don't know what you're going to have for your tea,' she said. 'I've never had a minute all day to get anything in. There's a bit of bacon, I think. Frankie had the last couple of eggs there were.'

He sat without answering. He struck his chest once or twice with his fist, trying to relieve pain and wind.

'Well, what will you have?'

Suddenly he flung his cigarette into the fire and shouted:

'It'd puzzle me to know, wouldn't it?'

'Who are you talking to?' she said. Her voice was restrained and haughty.

'Talking to? Talking to?' He shouted again, mouthing mockeries of her way of speaking. 'A bit of bacon. Frankie's had the last couple of eggs. Dear Frankie. Poor dear Frankie – '

'If you'd get home a little earlier it might make things a bit easier,' she said. 'As it is I keep tea things on the table from morning till night – and don't speak like that about Frankie!'

'Don't speak like that about Frankie,' he mocked. 'Mustn't speak like that about Frankie. Mustn't offend Frankie.'

'Frankie has to work like anyone else, doesn't he?' she said calmly. 'Frankie needs a meal before he goes off, doesn't he? It's sometimes the last he has.'

'Work?' he shouted. 'You call it work. I should like!'

'It's *his* work,' she said. 'You may not think so.'

'Four hours a night. Matinée for the kids twice a week. Work! – you call it work?'

'Well, if you don't know what you want,' she said, 'I haven't got time to stand here all day.'

She began to clear the table. She looked, as she so often did when they quarrelled, aloof and haughty. With maddening restraint she put cups and dishes together, her face composed, her whole manner calm and provocative.

After she had taken away some of the dishes he began to shout something else about Frankie, the supposed work he did and the way he fooled away the rest of his time, but as if remembering that she was the daughter of an army major who was above listening to cheap nonsense of that sort she simply held her head a little higher and began serenely to fold the tablecloth.

'Perhaps if he gave a bit more help here instead of chasing after women – '

Witheringly she looked down on the squat, yellow-moustached figure balancing his cup on his knees and staring at it through grubby spectacles and said:

'Don't be any more ridiculous than you can help. Women!'

'Yes!' he said. 'Women! Mrs Melford Turner's a woman I suppose?'

'And a very good customer of yours too. I suppose you don't mind that?'

'I wasn't talking about that.'

'Then I will,' she said. 'If Mrs Turner spent a penny here last year she spent fifty pounds. A lot of it thanks to Frankie.'

'Oh! of course, of course, it would be!'

'And another thing.' She was still serenely, haughtily calm. 'Perhaps I'm a bit more broadminded than some people in this benighted hole, but I don't see anything wrong with their friendship. It's very nice for Frankie. It's been a godsend for him to have somebody sensitive and intelligent like Mrs Melford Turner as a friend. They both love music – what else they do is their affair.'

'A boy and a married woman,' he said. He tried to light another cigarette. His hands trembled as they made gestures of mockery. 'I wonder what her husband thinks. Nice thing for the mayor.'

'Don't be so smug,' she said. 'I used to see you while you were married, didn't I?'

He had no answer to that. Pain burnt dully in his chest. His vision seemed grey. His belly rattled with dyspeptic rumblings and lack of food. Tobacco ash began to fall again on to his yellow drooping moustache and then she looked up to the ceiling and said:

'That sounds like Stella at it again.' She went to the door and opened it. The voice of a child crying came down the stairway and a moment later she was gone from the room.

Schofield sat for a few moments longer, staring through foggy spectacles at his cooling tea-cup, letting ash drop down his moustache, waistcoat and trousers. Then he went into the passage, put on his wet hat, scarf and mackintosh and went out into the town.

He walked as far as the square, went into the tap-room of The Prince of Orange and ordered a glass of oatmeal stout. Moodily he stood at the bar, stared into the dark depths of the glass and thought of Frankie Johnson. Frankie, dear Frankie, Frankie who had the last two eggs for tea, Frankie who had his breakfast in bed, Frankie who had the nice, easy, cushy job at the cinema, Frankie who was going to be a great pianist and who spent most of his time gallivanting with the wife of the mayor.

Never would be a pianist, he thought. Hadn't got the talent or the discipline. His hands were too small. He took things too easy, a lot too easy. Lois spoiled him hopelessly.

With a fumbling sense of martyrdom he drank his first stout and ordered another. He thought of dreary journeys on the bicycle, kids, wet napkins, messy tablecloths, cheap pianos, cold front-rooms, stupid children who didn't know C from G, people who never paid their bills. He thought of Frankie having bacon and eggs for tea. The oatmeal stout, heavy and smooth, put a soothing band of velvet round his stomach and presently he began to feel bolder about things, altogether less dispirited. He found time to take off his glasses. When he had polished them and put them on again he began to fancy he saw things more clearly, especially about Frankie Johnson.

It was time to put his foot down, he thought. It was time to be bold and tell Lois to her face that Frankie had to go. He ordered another stout and, mildly intoxicated, resolved that his simplest course was to go home, make a stand and have the whole thing out with her, once and for all.

'Damn Frankie,' he said. Unwittingly he spoke aloud, banging his glass on the counter. 'Blast Frankie.'

Carrie Waters, who had served him with his stout and was now preparing to play a game of skittles with three railwaymen who had come off shift, stood with the big wooden skittle cheese in her hand and laughed shortly and said:

'I see you're on the mayor's side, Mr Schofield.'

'Just as well,' one of the railwaymen said. 'Somebody's got to break the bad news one of these days.'

Friend? Bad news? Schofield hadn't thought of that. Feeling bold almost to the point of making inspired decisions, he drank the last of his stout and went into the street. In a fuddled way, as he walked up to the square, he began to tell himself that now there must be other people in Orlingford who wanted to get rid of Frankie. The mayor, for instance. Melford Turner. He hadn't thought of that.

Bad news? He pondered for a time on what the railwayman had meant by that. With some amazement he could only suppose it meant that Melford Turner knew nothing of Constance and Frankie.

Perhaps it was true that Melford Turner needed a friend? Perhaps he had been too busy as mayor to notice these things? It sometimes happened that the very people who were gossiped about were the last to hear that they were being gossiped about. That was common enough. In fact it had happened to himself and Lois in Brighton.

He walked across the square. The bold decision to go to Melford and tell him about his wife and Frankie seemed suddenly to offer a solution to the entire problem of getting rid of Frankie. Two eggs for tea – By God, he thought, when last did I get two eggs for tea?

Half-way across the square he became aware of figures coming down the lighted steps of the town hall. He saw them gather for a moment outside, under the chestnut trees, to say good night to each other.

'Good night, Mr Turner,' he heard a voice say; and another: 'Good night, Melford. I think that went very well, after all; all things considered.'

'Good night,' Melford said.

Then Melford was walking towards him, alone, across the middle of the square. He was hatless, without an overcoat, and carrying a bundle of papers. In the light of street lamps Schofield saw him clearly, remembered again what the railwayman had said about the mayor needing a friend, and then made up his mind to be that friend and stop and speak to him.

At that moment he staggered. Melford, recognizing just another of the drunks that preferred the safe open space of the square for the first uncertain passage of the journey home, looked swiftly at him, changed direction and walked on.

' 'Night, sir,' Schofield said.

Melford did not answer.

'Just a minute, sir,' Schofield said. 'Could I have a word? – just a word, sir. Won't keep you a jiffy – '

Melford, not bothering even to turn his head again, continued walking.

For a few moments Schofield stared tipsily after him and then staggered on. Well, perhaps after all – he belched and spat on the square – perhaps after all it was none of his business. He tried to belch again but this time the gases rising from his stomach stuck in a hard chill lump of pain. More drearily, with less boldness, he staggered on. The warm and soothing effects of the stout were wearing off. His spectacles were getting misty again. Indigestion began to gnaw at him with its narrow, obliterating pain and he knew that in any case he would never have had the courage after all.

One other person, towards the end of that winter, tried to speak to Melford of Constance and Frankie Johnson. Charles Edward Twelvetree, a retired solicitor of nearly seventy, a man of arid reservation and some of the chilled and bony aspect of a judge, came home one evening to say with shocked severity to his daughter:

'Agnes, do you know anything of these stories that are going round about Constance Turner?'

'I've heard them.'

'You've *heard* them? Why didn't you tell me?'

'I don't tell you everything, father.'

'But are they true? They can't be true, can they? They say she's having an affair with a boy from that music shop, one of that Schofield crowd.'

'Of course they're true.'

'But why didn't you tell me? It makes my position with Melford most difficult, not knowing about a thing like that.'

'I don't see how,' she said. 'If Melford's such a fool that he can't keep his wife amused it's no business of mine.'

'I think it's terrible,' he said. 'Terrible.'

'And I should think it's terrible to live with Melford,' she said.

With dry scorn she helped herself to a whisky, her third that evening, and sat down to read the paper.

At school Agnes Twelvetree had been a studious timid girl with a certain natural charm and a taste for literature. She wore her hair in thick brown pigtails tied with large black bows. Her mother, believing that brains alone are not everything and that food is more important to man than poetry, taught her to cook well. She learned to cook well the things that most people cook badly: omelettes, meringues and soufflés of various kinds. Her salmon soufflés particularly were always ethereal and she made a perfect orange jelly.

When she was twenty-three her mother died. Instead of marrying again, hiring a housekeeper or taking in an extra servant,

Charles Edward Twelvetree decided, aloud, that Agnes could look after him better than any woman in the world. He also indicated that it was her duty and right to look after him. He expected her to agree, and silently, without opposition, she did agree. She ran the house, cooked for him, darned his socks, played the hostess and went out with him to dinner. She even accompanied him on holidays, knitting and reading in drawing-rooms filled largely with elderly people in dour stuffy hotels.

The way ahead of her, at that time, did not seem bitter. At twenty-three she was full of hope that a young man would feel attracted by her, tell her so and take her away from a household presided over by a man who was something like a cadaverous grey idol dressed in clerical grey or tweeds. Twelvetree was an old-fashioned solicitor of almost ecclesiastical appearance who did not smile much. He regarded it as a sort of divine right that a daughter should look after a widowed father and he remained unaware, over the next thirty years, that there were a score of times when Agnes could have shot him gladly but was too nice to do so.

By the time she was fifty she was a grey round-shouldered woman of bitter tongue who spoke of men, love, marriage and the natural attraction of the sexes with a despising, caustic smile. She smiled with special acidity on men who praised her cooking. She did not want men; thank God she knew what men were. Scornfully she developed a hatred of men in general and her father in particular. With her acid smile, her outspoken rudeness, her face growing gradually not at all unlike her father's in its cadaverous austerity, she told men, the selfish breed, what she thought they were fit for and where she wished they were.

In her late forties, four or five years before Constance came to the town, Agnes Twelvetree started drinking. Drink had the effect of making her a much nicer person. It softened the caustic insults of her smile. It disclosed flashes of the original clever and quite charming girl who had once wandered, moon-shod, dazed and choking for the sheer beauty, with Keats and Shakespeare. It even made men like her. She was so much more human, they said, and some of her rudeness was quite witty after a drink or two.

'I think Melford ought to know about this,' her father said.

'If there's anything in it he can go about stopping it. If there isn't he can get the gossip stopped.'

She did not bother to answer. She filled her glass with what was really her fourth large whisky that evening and then folded the paper to another page.

'Somebody ought to tell him if he doesn't know,' her father said. 'I'll see that he gets to know myself if the worse comes to worse.'

She gave one of her searing, caustic smiles.

'You're all alike,' she said. 'You men. A woman tries to get a little happiness out of life and all you can do about it is to run to each other telling tales.'

'Happiness?' he said. 'You mean to say she's not happy there? In that nice house? With that fine business, with Melford?'

'What makes you think houses and men make people happy?' she said. 'Good God, since when have men and houses and happiness been synonymous?'

'Really, Agnes, the things you say.'

'Well, don't talk rubbish then,' she said. 'Mind your own business. Of course she's not happy. You could see that if you looked at her. She never has been.'

In acid silence she read the paper and drank her whisky. In twenty minutes it would be time to go to the kitchen and start to prepare a soufflé. It would, as always, be a wonderful soufflé and he would, as always, never think of telling her so.

'I can't believe it,' he said. 'That shy creature. It seems fantastic.'

Once again she did not bother to answer. What in heaven's name had shyness to do with it? Instead her mind went back to an evening, a few months after Constance's marriage, when she and her father had gone to dinner across the square. After dinner, while the men were talking and smoking, Constance had taken her upstairs. With painful shyness she had shown her the bathroom, and then added quickly: 'Or you can come into my bedroom. There's a much better light in there.'

Agnes Twelvetree, as much out of curiosity as out of need of a better light to see a face she was not particularly fond of, went into the bedroom. Her curiosity had arisen from the words 'my bedroom', and in the bedroom itself she noted the single bed. She noticed too the pile of records and the gramophone. She made some remark about them and Constance said in her shy quiet way:

'Oh! yes. I have my records up here. I like to play them at night-time.'

That was her first suspicion that Constance was not happy; that was why she turned sharply, with scorn, on her father when he spoke again:

'I'm not sure I won't go over to see Melford after dinner,' he said, 'and have a word with him and see how the land lies.'

'Don't be a damn fool.'

She drank her whisky in a harsh fiery gulp that had the effect of silencing her father completely.

'If all I hear is correct,' she said, 'Constance is not the only one playing at that game.'

Open-mouthed, chin-dropping, he looked at her astounded, unable to speak a word.

'Don't look so shocked,' she said. 'Yes: Melford.'

'Melford?' he said. 'Not Melford?'

'Yes, Melford. Don't look so surprised.' She drained the last of her whisky and got up in readiness to go out and make, once again, the perfect ethereal soufflé. 'What else would you expect of a man?'

Chapter Six

On a fine afternoon in February Melford put on a big snuff-coloured ulster, a brown mixture tweed cap, and thick fur driving gloves and drove out, in the trap, to Ascott St Mary. The day was cold but sunny. In a box he carried a few things extra to the Bourbon biscuits Phoebe Corcoran had asked him for. Carlsbad plums, a jar of Chinese cumquats, a tin of peppermint creams: these, he told himself, would be just a small way of showing that he had not forgotten all the kindnesses the girl and her mother had shown him during the snow of January.

At the last moment he added a box of sugared almonds. He did not know why, but something seemed to tell him that Phoebe Corcoran might like them. They were French, in delicate shades of rose, cream, and eau-de-Nil. He seemed to see her eating them. Perhaps he was wrong, but it would be a curious coincidence, he thought, if he were able to divine her taste as well as she had done his own about the quince jelly and the ginger.

'You've caught us at a bad time,' Mrs Corcoran said. 'Well, I don't say bad exactly – but Phoebe's laid up, Mr Turner. She caught a chill in that last bout of bad weather. She's had a little touch of pleurisy – there's always been a little weakness there.'

He said how very sorry he was and she said:

'Oh! she isn't all that terribly bad now. She's in bed, of course, but she can see people. She likes to. If she isn't asleep would you care to go up for a while?'

Five minutes later he was sitting by Phoebe Corcoran's bedside. She was wearing a rose-coloured knitted shawl over her white nightdress, and her hair, dark and freshly brushed, fell loosely over her shoulders.

'Well, this is a nice surprise,' she said. 'You're the last person I expected to see.'

'I didn't expect to find you here either,' he said. 'If I'd known I'd have brought you some flowers.'

'You always think of kind things,' she said.

Then he produced the Carlsbad plums, the cumquats, the peppermint creams, and the Bourbon biscuits. In return she gave him the sort of smile he liked to see on her face. Her eyes were very bright and her face was sharply flushed, as if her colour had actually come up suddenly because he was there.

'You shouldn't spoil me like this.'

'Well, here's just one more,' he said and gave her the box of sugared almonds.

'Oh! Mr Turner, now you're spoiling me completely.'

'I had an idea you might like them.'

'May I undo them? Are they something special?'

'Undo them,' he said.

When she finally undid the wrappings of the box and revealed the nested almonds in their delicate egg-like colours it was very much as he hoped and expected. She was delighted beyond words at the sugared almonds. She not only loved them. She gave the impression, as he had hoped, that they were her favourite things.

'If you spoil me like this, Mr Turner, I shall just stay ill all summer.'

'Oh! no,' he said. 'You must get well as soon as you can for the spring days.'

He did not care for illness in people; sickness made him curiously distressed and uneasy, in much the same way as he was distressed and uneasy for animals in pain. He was not very good at pain himself, but he disliked it still more in other people.

'It's almost like spring today,' he said. 'It's cold of course, but I couldn't help noticing how high the sun was getting.'

'I'll be out soon,' she said, 'but it's tempting to stay here. It's so warm and cosy when you go under.'

After saying this she suddenly slid down from her pillows. She put her arms under the coverlet and drew it round her closely, leaving only her face and dark loose hair revealed. She lay on her side, looking at him quietly for a few moments and then said:

'I didn't realize you were so tall.'

'I didn't think I was.'

'From down here in the bed you look terribly tall.'

Something about her way of lying there and saying this managed to give the impression that she liked tall men, just as she liked sugared almonds and men who surprised her with presents she hadn't expected.

He did not think it either polite or tactful to stay with her very long that afternoon. He left after half an hour, asking her before he went if there was anything he could do for her or bring her next time he came.

'Just bring yourself,' she said.

She gave him, from half under the coverlet, with her bright flushed cheeks, another smile; and he promised to come again on Sunday.

The following Sunday he drove over again in the same big ulster, tweed cap, and gloves, on the same kind of cold sunny afternoon, to take her some flowers. There were daffodils and mimosa in a large bunch, with separate bunches of big dark violets tied in leaves. She had been sleeping before he came in. She looked over-flushed and uneasy and not so well as before.

And suddenly as he sat by the bed he was sharply aware of wanting her to get well in the same way as he might want a sick dog or kitten to get well. He felt physically wretched for her. As with an animal he felt a continual urge to stroke and comfort her.

'There's nothing to worry about,' she said. 'I just started to run a bit of a temperature. I do that if I get excited.'

He was too dull to divine what in any way might have excited her and she said:

'That's the trouble with knowing you're going to have a visitor.'

He stayed a little over half an hour that day. In the warm room there was a strong scent of violets, with odours of mimosa and daffodil underlying it. His urge to stroke and comfort her also grew stronger and at the last moment he actually stooped down and put his hands over her shoulders and patted her, with heavy kindliness, as if she were a dog.

'Now you get well, young lady,' he said. 'We can't have this nonsense any more.'

After that he began to go over to see her twice and sometimes three times a week. He always took little gifts from the shop, together with bunches of flowers, and patted her like a dog. In that soft animal way of hers, staring up at him from under the coverlet, sometimes mutely, always large-eyed, wanting to be fussed, she evoked in him feelings of a kind that women like Constance and Mrs Marchmont had never aroused.

He felt for her very much as he once felt for Pilfer. She was an animal who did not repel him. He could express himself in the same unembarrassed way as he did with a horse. And presently, in that same way, he found he could touch and hold her hands. Once he looked at these hands and told her:

'This isn't you yet. We've got to get more colour into these hands yet,' and then stroked and patted the hands in his own heavy tender way.

After one of these visits he came downstairs and met Mrs Corcoran waiting at the foot of them. He had, he thought, possibly misjudged Mrs Corcoran. Not all Londoners, it was now obvious, were quite so bad as he had imagined. Not all were 'mullocking people', as Orlingford folk would have said. Mrs Corcoran was immaculately spruce, smart, and well-dressed. With her rings and ear-rings, her silk afternoon blouses, her high-heeled shoes, she brought quite a touch of town quality to a country pub. Perhaps in the evenings, when she put on even larger rings and longer ear-rings, she was, he thought, possibly a little over-dressed, but she was always so friendly that he thought it did not matter.

'Well, Mr Turner, been to see your patient? You know she looks on *you* as her doctor, don't you?'

He said something about making her cheerful and comfortable as far as he could and she said:

'I think you've done more than that. She's a girl who needs a lot of nursing back when she gets low.'

'Well,' he said, 'as long as you don't mind my going up and sitting with her – '

'Mind?' she said. 'Gracious, you're a blessing. Besides, I think we know a gentleman when we see one don't we?'

Larks were singing on an April day when he went to see her for the last time but one in her bedroom. Her bedroom window, facing south, was open to the sun. But a sharp breeze ran with white combings through the corn on the opposite hillside and he thought it was one of those treacherous, too bright days, that were not to be trusted.

Several times he got up and closed or half-closed the window, fearing a draught, until finally she said:

'Don't keep jumping up and down. Come and sit by me. You make me quite nervous, jumping up and down.'

'I don't want you to get cold.'

'I won't get cold.'

'You mustn't take risks, though – '

'I'm as warm as a kitten,' she said. 'Come on, sit down.' She put one hand out of bed and patted the seat of the bedside chair. 'Come on,' and it might have been that she, at this time, was calling a dog. 'Come on. Sit down.'

He sat down.

After some moments she said:

'They were lovely flowers you brought me today. Those jonquils. Where did they come from?'

'My garden.'

She seemed to ponder this for a moment or two and then said:

'Won't your wife be jealous? You gathering her flowers and taking them for another girl?'

'I shouldn't think so.'

'I should be,' she said. 'I think I should be jealous about you.'

It made him feel quite flattered, almost important, to feel that someone could be jealous about him. He smiled a little and she said:

'What is she like, your wife? I've never met her.'

He could think of no way of describing Constance except to say that she was shy.

'Shy?'

For a single moment he thought that Phoebe Corcoran was laughing at him.

'You did say shy, didn't you?'

'Yes,' he said. 'She's really very shy.'

Then there was, as he saw from the way her eyes were dancing, no doubt about it. She was laughing.

'You don't mean it, do you? Shy?'

He said yes, he meant it, but what was amusing about it?

'Oh! nothing,' she said, and she smiled and shrugged her shoulders. 'Only it isn't quite what I'd heard about her, that's all.'

It had not occurred to him that anyone, least of all Phoebe Corcoran, would have heard anything about Constance. It did in fact surprise him and he said:

'Heard? What have you heard about her?'

'Oh! you hear all sorts of things in a pub,' she said. 'You know what pubs are.'

She was lying in her favourite position in the bed: on her side, hands tucked under her face, her neck hidden by thick soft hair. Her eyes held him in long upward glances, so that she looked more than ever like a furry sleepy animal as she said:

'I think you'd better ask her. I'm not telling tales out of school.'

It was all so strange to him that he could only stare at her in answer.

'Don't look so shocked, duckie,' she said. 'It's just something I heard.'

'What?' he said. 'What did you hear?'

She seemed to draw closer under the coverlet. There was something secretive about her as she lay half-hidden under her mass of thick soft hair.

'Come here,' she said. 'You won't be angry if I tell you this, will you?'

He said he didn't think he would be angry.

'You won't scold me, will you?'

He shook his head.

'You'd better come closer,' she said. 'I think I'd better whisper this.'

He did not ask himself why it was necessary to whisper; the next moment she drew her hands from under the bed-clothes and held his face with them, putting her mouth close to his ear.

'She's playing games,' she said. 'That's the story I heard.'

Playing games? He was dull enough to ask her what games?

'You know what game,' she said. 'She's got a fancy boy.'

With amazement he drew back his head and stared at her. He recoiled from the words fancy boy. But whether she was actually laughing at him or not he never knew.

'I think it's true, duckie,' she said. 'If I've heard it once I've heard it fifty times.'

He had nothing to say. The look of intense and baffled astonishment on his face was so great that she said:

'You mean you didn't know? You hadn't heard? – Oh! you're angry with me, duckie, aren't you?'

He was not angry; he was groping about in a maze, one of the few outlets to which was his own curiosity.

'It's a musician, a pianist, or something,' she said. 'I think he plays in a cinema.'

He was still groping through his maze of astonishment, dumb and unapprehending, when she gave a little cry and said:

'Oh! duckie, I've just realized. I thought it was because you knew that you were always coming over to see me. You know? I thought it was because you and she – '

She was no longer lying on her side. As she spoke she turned and lay on her back, mouth slightly parted, hands free, eyes holding him with a deeply surprised expression of tenderness.

'I think you're a wonderful person,' she said. 'All the time I kept thinking you only came over because of her – you know, because you knew all about her and you wanted someone else – '

Impulsively she lifted her arms and drew him suddenly down to her.

'Now I know what you came over for,' she said. 'You came over just for me.'

She drew him farther down against the bed, until he felt the warmth of her body and the sheets. She kissed him several times and called him duckie. During one of these kisses he heard a breeze lift from across the fields, catch the open window and blow it sharply shut against the catch. The singing of larks, which he had heard all afternoon, was suddenly cut off from him. The spring air was very quiet. All he could hear was the sound of her warm quick breath and the steady beating of his own blood, which in some strange way she kept from racing.

Then finally she smiled up at him and said: 'It's nice to have you. I'm glad. Even if she doesn't want you there's someone here who does.'

Later that day he drank three whiskies, got into the trap and began to drive home in a mood of hardening resolution. At first his thoughts, fired by the whisky, were very clear. Once or twice in his married life it had been apparent to him that the only possible way of dealing with Constance was to bully her. Now it seemed to him beyond doubt that this was a third.

As he drove he grew angry. It was a monstrous thing, a cheap thing. He was mayor and he was humiliated. Of course he had been absorbed in the business of his first year as mayor; he had been distracted and overwrought by the terrible affair of Hyde; he had never been close to Constance. But how had it come about that he didn't know? Everyone else knew. He supposed even people like Charles Edward Twelvetree and Miss Mackness and Dot and Carrie knew. If it had got as far as Ascott St Mary then all the county, all the hunt people knew.

He did not like being made a fool of; he did not like being laughed at behind his back. Why had no one given him a clue? Then he remembered that perhaps that was what Rampling, Captain Whitling, and Beety Beeton had in fact been trying to do on that night before the meet when they chivvied him and pulled his leg and threw out those hints about escaping. He didn't know. How was it possible to know? – either about that or any other thing?

He knew only that, now or never, he must have it out with Constance. He must face up to it. He did not know what he would say to her or how he would say it; but he knew he must face up to it. He knew he must be firm. If necessary he must bully her. As with an animal there were times when you had to show that you were master.

Half-way home the effects of the whisky began to change from those of resolution touched by an exhilarated self-confidence to a sort of dyspeptic, uncertain gloom. The whisky, which he had drunk too quickly, had given him wind. He stopped the trap, stood up and belched several times behind his hand. A flat ache settled in the pit of his stomach. He began to feel listless and altogether less certain about everything. He even wondered if he had caught a chill standing several times at the open window of Phoebe Corcoran's bedroom.

He drove home for the rest of the way at a walk. Through uncertainty the situation developed into one of deepening complexity. He could no longer see the best way of tackling it. It was terribly embarrassing to speak of this sort of thing. Then gradually his better nature began to assert itself. The paling influence of his mother came back. There would be an awful scene, a row, ghastly things would be said, things that would be regretted.

And when you were married to a woman and yet in a sense were not married – how could you assert that something in her own reactions to that situation were frivolous, monstrous or unfaithful? He did not like the word unfaithful; it was a most uneasy word. He could only hope that it hadn't gone as far as that. It was all awfully complicated and worrying and embarrassing and somehow slightly indecent.

Gradually he knew he was approaching that same situation of cowardice and sheer physical paralysis as on the night when he and Constance had spent their honeymoon by the sea. He knew that he could not go to her and do what had to be done. They had never spoken of that night; how could they possibly speak of it? All his subsequent approaches to her had been worse than futile.

Some time before he reached home he knew that he was too much of a coward to do anything about it – at least not yet. Later perhaps he would. He would keep his ears open. He might even go and ask Charles Edward Twelvetree for an honest man-to-man opinion about it. Yes: he might do that. He would wait, and perhaps things would resolve themselves.

By the time he had changed his clothes, had a bath, and drunk another whisky he found that Constance had begun her dinner. Some time before this he thought it would be at least decent, and less embarrassing, to think of a good excuse for being late, and as he sat down at the dining-table he said:

'Sorry I'm late. I've been over to Ascott St Mary. These new people have offered me the fishing there. They say there are some very good bream and perch in that stream. They'll let me have it very cheaply and I can invite one or two people over this summer. I haven't done much fishing lately and it will be rather fun to start again.'

She did not comment on this except to say that it would be nice for him.

'Fishing's a curious thing,' he said. 'You can't stop it once it gets hold of you. I wouldn't mind betting that when I start I'll be over there all hours of the day and night. Of course it's the breeding season now. We don't start till June.'

He tried not to look at her much during dinner. He tried not to think of the things he had been told about her.

When the meal was over he excused himself, left the table quickly and strolled down towards the orchard with his pipe in his hands. A pale April twilight, prolonged by a quarter moon, lay without wind over the apple trees that were still tight-knotted with sprigs of leaf and blossom. Everywhere the jonquils, with beaked buds of later narcissus part-broken among them, were thick in the grass about the trees.

It was a beautiful evening, still and clear. There was perhaps a promise of frost in the air. But everywhere across the orchard a light fragrance of jonquils floated and as he smelled it he remembered Phoebe Corcoran. He remembered her thick brown hair and the way it grew softly and abundantly in her neck. He remembered how he had kissed her and had not been disturbed about it and how, softly, without demand, like a furry animal, she had looked up at him from the warmth of the bed.

It was very pleasant there at Ascott St Mary. He knew it would be still more pleasant in the summer-time, by the stream, with fish rising in deep pools under the dark shadow of alder trees. He looked forward to the fishing. It was curious how, as he said, fishing got hold of you when you once got started.

By July, with the close-season over, he was beginning to get away for the fishing as often as he could: generally twice a week, occasionally more often. Thursday was his best day: then he would close the shop at one o'clock, have lunch and be away in the trap by two. But Monday, always slack in the shop after the week-end, was also good, and sometimes he also went late on Saturday afternoons.

The fish in the stream were mostly roach and perch, with occasional rudd and silver bream. Sometimes he happened on big feeding schools of perch when he had only to drop in small red worms that Brown got him from the dung-heap and he could pull out fish by the score. The twilights were long and slow to darken. In the meadows along the stream, three of which belonged to The George and Crown, hay-making went on all through the last weeks of June and on into July and as he fished he would hear the sound of hay-mowers working, the occasional shudder of a horse impatient in the shade and the voices of women laughing and talking as they worked on swathes of whitening hay.

Sometimes when he came in from fishing, the pub would be closed. In the cool back parlour there would be draught beer and bread and Cheshire cheese to eat, with spring onions if he wanted them. 'But if you take a spring onion then I must have one,' Phoebe would say, and sometimes he was there until past midnight, supping his beer, hungrily helping himself to more bread and cheese, with a touch of his favourite mustard on top, and snapping at the crisp young onions.

One evening he taught her a word she had not heard about the onions.

'The onions are very frem,' he said one night and she said to him: 'That's a queer word. Frem? I never heard that one before.'

He almost said, 'Ah! but then you're a Londoner,' but instead he told her that that was one of their good local words. It meant crisp. You used it about things like radishes and young fresh lettuces that almost cracked as you ate them, and especially about things like water-cress and celery.

'Frem,' he said. 'Yes: that's a good word. We have some good words here.'

'I think you're so clever,' she said. 'Knowing about words and things.'

'Oh! I'm just interested,' he said. 'I like these old words. I made a list of them at one time. I even thought of getting them printed.'

'Printed?' she said. 'What a wonderful idea. Printed! – I shall never keep up with you.'

Sometimes she slipped out of the pub and came along the river path to meet him. He had been greatly flattered by her interest in words and one evening, as they walked back together through fields of still uncarried hay, he even told her the names of the meadows that bounded the stream.

'This one here is Linch Meadow,' he said. 'Linch – meaning

hill, and meadow. The meadow under the hill, you see. And that one, the one we just came through, that's called Water Seeks. That just means water-course – seeks meaning course. And this next one is The Rows – that's from a very old word meaning corner. I think in fact it's an old Norse word.'

Listening to all this she said again how clever he was, how much she admired him and how it would never be possible for a girl like her to keep up with him.

'I don't wonder they made you mayor,' she said. 'I shouldn't think anyone else stood a chance for miles.'

One evening towards the end of July he was fishing farther upstream than usual, in a narrow stony place where water dribbled over, in a field called Stanch Meadow. It had been a very dull evening, the water dead and with hardly the quiver of a swim running, and as he stared at the tip of his float, scarlet and motionless on the flat-skinned surface of the stream he made a mental note to tell Phoebe the name of that field. The word Stanch meant Staunch. Thus the name Stanch Meadow meant a place where a dam had been. In fact he was sure there were signs of a dam still there.

He pulled out his line, found that his bait was missing and put a square of bread on the hook. A minute later he was fighting a fish that kept boring away towards the big stones of the stream-bed, twisting and leaping. Once or twice it leapt clear of the water. It was a very big, undocile, powerful fish and it was not like anything he had seen before.

Twenty minutes later he was back in The George and Crown with a trout, weighed on Mrs Corcoran's kitchen scales, of two pounds thirteen ounces. Flushed and trembling as a boy, he saw the fish weighed, then weighed again and finally laid out on a dish on a table in the private bar. He saw Brown, solemn as a preacher, stand above the fish and pronounce:

'Never have been no trout in this river. Never. Not since I was a boy-chap and that's been a minute. Never been nothing here but roach and perch and rudd and bream and a jack or two. I don't see for the life of me how a trout could have got there.'

Presently the bar was full of drinkers admiring the big, mystifying trout. It was a masterpiece of a thing, they said. It was a knock-out. With pride Melford heard them speak of the fish, of himself, and of the way he had caught it as something that was already like an eclipse or a comet, one of those events that happened only with great rarity over the years.

'You must be born under a lucky star, Mr Turner,' Mrs Corcoran said.

He called for drinks. He bore the fish into the tap-room. He invited everyone there to take a drink with him. Then everybody raised glasses of beer and said again that the trout was a masterpiece. It was agreed again that there never had, in that river, been a fish like that, or for that matter a trout at all, and then a small old weasel-faced thatcher named Sherman said:

'Oh! ain't they?'

The tap-room became suddenly hushed. Glazed, one eye stiff like a dark shining blister, the fish lay on the altar of its plate. The thatcher Sherman gazed down on it and said:

'Ain't they? Oh! yis they is. That there fish is kin to one I had on a worm over twenty-one year ago.'

'No?' people said.

'Don't you remember?' Sherman said. 'Some on you perhaps ain't old enough to remember. But I know – I remember – it was Major Beeton's father who first put trout there.'

'Stocked the stream?' Melford said.

'Stocked the stream, sir,' Sherman said. 'Five thousand fish. What the heronshaws didn't get the others did. Chased every jack one out in no time. I'll be damned if I don't begin to think they was only two left – mine and yourn.'

Melford ordered more drinks. His health was toasted. He drank several whiskies. The fish was borne from bar to bar on its dish and someone said that if you counted its scales you could tell how old it was. Someone else, followed by several more people, said that it would be a crying shame if a fish like that couldn't be set up, in a glass case, with the weight on and the date and place and Mr Turner's name.

'You'll get it set up of course, sir, won't you?' Brown said, with something like reverence, and Melford knew that he would.

He must. His achievement had to be commemorated. The fish would look splendid in a case. He would have it hung either in the hall, so that people saw it as soon as they came in, or over the mantelpiece, in the sitting-room. Or perhaps in his bedroom, side by side with the badger he had shot as a boy.

'You leave it to me, sir,' Brown said. 'I know where I can get that done. You must have a thing like that done properly.'

He drank several more whiskies. In the course of the evening he supposed forty or fifty people, perhaps more, came in to admire the fish, to congratulate him and to say what a master-piece of a thing it was. He felt that he was responsible for a great achievement. He thought he was a wonderful man. No: more than that; he began to be sure that he was a wonderful man.

Finally, when the bars had emptied, he walked with Phoebe through the garden at the back of the pub, into the meadows beyond and along the stream. He was a little tipsy; he insisted on showing her the exact spot where the fish had been caught.

'Stanch Meadow.' He explained about Stanch Meadow. He explained about it, together with the meaning of the word Stanch and the fact that he was sure there was a dam still there, several times. 'Here,' he said, 'just here. This is where it was. Exactly in the middle there, before you get to the stones.'

All across the meadows, under a sky prickling softly with the subdued stars of summer, there was a drowsy ripeness in the air. A smell of overflowing summer water, thick and heavy, with a fragrance from a few uncarried cocks of hay, seemed to complete for him an evening of wonder. He felt generous and happy. He felt almost as if Providence had singled him out, by that aston-ishing coincidence of the fish, for a special blessing.

'I'm going to have it set up, of course,' he said. 'Brown's going to see to it. What shall I have put on it? "This trout – this speci-men of trout, weighing two pounds thirteen ounces, was landed by G. Melford Turner, Esq., at Stanch Meadow, Ascott St Mary, 23 July, 1924." How would that do?'

She said she thought it would do, and then asked him where he would put it.

'Oh! in my house somewhere. Perhaps in the hall, where people can see it.'

What people? he thought suddenly. How many people? Constance would not be interested. People like Tom Spencer and Charles Edward Twelvetree would come in and he would ex-plain to them the miracle of its catching. To them and a few others the legend would be presented and become well known. How many more?

Not many more, he thought. And suddenly he seemed to see it in a better place. Many more people would see it if, by some chance, it could hang in a place of honour over the bar in The George and Crown. Hundreds of people would see it there. Other fishermen would see it; people from the hunt would see it. Men like Captain Whitling and Rampling and Beety Beeton would see it and perhaps, in consequence, not take him quite so lightly.

'On second thoughts I think I'll make you a present of it,' he said.

'When it's stuffed?'

'It isn't really stuffed,' he said. 'Set up is the proper term.'

She seemed to accept without further comment the idea of receiving a dead fish as a present from him and he said:

'Of course you needn't keep it absolutely for yourself. You could hang it in the bar.'

'Supposing we ever went away?'

'Then it would be up to you,' he said. 'Either to leave it or take it away with you as something to remember me by.'

They sat down, some minutes later, under a hay-cock. He still felt tipsy, harmlessly and pleasantly tipsy, in a warm and expansive way. She folded him against her, moving with the lazy squirming movements of an animal settling down to rest. She plucked at his hair with her fingers and said:

'I was naughty about the fish. I never thanked you for it, did I? But you're always giving me presents and I don't seem to do anything but thank you.'

'No need to thank me.'

'Don't you ever get tired of giving me presents and bringing me things?'

'No,' he said. 'And I don't think I ever shall.'

'You sound happy,' she said.

Very naturally he was happy. Who, he thought, wouldn't be happy? Who, in his special circumstance, could help being happy? Apart from the fish he had gradually grown, that summer, into the easy habit of a life with neither urge nor distraction. That was how fishing took you; you stopped worrying and fretting about things that did not matter. All that mattered was the water, the line, the float, and finally the fish on the hook streaming away into dark water. Before you knew where you were you were woven irresistibly into a web of pleasant aimless things.

'Do I make you happy?' she said.

Yes, he said, she made him happy.

'I'm glad about that,' she said. It was very quiet. From over the meadows, under the subdued stars, in the warm air, there was hardly a sound except an occasional dribble from the stream, in the place where he caught the fish among the stones. 'Because I've got something to tell you. Oh! not just now – before you go, I mean.'

Part 3

Chapter One

For the rest of that summer the house on the square was like a schoolroom in which Melford and Constance stayed long enough to observe a certain curriculum and then run free.

Constance did not trouble about the fishing excursions because she was not interested in Melford's comings and goings; nor was she interested in fish and how you caught them. She listened respectfully to the story of the large and mysterious trout that had been caught in a stream where there were no trout rather as she might have listened to the story of a fox turning and chasing its pursuers at a hunt meeting. It was an extraordinary event if you were interested in fish and foxes. She was not interested. It would have been exactly the same if Melford had hunted tarpon and tiger.

Apart from her duties in the house only her little oppressive urban programme as mayoress kept her from escaping every afternoon. She was a very dutiful mayoress. They had been wrong, people in the town, when they had doubted the qualities of the Untouchable Mrs T. as mayoress. They did not fail to notice that she was not so untouchable now. She made conversation more easily. She did not seem so shy. She did not look completely through you with her big lost brown eyes in the way she had done two years before.

Whenever she gave a tea-party in the house or a small garden-party on the lawn behind it she seemed also perfectly happy. At these parties she always saw that there were wonderful things to eat. Little old ladies who lived alone or in pairs or in almshouses or on frugal pensions could be seen lifting the edges of elegant crustless sandwiches and peering into them and exclaiming in whispers: 'What are they? Real salmon! And best butter!' She always saw to it that there were plenty of fresh bridge-rolls with varied fillings and that Mrs Butterworth cooked enough rock cakes, curd tarts, plum cakes, and sponge fingers. There were varied and delicious things like best Scotch short-cake, gingerbread, chocolate biscuits, apricots, and peaches from the shop. Mrs Butterworth and Edna put on their best cream uniforms and saw that everybody had plenty of everything and that there were ample fresh supplies of tea. And at the very end, before everyone went away, Constance always took aside the little old ladies who lived frugally and alone and told them not to forget to go out of the house the kitchen way. A few minutes later they could be seen hurrying across the square or through the churchyard with enough food to last them a day or two: sandwiches and cakes in bags, jellies in basins and sometimes an occasional ham-bone.

They were not only grateful for these things; they were almost endeared to her because of them. And they noted too that, before the end of the parties, Melford always arrived. He handed round plates and dishes, patted the old ladies, made jokes about being the isolated member of his sex and what was one among so many? Excited and giggling, the ladies thought him frivolous. He was not stuck-up. It did not matter what part of the town you came from or who you were or what party you voted for, he was not above taking a cup of tea with you, asking after your family and wondering if there was anything he could do for you. That was the sort of man he seemed.

But if Melford was clear enough, Constance gradually became and remained, because of all this, something of a mystery. If it was true, as people said it was, that she was running on the loose a little, how did you account for that state of composed, almost preserved, happiness at home? If it was true – but was it true? In a little town like Orlingford people were always over-fond of talking. When there was nothing to talk about they naturally fancied there was or they made something up and that was how things started.

Was it true? Constance and Melford did not seem, the ladies thought, like two people who are dissatisfied with each other, let alone unfaithful. At the parties and garden-parties they moved and talked and laughed among the guests in a way that could not fire suspicion. On Sundays they went to church together. They were often together at dances, fêtes, and bazaars. They were generous with subscriptions, help for the sick and diversions for old people who lived alone. Melford was especially energetic in work for the disabled, the tubercular, and the blind. He could not bear these forms of physical suffering and sometimes at bazaars or concerts arranged for such causes he spoke fervently when he said:

'I know it affects my wife just as deeply as it does myself. Believe me, this is a cause very near to both our hearts.'

You could not deny the evidence of your own eyes that Constance and Melford were so often together or that so often they had the same causes at heart. But the same eyes that saw them together, the eyes of ladies who knitted egg-cosies for bazaars and bed-socks for hospitals and thought that Melford was frivolous at tea-parties, did not notice other things.

With one exception, Agnes Twelvetree, they did not notice that Constance never looked at him. She never lifted her eyes, looked straight into his and held the glance between them. Melford could be jocular, frivolous, and even mildly flirtatious with ladies who came to tea, but he did not joke with Constance. He had no diminutive for her name. There were men who called their wives by perfectly stupid and idiotic names like Bubbles, Waffsie, and Kiddo; and a new fashion was springing up by which everyone, even a casual acquaintance, was called a darling. Melford called his wife neither darling nor dear, nor by diminutives, idiotic or otherwise. She in turn, except to a few friends who had known him all his life, had nothing by which to call him except Mr Turner, my husband, or the mayor.

They did not notice, either, that she never spoke of Melford and herself as 'we'. It escaped them all, again with the exception of Agnes Twelvetree, that she separated herself from him, no doubt unconsciously, in conversation:

'I will ask my husband. I shan't be there, but I know the mayor will. If Mr Turner has agreed to it then I'm sure you can count on his support. Yes: I hope to be coming too.'

Only Agnes Twelvetree, who had acquired a gift of malice in observation and a certain knack of mimicry about men with which she sometimes amused her guests at supper, noticed these things. It was she who was quick to notice things like Melford putting a little finger in the top pocket of his waistcoat or the fact that when in doubt about something his brain was not quick enough to grasp, he was inclined to stare at you, as she put it in her malicious way, like a dray-horse that wanted to be excused.

It was she too who noticed, towards the end of that summer, a great change in Constance, in her appearance and her way of doing things.

Towards the end of an afternoon late in August Constance stood against the window of a top room of Pollards' Mill, brushing her damp hair. She had been swimming all afternoon but the water, with the sun dropping westward, had suddenly become too cold for her and she had left Frankie Johnson alone in the pool. At the edges of the water there were already little drifts of yellowed willow leaves.

The brush was backed with tortoiseshell. At the last moment before leaving the house, she had slipped it into her handbag in addition to her comb. Her hair was soft and thick. After swimming it tangled quickly and she preferred to brush it dry.

Suddenly the sun caught gold-bronze light from the brush-back. The light lifted swiftly, leapt up and swivelled away. A moment later Constance was staring, far off, high beyond the turning leaves of the willows, at a strange object in the sky.

She could not decide, for some time, what this object was. It was exactly the colour of the flash of light from the tortoiseshell. It flashed gold-bronze against the deep blue August sky. It seemed, she thought, like a distant aeroplane catching the light of sun or a balloon that had actually caught fire above the town.

She watched it for a few moments, unable to make up her mind, and then suddenly the strange fiery gold object in the sky excited her. She leaned out of the window and called down:

'Frankie! Come up a minute, come up here! I want to show you something. There's something strange out there in the sky.'

He was practising a new way of holding his breath under water. Properly done, it meant that you could stay under for two minutes or more. He had so far achieved ninety-eight seconds. He was still under water when she shouted and it was some time before he came up to say:

'Did you call me? What did you say?'

'Come up here. There's something odd out there in the sky. It's a balloon or something – a strange balloon.'

'I'm practising holding my breath.'

'Oh! I know, but Frankie! – come up, my sweet. It's so extraordinary. It's beautiful really – I think it's floating away –'

'Oh! in a minute.'

'No – now, please, now. Before it disappears.'

It did not disappear. It remained with its curious ethereal effect of being part real, part amorphous, solid and yet burning, until he finished practising his breathing exercises and came up to her five minutes later. During that time she experienced a sensation, over and over again, of exhilaration, of being uplifted in a strange way, as she was sometimes uplifted by music, and when he finally reached her she was still excited.

'Look at it, Frankie. Over there. It's never moved. Is it a balloon or something? Perhaps it's one of those balloons they send up at fêtes – but if it's a balloon why doesn't it float away?'

Frankie Johnson, rubbing his wet hair with a towel, stared across the sky above the willow trees and said flatly:

'It's the weathercock on the church, you ninny, that's all.'

'Oh! it can't be –'

She did not go on. She was suddenly very quiet. It was all a trick. She supposed it was simply that she had never been looking that way, at that time, in just that stage of light, and so had never seen the weathercock like that before. She had been so enthralled by the experience of believing in the reality of that fire in the sky, that strange, fiery tortoiseshell light, that she felt she had watched a phenomenon, and it was some minutes before she could bring herself to believe that she had not been cheated.

Then in a low voice she tried to explain:

'You see, I was standing just here. The sun caught the back of the brush. It's just that colour, you see, and then suddenly –'

It was almost as if she were speaking to herself.

'I've done a hundred and three seconds now,' Frankie Johnson said.

'Even now when you look at it,' she said, 'just before you get your eyes focused, it looks like something strange –' and again it was as if she was speaking to herself.

'I think I'll go down and have one more try,' he said.

'One more try at what?'

'Holding my breath. It's this new method. A man I met at the barber's told me.'

'That's a thing I can't do,' she said.

'It's easy,' he said. 'Simple. Come down and watch me.'

She went down, sat on the edge of the pool and watched him. He dived. She saw his body, brown from many afternoons in the sun, turn fish-wise and disappear. After some time he broke water, laughed and spat water out and said:

'A hundred and nine! How's that? I'll make two minutes by next week if I keep at it.'

'You look exhausted,' she said. 'Give yourself a rest now, Frankie.'

'Oh! please,' he said. 'Don't be such a fuss.'

After that he dived several times more, disappearing, staying under, then breaking surface with shouts of his numbers. He was twice above a hundred; once, when weed tangled him, as low as twenty-nine. Each time, because she remained bemused and puzzled by that trick of light that had turned itself into a weathercock and cheated her, she was not really aware of how long he stayed under.

Suddenly she had a strange feeling that he was not coming up. The pool was deserted. In her bemusement she was not sure how long he had been down. Then a great leaping electric shock of terror went searing through her. She jumped up, staring at the water, three parts black in shadow, and then started to yell:

'Frankie – '

'A hundred and twelve,' his voice said. She saw his head break water and a hand wave beyond a six-foot clump of reeds.

Her own voice died; she was too frightened even to say that she was frightened. She smiled and tried to say 'Good' in answer to his shout of 'How was that, my pet?'

Without words she watched him drying and dressing himself. He looked young and vigorous. He towelled his body into a burning flush, talking a good deal. His hair, darkened by water, became a fair gold again as he dried it, shaking it down like a straw fringe over his brilliant white-blue eyes.

'Lend me a comb, sweet.'

She was staring at the pool; she was gazing, with undiminished fear, at shadow on empty water.

'Sweet. Daydream. Comb, please. Dreamy, I said a comb.'

She came to herself. She found a comb in her handbag, smiled and gave it to him. There was a sudden dark singing in her heart as she watched him comb back the still damp, vigorous hair. He always looked so exhilarated and fresh, so purely physical, in his blond English way, after swimming.

'Thinking about something? Or just lost in admiration?'

No: she was not lost. She was not thinking. She said a few words without knowing quite what they were. Then she made a great effort to recover composure and said:

'Well, I was really. I was still wondering about that weather-cock. I still can't believe – '

'Disappointed in you.' He was standing in nothing but his trousers. He retracted his belly, throwing up the spare brown cage of his chest. 'Thought you were admiring me. Look at these for muscles.'

He grinned, proud of himself despite the mockery, and danced from one foot to another.

'I didn't think the spire was so high,' she said. 'I went up there once. It didn't seem so high,' and then she added stupidly: 'Of course I didn't go to the top.'

'Well, hardly, dear.'

He was still dancing to and fro on his bare feet. Now and then he burnished and beat the solid muscle of his chest and shoulders with the flat of his hands. He had fine spare muscle, with only small quantities of fine gold hair on his chest, and looked more like an athlete than somebody who did nothing but jingle a cinema piano several hours a night.

And after watching him and wanting to change the subject again she said:

'You're very proud of yourself this afternoon.'

'Well, naturally. So would you be if you could stay under as long as I did.'

She wanted to say 'I thought you were never coming up. I thought I'd lost you,' but the words seemed naïve and silly now. Only the shock of it all was still there; the sinking ache inside her diminished only to become more tense. It was impossible to explain about this and she was glad when he said:

'Always think the most of yourself. In case nobody else does.

How far could you see from the church-tower by the way? What was it like up there?'

'Oh! high,' she said stupidly. What was the matter with her? Why in Heaven's name did she say things like that? 'You could see the town and the fields all round.'

He buried his head in his shirt and pushed it out again, ruffled.

'High? You don't mean it. What did you go up for?'

'To see some fox-hounds.'

'What?'

He gave a guffawing laugh. Astounded by the idea that some-one could climb a church-tower in order to see fox-hounds, he looked at her as if she were mad.

'Fox-hounds? Up there? How did *they* get up?'

'No, not that,' she said. 'I didn't mean that. I meant we went up to see the hunt go past – it was away over here somewhere. Across these fields.'

'Well, my God,' he said. 'My sainted Aunt Johnson.'

He stood buttoning his shirt, laughing again, loudly, unkind. She was so hurt that the ache inside her sank lower than ever, darkening. She tried for the third time to change the subject and said, going towards him:

'You're just like a man. Comb your hair first and then put your shirt on afterwards. Instead of the other way round. Here, you're all ruffled again, let me comb it. You're just like a man.'

The laughter went from his face. Nothing of it was retained but a small, arched smile.

'And what else do you suppose I ought to be like?'

'Give me the comb. I'll comb it.'

'I'll do it myself,' he said. 'I like to comb my own hair.'

'Let me do it, sweet,' she said.

'I'll do it!' he said. 'I can do it. I'd like to do it myself if you don't mind. I'm very particular about my hair.'

He snatched the comb from her reach, finished dressing and then combed his hair in savage gloomy sweeps.

They walked most of the way back to the town in silence. It was, she knew, stupid to quarrel, to seem upset and silent about a little thing like a comb, but she could not explain and she could not help it. Below it all was the dark sinking ache of her fear:

fear of losing him, fear of a change in him, of not being wanted.

Along the path, as they came up earlier in the afternoon, she had noticed the first dew-berries ripening, and they had stopped to gather some. Now he noticed them again and stopped by the hedge-side, plucking with over-scrupulous care at the soft fat berries so that he should not burst their bloomy skins.

The act of gathering the berries so deliberately seemed to mock her again. She felt deeply hurt for a second time. She walked slowly on and he did not follow her. Presently there were thirty or forty yards between them and when she turned to look back he was still standing by the hedge, plucking at the berries and eating them in the same arch, deliberate way.

It was not until she reached the stile at the end of the path that he caught up with her again. This was the place where a farmer named Wheeler had once seen her rain-soaked and dishevelled, with blood on her hands, and had gone home to tell his wife of the slightly crazy Mrs Turner he had seen.

Beyond this point they always parted. He took a back-way cinder-path that went past small-holdings towards the station. She went on through the churchyard.

Now he had blue ripe berries in his hands. He held them out to her. Some of the skins had burst and his hands were stained.

'No, thank you.'

She was hurt and knew that it was stupid. She knew it was childish and she could not explain.

'No? Awfully good,' he said.

She stared at the ground.

'Please yourself,' he said.

He crammed more berries into his mouth. She did not watch him climbing the stile. From the other side his voice became purposely formal. It seemed as if meant to taunt her.

'Sure you won't change your mind? Just one left,' he said. 'Last one.'

As if all her old dismal obliterating shyness had come back, she continued to stare at the ground, not speaking.

'Refused,' he said. 'Offer not accepted.'

She had nothing to say.

'Well,' he said, 'I'll say good-bye.'

When she looked up again he was twenty yards or more down the cinder-track.

'Frankie, don't go like that.' She tried to speak quietly, un-reproachfully. Nothing in the nature of that sharp rift had ever happened before. 'Frankie, that's an awful way to go.'

He walked on, not turning.

'Frankie, aren't you going to say good-bye?'

He turned and stood still.

'I said good-bye.'

With deliberation he licked smears of berry-juice from his fingers.

'Not that way. I don't mean that way.'

After licking his fingers he looked at them carefully, separately, almost as if to say, 'Well, which way?'

'Will I see you tomorrow?' she said.

He shrugged his shoulders. She was so hurt by the gesture, reading into it 'Who knows? Who can say? Who cares? It's up to you', that suddenly anger woke her pride and she was over the stile, head up, saying nothing, suddenly walking away.

He was so proud of himself that day, so proud of his taut neat body and thick bright hair and his feats of staying so long under water, that she went home and, that night, did an amazing thing.

Hardly aware of it, blind with bitterness, she put into a letter all the lacerations of the afternoon. 'Don't be cheap with people,' she wrote. 'That's not you. It doesn't suit you. It's easy to jibe at people but there were things you didn't understand this after-noon and I couldn't explain to you – and because you didn't understand all you could do was to be cheap, wasn't it? Don't do it, Frankie. It doesn't suit you. You're above that. People will only hate you.'

As she went out to post the letter she was hardly aware that she did, in fact, hate him herself. She hated him darkly, without reason, with her own pain.

She had no sooner dropped the letter into the box than she bitterly regretted it. Hatred turned in on herself, with endless lacerations. She did not sleep well. She had another of her white, staring nights, tossing starkly, wondering if he would come next day.

In cold trepidation she went to meet him earlier than usual the following afternoon. To her joy and astonishment he was sitting on the stile, waiting.

'Frankie,' she said, running to him. 'Oh! my God, Frankie.'

In this way she built up strange agonies of mind. She did not grasp at first that the curious little quarrels that began to spring up between them were the result of fear. She did not grasp that, most of the time, it was she who made them.

'You didn't used to talk like that to me. You never said things like that. You never say you love me. Not in the same way, not like you used to.'

Throughout August and September she became more restless and tautened. She never confessed that she was frightened. She was too proud to let him see that a moment when she thought he had drowned while swimming had let loose a whole dark fleet of fears.

'Come tomorrow. Stay a long time. Don't be late, will you? Because the next day's Sunday – had you forgotten? I don't see you till Monday and that's more than a day.'

If September had about it a curious unreality it was possibly because the town and the low land about it lay suffocated in a hot, humid spell of weather. It was too early for a true Indian summer. Thick overnight mists hung in low-lying places and smouldered into oppressive brilliant days.

On one of these days, heavy with late corn-smell, darkly mellow with elderberries that hung bagged and glistening above the mill-pool, a breathless, soft day, perfect for swimming, she waited at Pollards' Mill for most of the afternoon. Frankie Johnson did not arrive and after nearly an hour and a half she walked slowly back to the stile.

Again, to her astonishment, he was sitting there.

'But where have you been, Frankie? What happened?'

'Here!' he said. 'Here! Where else would I be? We said here. Where the hell do you expect me to be? Here – at the stile, where we said. That's where.'

Bickering broke out. Under the trees it was hot and suffocating. Glaring, he accused her savagely:

'The trouble is you don't know what day it is. Half the time you're in a daydream. I say things and you never listen.'

'We didn't say here, Frankie.'

'Oh, for God's sake,' he said, 'what does it matter? Things never go right nowadays. Don't let's squabble about it. It's finished. Let's pack it up. It's all over now.'

Chapter Two

It was Agnes Twelvetree who first noticed the effect of these things on an evening in October.

'I suppose,' she said as she walked with her father under the chestnut trees across the square, 'we shall be having Gertie Butterworth's celebrated rabbit and knuckle-end pie again to-night.'

'I don't think it's bad,' her father said. 'I think she cooks quite well.'

'Cook!' she said. 'The woman uses shop-lard.' And then added before her father could speak again: 'Butter by name all right, but lard by nature.'

She and her father lived in a pleasant, lime-shaded street leading off the south corner of the square. Two or three times a year, perhaps four, and always at Christmas-time, they walked across the square and took an evening meal with the Turners; the same number of times the Turners walked across the square and took a meal with them. The only differences in these events were that Agnes Twelvetree's cooking was better and more imaginative than Mrs Butterworth's and that whereas the meals at the Twelvetrees' were called dinner those at the Turners', because Melford hated to be thought ostentatious, were called supper.

Every October the rabbit and knuckle-end pie, the knuckle-end being of ham to give the pie a saltier, smoky flavour, appeared without fail. It graced the year as surely as an equinox.

'I can tell you what else there'll be,' Agnes Twelvetree said. 'Chicken broth with pearl-barley. I think,' she went on with malicious afterthought, 'that when Gertie gets to heaven the pearl-barley gates will open to receive her.'

'Agnes.'

'After that the ham and bunny. Squiggle potatoes – I fancy she puts them through a cake-icer. Brussel sprouts as big as pincushions. And gravy, of course, plenty of gravy. Thick and dark brown. I think she makes it out of heel-ball.'

'Agnes.'

'And then trifle. I think she waits till Melford has an autumn-cleaning in the shop. Then she begs something of everything except sardines and puts it through a mincer. Pops custard on it and then does algebra in angelica on top. And then of course Angels-on-Horseback to end.'

'Agnes: sometimes you're too bad.'

'What a lovely smell there is tonight,' she said. 'I love that wonderful smell of watered dust after rain.'

She had taken two or three whiskies before setting out, so that now her malice had a velvet quality. When she and her father arrived at the Turners' house Melford, knowing her preference, gave her another. He rather liked Agnes Twelvetree. She was clearly the sort of woman who never bothered about men. And as he lifted his glass he turned and said to her:

'Well, Agnes, here's to the health of your new baby.'

'And here's to yours,' she said.

'You mean her car, I suppose,' Twelvetree said. 'Have you seen it yet, Constance?'

'No,' Constance said, 'I didn't even know you had a car.'

'It came last week,' she said. 'After I've killed two more cows you must come with me for a drive one afternoon. Melford, I hope we haven't got beef tonight? I think the cow I killed last Sunday ought to be hung a little longer.'

Melford laughed heartily, opening his mouth wide, and felt in great spirits. He wished there were more women like Agnes Twelvetree; she was very sporty; she almost had the outlook and feelings of a man.

'What kind of car is it?' he asked.

'A Talbot,' she said. 'I'm going to think of a name for her that will indicate something French and fast. How do you think Cocotte would do?'

'Oh! awfully good,' he said, by no means certain of the meaning of the word.

'You ought to get one too,' she said. 'Constance could learn to drive and get out more. It would do her good. Everybody's getting a car now. I'm afraid it looks like the end of horses.'

'Not,' said Melford staunchly, 'as long as I'm alive. I see no future in a world without horses.'

'I do,' she said. 'Butchers would then have to give us real meat for a change.'

At supper it was as she had predicted. The meal began with chicken broth plentifully sown with pearl-barley; there were fried croutons of bread to float in it. Her father ate it very slowly, sitting upright, judicial, and embalmed, as if he were dealing with difficult evidence that needed careful digesting.

To follow there was, as she had said, Mrs Butterworth's ham-and-rabbit pie, with its accompaniment of brussels sprouts and potatoes. She did not comment on the pie but waited for Melford to do so instead.

As she had hoped, he tasted it, then tasted it a second time, then laid down his knife and fork and said:

'You know, Charles Edward, there's something about a young cornfield rabbit that takes an awful lot of beating.'

'Undoubtedly,' Twelvetree said. 'I think that's absolutely right.'

'The flavour,' Melford said, 'is something miles different from a winter rabbit. You take this rabbit. Probably born – when? May? Early June? Fed all its life on corn – and the young corn, mind you. That's the point, I think. The young corn. Don't you think so?'

'Oh! absolutely.'

'Milky,' Melford said. 'That's what they are. Milky.'

Aware that he said this every year, Agnes Twelvetree did not listen much. She sat watching Constance instead. She noticed that a brooch at the neck of her dress had come undone. The pin stuck upwards, so that each time Constance bent down to her food it seemed visibly to prick her throat. It troubled and fascinated Agnes Twelvetree that Constance did not seem to notice it at all.

Then, because the pie was rather too salty, she began to drink more burgundy. Constance hardly touched wine and presently Melford was filling up Agnes Twelvetree's glass quite frequently. And he was glad when, after two more glasses, she began to be malicious again.

By the time the trifle had arrived, green with its design of algebraic angelica, she had mimicked most of the people he hoped she would mimic. Her imitation of Foghorn Spencer reading the lesson in church was always her best, he thought. 'Like Gabriel himself reading the register.' But he liked too her imitations of Fossett-Brown, the auctioneer who suffered from duck's disease, the tall wand-like Mr Prout, the organist, who bounced on the balls of his feet and carried his bowler hat on his ears, and Bish Thompson, who kept the fire-horses that, at the call of fire, always lay down.

They were all very good and made him laugh a good deal. He did not notice that her victims were all, with rare exceptions, men. One of these rare exceptions was a Mrs Cunningham, of whom, as the trifle came to an end and Edna cleared the dishes in readiness for Angels-on-Horseback, she said:

'She is *so* good. I think when she pricks her finger she bleeds Communion wine.'

Between the trifle and the Angels-on-Horseback there was a slight gap in the conversation. Her father never talked much; Constance, she thought, seemed even quieter than usual and for some part of the time had not been listening. Melford was content to listen to her mimicry and suddenly she filled the gap by saying quickly, casually, and as if it were an afterthought:

'Oh! they tell me you caught a wonderful fish, Melford. A pike or something.'

'Trout.'

'Nearly a three-pounder,' her father said.

'Two pounds thirteen ounces.'

Dryly Agnes Twelvetree looked round at the walls of the dining-room.

'Isn't that the sort of fish that gets itself put into glass cases? I don't see it here.'

'Didn't you get it set up, Melford?' Twelvetree said. 'I thought you did.'

'I did,' Melford said. 'But I gave it to the people at The George and Crown. After all, it was caught there. It was sort of nice for them, I thought. Their river. Their meadow. You know. Nice for them to have it, I thought.'

'Extraordinary fish to have been in that stream,' Twelvetree said. 'How do you suppose it got there?'

'It seems,' Melford said, 'that Beety Beeton's grandfather put trout in that stream over twenty years ago.'

He got up and filled Agnes Twelvetree's wineglass for the last time. She rewarded him by putting Beety Beeton into the clear, pleasant aspic of her malice, lifting her glass at the same time:

'Good old Beety. He always looks as if his father was Humpty-Dumpty and his mother a prize bloodhound. I suppose Beety was the only one they could keep out of the litter.'

She was pleasantly, unaggressively tipsy as she and Constance left the table and went upstairs. And again Constance said:

'Would you care to come into my room? There's a better light in there.'

Agnes Twelvetree sat under the light of the dressing-table, making a pretence of arranging her prematurely grey-white, rather straggly hair. In the mirror she again noticed Constance's brooch, unpinned at her neck. It had worried her throughout supper and now she got up and said:

'Your brooch is undone, Constance. Didn't you notice it?'

'No.'

'You might have pricked yourself. Let me do it up for you.'

So close to her, doing up the brooch, Agnes Twelvetree could not help noticing a bruised, glimmered look about her eyes. Normally dark clear brown, they were now oddly dull and compressed. The whites were bloodshot. She did up the brooch and said:

'It was very generous of Melford to give that prize fish to the new people at Ascott.'

'New people? What new people?'

'Didn't you know there were new people?' she said. 'They've been there since Christmas. A woman named Corcoran and her daughter.'

'Oh! yes. They've been very good to him. Only I thought it was still Mrs Duncan.'

Tipsily, with a sudden flash of her general hatred for men, Agnes Twelvetree said:

'You mean Melford has been going over there all this time and never told you?'

'I never asked. I wasn't interested.'

'Perhaps it's time you were.'

In the mirror she noticed, now, for the first time, how untidy the room was. The coverlet of the bed was turned back. The bed was covered with records, newspapers, and magazines. A dressing-gown, a petticoat, and some more newspapers lay in a chair. It was as if Constance had been busy searching for something and had suddenly remembered her supper-party and then left it all, forgetting to do up her brooch at the same time.

'I tell you what,' Agnes Twelvetree said, 'let's drive out there one afternoon. I'll try not to kill you. They do very good teas, they tell me.'

'I know. I've been. But I'm not very free in the afternoons.'

Agnes Twelvetree got up and went to the window and looked across the square. The window was open. Another little shower of rain had fallen on the dust and the mild October air was fresh with sweetness.

'The country looks lovely. We ought to take advantage of this spell and have a trip over there.'

'Why?'

'Well, it's so nice. I'm mad about the car –'

'Why?'

Warmed and talkative with drink Agnes Twelvetree, surprised, turned suddenly from the window and found Constance looking at her with staring eyes.

'Why?'

Agnes Twelvetree wished for a moment that she was drunker than she was. The eyes staring at her were brimming with a terribly dark uneasiness and she said:

'Oh! nothing. I thought you didn't get out much –'

'Tell me what you were going to tell me.'

Agnes Twelvetree was fond of mimicking people in strange attitudes; she was fond of talking about people in her malicious aspic way. But there was nothing in Constance's face that she felt like mimicking and she did not feel malicious as she looked at it. She simply felt a terrible uneasiness of her own and began to say:

'Constance, it doesn't matter –'

'Say what you were going to say.'

Outspoken but no longer malicious, not quite drunk enough to be proud or pleased about it, Agnes Twelvetree said with cowardice:

'Oh! everybody knows. I thought you knew.'

She knew that that was stupid; she knew that Constance did not know and with renewed cowardice she said:

'You know how people talk. They're always talking.'

Constance did not answer this time. The huge, staring eyes, unhappy in preoccupation, were fixed on Agnes Twelvetree with a kind of devouring paralysis. It was that which finally unnerved her into saying with a rush of her customary frankness:

'Well, it's Melford. It's a girl there. This Corcoran girl. It seems it's been going on a long while. You'd got to know some-time.'

A dart of unhappy fire sprang from the remote colourless depths of Constance's eyes.

'Was that what you meant when you congratulated Melford?' she said.

Agnes Twelvetree did not answer. Sharply she remembered her toast to Melford, at the beginning of dinner, in reply to his about her car: 'And here's to yours.' It was terribly unfortunate. She had not meant it that way. It had been one of those things that just sprang out. She had not meant it that way.

'I think we should go down,' Constance said.

That night Agnes Twelvetree sat for a long time at her bed-room window, staring over a warm autumn garden that copper beeches divided from the fields beyond. She did not feel mali-cious. She sipped slowly and with sour determination at a glass of neat whisky, looking at the stars. That evening she had said a great many stupid things that she regretted. Wouldn't she ever learn to keep her mouth shut? Like a fool she had gabbled until it was too late, until she didn't remember what she was gabbling. That was how she always ended: a sour, mimicking, careless, gabbling fool.

But it was not because of this that she did not feel like sleep-ing. She roamed about the room, looking at the stars appearing and reappearing from light cloud above the beech-trees. She gulped at her whisky, remembering Constance's face. She could not get out of her mind the strange remoteness of the eyes, the devouring, brooding sense of trouble. Her own keen, too-sharp eye had focused, caught, and uneasily kept it all.

Rain fell for a few seconds on the leaves of the beech trees. The spots pattered separately and quickly and then were silent. She walked about the room in darkness, drinking her whisky, and again there was a smell of rain-sweetened dust in the air.

'Constance,' she kept thinking, 'my good grief, Constance, what is it? What's happened to you? I wish to God I could help you.'

It was soon after this that Melford spoke enthusiastically of the hunting season to Mrs Corcoran. That day there had been a keen white touch of frost in the air.

'Well, it won't be long now,' he said. 'Let's hope the weather treats us a bit kinder than last year.'

'Let's hope so,' she said.

Soon it would be November. Already some chestnuts were bare of leaves. The poplars and willows were raining yellow by the river. The fishing season, as far as he was concerned, was over; now he could concentrate on hunting again. Soon he would be riding home in the blue, charming, misty afternoons. Oaks would begin to flame across fields of young wheat and gradually black arms would begin to stretch wet and naked from skeins of yellow elm.

He wanted very much to make it a bigger season than last year. He would be able to give more time to it. He had in mind to buy himself another hunter and take in another two or three meetings. For one thing he would not be mayor. He was glad everyone had seen his point so readily, at the last council meeting, when he had announced quite frankly that he thought the office ought to go round.

He had no idea, when the year of his mayoralty began, what a tie it could be. He had fairly flung himself into it; the few days of fishing and hunting had been his only recreation. Once or twice he had the impression of being a stranger simply lodging in his own house. He had never spent so many hours over papers, had never signed his name so many times or signed so many cheques. It had cost him rather more than he had bargained for and now, though he had enjoyed it, he was glad that it was over.

'I hope to be a lot freer this season,' he said to Mrs Corcoran, 'especially once we get Christmas over.'

She commented on this by saying a curious thing: 'It all depends on what you mean by free.'

He had never been quite certain, or really quite at ease, with Mrs Corcoran. She had been very kind, but her excessive niceness of manner sometimes made him suspect her. At times he had more than a suspicion that she was what his mother would have called false. She wore too many rings; she greeted all her gentlemen guests with too large, too sweet, and too friendly a smile; she spoke in that glib, facile London way that was a shade too quick for country people.

Another thing was her excessive perfume. She had only to move her arms or take out her handkerchief and it seemed to spread from her like a cloud.

'I wonder if you'd mind stepping into the back sitting-room,' she said. 'I want to speak to you about a little matter.'

He stepped into the back sitting-room. She shut the door. Thick perfume wafted about him. 'Sit down, dear,' she said and her rings made florid circles in the air.

He sat down on a sofa and, too late, noticed that she preferred to stand.

Suddenly he had an uncomfortable suspicion that she was going to ask him to lend her money; instead she said:

'Of course I know what's been going on between you and Phoebe.'

'I suppose you do.'

'Oh! I don't object. I like a bit of fun myself. Everybody does.'

He did not know what to say.

'In fact one can well understand the girl wanting to,' she said, 'with a gentleman that's been as nice as you've been.'

She came and sat down on the settee, at the same time offering him a cigarette. He said: 'No. No thank you,' and she lit one herself, inhaling sharply, blowing exhaustive smoke clouds.

That was another thing, he thought. She smoked too much. He waited for her to speak again but before doing so she picked a shred of tobacco from the tip of her tongue, flicking it away with a finger-nail.

Then she turned to him and again a great saccharine breath of perfume oppressed the air.

'But I think there's quite a difference, don't you,' she said, and she seemed to speak with calmness, 'between having fun and giving a girl a baby?'

He felt his veins run cold. She let cigarette ash fall on her dress. With her ringed hand she flicked it away from her heavy thigh.

'I should have thought you'd have known better than that,' she said. 'A married man. Old enough to be her father.'

'May I change my mind and have a cigarette?' he said.

'Of course, dear, of course.'

She gave him a cigarette. His hands were shaking. He tried hastily to find his matches and she said:

'Have a light from me, dear.'

Unsteadily he took a light from her cigarette, quivering. He hated her calm familiarity, that London way of calling him dear. He blew smoke, dragging a short sharp sigh.

'Better?' she said. 'Don't upset yourself, dear. There's nothing to be upset about.'

His mind started to fumble its way back to the summer.

'How –'

'Four months,' she said. His mouth filled with nausea. 'She didn't want to tell you before because she wanted – well, you know, one can never be sure, can they?'

He remembered suddenly the evening when he had caught the trout; how Phoebe had begun to say to him, in the meadow, 'There's something I want to tell you,' and then had added some moments later: 'No: I won't. Not now. It's too nice an evening. It can wait till some other time.'

'I'm not blaming you,' Mrs Corcoran said. 'And I'm not blaming Phoebe. I'm the one to blame. I let you go up to her bedroom that time she wasn't well –'

'Mrs Corcoran, I assure you –'

'Well, does it matter, dear?' she said. 'When and where?' She shrugged her heavy shoulders and gave a sideways, unpleasantly friendly smile. 'It happened sometime.'

He swallowed the nausea that was in his mouth. It burned down his throat, leaving him with nothing to say.

'You know I don't think you quite appreciate,' she said, very slowly, 'that you're very attractive to a certain type of woman. You've got that particular sort of nature.'

It was insidious, that voice of hers. It embarrassed him. Her thigh was close to him on the sofa and now, turning to speak to him again, she pressed it closer.

'Yes!' she said. 'No larking. I know one or two women who've been in here.'

His brain, fumbling and clogged, could devise no kind of answer.

'And they're not the only ones.' She was very close to him. Perfume wafted thickly about him, mingling with cigarette smoke. He felt fogged and unhappy. 'There's a lot of lonely women about the world, dear. You'd be surprised.'

He was beyond surprise; he had simply a feeling of being trapped and mesmerized.

'Well, I know you'll want to think this over,' she said. 'Did you think of staying the night, dear? Perhaps we could talk about it later. When things are quieter. When Phoebe's gone to bed – I don't want to upset her any more if I can help it.'

He wanted to run from her as he had once run from Mrs Marchmont.

'Well, no. I wasn't. I think I'd rather talk about it now.'

He got up. He felt better standing up. She crossed her heavy legs on the settee. Cigarette ash had again fallen in her lap and she shook it free of her thighs. He thought of Phoebe. He wondered if she needed him, if she was hurt and what she thought about it all. It was a desperate business. It was a terrible business whichever way he looked at it and he said:

'Where's Phoebe? Couldn't we all three talk?'

'I think you and me should talk,' she said. 'Why don't you come and sit down?'

She patted the sofa, close to her big, bulging thigh. He ignored it and walked about. He felt certain now that she was another Mrs Marchmont, seeking to drag him down. It revolted him physically that she might think him attractive. He pulled nervously at his cigarette, trying not to look at her and she said:

'You're all to pieces, dear. Why don't you sit down? Why don't you let me get your bed made up and you relax and then we talk it over later?'

No, he thought. Now. It was all he could do not to break out of the room and start running. Nausea rose acidly into his mouth. Somewhere far off the pleasant prospect of winter lay shattered. Ashily he stared and said:

'I'd rather talk it over now.'

He knew he meant 'Get it over now,' and she smiled.

'Sure?'

'Yes, yes,' he said. 'Now.'

'All right, dear. If that's how you feel.'

In silence she found another cigarette, lit it from the old one and then drew on it slowly. The whole process seemed to take minutes, during which he simply stared.

'Well, dear, it's like this.' With deliberation she blew smoke and watched it. 'There's three people to consider. Phoebe, the baby, and me. That right?'

'You?'

'Well, of course. I keep a public. I've got a name to think of. And who's going to look after the girl when the time comes?'

Yes: that was true. He saw that. That was fair.

'You want to be fair, don't you?' she said. 'You don't want to be mean or anything like that to anybody I hope, do you?'

'Oh! Good Heavens, no.'

He nearly said he wanted to be generous, he didn't want to hurt anybody, and that he was too fond of Phoebe to do a thing like that. But he simply felt sick again and she said: 'All right then. It all comes down to what you're going to offer.'

It was like a business proposition. It was cold and awful. Muddled and shocked, he found himself saying something about what had she in mind?

'It isn't what I have in mind,' she said. 'It's what *you* have in mind.'

He had nothing in mind; he started to say something about seeing everything right and she said:

'Yes, dear. But *how* right?'

Something made him say 'A hundred.' He meant to qualify it somehow, add to it, propose it perhaps as an instalment, but before he could go on she gave a dry sharp laugh.

'I don't think so, dear.'

Where was his cap? He had left it in the lobby somewhere. He had a wild idea of going out, grabbing it and starting to run.

'You'll have to think harder than that,' she said. 'Confinement. Doctors' bills. Phoebe off duty. Somebody extra to pay. The baby to feed and clothe and educate – don't you think one would do a lot better to think it over?'

'You say,' he said. 'You give me an idea.'

He felt beaten. He made the grotesque mistake of running his hands through his hair. Sweat had broken out coldly along the pores of his forehead. It was wet on his hands. He knew that it was not cowardice about Phoebe that was distressing him but cowardice about Mrs Corcoran. He knew it and knew, at the same time, there was nothing he could do.

Then quietly, with a look of oblique scorn, blowing smoke and flicking ash off her florid thigh with her ringed hand, she said:

'I'd got in mind something like a thousand.'

He had some fantastic impulse to strike her. As with Constance in those impossible moods of hers, the only solution seemed to be to bully her into sense. Women were like that. There were times when words were of no use at all.

Instead he began shouting. What he said was so incoherent that it sounded like a goat coughing.

She said simply:

'There's no need to lose your temper. The thing had much better be settled quietly. Otherwise there'll have to be solicitors and court-cases and orders and things in the papers. And in the end you'll have to pay anyway.'

He had the courage to say frigidly, 'I'll see my solicitor before I pay anything like that sum.'

She lit a third cigarette. Again she picked a shred of tobacco from her tongue.

'All right. They'll make a paternity order against you whatever you do,' she said. 'Of course I never said you should pay anything now. I wouldn't dream of that. The baby – well, one never knows, do they? Pay a hundred now. To help her.'

Some of his resolution had begun to come back. It was not much, but he said:

'I'd like to see Phoebe. I'll consider things a bit better after I've talked with her.'

'All right, dear, see Phoebe,' she said, and again she seemed to speak with calmness. 'I think she's in the garden somewhere.'

With angry relief he went out. He was overwrought and trembling. In the lobby he stopped to pick up his cap. His cigarette was out. He dropped it on the carpet and crushed it hard with his heel.

In distress he strode about at the back of the pub. The afternoon was fresh and sunny. In an effort to calm himself he blew his nose hard several times and wiped sweat from his forehead. He could not think. His mind was a mass of indecision, muddle, hopeless confusions, incomplete and groping ideas about being outwitted and cheated. But somehow, in the centre of it, it registered a single clear and amazing thing.

It was that the girl hated him. That was why, he thought, she had left the telling of it all to her mother. That was why she and her mother had, as he felt, hatched up a conspiracy. The pair of them despised him.

Presently he decided that if she hated him that was that. That was the end of it. He was well shut of it all. He would pay up. That was what fools had to do. Pay up and look pleasant and try to forget it all. But first, if that was the case, there were words to say to the girl.

With this one fixed thought in his mind he walked into the garden. It was a long garden, with a central path running between currant bushes and clumps of yellow chrysanthemums. He could smell the strong odour of the chrysanthemums as they shone there in the sun.

At first there was no sign of the girl. At the end of the garden a tree of late hard apples, like round grey-pink stones, gleamed on otherwise bare branches against a thin blue sky. Then he saw that she was sitting under the tree. She was sitting on a box sorting bruised and maggot-eaten apples from one skip to another. Her head was down. He saw the crown of her hair catching the slanting light of sun. In the air was a strong, mellow winy smell of apples. And beyond the garden, in the meadow where he had caught his fantastic trout, he could hear the already half-wintry whistle of snipe somewhere along the river above dry frosted reeds.

She looked up. He had nothing to say. He looked instinctively at her body and then at her face. The sun fell full on her face giving it some of the bland and mellow appearance of the apples she was sorting.

It was broad and soft with ripeness. It was full of a smooth and ageless tranquillity, the skin full blown. Women carrying children had always had about them, he thought, a repelling distortion. He had always been embarrassed by pregnant pinafores coming into the shop. They sent shivers down his spine. But until now he had never really looked at the faces. He had never noticed the expanding breadth, the mellow stretching of the flesh, the shininess and the beauty.

She started smiling and then got up. Before he could say anything she stood against him and he held her without a word. Her body was not big; he was able to hold her closely. And again her hair was like that of a fluffy animal, a fox-cub or a kitten, and his thoughts of her were entirely without hatred.

He said at last: 'I've fixed things with your mother all about – you know, the other business. There's no need to worry. Don't let's talk about it.'

'I'm glad,' she said. 'I didn't want to talk about it.'

'Why didn't you tell me before?'

'I didn't want to tell you before,' she said. 'What was the need? There was plenty of time. I didn't want to upset you.'

'And you don't hate me, do you?' he said.

'Hate you? Me?' she said. 'Why ever in the world would I hate you?'

Several times before going home that evening he looked at her face. She had always been a pretty girl but now, he thought, her face was full of a strange, dedicated, waxen sort of beauty. It was a queer thing, he thought, but he had seen something of that same waxen unearthly beauty on the faces of nuns.

Going home, letting the horse fall into a walk as he drove into a frosty yellow twilight, he spent a long time searching for a word to describe her face. He felt eventually that the word was transformed – and then decided no, transfigured. Transfiguration – he hadn't the slightest idea why he should go to such pains to think of that word, but it made him happy. It drove out, for the last time, all feeling of being cheated, that awful interview with Mrs Corcoran, and his thoughts of hatred. It put on all his thinking, which was never very rapid, a clear and embalming sort of hush. Somehow in his blundering way he had managed to work himself free of confusions. He had come out into the reality of a new experience, and did not know fully what it was.

He was even able to think about Constance. There had never been, and never would be, any question of transfiguration about Constance. Nor love: he knew that now. Better to face up to it. There was, and could be, no love, no transfiguration, nothing of that. He knew what love was now because, he thought, in spite of himself, Phoebe Corcoran had taught him.

All that remained now was to tell Constance so. He had always been honest. The fairest thing now was to go to her and, like the gentleman he hoped he was, tell the truth. There was a point in life when the kindest thing was to make a clean, clear cut.

That was what he would do: make the clean, clear cut. That, he thought, was the simple solution.

The following Sunday morning, after church, he walked as usual into the bar of The Prince of Orange. As he entered he raised his bowler hat. Carrie Waters reached for his tankard. And then, to her great surprise, he said, for perhaps the first time in twenty years, certainly for as long as she could remember:

'No. I don't think I will, Carrie. Give me a large Black and White instead.'

He took several gulps at the whisky. He made some remark about the air being a bit sharp after the frost that morning: very cold in church. He stood leaning against the bar, forgetting to tuck his little finger into his top waistcoat pocket.

Carrie Waters, who knew more about his life at that moment than he knew himself, made a pretence of polishing glasses and watched him closely. He had begun to know what it felt like not to sleep at night. His eyes were slow and baggy. She said:

'Feeling all right, Mr Melford?' hoping to draw him out, perhaps, on topics, that had been common gossip for six months or more. 'You look a bit dicky. Look as if you got a cold about you.'

No, he said, he was all right. He didn't know that he had a cold about him. He ordered another whisky and she said:

'You mustn't get a cold just as the season's starting. That'd never do.' And then, probing him again: 'Is it right that you're not going to be mayor again this year?'

Yes, that was right, he said.

'Well,' she said, 'I can't blame you. I'd rather it was your pocket than mine.' And then, in still another probe: 'Anyway, it'll give you more time to yourself. You could do with that, I expect, couldn't you?'

Yes, it took up your time, he said.

That was all she got out of him. He felt he could have managed another whisky, but he knew it would look conspicuous and suddenly he raised his hat and left the bar.

Ten minutes later he was sitting at the dining-room table. Constance sat at the other end. It was like any other Sunday of their married life, quiet, somehow sanctified by the silence of streets outside and the smell of roast beef inside, except that now, at last, he was about to tell her of Phoebe Corcoran. Why he had chosen to tell her at Sunday dinner he did not know.

Edna set the roast beef and Yorkshire pudding in front of him and he began to carve the beef. He liked the first outer cut of the meat himself and he set it aside. After that he carved two slices of underdone meat for Constance and put a piece of Yorkshire pudding with them and Edna took the plate down to her and served her with vegetables.

Then he served himself not with beef but with a piece of Yorkshire pudding. There was always that difference between them: that he preferred to eat his pudding first, separately, in the old Midland way. There was no doubt it tasted better that way.

This meant that Edna always had to go out of the room and then come back again. Sometimes he enjoyed the pudding so much that he took a second slice. In that way Constance had often finished her meat before he had even begun.

Today he took a second piece of pudding for the same reason that he had ordered a second whisky. He was nervous; his mouth felt raw and dry. He tried to make the pudding last as long as possible. But when the final yellow forkful had been put in his mouth there was nothing for it but to ring for Edna to come back.

Then when Edna came back he indulged in a few pointless

pleasantries. Edna was vague. She had a way of forgetting simple things like gravy-spoons and mustard. He liked to mystify her about these lapses by saying: 'Edna, Edna, haven't we forgotten something? Come now, where's that thinking cap?' – words he used practically every Sunday and which he used again today.

'I don't think so, sir.'

'Thinking cap, Edna, thinking cap.'

It was easy and amusing to have a girl confused, mystified, and blushing.

Today it was not much fun; it simply helped to postpone the moment when he would have to be alone with Constance to face the big staring eyes that had so troubled Agnes Twelvetree, and to make the clean, clear cut.

'Horse-radish, Edna, just the horse-radish.'

'Oh! I'm terribly sorry, sir – '

'That's all right, Edna. But beef without horse-radish is like – ' it was on the tip of his tongue to say 'a woman without a hat,' but he changed his mind and said, 'lamb without mint-sauce.'

Then there was nothing for it. He was alone with Constance. Blood was pouring from the beef on his plate. It was time to make the clean, clear cut.

'Constance – '

He made himself look up from his plate. Surrounded by the familiar and sanctified paraphernalia of roast beef, pudding, and horse-radish he felt in some way protected and insulated in what he had to say.

To his astonishment she was standing up.

She was folding her serviette, putting it into its ring. Her eyes were large and calm, with that peculiar distance about them that distressed him so much. He had a sudden feeling of being unfairly frustrated, of having somehow made a miscalculation, and said with a sense of injury:

'Where are you going? Couldn't you wait till I've finished?'

'I'm going to catch my bus.'

'Bus?'

He had never heard of Constance catching a bus in her life. He supposed she sometimes did, but certainly never on Sundays.

'Bus?' he said again. 'What bus?'

He thought she gave a contemptuous touch to her lips with the serviette before laying it on the table.

'The bus to Ferrywood. I'm going with Miss Mackness to see Hyde. She's been asking me to go all summer.'

'Hyde?' he said. 'Why on earth didn't you tell me? I'd have put a few things in a parcel for the chap. You might have told me.'

'Why?'

'Well, I don't know – I don't – well, you might have told me.'

'Oh?' she said. 'Must we start telling each other everything?' she said and he thought her voice was bitter.

'What time will you – '

'I've no idea,' she said. 'Does it matter?'

She went out. He stared at his plate, then finished his beef, mopping up the blood with potatoes. His eyes were dense and baffled. He had worked himself up to a pitch – and now there he was, cut short, frustrated. Mentally he groped about for a few moments. His thoughts were vague and stupid. It was a desperate business and now he would have to face it and begin all over again. Then he remembered that it was Sunday and that always on Sundays there was hot apple-pie and cream for dessert and he began to feel better.

The bus carrying Constance and Miss Mackness went southward. From the garden Constance had picked a bunch of salmon and bronze chrysanthemums, which Miss Mackness carried. She had brought a parcel of sweets and biscuits from the shop. Sharp November sunlight lay motionless on the countryside. Across the distances the fading frosted oaks looked not at all unlike great bronze clumps of shaggy cool chrysanthemums themselves.

It had been many months since she had last seen Hyde. But between them, though she knew nothing of it on her side, there existed a state of communion. Every Sunday morning she permitted Miss Mackness to gather flowers for Hyde from the garden; every Sunday afternoon Miss Mackness boarded her bus, rode out to the mental home in its pleasant landscape of birch and pine and presented the flowers to Hyde. 'From Mrs Turner, dear.' After that she talked and walked with him and occasionally held his hands.

As time went on he grew to expect the flowers. They expressed not only Mrs Turner; they expressed the outside world. In this way Mrs Turner began to stand for the outside world. And presently he began to brood on Constance as he had once brooded on Melford. In his solitary fashion he brooded far back on incidents that had troubled him at the time: a moment at Pollards' Mill when he and Miss Mackness had seen Constance and Frankie at the pool, another when they had seen them laughing in the snow, and still another when he had begun to shout it all at Melford on that fatal evening in the shop.

Gradually time and solitude began to magnify these things. It magnified especially the incident in the shop. What he had said that evening had become nebulous; he could not remember it perfectly. He was aware only, as he thought, of having wronged Mrs Turner. He had revealed things about her he had promised not to reveal. The substance of it all was vague. But gradually the reproach of it was sharpening, growing, persecuting him, filling him with brooding shame.

All the time he kept this to himself. He could not even speak of it to Miss Mackness, who walked in the grounds with him and spoke gently and held his hands. And every time the flowers came he was made to feel more impotently, more broodingly ashamed. He had wronged her; and now she gave him flowers. Instead of setting things right, he thought, it made things worse. In his darkest persecutions he wept for her.

'I haven't told him you're coming,' Miss Mackness said. 'I thought it would only excite him. He gets excited enough as it is at the thought of seeing me.'

Hyde, his skin like parchment, walked with the two women in the sunshine. At first, except that his mouth had fallen open into a surprised dark gap on seeing Constance and except that he wore a flat black cloth cap and that his face was slightly plumper, he looked like the Hyde of the shop. His thin, flinty mouth had never talked much. Now it simply fell open and, like his eyes, stared with a kind of barren politeness into the bright November afternoon.

'You see, the grounds are lovely,' Miss Mackness said. 'They have these big trees and all the lawns and places to walk in. In the summer they have sports and cricket matches. You have cricket, Jim, don't you?'

'Yes,' he said. 'Nice cricket.'

Inside the house, together with other visitors, they took tea with Hyde at a square unpolished table, drinking from plain white cups. Several times Hyde dropped crumbs of cake down his chin.

'He has new false teeth now,' Miss Mackness said. 'He's only had them ten days. He's not really used to them yet. You're not really used to them yet, are you?'

'What?'

'Your teeth – you're not really used to them yet, are you?'

'Not yet,' he said. 'I have to take them out a lot,' he said and made a gesture towards his mouth as if he were just thinking of doing so.

'No, not now,' she said. 'Get on with your tea now.' And then brightly to Constance: 'They get all that for nothing. All their teeth and everything. All for nothing.'

Several times when she looked up suddenly Constance found herself imprisoned by the triple stare of Hyde's eyes and mouth. When she surprised him like this the upper set of his loose new teeth dropped against the lower jaw with a chatter.

She felt strangely unnerved by Hyde. She realized how much he had changed. She felt as if she were waiting for an explosion. In a moment he would run at her and yell. In turn Hyde saw before him a pair of big brown eyes, expanded, fixed, constantly staring: staring, as he thought, reproachfully. Constance, unnerved and troubled, did not speak much. But he understood that. He knew why that was. He knew why she could only think unkindly towards him. It was because she had not forgotten, or forgiven him, the things he had said of her.

So he kept up the dark, speechless stare. And it was not until they were ready to come away that he tried suddenly to speak to her. He wanted to apologize for the things he had said, or felt he had said, that evening in the shop. But it was such an old, complicated business that he got no farther than saying 'Mrs Turner, I want to –' before the upper set of his dentures quivered and slipped with a snap. They hung loose for a moment before he sucked them back again. When he recovered there were big slow tears in his eyes.

'I think he was trying to thank you for the flowers,' Miss

Mackness said as they rode home in the bus. 'He's always very touched by the flowers.'

Constance did not answer. She stared unhappily out of the bus windows into darkness. She had seen a great, gnawing trouble in the face of Hyde. It haunted her. She did not know what to make of it. She only wished she had never gone to see the strange parchment figure, with its ill-fitting dentures, imprisoned with its cares.

She arrived home in a tense and brittle mood. Something made it seem imperative that she should speak to Melford. She found him in the sitting-room alone in the house, smoking his pipe before the fire. About him lay a scattered collection of half-burnt spills.

In the room only one standard lamp was switched on and she stood just outside the circle of its light. Her hands were dry and cold and she rubbed them tensely together.

'I had an idea,' she said, 'that you had something on your mind at dinner-time. If it was about the girl at Ascott St Mary I know already.'

Shocked and unprepared, he could only stare at the bowl of his pipe, then press hard down on it with his thumb.

'Don't think I blame you,' she said. 'I don't blame you. That's the last thing I want to do.'

He wished to God he could think of something to say.

'It isn't your fault,' she said. 'I don't blame you. I've known some time. It doesn't make any difference to me.'

She knew that, somehow, that day, between the episode at dinner and her impressions of the melancholy parchment face of Hyde, something had made a difference. Quite what it was she did not know yet, but suddenly she blurted out:

'I'm terribly sorry about it all. I'm really terribly sorry. More than I can say. I wish there was something –'

His pipe was out. He leaned forward and knocked it hard on the wooden fender. The sound startled her and stopped her from going on. Half-burnt tobacco fell all over the hearth and he said:

'As long as you know. That's the main thing. I've been trying to get down to telling you.'

As long as she knew. He could not see her face; he would not have dared to look at it if he could. Anyhow, somehow – as long as she knew. Well, she knew now. The worst was over. It was not quite the clean, clear cut, but she knew.

'Yes,' she said, 'as long as I know.'

He did not detect in her voice a note of repressed anger that made it seem almost chill and callous. He was too relieved for that. He had always feared some pointless, nagging exposure of their differences – what was called having it out. They had never had it out. Perhaps it would have been better if they had. But she was a difficult person to approach, to have it out with, and perhaps – well, the only decent thing now to do was to say that he, too, was sorry and then retire and get himself a whisky.

He began: 'All I can say is – ' and then she cut him short. She cut him short in a voice that was now, in its quiet way, hard and ruthless. He still did not notice its growing tightness of tone and she said:

'In the same way I suppose you know about me and Frankie. Everybody else does.'

Frankie? Who was Frankie? What Frankie? He had never heard of Frankie.

She had never wanted to tell about Frankie. That part of her life was locked away and enshrined. She did not want to share it. Over and over again she had determined not to tell of Frankie.

'Frankie who?'

Then, in the same chill and passionless way, she was telling about Frankie. She might have been reciting something from a directory at a post office. She seemed to strip it of all emotion. She made it seem a trite, ordinary, unimportant thing, something she might have done out of boredom, off-hand. That was her only way of keeping it to herself while telling it at the same time and she ended by saying:

'I can't tell you more than that. But I daresay everybody else can if you want to know.'

He did not speak; he did not want to know. Immense

buoyant relief was all he was capable of feeling. Except that he wanted his whisky. He wanted that very much and he made the mistake of saying:

'Well, as long as we know. As long as we both know.'

Her normally quiet voice raised itself with chill sharpness. Suddenly it was like the tearing rip of scissors.

'That's all it matters,' she said. 'That's all it means? We know? We both know. So long as we both know that's all that matters. You talk like a doctor!' Her voice was rising to a shout. 'What do you suppose is the matter with me?'

After all, he thought, there was going to be a scene. He picked up a pipe-cleaner and poked with it at the stem of his pipe. He still could not look at her and she shouted, hoarsely now:

'You'd be able to tell me if I was a horse, wouldn't you? You would tell me if I was a horse. Didn't you ever think of me as a horse? That might have helped us both. Do you think of Miss Corcoran as a horse? You should do,' she said, with new, jibing bitterness, 'then you'd know what it was to have one of those two-horse affairs on your hands!'

Half-blindly he prodded at the stem of his pipe, staring down. She came forward, distraught in the lamplight.

'Couldn't you even look at me while I talk?' she shouted. 'I believe if I stripped naked you couldn't even look at me could you?'

He heard something rip. It was actually the rip of her handkerchief, as she tore at it with both hands. For a single miserable moment he thought that she might be ripping at her clothes and he stared lower and lower and harder and harder at the pipe in his hand.

'Does Miss Corcoran strip naked?' she said. 'How do I compare? You wouldn't know, would you, because you've never seen me. I'm quite nice without my clothes. Wouldn't you like to see? I'm quite nice without them?'

'Steady, steady,' he said and again it was as if he were speaking to a horse. 'People will hear – people will be coming out of church.'

'Steady, steady!' she mocked. 'Church!' Her voice cracked in a shout. He did not know what to do. He could only suppose her nerves were breaking. 'Does Miss Corcoran stand steady? Good girl, stand steady!'

He was glad that neither Edna nor Mrs Butterworth were in the house. He jabbed blindly at the stem of his pipe. Then he heard her yell something about 'All I had was the sound of the sea – that's all I had for my wedding-night – sea-love, hours of it, tides of it, oceans of it, and wondering where you were,' and he could only think that she was finally beside herself, raving, beyond the bounds of coherence, quite mad.

'I wish Miss Corcoran luck,' she said. 'She needs it,' and added in the same breath, 'I saw Hyde today. He's changed. Sometimes I think I'm like Hyde – going off my head.'

'You're tired,' he said and gave another clumsy jab at his pipe-stem.

'And dirty,' she said. 'The bus was dirty. I'm going to get my bath.' Her voice lowered; it taunted him at its chill merciless new level. 'Wouldn't you like to see me? You've never seen me. I'm not bad, really. Come and see me. Come and see how the two of us compare.'

'I'm going to get a whisky.' He was shaking. He was quite incapable of dealing with so ruthless a situation. He thought he could hear voices on the square. People were coming out of church. They would hear her shouting. 'I wish you'd try to control – '

He turned with a gesture of reprimand. She had gone. Voices, as he feared, were growing louder on the square. With agitation he remembered that sometimes after church people dropped in – the Twelvetrees, somebody from the council, odd friends who were passing. He blew down his pipe-stem. The filter was clear now; he could light it up again.

He sat for a few minutes longer assembling his pipe, then filling it with tobacco. It was a terrible scene; he hated such scenes; he hoped there would never again be a scene like that. She had lost control. It was terrible to hear that shouting.

He had failed to detect in her voice any note of remorse or sorrow – something of the locked, gnawing sorrow she had first caught, that afternoon, in the face of Hyde. He had heard only the bitter taunts and the shouting. He was incapable of realizing that she might conceivably feel sorrow about it all, slow-brooded, haunting, devouring sorrow. That was beyond him.

'A horse,' was all he could think, 'as if I would compare her with a horse.'

A minute later he went out to get a fresh bottle of whisky from the little pantry across the passage where he kept his wines.

From upstairs he heard a door bang and then a shout. He looked up the well of the stairs. A single light was burning on the landing. Underneath it Constance was standing with nothing but a white bath towel round her body.

'Is that you?' she shouted. 'Have a look at me.'

While he was still staring she threw off the towel. The gesture of dropping the towel left her arms stiff in air. She stood quite naked, facing him. Her body, brown from sun, looked stiff and golden under the light of the single lamp. Her hair, let down and then tied sharply back for her bath, seemed to throw her entire face forward, aggravating the shadows of the large staring eyes.

'How do I compare?'

He tried to say something. He succeeded in giving only a choking grunt. At the same time he looked behind him. The stairs faced the door leading to the square. At any moment someone would be coming in without knocking and would see her there, naked and mad as a hatter at the head of the stairs.

A moment later she gave another shout. He looked up again to see that she had turned completely round. He was staring at her stiff forked legs, the soft round buttocks, perfect as a white half apple, and the back of her screwed-up hair.

'Now you've seen all of me. How do I compare? How does Miss Corcoran compare?'

Hardly had he begun to say 'For God's sake,' when she laughed again and turned round. Again her arms were stiff. The front of her body was thrown forward, full and young, unnaturally tensed, the breasts hard and divided.

'Don't look so shocked!' she shouted. 'No one will hurt you.'

She laughed again. Her arms sagged a little with the effort of laughter. And for a moment he was chilled by a terrible impression. It was also a grotesque impression: he was reminded suddenly of one of the church windows he stared at every Sunday beyond the altar. Standing there, naked, looking down, arms half-loose about her head, she looked to him, he thought, like a person crucified.

Next day she began to face life on the square in a state of deeper remorse. Her sorrows about everything came sweeping back, settling like an actual ache on her heart. Her mind was empty. In a way she could not explain she felt dispossessed of her true self. The woman she had been had been left behind somewhere, beyond Hyde, beyond the scene with Melford and the moment when she had stripped off her clothes. In that moment she felt she had done more than merely strip herself. After it she felt sere and spiritless, like a husk. What she had been was not there any more.

She also began, that morning, a new routine. She did not go down to breakfast. For the first time she did not sit at the big mahogany table, eat porridge, wonder if the bacon was crisp enough and listen to Melford praise, as he read of racing affairs at Epsom and Newmarket, the excellence of the ginger marmalade.

She was never, in fact, to go down to breakfast again. That morning she formed a permanent new habit. 'I don't feel quite myself,' she said to Mrs Butterworth. 'I don't want breakfast. You can bring me some soup at lunch-time.'

'You stay there,' Mrs Butterworth said. 'I would if I were you. It's dreadful foggy. There's nothing to get up for.'

She was not herself; there was nothing to get up for. Thin fog lay on the square. A lamp in a rose-pink shade burned by her bedside. She lay for a long time watching fog drift past her windows. At nine o'clock, when Melford came upstairs to clean his teeth and listen outside her door for some sound of movement, she was playing records.

At twelve o'clock she had chicken and soup with toast. The fog had lifted. A pale orange wintry light, from the thinnest of blue skies, lay across the chestnut trees. Music from the records had lulled her several times into a half sleep. She woke each time to find that the ache in her heart had not lifted. It was a dull, tenacious physical pain.

Just before two o'clock she got dressed, put on her winter coat and gloves and went out to meet Frankie. The extraordinary pain in her heart was still there. In the hall, as she went down-stairs, she met Melford. She did not speak; she stared past him. He looked at her as she came downstairs as if he too would never see quite the same person again, but only a naked, cruci-fied taunting woman standing in a nightmare of embarrassment at the top of the stairs.

'How do you feel?' he said. 'Any better?'

She walked past him, out of the house and into the square. It was not herself walking. The old impression that a strange amorphous creature was behaving for her grew stronger. As she walked away to the churchyard Agnes Twelvetree crossed dia-gonally the same corner of the square, thirty yards away, and waved her hand. Constance did not see her and did not answer.

She walked through the churchyard, out towards the country-side. She began to feel less empty and dispirited as she remem-bered that now, for a month or more, she had been seeing Frankie at a new meeting place that she herself had found.

Two miles to the north-west she had discovered a green lane that led, two hundred yards away, to a church that stood alone among big tense roundels of English yew. It was surrounded by tussocky pastures of arrow-head and ant-hills. When she had first discovered it, by accident, on a day in October, a few stray harebells still bloomed about the ant-hills and yellow crab-apples stared from the thinning hedgerows.

The church was squat, plain-windowed, and without a tower. High pine pews, of the kind where families worshipped in hassocked privacy, sometimes with foot-warmers, stood on either side of a nave flagged with tombstones. Services, she had dis-covered, were held on alternate Sundays. But the church was always open. Sparrows quarrelled in the porch and house-martins nested under the water gargoyles and the eaves. On all sides rough tussocky pastures folded away without a sign of another house, empty and silent except for sheep coughing on quiet misted autumn afternoons.

She did not grasp that this, with its black-green yews, its grave-stones, its air of being severed from the vain landscape of existence, might be a pathetic place for meeting: still more a pathetic, impossible place for love affairs. She failed to grasp that a man could possibly be bored by it all. She did not sense that precisely the things that appealed to her most – the silence, the isolation, the separation from ordinary living – might be the things that made Frankie Johnson most impatient.

'Let's find that grave-stone of Susannah Whitworth again' – by November he had seen that head-stone, with its inscription, its date of May 1796, something like a dozen times:

> *Under this sod*
> *A gentle creature lies:*
> *Susannah Whitworth,*
> *A score less three she dies.*
> *Look down, O! traveller,*
> *Upon this sod,*
> *And look You down*
> *From Heaven, upon her, God.*

Like her he found it pleasant to wonder, for a short time, who Susannah Whitworth, 'a score less three', might possibly have been. It was an idle and pleasant amusement, up there among the solitary quietness of the enormous yews, to speculate on whether she had been blonde or brunette, married or single, dull or vivacious, and why and how she had died.

'She must have come here. She must have walked about here. She probably sat in this same pew where we're sitting now.'

It did more than amuse her to try to pick up, as a woman picks up a dropped stitch at knitting, this link with a past. It excited her, extending her sense of wonder; it caused her presently to identify herself, at first without knowing it, with the gentle creature who had died. 'I get a feeling about her. You know that queer feeling? – that you've been somewhere and done something and been somebody before? That's how I feel about her.'

After the fourth and fifth time of hearing this, of staring as before a puzzle of heiroglyphics at the head-stone of 1796, he knew that he was not amused. He was not excited. Whatever else the stone did it did not extend his sense of wonder. It did nothing to make him suppose that it would have been better to be Susannah Whitworth, or her lover, if ever she had one, in the reign of George the Third, than it was to be Frankie Johnson, playing a piano in front of a cinema screen, the lover of a married woman, in the reign of George the Fifth. He certainly knew, if it came to the point, which of the two he preferred.

His life, he often thought, was not unlike a cinema screen. On the screen figures were larger, sharper, lighter than reality. That was like himself. He too was bigger, sharper than the general run of Orlingford's humdrum male existences. His secret affair with Constance was not unlike a film. He knew exactly the music he would play to it. Stealthy music, *pianissimo*, intensely tremulous; music searching, tender, and perhaps in a minor key – he remembered the first tremulous summer days by the mill-pond, her shyness, her remarkable eagerness, the way she had first undressed for him, her stammering confession that, although she was married, he was the first to give her love. He felt sometimes inclined to boast about that – who else could say what he could say?

'Dear Susannah. I've a queer feeling she came up here to meet somebody too.'

'More likely she was fat, anaemic, and died of a chill on the kidneys,' he said, 'I shouldn't wonder, up here.'

'Don't be scornful,' she said. 'You never know.'

'I know this,' he said, 'Susannah, with three off a score, is becoming a bit of a bore – '

'But don't you ever *feel* about people in that way, Frankie? Don't you ever get that strange feeling? – that sort of unearthly idea that you've been here, seen everything, and been through it all before?'

'Going through it once is quite enough.'

'And don't you ever get the idea that you'd like to be someone else? For a change? – to see how other people feel about things?'

'Being Frankie Johnson is as much as I can manage,' he said, 'and I make quite a good job of it too.'

'Vain,' she said. 'Vanity. Vain – that's what you are.'

'Who praises me if I don't?' he said. 'Nobody that I know.'

'I do.'

He said he'd bet she never mentioned his name to anyone in a month of Sundays. It was true too that she hardly ever spoke of him. But a queer look came over her face as she said:

'I'm always praising you. To myself, that is. You don't know how I praise you every night and thank God I've got you.'

He had nothing to say to that. She was, after all, always telling him what a wonderful person he was. Just as Lois was always telling him. It was odd, he thought, how it was always women who understood him best: far better than men. Constance, Lois, the pay-box girl at the cinema, Miss James, a short plump well-formed girl with bright blue eyes who displayed several flashy bracelets on her white arms in order to impress her customers. She too was always telling him. In love scenes he played Rachmaninoff and Mendelssohn specially for Miss James, knowing that she stood in darkness at the back of the cinema, behind the tenpenny seats, sobbing tears of grieving, melancholy joy.

Miss James, who also wore low-cut shirt blouses and long pearl-drop ear-rings and did her hair in a piled-up fashion so as to look taller than she was, had been engaged for several years to a respectable solid telephone operator on the night exchange. Every night he called to collect Miss James from the cinema before going on duty at ten o'clock. This did not prevent her from slipping down as often as possible to the artistes' room to kiss Frankie Johnson and tell him how wonderful his music was.

It was Miss James who had first started this sort of thing. It was no fault of his, he thought, if Miss James sometimes pursued him. He could not help it if girls got themselves engaged or married to men who subsequently did not excite them much. What was an impassioned, rather flashy little girl like Miss James doing with a solid night-exchange operator who wore a bowler hat? Between the telephone exchange and the semi-theatrical life of the cinema it was not surprising if Miss James grew bored and unsatisfied. Women wilted, like flowers, from lack of attentive nourishment; and he was not surprised that Miss James cried out, in sentimental Mendelssohnnic moods, for kisses in the artistes' room and on back-stage stairs.

He was young and good-looking too and they praised his music. 'That brilliant boy,' people said. With tears of inexpressible sentimentality in her eyes Miss James spoke of the piano, played by him, as 'fair talking'. She did not know how he could change so quickly from interpreting the moods of love to the stern thunders of fate, villainy, and revolver fire. He played with slick, dazzling improvisations. Miss James knew of people who came to watch films and yet were content to sit in darkness, with their eyes shut, simply listening to him.

'I often sit with my eyes shut too. I don't care about the film. I can *see* it all in the way you play.'

He seriously believed he could have achieved the conquest of Miss James some time before he did. Matinées on Thursdays and Saturdays left an interval between afternoon and evening performances of about an hour. It was hardly worth the trouble of going back to Schofield's music shop for tea. He generally joined the other fellows in the temperance café across the road, where they had tea and soft-boiled eggs with toast and talked of the afternoon's races and the results in the evening paper.

When Miss James surrendered to him on an autumn Thursday afternoon, in what had once been a dressing-room in days when the building was a variety theatre, she confessed she had surrendered to others before, but not to the telephone operator. She was eager also to know how life, in the shape of love, had treated him. He lied by confessing 'Oh! quite a few. You know,' speaking of conquests with married women that were unachieved.

'I believe you're an awful dog,' she said. 'All along I felt you were naughty. Married women – well, I'm near enough married too.'

After that excursion with Miss James it was natural, if only because she wished it, to go on to others. She encouraged him too in the invention and expansion of a myth. It was the myth that, in a mysterious way, he was a great destroyer of virtue, especially married virtue. He was a great hunter. Birds had fallen to him in great bags, as if from a punt-gun. He spoke of them all with casual vanity, always with that smile of his, telling Miss James, with truth, that none of them was like her. The notion of these experiences suited Miss James. For a girl who was on the short side, with rather dumpy legs and a fattish figure, it flattered her too that she was attractive enough to be counted among such conquests, one of whom, as she knew, was Mrs Turner, wife of the mayor.

And after Miss James he would go home to Lois. There is no

lover quite so complete in fanaticism as a blindly adoring sister and at home, behind the Schofield shop, another conquest was resumed. While Schofield went early to bed with charcoal tablets and hot peppermint and fought the pessimistic worms of dyspepsia knotted all over his stomach, Lois stayed up, kept the fire going and, at no matter what hour, cooked eggs-and-bacon and fresh tea for Frankie. There was no one like Frankie. She always wished she had been like Frankie. Frankie had the same brilliant eyes, the same hair, the same ever-ready smile as her father, who had died too early, leaving her with Aunt Johnson. She had greatly loved her father; and after all a major, a regular army major, was something of which to be proud. So in Frankie she saw, adored and clung tenaciously to the image of a man who, though she did not know it, had often promenaded the sea-front late on summer nights, looking with half-smiling disdainful invitation at the faces of women caught like butterflies in the pale net of their veils.

Then there was the piano. She had always wanted to play the piano. Aunt Johnson's choice for her of the violin had been a frustration and a catastrophe. She had grown up to hate the violin and in turn to envy all, especially Frankie, who played the piano. She believed, because of this, that Frankie could be great. With that brilliant ear, that amazing aptitude, she thought, there was no telling what, eventually, Frankie would do. Of course in a town like Orlingford no one could see that; not even Leo could see that. It was only she – more even than Frankie himself, she sometimes thought – who saw it, cherished it, and knew exactly what it signified.

All these things were part of a reason why, in his meeting with Constance on the afternoon when she had failed to speak to Agnes Twelvetree on the square, he was not really listening to what she had to say of Susannah Whitworth, who had died, a gentle creature, a hundred and thirty years before. Susannah was not a conquest; and nor, if it came to that, was Constance any more.

That was why too, a few weeks before, he had not been able to share her strange mystified mood about the phenomenon of a weathercock floating in the sky. He could never know that, in a way, he had died that afternoon. It was impossible for him to know that she, in some instinctive sort of way, had felt that she had lost him.

That was why, also, he had no conception, that afternoon, of the existence of any pain in her heart; and why, when he left her later, just as twilight was falling, he stepped out rapidly, almost running, with a feeling of being free, of having escaped her. He was growing a little impatient of love in autumn churchyards.

It was also why, less than two minutes later, when she came to go into the orchard at the back of the house, taking the short-cut through the garden, he failed to hear her scream.

Chapter Three

Hyde walked out of the mental home on Monday morning at eight o'clock. After the clear sunlight of Sunday it was very foggy. A thin white hoar frost edged all the grasses and the trees. On Monday mornings, Hyde always noticed, there was a certain air of flatness about the home. No one seemed properly alert after Sunday. Nurses groped about with sleep in their eyes. Consequently, at a few minutes past eight, no one saw him crush a slice of bread into his pocket, let himself out by a door above the furnace shoot and walk away into a belt of pines.

By ten o'clock he had reached a place called Black Top Bridge. The fog had lifted a little, but everywhere frost was still stiff on trees and grasses. He stood on the bridge, a big double-arched span of dark red brick, and looked at the railway track below. It was a double track, taking traffic from London to Manchester, Sheffield, and the north. From London it came up a long hard gradient of more than three miles, entering a tunnel of half a mile a few hundred yards beyond the bridge. On both sides were big woods, mostly old oak and ash with undergrowth of hazel, so that as the trains roared along the track the woods were full of shattering, sweeping echoes. Away up the track, northward, the two entrances of the tunnel were like the pupil-less eyes of a statue. That morning, in the fog, trains from the north shot out of them with bright, enlarging lights, giving them the uncanny quality of seeing eyes.

He knew the track and the woods very well. There was hardly a path and a riding he did not know. As a young man he had often stuffed a packet of bread and cheese into his pocket, much as he had done that morning, and taken his stick and called his terrier and walked the three miles from Orlingford to Black Top. He called his dog a tarrier; it rabbited very well.

In those days the woods were full of pheasants and foxes. Perhaps they still were. In spring they were thick with primroses and white anemones, to be followed by bluebells as lush as corn. In summer they were full of small wild strawberries, which spread, like the primroses, all down the railway-banks that by June were golden and white with broom and moon-daisy. You had to be careful of game-keepers, which was why he knew the tracks so well. He knew how to double back and recross his tracks and slip out and up the line. One day he had slipped the keepers only to find himself facing a ganger inspecting the line, but he had managed to climb over the top of the tunnel, where there was plenty of cover between the black brick ventilators and the seedling bushes of hawthorn and wild rose.

They were great days with the tarrier. There were no cars in those days. Only trains, people on foot and the lucky ones who rode. He thought nothing of walking twenty-five miles or thirty miles on a Sunday. The tarrier, the fresh air, the primroses, a rabbit bolting on a summer afternoon: part of his desolation rose from the fact that war had started to change such things. The woods, that morning, looked just the same as ever and in spring-time primroses would flower down all the cuttings, but he knew that it was not the same. He knew, quite rightly, that it would never be the same again. Passchendaele, for him at any rate, had left a cancer in the heart of it all.

Some time later, when the fog lifted and the sun began to come through in a thin November orange, he felt he was too conspicuous on the bridge. He slipped into the woods and sat down. Long before this he had taken out his teeth. They still hurt his gums a good deal. Now he put them in again and began to eat his bread, chewing slowly and reflectively.

As the fog lifted still more the air warmed with thin sunshine. Wet coppery oak leaves still hung on most of the trees but now, frost-freed, they fell almost continuously, but without sound, in the windless orange air. Nothing else moved except, after a time, a half-grown rabbit, and then another, which came out from under a clump of hazel root and sat quivering in broken sunlight, among falling leaves.

He did not feel lonely with the rabbits. He could almost persuade himself that he was back in the old days, in the good days, before the war. He wanted only the tarrier to complete the scene.

It was the thing, in those days, for every young chap to have a tarrier. What else had you to worry about once you had a stick, God's air, and a little dog?

He had never been lonely in those days. It was impossible to be lonely then in the way that he was lonely now. In the mental home he often sat grieving in the shadow of melancholy – though not grieving, as Miss Mackness might have been surprised to hear, for herself. He brooded on the absence of a dog. He had never forgotten seeing his first boxer in a Picardy farmhouse. He had seen it square up, deathless, strong as a lion, to a raging boar that had broken the door of a sty. It did not yield an inch. The boar, fanged and ugly, looked like a slobbering ogre that could not grasp the meaning of the spirit defying it. It had a heart forty times as big as itself, that dog.

So every Sunday, when Miss Mackness visited him, two things were on his mind: Constance Turner and his boxer. Somehow Miss Mackness, with the help of her mother and sister, managed to feed and exercise the dog. He asked her many questions about it every Sunday.

By contrast he had no questions about Constance. Partly because he could never remember exactly what he had shouted about her that evening in the shop, he had nothing to say except:

'Thank madam for the flowers. You'll thank madam for the flowers, won't you?'

He was more than overwhelmed by that weekly gift of flowers; it persecuted him with feelings of shame. He had wronged her and she gave him flowers. He could not fathom that. To that, throughout all his brooding for the rest of the week, he could find no answer.

Bad as this was, it become still worse on the Sunday she visited him. Week after week Miss Mackness brought him a scrapbook of gossip from the town: birth and death, accident and scandal, the fact that Melford was entangled with a girl at Ascott St Mary, gossip she had heard of Constance and Frankie. He listened to it all impersonally.

Then, that Sunday afternoon, he saw her face. It suddenly meant more to him than all the gossip in the world. He saw the unhappiness in the large, staring eyes. In almost the same way as she saw beyond his ill-fitting teeth to the darkest of his cares below he thought he saw her sorrow, her uncertainty, and her breaking grasp on things. He could see how greatly, uneasily, she had changed.

After she had left that afternoon he could not sleep. Just as he had brooded and persecuted himself about Melford he now began to brood and persecute himself about her. It became fixed in his mind, irretrievably, for the last time, that he was responsible for it all. He was to blame for that haunting change in her. If he'd kept his mouth shut, he thought, it would never have happened.

He spent the rest of the morning in the woods, watching the rabbits and an occasional bird, listening to the rush of expresses on the line, sucking the bread from his gums and trying to work out a way of seeing Constance without being seen.

About two o'clock he tried his teeth again. They were still uncomfortable. He wrapped them back in his handkerchief. Then he put them in his pocket and walked through the wood, parallel with the line, and out on the other side.

He knew a dozen cross-country cuts, by green lanes, footpaths, and cart-tracks, to Orlingford. By half past three he was in sight of the town. The colour of the dying afternoon was a soft salty blue, with a glow of darkening copper from mist about the sun. Flocks of starlings swished over empty fields, homing somewhere to woods in open country.

By four o'clock he had made up his mind. He had remembered Constance's walks in the afternoons. For a few minutes he waited about by the orchard gate. He was shaking all over. Repeatedly he gripped the teeth wrapped up in his pocket. After waiting for some time and thinking that she was not coming after all he suddenly had an idea of going through the orchard, into the yard at the back of the house, and somehow finding her there.

He had hardly walked a dozen yards under the apple trees when he heard the click of the orchard gate behind him. He turned and saw her come into the orchard, shutting the gate behind her.

He stood on the path. Toothless, hands loose at his sides, he suddenly felt overcome with helplessness. It was hard to remember what he was there for. He shuffled forward, opening

the dark gap of his mouth, and began to try to speak to her.
'Madam – '

She saw him and screamed. She put both hands to her mouth
almost at once, stiffling the scream to a short sharp yell. She was
struck by a double illusion: first that she was seeing Hyde and
then, a second later, that she was seeing a stranger. A second
later still she felt it was all a trick. In the darkening twilight
neither Hyde nor stranger was there.

The last she heard of him was the click of the side-gate as he
opened it and rushed through. She thought she heard him running through the churchyard. And then there was nothing: she
was alone in the orchard, mist gathering about the upper shape
of the church, a black curtain of starlings swishing over, a
hooter blowing a half past four shift down the valley.

'It couldn't have been,' she thought. 'It wasn't. I must be seeing things.'

Half an hour later Hyde had worked his way round the back-
gardens lined with gas-tarred fences at the back of the house
where Miss Mackness lived with her mother. Rows of outhouses
and hen-coops with roofs of corrugated iron lined the fences. He
climbed a fence, stood peering for a moment about the ash-paths
and then gave a short low call.

A few seconds later his boxer came out of its kennel. He
picked it up, lifted it over the fence and then climbed the fence
and began running, with the dog, out towards darkened fields.

Next morning, for the second time, Constance did not go
down to breakfast. Thicker fog covered the square and she lay
all morning, under the rose-pink lamp, staring at the windows.
She did not play her records. Her queer illusion about the
meeting with Hyde had never left her. She had told no one about
it: largely because there was, she thought, no one to tell. For a
day she had not exchanged a word with Melford. And Miss
Mackness – was there any point in alarming Miss Mackness?
She supposed people did sometimes get out of mental homes.
She supposed too that they were soon recaptured. Perhaps Hyde
was already back again. Perhaps, after all, it was an illusion;
she had never seen him; he had never been there.

At half past eleven, just as the fog was lifting a little, Melford burst suddenly into her bedroom without knocking. He looked white and scared.

'I'm sorry,' he said. 'But Miss Mackness is in a terrible track about something.' His agitation had forced him into using another of his local phrases. 'A terrible track. Hyde is out. Escaped. They're looking for him. It seems he was here yesterday – somebody saw him in the churchyard. He came for the dog, it seems.'

'Dog?'

'His boxer. It's gone. It seems that's what he came for.'

She got up, dressed quickly and went downstairs.

To her surprise Agnes Twelvetree, wearing a big grey boa-constrictor Scottish scarf and heavy leather driving gloves, was waiting in the hall. Her face was flushed with whisky and a touch of temper.

'Poor devil,' she said, 'they're after him like a rabbit.' Constance heard her swear shortly, crisply, and for the first time. 'Hordes of bloody men with sticks chasing about Black Top woods, looking for him. The bloody cowards. The brave heroes. Are you coming?'

'Where?'

'I'm going out to Black Top,' she said. 'I've got a flask of hot coffee and a bottle of whisky and some rugs. I'll bet none of them have thought of that.'

'I'll come,' she said.

'You think the Mackness girl would like to come?' Agnes Twelvetree said. 'Poor kid. It's like catching a stray kitten or something – he might know his friends. Always a good thing,' she added with her bluff acidity, 'to know your friends. Sometimes they're hard to recognize.'

'I'll ask her,' Constance said.

The strangest afternoon of her life began. With Miss Mackness sitting in the back seat and herself side by side with Agnes Twelvetree, she drove out into a still, blue afternoon of deepening mistiness across a leaf-brown countryside. Before driving away Agnes Twelvetree took several hard pulls at a whisky flask and said once:

'Well, if anyone had told me I'd ever be chasing across the countryside trying to find a man' – and then laughed with aggravated bitterness, stopping only because she realized that Miss Mackness was hardly in a mood to answer.

It was, in fact, only Agnes Twelvetree who talked as they drove along. Miss Mackness, nursing the first of her winter chills, gave adenoidal sniffs in the back of the car as if weeping, and kept her mouth in a scarf. Constance could think of nothing but her strange illusion about Hyde in the orchard, filled with fresh remorse because she had been too frightened to speak, to give him food or ask what he wanted.

'All this is my fault,' she thought and hardly heard Agnes Twelvetree say:

'It's like following hounds when you're not really on horse-back. You can get a free view without the expense and fag. All I can say is that my sympathies are with the fox. I hope he gets away.'

Tactlessly, whisky-free, Agnes Twelvetree drove with aban-don towards the woods at Black Top. On the bridge where Hyde had stopped to gaze at the gleaming eyes of south-bound trains a number of policemen, with onlookers leaning on bicycles and stray dogs and children, stood talking and peering down at the line.

Agnes Twelvetree stopped the car, leaned out and said:

'Any sign?'

'Not yet, madam,' a policeman said.

'When you find him I've got hot coffee,' she said. 'Don't forget.'

She drove on, slower now, through red-brown woods still dripping with mist. From Miss Mackness came a single suffo-cated sentence:

'We used to come here primrosing sometimes.'

Where the woods ended Agnes Twelvetree stopped the car, turned it round and assumed some of the attitude of a general. A rabbit bobbed from drying bracken in a ditch. After the car had stopped abruptly she got out and gave orders:

'You,' she said to Miss Mackness, 'can sit here and keep your eye on the road. I'm going to try that riding we passed back there. I saw a keeper's hut. He might be there. Constance, you try the footpath – the woods are so big you never know where he might be.'

'We saw young foxes here once,' Miss Mackness said in the same suffocated voice. 'Cubs. Little foxes.'

Constance began to walk in the woods. In a dripping half-mist, with occasional orange breaks of sun, the undergrowth looked as pale and delicate as stalks of giant cow-parsley. Leaves pattered down on leaves and among the leaves invisible pheasants walked with daintiness.

She walked for perhaps twenty minutes and then heard coughing. The mist had thickened. It was some time before she recognized the outline of Hyde sitting in a small hollow, by a pond, under the black-green of an enormous holly-bush, about which a bank was carved with fox-holes. He was twenty yards or so from the path, and the white boxer was curled on the floor of leaves at his side.

It sprang to its feet as she came closer. Hyde sprang up too, startled. His black cap gave his face the same flattened parchment look of unreality she had noticed on Sunday. His teeth were not in and his mouth dropped open darkly.

He stood shivering, either from fright or cold, perhaps both, and could not speak to her. He could only make some quivering motion with his hand towards the dog, which sat down promptly, laughing redly with its tongue.

'Hyde,' she said, 'Ada's here. Ada has come for you, Hyde – come and see her. She's come to look for you.'

He gave a strange twist of his head, so that she could not tell whether he was nodding or shaking it.

'Please, Hyde.'

Then she noticed something. He had actually found from somewhere among the leaf-covered roots a solitary autumn primrose. He had tucked it into the lapel of his jacket. It was still fresh and he had made a buttonhole of it with a leaf.

'I see you found a primrose.'

The dog licked itself. He looked down at the dog. She remembered Miss Mackness and her primroses.

'Ada told me you used to come here for primroses,' she said, but he did not answer. The same great blankness of care, on the surface almost negative and polite, covered his face: the same emptiness as she had seen on Sunday.

By now the mist had thickened, making the pond black,

cutting off everything but the nearest trees. There was no sign of sun. The air dripped moisture and presently she sat crouching under the holly-bush with Hyde, among the fox-holes, in the heart of a grey-white cloud on the edges of which birds walked with stealth on beds of leaves.

'Hyde. They've come to take you back home, Hyde. Aren't you hungry? Isn't your dog hungry?'

She heard a pheasant, far down another corner of the woods, give a chucking, choking cry as it prematurely settled to roost in the darkening afternoon. In a false twilight the tips of the trees dissolved upwards into cloud. In another hour or less it would be nightfall.

She suddenly felt uncannily and uneasily that Hyde and the dog and herself were quite alone, cut off, imprisoned in cloud. Leaving only primeval mist and the bone of dying branches, the world she knew had faded out.

She was not, however, afraid of Hyde. She felt, on the contrary, a strange sense of security. Once or twice she held his hands.

His hands were chilled. The veins were enlarged and rubbery. 'Hyde, it'll be dark soon. Miss Twelvetree brought us. She's got whisky and hot coffee in her car. You're cold – come and have hot coffee. Come and have a whisky.'

'I – '

He tried to speak for the first time. Toothlessly his mouth failed to frame the first syllables and he slobbered.

'Come and have a nice whisky.'

He was suddenly speaking with incoherence of some event in the past. It was hard to hear what he had to say. The vast mystery of his grievances, always impossible to set out rationally, had become tangled with the vaster reproaches that he had somehow been guilty of wronging Constance. She gathered, presently, that he was making some sort of apology for trying to meet her yesterday and she said:

'That's all right, Hyde. You just startled me that's all. I just wasn't expecting to see you there.'

He fingered the fleshy neck of the dog, not looking up.

'But I didn't tell anyone, Hyde,' she said. 'I didn't tell a soul. I knew you wouldn't want them to know you were there.'

Not quite with suspicion, but furtively, he looked up.

Another pheasant croaked. A trail of starlings went over, invisible above the tree-tops, lost in mist. Brown wet leaves suspended themselves in slow flight, dropping soundlessly.

'Shall we go back before it gets dark?' she said. 'Come along, Hyde, come back with me.'

She tried to take his hands again but suddenly he clawed them back, staring with hostility.

'You're going to tell them now though –'

'I'm not going to tell them.'

All about the black saplings the mist was a queer dead colour, darkly gleaming with wetness, and she had the sense to say:

'All right. You wait here and I'll fetch you a rug and some coffee. I didn't tell them yesterday, Hyde, and I won't tell them today. I know how you feel. You stay here and I'll fetch the coffee.'

He seemed to agree to that. He clung with both hands to the dog.

'I'll be a few moments. I think I'll find you again. I'll remember the holly tree.'

He stood up. His hands were shaking. Before she could move he seized her by the shoulders and began to blubber. Her head jerked upward as he shook her.

'You're not going. You stop here. Don't you go. Don't you move from here.'

Black saplings swayed in dead-coloured mist as her head rocked to and fro. She tried to scream. Another pheasant croaked on the edge of the woods, down towards the railway line. She felt her breath constrict and suddenly the woods were blacker.

For the next few moments his mouth was close to her face, yelling grotesquely. She tried to scream a second time. Then, for some reason, the boxer began barking.

Hyde looked round at the dog. A train roared through the cutting, filling the woods with echoes. The dog kept up its barking and suddenly Hyde's hands were loose on her neck and he was yelling at the dog:

'Shut up, blast you. Keep quiet, damn you, shut up!'

A moment later he bolted. He crashed away through saplings.

In a wood free of train echoes the dog rushed after him, barking joyously, as if away on adventure.

She stood for a moment or two, dazed and trembling, and then walked back to the road. Presently the wood was full of shouting men, running down towards the railway line, crashing through dark mist, with the bark of a dog to direct them.

And when, ten minutes later, she saw Hyde being frog-marched by two policemen along the road beyond Black Top bridge it was, as Agnes Twelvetree said, exactly like a fox-hunt, except that you didn't have the fag of riding and didn't have to pay.

Chapter Four

There was only one person to whom she could speak of all this. She could speak to neither Miss Mackness nor Agnes Twelvetree. But easily, without fear of impatience or ridicule, she knew she could speak to Frankie Johnson.

'You've heard people talk about facing death, haven't you?' she said. 'That's what happened that afternoon. I knew. It was the end and I knew. It was a terrible thing, Frankie.'

She was also able to explain her former feelings of hallucination: how she had felt, as Hyde came from the orchard, that she was crazy, that she must be seeing things.

He listened, as he always did with women, sympathetically. He was, with his soft reflective eyes and easy, ready smile, a good listener. Women liked talking of their troubles; they liked it when you listened. They took their troubles to heart in a way that men never did. They liked it when you gave them sympathy. And if you listened long enough they generally gave you, in return, the things you wanted.

That year winter came early. Presently, in December, there was a fall of snow. Earlier, in November, Melford had finished his year of office as mayor. He now had more time for hunting, for taking the waters at The Prince of Orange, going over to Ascott St Mary, or meeting people like Charles Edward Twelvetree and Foghorn Spencer at the Waverley Club, where you could play billiards, cards, or chess and finish up with cold suppers of ham and beef and a glass or two of port. By early December he had already hunted three times and had also formed a new habit of walking down to the Waverley Club four or five nights a week, staying until eleven, at which time the lamp-lighter had begun to put out the street lights, riding from lamp to lamp by bicycle, carrying his long pole. It was a pleasant sharp walk of ten minutes to the club. Big roaring coal-fires always burned in the rooms there and he was always sure of meeting friends. Sometimes he won four or five shillings at bridge or solo and then he greatly enjoyed the walk back through darkening streets, where one by one lamps were winking out and only a few late footsteps, like his own, made echoes on empty pavements or among the few last fallen leaves of limes.

His friends at the club never spoke to him of domestic affairs; it was tacitly understood that whatever happened at home or at Ascott St Mary was his own business. Nor was Constance ever mentioned; it would have been an embarrassment to men who had known him all his life to say anything of a woman who, as everyone now knew, never got up for breakfast, had her own bedroom and spent a lot of her time with a pianist: a fellow who, like herself, suffered from the stigma of not being Orlingford bred and born. There was a great difference, as everyone knew, between the rest of the world and people who were Orlingford bred and born.

Then, early that autumn, Melford began to be aware of a new face at the club. Tom Blackman was a bachelor of fifty who had come down from Staffordshire to breed and raise cattle on a five hundred acre farm between Orlingford and Ascott. On this strong heavy land, mostly of meadows richened by the silt of winter flooding, he was about to raise, as he claimed, the best cattle in England. He was a big man, with broad shoulders made to seem broader by ample jackets of best quality Highland tweed, thick as blankets, and mostly in wide herring-bones of an oatmeal shade flecked with tufts of brown and yellow. His voice, like his dress, was thick, homely, and loud. He wore small crushable tweed hats that made his long red face, with its restless blue eyes, seem unduly large, fleshy, and in some way warmly ferocious. He walked aggressively, rowing himself along with the single oar of a heavy polished thorn-stick, and in wet weather wore bright yellow gaiters with leather buttons and a weatherproof with wide cape shoulders.

Blackman worked with restless skill at making money. At the farm he kept open house, with plenty of meat, spirits, and beer, for whoever cared to drop in. Young pig was sometimes served whole for dinner, lambs were spitted to roast at the old-fashioned open kitchen fire, and his own sirloins were vast and of good quality. New friends like Melford could go and shoot there and be sure that pheasants would rise in droves from larch and hazel coverts; partridges and duck in generous numbers from the lower open land and the meadows; and perhaps snipe and woodcock from brown beds of naked osier by the riverside.

Blackman came into the club almost every evening, played tireless games of billiards and solo-whist, ordered thick sandwiches of fat ham, drank Dublin stout with them and made bets on everything. Men who had quietly played for many years with bets no larger than two shillings a rubber at bridge and a shilling a horse at cribbage now found themselves caught up with a man who waged in sovereigns and loved to bet on anything from the cut of a card to the number of pips in an orange. Unable or unwilling to bet, a few older, staider members dropped away, hid themselves in corners and read local evening papers. But others, especially younger men, liked Blackman. And what was losing a bet or two, even of a sovereign, when you could go over to Blackman's farm, any time, without invitation, and eat and drink your bellyful and come home with a brace of pheasants or perhaps half a sheep in a bag?

Unlike Melford's hunting acquaintances at Ascott St Mary, Rampling, Captain Whitling, and Beety Beeton, Blackman did not taunt Melford. He simply made him feel that his life had been humdrum, unadventurous, and hardly worth while. With shrewdness and ox-like vigour Blackman threw himself into the adventure of making money in a way that made Melford feel small and conservative to a point of timidity. He had never made a bet of a pound in his life. To see Blackman make a bet of five or ten pounds on the number of lumps of sugar in a basin or the turn of a card or a domino filled him with the same amazed and uneasy admiration he felt when, at circuses, he saw men swallow swords and fire.

He was amazed too by what he thought was Blackman's irresponsibility. He was dumbfounded by Blackman's frequent habit of suddenly getting up from a card table, asking the club-steward to telephone for a taxi and disappearing in five minutes, without apparent preparation, to catch the night express to Scotland. There Blackman bought pedigree cattle, prize bulls, or sold herds of his own, offering friendly proof of the profits by buying everyone unlimited drinks on his return less than two days later. In the same way he thought little of waking at one o'clock in the morning, cutting himself a few thick slices of his favourite ham from the pantry and then driving himself, by car, to the West Country, coming back the same evening to bet more heavily than usual with notes taken from fat crocodile wallets drawn with an open flourish and yet somehow without ostentation from inside the hairy, handsome tweeds.

There were men who dismissed Blackman as a dealer who did not farm; others sat back and waited for a crash. Melford simply admired. He could not help being attracted by a man who lived with so much vigour, so much fearless shrewdness and so much luck.

So, in a strange way, utterly unlike each other, the two men were drawn together. Perhaps because it took his mind from thoughts of Constance and Phoebe Corcoran, Melford found himself looking forward to evenings when he could play solo-whist or bridge with Blackman, drive out to the farm for supper or shoot over Blackman's fields on blue sharp winter afternoons. In the same way Blackman, perhaps because he saw in Melford's stiffish undemonstrative manners a certain quality he did not possess, found himself looking forward to meetings with Melford, especially late at night, when he liked to walk with Melford from the Waverley Club to the square.

Most evenings Blackman drank heavily but was never drunk. He seemed to need and absorb alcohol as another man might need and absorb sugar. Alcohol fired his body with vehement, even violent energy. Melford did not need alcohol. He drank for company. He drank like a good Englishman, with mild enjoyment, with restraint and because another man might take umbrage when drinks were refused.

As a result he was never really drunk either. Only, on the walks home at night, in the cold air, he experienced a feeling of being more expansive, a little bolder, not quite so cowed as he had been. A little more like Blackman, in fact, he sometimes thought.

'I hope you're not paying for that kid over at Ascott?' Blackman said.

The affair of Phoebe Corcoran was something very delicate.

It was never mentioned, in Melford's presence, by his friends. He supposed they all knew of it. He supposed too that they were too decent, too tactful to mention it.

'Never pay for kids,' Blackman said. 'Only Joe Muggs pay for kids.'

Always Blackman made life sound easy. He stripped it of doubts. Affairs like that of Phoebe Corcoran were trivialities to be flicked aside.

'You weren't the first, were you?' Blackman said. 'You bet you never were.' And when Melford seemed to hesitate: 'Well, good God, man didn't you *know*?'

Melford, who did not know and could only remember all his encounters with Phoebe Corcoran with what now seemed like soft-hearted affection, could only begin:

'Well, I – '

'Good God man, never worry about a thing like a kid. Women like it. They respect you for it. I had three up in Stafford. Different women. For all I know might have had more. I never paid a penny – damn it, they loved it. They still write to me. Send me Christmas cards.'

Melford, regarding his old self dubiously, was too diffident to mention that he had paid for the child already and Blackman struck him with heavy affection on the shoulder.

'Once you pay you're sunk,' he said. 'They stop looking up to you. Anyway they can always pin it on somebody else. They always find another mug.'

In the same broad bold way Blackman spoke of Frankie Johnson. The difficult painful entanglements of Constance became miraculously unravelled in Blackman's hands.

'Give him a bloody good hiding,' he said. 'And then go home and give her one. That'll cure it, man.'

Melford could not bring himself to contemplate these cold coarse remedies. The last thing he wanted in life was to exchange blows with a cinema piano-player, still less with Constance. At the same time he was fascinated. He half-wished he could be like Blackman, able to pick women like fruit, taste them with swift rough enjoyment and then throw them away like apple-cores.

On an evening in January snow was falling as they walked

home towards the square. Soft flakes floated in and out of the light of the few remaining street lamps.

In a few weeks the hunt would meet at Ascott St Mary. Melford remembered the big momentous snow of the year before. He remembered Phoebe Corcoran, whom he had not seen since Christmas, and he said:

'We don't want snow. That'll put the tin-hat on the Ascott meet. You'll like that meet, Tom. That's the best of the year.'

Suddenly Blackman stopped in the street and rattled his thorn-stick on a line of iron railings, shaped like spears, that enclosed a chapel yard.

'How many, Melford, how many?' he said. 'Spikes, man, spikes?' he said when Melford hesitated.

He rattled the railings a second time with the thorn-stick. Little flakes of snow were shaken dustily from the crests of the spears and the sound echoed about the dark chapel in the snowy night air.

'I lay you five to one there's not more than fifty. Under fifty – five to one.'

The fat crocodile wallet came swiftly from the folds of hairy tweed. Blackman counted out five pound notes with little snaps of his fingers.

'Money down, money down,' he said and in another moment Melford had put his own single note on top of Blackman's five, which he still held in his hand.

Blackman, laughing, spiked the notes on a spear of the railings. He laughed again and then strode to the end of the chapel-yard and spat.

'End to end,' he called. 'You start. Count from your end.'

Melford began counting the spears. He found himself laughing too. Across the street the figures of a home-going couple moved towards a corner street lamp, huddled arm in arm. Snow was blown from the sloping buttresses of the chapel in a sudden turn of wind and Blackman shouted:

'Come on, man, no whispering. Keep your voice up, man. How many?'

'Thirty-five, thirty-six – '

'Make it ten to one!' Blackman said. 'By God, it's close – it's close! It's going to be close – ten to one!'

His voice choked. Laughter echoed about the dark chapel. Blackman rattled his thorn-stick hard against the spikes and the iron gave out a singing frozen sound. The couple across the street paused under the street lamp. Lifting their faces, they gazed in curiosity through the dancing whirl of snow and Blackman shouted:

'Fifty-four, you lucky bastard. Fifty-four. You lucky old – Just beat me! Fifty-four.'

Blackman laughed again, his voice choking with excitement. He whipped the pound notes from the spike of railing as a butcher whips bills from a hook. The fat crocodile wallet came out of his pocket again and he paid out a second five pounds boldly and happily, his voice big and free with new gusts of laughter.

'And don't keep saying no! If I bet, damn it, I bet, don't I? Here, take it, man, take it – I'll get it off you some day.'

In the act of taking the notes Melford looked up and across the street. The two figures under the lamp-light were beginning to move across the road. They were now thirty or forty yards away.

Suddenly something in the half-inclined, sideways fashion the woman held her head seemed to him familiar. A moment later he recognized Constance and, too late, without knowing it, let his mouth fall open in surprise.

'What's up?' Blackman said. 'What are you staring at? Who are they?'

'Nobody. Come on – '

As the couple reached the opposite pavement Frankie Johnson stepped back, letting Constance go first, and then walked with her at the kerbside.

In that moment Blackman recognized Constance too. He gave a short whistle and gripped Melford by the arm.

'By God, is that him? In you go, man. What are you waiting for?'

'No, Tom,' Melford said, 'we don't want that.'

'Go in!' Blackman said. 'Get in there. Go after him. Pluck and truss the bastard.'

'I'd rather not.'

'You mean you're going to let them go? You catch 'em bloody red-handed and then let them go?'

'It's been going on a long time and I'd rather –'

'It wouldn't have gone on five minutes if you'd given him a damn good hiding. Go on, give him a good hiding and then go home and give her one too.'

'No, no, Tom, honestly.'

'Go home and slap her a few times,' Blackman said. 'She'll start thinking the world of you.'

'Stop chivying me, Tom,' Melford said. 'I'd rather leave it all alone.'

Head down, he deliberately fumbled with the money Blackman had thrust into his hand. When he looked up again Constance and Frankie Johnson had disappeared. Eleven o'clock started chiming from the church beyond the square and as the notes ended Blackman whipped the air with his thorn-stick and said:

'Pity. Damn pity that. I'd have lent you my stick to do the job with.'

The two men walked towards the square. Melford was relieved to see it empty except for Blackman's car parked under the chestnut trees.

Blackman laughed again and gripped his arm. 'Well, you've got to use your strength up on something, man. Come and help me swing the car.'

Snow was already falling in larger flakes. Already it was settling smooth and white on the open square. Melford, breathing with relief, sucked heavily at the sharp snow-fresh air. The idea of an encounter with Frankie Johnson had made him feel a little sick. He was glad it was over. He was not the man for that stuff. Like Schofield, he knew he hadn't the courage for that sort of thing. Some things were better left alone. He drew the line at fighting.

As Constance said good-bye to Frankie by the wall of the churchyard snow was falling in still thicker, larger flakes. He was not wearing a hat and she turned up the big collar of her winter coat and held him close inside it, shielding his face and hair.

'Whenever it snows,' she said, 'I remember the time you first kissed me. I always think of that.'

'Was it snowing?'

'I remember a big flake on my face,' she said. 'I remember looking up and saying you were not to.'

From the church steeple the clock struck a quarter. She lifted her face a fraction to listen to it. In the thickening snow the chime seemed slightly muffled. Every change of air affected the sound of chimes. In windy air, from the west, they had a rippled swinging sound. On crisp bright nights they seemed to split, cold and short, and sometimes in summer, especially in thundery weather, they had a slow, ripe, dying sound.

'And there's another thing I always think of when I hear that clock,' she said.

'What?'

'Honey.'

A spasm of hunger sharpened his irritation.

'Honey?'

'I read once how some bees made a hive in a church bell. For years. Then one day the bell wouldn't ring. There were sixty pounds of honey. I thought I told you once before?'

'You'd believe anything, wouldn't you?'

'But it's true,' she said. 'It's true, darling. I read it. It was in a paper. The sexton found sixty pounds of honey.'

'In the church tower? Very high?'

'Very high,' she said, 'in the church tower.'

'Another tall story,' he said.

She laughed and said how clever he was, so late at night, to make a joke like that. Then she stirred from under the big turned-up collar of her coat, lifting her face much as she had done when he first kissed her, and said:

'You must go now. You'll get cold without that hat. Will you come tomorrow?'

'Yes.'

'Whether it snows or not?'

'Yes.'

'Even if it's ten feet of snow?'

'Even if it's ten feet,' he said.

She lifted her face and kissed him. Snow fell on her face. One single cold fresh flake lay on her forehead and she said:

'I nearly forgot. There was something else I had to tell you.'

He did not answer. 'Don't you want to hear?'

'H'm.'

'I'm going to have a new dress for spring. A yellow one. Silk. I've been to Miss Wilcox's to be measured today.'

She did not notice that he did not really answer again and she went on:

'Do you remember I had yellow once before? I like yellow. But this is different. It's going to have small green cuffs and collar and a green belt and four or five buttons on the sleeves.'

'Sounds nice.'

'I've always liked yellow. I suddenly thought of it. The day before yesterday. Everything was so grey with that mist hanging everywhere and suddenly I thought how nice yellow was.'

'Yellow makes me think of eggs,' he said. 'Lois will be waiting up –'

'Oh! I'm sorry,' she said. 'Here I am talking. Drivelling on about my dress. But I wanted to tell you. I want to be fresh and nice for you, in something new, when the summer comes.'

Hungry, thinking of bacon and eggs, he took the short-cut back towards the square. He hurried, hoping Lois would be waiting up. She always cooked the eggs quickly, on a gas-ring, serving them straight on to the plate. They were better that way.

At the corner of the square he came upon Melford and Tom Blackman still trying to start the car. Blackman was cranking the starting handle while shouting instructions to Melford, who stood by the door, manipulating hand controls on the driving wheel.

Just in time Frankie thought he recognized Melford in the light of the side lamps. He turned direction quickly and crossed the road. At the same moment Blackman raised his head and called to Melford:

'We'll have to push the blasted thing, Melford. Here – we'll get that chap over there to give us a pound. If we can just get it to the hill –'

Melford turned too, in time to recognize Frankie Johnson. He muttered something swiftly to Blackman, who said, raising his voice:

'Oh! it's bloody Johnson, is it? Here Johnson, somebody wants a word with you – Johnson!'

Urgently Melford began saying, 'It's all right, Tom, it's all right,' but Blackman took no notice. He advanced several paces into the road, swinging the starting handle. His big rough tweed overcoat and his heavy gauntlet driving gloves made him seem cumbersome and threatening. He made another hostile swing with the starting handle and called:

'Hey, Johnson, come here a minute. Here, you're mummy's music-boy, come and face it. Somebody wants a word with you!'

'Tom!'

'Come on, music-boy. Don't be frightened. I'll give you the note, Johnson.'

He bent down and struck the starting handle on the road, thinly coated with snow.

'Tom, better stop that,' Melford said.

Blackman took no notice. Laughing, he struck the road again with the starting handle and called:

'B flat, Johnson. B flat – and bloody flat you'll be too if you don't look out.' He laughed and stamped his feet hard on the road several times, with the effect of running. 'Oh! don't run, music-boy. Don't run. Look at that, Melford. Music-boy's running.'

He stamped his feet several times again, laughing. Then he stood in the road, slapping one big gauntlet glove against his knee, and called:

'Steady, music-boy. Don't fall. Pick your feet up, music-boy. Don't run too fast now – '

Round the corner Frankie Johnson stopped running. He had run as casually as he could: not, he told himself, because he was afraid but because he wanted to avoid a scene and mostly because he hated jeering, mouthing men like Blackman. Like Melford he drew the line at fighting. It was simpler to get shut of big mouths like Blackman by running. It might look undignified but it was the simpler way.

Walking again, head down against the snow, he felt angry. He was angry at being called music-boy. He was angry that he should have taken the short cut back towards the square and have fallen into the trap of meeting Melford and Blackman. It riled him to be called music-boy. That was just the sort of taunt you would expect, as Lois always said, from a town like

Orlingford, where nobody had a scrap of superior feeling and where men like Blackman set the tone of things by jeering at people who did not share their hunting, shooting, coursing way of living.

He was angry too when he reached the Schofield shop and found the living-room empty and the gas turned low. There was no sign of Lois, who always waited up for him, and the fire had hardly a glimmer of life under its caking pile of slack.

He stamped snow from his boots. He shook it from his overcoat and then turned up the gas. From the back kitchen came sounds of someone stirring a spoon in a cup. He went into the kitchen and found Schofield, grey-faced in a grey dressing-gown, mixing a charcoal powder. A kettle was simmering on the gas-ring and two eggs and a packet of bacon lay ready for cooking beside a frying pan that had a thick daub of white fat on its rim.

'Where's Lois? Isn't Lois up?' he said.

'Her cold got worse,' Schofield said. 'She could hardly breathe. She was in bed by eight o'clock. She left your supper ready.'

'I've got to cook it myself, I suppose?'

Schofield did not answer. He set his cup on the table, pressing both fists into his body just below the ribs. He held his breath, pressing hard, and presently a great sour rush of wind belched up, noisily relieving his congestion.

'Don't mind me,' Frankie Johnson said. 'Be sick all over me if you feel like it.'

Grey and drawn with pain, Schofield could not prevent a second rush of wind from belching up.

'That's right!' Johnson said. 'Be sick. Come closer.'

Schofield's mouth began trembling.

'I been trying for nearly two hours to get that up,' he said. 'Do you know what it's like?' – he beat his body with both fists – 'to have it sticking there? Like a lump of lead? Hour after hour? Gnawing? What the devil's the matter with you?'

'I'm hungry, that's what.'

'Then cook your supper and eat it and stop maundering and go to bed.'

'Who's maundering? I come home tired and hungry –'

263

'Hungry? Hungry?' Schofield said. 'I wish I knew what it was like. Hungry? – I never wanted a bite all day.'

'That's your funeral,' Johnson said.

The two men stood in the centre of the little kitchen, glaring. Then Frankie Johnson turned up the gas-ring. Forks of blue flame shot up about the kettle. He took the kettle off and slammed the frying pan down on the ring. Flames sprang in a flat circular fan about the edges and Schofield rushed forward, seizing the pan, and said:

'What do you think you're doing? You want to set the place on fire?'

'I'm trying,' Johnson said, 'to cook my supper.'

'You couldn't cook pussy. You couldn't cook water. Turn the gas down unless you want to get the fat a-fire.'

'Fat a-fire,' Johnson said. 'Fat a-fire. I've got to get the fat started, haven't I?'

'Give it me for God's sake,' Schofield said, 'before the place goes up. Go and sit down. I'll do it. Go and sit down.'

He seized the frying pan, turned the gas low and stood over the stove. He said again that Johnson couldn't cook pussy and the answer was quick, affronted, in anger:

'I'm a pianist, not a skivvy. You don't expect me to do everything, do you?'

'Pianist?' Schofield said. 'Pianist. You never will be.'

'No? I'll say this – I can show you round when the day comes.'

'You never will be,' Schofield said. Fat was smoking blue in the pan. He had wanted to say it for a long time. They had quarrelled often but he had never managed to say, with quite the precise finality he desired, what he wanted to say. 'Never. You never will be.'

He threw three slices of bacon in the pan. The rashers hissed and began to curl. Schofield stuck a fork into one of them and said:

'One thing – you never practise. Another thing, it comes too easy. You never had to bother. And another thing – I'll tell you another thing.'

'What?'

Schofield broke first one egg and then another into the pan, beside the curling rashers of bacon. He was calmer now. By the tiniest fraction he turned down the gas. He was altogether calmer. Now, at last, he was saying what he wanted to say.

'You've got no ear.'

'Thanks for telling me. Thanks. Nice of you. No ear, my God ! – '

'Your eggs are ready,' Schofield said. 'Go and sit down. The bread's there. Cut yourself some bread.'

He slid eggs and bacon from the pan to a plate. He carried the plate calmly – above all he wanted to keep his calmness now – into the living-room, setting the plate in front of Frankie Johnson.

'You've got no ear. This.' He tapped his left ear with a finger. 'That's what.'

'Go to bed. You'll get belly-ache again.'

'Listen,' Schofield said. He went over to the piano. Hiding the keys with his body, he struck a note. 'Now – tell me what that is.'

Frankie Johnson, eating bacon and eggs, did not answer.

'Go on.' Schofield struck the same note a second time. 'Tell me.'

'E flat.'

'Natural, natural, natural ! E natural !' He struck the note repeatedly, turning, not shielding the keyboard now. 'Look – look for yourself – look. See ? There it is – natural, natural.'

'You're talking about pitch, you damn fool – pitch ! – perfect pitch, not ear ! E natural – egg natural – what the devil's that got to do with it ?'

'All you think about,' Schofield said, 'is stuffing. Lounging about. Reading the papers in bed. Slopping round. Four hours' work a day.'

'It suits me,' Frankie Johnson said. 'Why should you crib ?'

'I don't crib. I'm not cribbing.' Schofield took off his spectacles, breathed on them and then polished them for a few seconds before putting them back. Then he looked steadily through them at Frankie Johnson. Now with his spectacles perfectly clear, he felt calmer than ever in what he wanted to say. 'I'm not cribbing. I'm telling you.'

'What ? Go to bed. Have a sleep. You'll feel better.'

'Are the eggs nice?' Schofield said. 'I hope so. Because they're about the last you're going to eat here.'

'How's that?'

'You're going. You're packing your bags,' Schofield said.

'Oh?' Johnson said. 'That's news. Does Lois know?'

'Lois knows,' Schofield said. 'I told her. That's why she went to bed. I told her. We had a bit of an up-and-a-downer. You never paid her, did you?'

Frankie Johnson, head close over his plate, mopped bread into egg and bacon fat as if preoccupied.

'Did you?'

'She said – '

'Never mind what she said. You never paid. No wonder my guts are bad. No wonder I never get rid of it. No wonder I slave and never get anywhere. I didn't find out till today. You've been dishing me, haven't you?'

'That's your look-out – '

Schofield reached out and gripped the bread-knife. He held it point outwards, towards Frankie Johnson. For a moment or two his calm snapped. Behind his spectacles his eyes seemed distorted. He saw a pair of open yellow lips mopped by final crusts of bread and the pale habitually smiling face of Frankie Johnson held stiff by fright, in the glare of his own hatred.

'Here, put that knife down. Go on – put it down before you do some damage.'

Schofield put the knife down. His calm was back. He was glad it was back and he smiled.

'Finished your eggs?' he said. 'Then get up to bed. You'll want some sleep. Your train goes at half-past seven. Lois has packed your bag.'

'Oh?' Frankie Johnson actually smiled. 'Really? I'll go when I like and how I like – '

Schofield gripped the bread-knife for a second time.

'If you're here when I get down to breakfast,' he said, 'I'll cut you.'

Unsmiling, he made a single brisk gesture with the knife before putting it down. Inside him the sour gases were gathering again, tightening into pain. In spite of them he managed to retain his calm, speaking steadily, without anger, for the last time.

'Get to bed,' he said. 'Get your sleep and get out before I do something I'm sorry for. You had a good run, Frankie. But it's over now. Everything comes to an end.'

Chapter Five

A sudden turn of wind in the night brought rain. By morning the streets were clear of snow. By afternoon, when Constance walked out across the town, wearing a bunch of violets, the sun had dried the paths, the grass and even the soil in the public gardens. The violets had been grown by Britton, in a frame. He brought her fresh bunches every four or five days or so and now she wore them, as always, upside down.

On the seat where she usually met Frankie Johnson an oldish man sat playing at rolling a ball to a child. The ball was bright red. The sun shone on flower beds cut into the grass, revealing the first leaves of daffodils.

Perhaps twenty times in half an hour the oldish man rolled the ball along the path for the child. Sometimes he rolled it with his hand. Sometimes he pushed it with his foot or struck it with his stick. His hair fell in short stiff white curls from under a bowler hat. The child, a boy, ran on soft dumpy legs, pin-toed, to fetch the ball, laughing sometimes and dropping it. On the face of the oldish man was a look of contentment. His eyes were blue. Transparently they reflected a world where, for ever, he could go on happily rolling a ball for a child to bring back to him.

She sat watching this for some time and then walked away. She was afraid to walk too far. It was easy to walk down one path, hidden by rhododendron bushes, and miss a person coming along another.

By three o'clock she was back at the seat again. The ball rolled past her feet, red in the sun. The child cried out with wordless noises, stooping to catch it. In the act of picking it up he caught it with his foot, kicking it out of reach again. His wordless noises became laughter. The ball ran on and he could not catch it. He stood in doubt, puzzled, large-eyed, watching it run faster and faster away from him until finally the man, as if training a puppy:

'After it, Peter. After it now.'

She sat down. She stared at the sun on the grass and on the unexpected premature shoots of daffodils. Presently the child brought back the ball. He clutched it to his chest with two hands. His cheeks too were like a ball in the sun.

As he approached and, in the final moment, looked first at the man and then at herself, he put the ball in her lap. She smiled down at him. In reply he made wordless murmurs that she did not understand. The man touched his hat, translating these murmurs, saying:

'I think he wants you to throw it, ma'am.'

She stooped, rolling the ball gently along the path. The child crowed with pleasure and ran after it on wobbling feet. He caught the ball quickly and brought it back, putting it in her lap, resting his hands on her knees and looking up at her.

She smiled again and threw the ball. Again he brought it back and again she rolled it away. Then after this had happened several times the man said:

'No, Peter. Not to the lady. You mustn't bother the lady.'

The man reached out, taking the ball from her lap. A great change came over the face of the child. A cloud seemed to settle on the shining red cheeks and the large shining eyes. His mouth quivered and the man said:

'Oh! Oh! Here, here. Dropping your lip. That'll never do.'

'Let me throw it,' she said.

Again she threw the ball. The child broke into a choking crow of laughter. He ran down the path in the sun and she sat staring at her empty hands in her lap, thinking of Frankie Johnson.

Suddenly the man said:

'It's quite like spring. Funny how it changes so quickly. Last night I thought we were in for a deep one. And now look at it. You can fair feel the sun.'

She said 'Yes,' staring up the path. Nothing moved except the red bouncing ball, the running child and a sparrow or two pecking at grass beyond. In the sun, after the brief snow, the grass seemed intensely green. Snow-washed, it seemed to have a sharp and painful brightness and the man said:

'We're not out of it yet though. We've a long way to go yet. Get March here and we might begin talking.'

The child brought back the ball. As it rested in her lap he fixed his eyes on her in solemn admiration. His lips made noises, lengthily, and the man said:

'He's quite taken to you. He's trying to make a speech or something.'

'Can he talk?'

'Not yet. He makes himself understood though. It's easy to understand him when you know.'

'What is he trying to say?'

'What is it, Peter?' the man said. 'What does Peter want? What's Peter trying to say?'

The child put one hand into hers. He made new, more urgent noises, pressing her hand.

'I think he wants you to go for a walk with him,' the man said. 'No, Peter, no. The lady doesn't want to walk. No, Peter. No. The lady wants to sit in the sun.'

As the man made these remarks the lips of the child began trembling again. The wide eyes became clouded. The man said, 'Here, here. This will never do,' and suddenly Constance said: 'I'll take him. I'd like to walk a little way.'

Slowly, with the child, she walked about the paths. The sun was perceptibly warm on her face and almost too warm on her gloved hands. Beyond the rhododendrons, somewhere high up in the branches of willows, a thrush was singing. The red ball ran shining across the extraordinarily bright green grass dispersing flocks of sparrows. The sky had almost cleared itself of cloud and was now a pale mild blue, so that it was almost impossible to believe that the year was not later than it was.

Walking back, she took off her gloves. The palms of her hands were sweating. She was afraid of betraying her nervous anxiety, but quickly she looked at her watch. It was almost a quarter to four.

Something made her shake the watch once or twice and then listen to it. The child saw these actions and made noises of his own and came to listen too. At the same time the sun became partially hidden by the westerly branches of the willows. The shadow cast on the grass was broken up, lacily, and for the first time there was a hint of coolness in the air.

At intervals, all the way back to the seat, the child stopped to put his ear to her watch. Occasionally he laughed out loud, almost like an echo of the thrush, shrill and sweetly. At the seat the man said:

'I can see he's found your watch. That'll keep you busy. You've started something now.'

Time, she suddenly felt, did not matter. As she sat down on the seat, holding the ball in her lap, letting the child listen to her watch, she was aware only of a single dark gnawing impression. She had a curious premonition of disaster.

'You can keep him quiet for hours with a watch,' the man said. 'No, Peter, no. Not the lady's flowers.'

The child, tiring unexpectedly of the watch, stretched up to touch her violets. Making new noises, he fingered the stuff of her coat below the flowers. The man started to reprimand him gently again but she said:

'He wants to smell them, that's all. There' – she lowered the lapel of her coat so that the nose of the child could reach the violets – 'you can smell them now.'

The child pressed his nose upward to the violets, giving a kind of whispered sneeze.

'That's his way of smelling,' the man said.

The child drew his face back and gazed at the flowers, which seemed to fascinate or trouble him. His face grew solemn as he looked at the suspended purple heads, his eyes puckered.

'I got an idea he's wondering,' the man said, 'why they're upside down.'

Before she could speak the child made a sudden snatch at the flowers. Two or three violet heads were pulled from the loosened bunch, clenched tight in his fingers. The man made noises of dismay and got up suddenly and said:

'Peter, Peter. That's wicked. That's naughty. Peter, what did you do?'

The child made minute gestures of defiance with the violets, his lips taut.

'Peter, that's very very naughty. Peter – I think we'd better go home now. Come along, Peter, it's time to go home.'

Defiant, giving a short wilful toss of his head, the child made a second grab at the violets.

'Peter ! – '

'It's all right,' Constance said. 'I'm going to give them to him. He wants to have them, that's all.'

'No, no,' the man said. 'No. Not after that. Not after he's been so naughty.'

'Oh ! yes. I want him to have them,' she said.

'He doesn't deserve it,' the man said. 'He deserves a good smack-bottom, that's what he deserves.'

'There,' she said.

She unpinned her flowers. The boy held out both hands.

'Can you carry them ?' she said. 'Hold them tightly, won't you ? Don't drop them now.'

'It's really more than he deserves,' the man said. 'Those nice violets. It's really too good of you. Now say "Thank you",' he said sternly. 'Say "thank you" to the lady. He can say "thank you" in his way.'

The child made bubbling noises, smiling at the same time. Then he pressed his nose to the flowers and smiled a second time. A moment later the man picked up the red ball, which had fallen on the path behind the seat, and then raised his hat and said :

'Say good-bye to the lady now, Peter. Come along now. It's time to go now. Perhaps you'll see the lady another day.'

The child made a little gesture of farewell with his hands. One or two violets fell from the bunch. She stooped and picked them up and said :

'Now don't drop them. Take care of them, won't you ? Put them in water. Good-bye.'

'Good-bye,' the man said. 'Good afternoon. It's very kind of you to give him the flowers.'

She sat down. Fifteen or twenty yards up the path she saw the child turn and make an attempt to wave his hand. A few more violets fell from the bunch. The man raised his hat for the second time and then, because the child was not walking fast enough, picked him up in his arms and carried him away.

She sat there for some time longer. The sun went down. The grass lost its rare, snow-washed brilliance. In a gathering twilight of grey tawny light the thrush continued singing, grey-brown itself on the high grey willow branches.

She knew, all the time, that there was no point in sitting there. Her hands had stopped sweating; she simply struggled with the cold renewed premonition that something had gone wrong disastrously.

While it was still light she got up and walked away. Unconsciously, almost from the first step, she fell into her old habit of walking with her head down. As a result she saw, every few yards along the path, occasional violets that had fallen from the bunch she had given to the child.

She started to pick them up. Soon, almost without knowing it, she had retrieved half the flowers she had given away. Once or twice she actually ran forward, glad to be able to find them again. She was glad too that they were still fresh, not dusty, and that the scent was still rich and strong.

From some distance away a park-keeper, starting his round of shutting the gates at sunset, watched her walking, running, stooping and picking up some object from the path. He could not see what these objects were. He had heard his wife say from time to time how odd Mrs Melford Turner was, how strangely she was known to behave. Now he could see for himself how strange she was.

As she went out of the gardens, stooping to pick up the last of the violets, she reminded him more than anything else, he thought, of men who had come back from war with shrapnel in their heads, their balance disturbed: the lost ones, the shell-shocked, the harmless ones, the ones who, half-demented, could only half-remember.

He had them in the gardens in the summer sometimes. They too talked to themselves and ran about the grass, picking up objects no one else could see. They made friends with birds and, as he had often seen, talked earnestly to space, telling their troubles to flowers.

Soon after seven o'clock that evening she stood in the Schofield shop. She had to wait for some minutes, as she always did, before anyone answered the bell. While she stood there the gas blubbered in its mantle above her head and a grey Schofield cat played with a length of pink tape someone had tied round a bundle of sheet music and left on top of a piano. The feet of the cat skidded occasionally on the polished surface of the piano, scratching it gently.

It was Lois Schofield who, after some minutes, answered the bell.

'Oh,' she said. Seeing Constance, she remained aloof, standing on top of the stairs. 'How do you do.'

The cat scratched at the smooth surface of the piano with its paws.

'I wondered – ' Constance fell instantly into her habit of pulling at the fingers of her gloves. 'Mrs Schofield – I wondered – is Frankie here?'

Mrs Schofield remained standing at the top of the stairs. Except for the sound of gas plopping in the mantle and the scratching of cat's' paws there was no sound in the room for several seconds.

'We were going for a walk this afternoon.' Constance stretched the fingers of her gloves nervously without knowing it. 'I think we must have missed each other – '

'I'm afraid Frankie's not here. He's in London.'

'In London? He didn't say – '

'It was very urgent. He went suddenly. This morning. First thing.'

The cat, playing with the pink tape that tied the sheets of music together, made a sudden feint with its paws, almost falling from the piano. Mrs Schofield said in sharp scolding tones:

'Miss – Mitzy – get off there.'

Constance said: 'What time is he coming back? What train? I might go down to meet him.'

'Mitzy – Miss – will you get off there!'

The cat rolled on to its side, showing leaden pads, and Constance, looking quickly from it to the top of the stairs, became aware that Lois Schofield, in contrast to her usual habit, had never smiled. Both she and Frankie had that same habit of the ready smile. Now the absence of it gave her face, with its cup of smooth-brushed yellow hair, a certain cool hostility.

'He isn't coming back,' she said.

'Not today?'

'Mitzy, will you do as you're told and get off there?' She glared at the cat, which swayed the stalk of its tail. 'Miss!'

The cat sat upright, quiet, and began to wash itself. Constance said again:

'Not today? You mean not today?'

'Not at all.'

It was as if someone had slit off her hands. She suddenly could not feel any sensation of life in her fingers. Then she realized that she had pulled so nervously at the fingers of her gloves that all ten of them were stretched out, like those of a scarecrow, dead and empty.

She made some hasty attempt to pull on her gloves again and Mrs Schofield said:

'He had to make up his mind very quickly. There was no time – '

'Why?'

'It was something he had to decide about very quickly.'

'Yes, but – I saw him yesterday. He didn't say a word. Why? He didn't tell me.'

In spite of herself Lois Schofield smiled.

'How could he tell you? He didn't know himself till late last night.' It was as if she had said 'Why should he tell you?' and Constance, without knowing it, started to pull at the fingers of her gloves again.

'You mean he's not coming back here?'

'I shouldn't think so for a minute. Not with the job he's got now.'

The cat began to play again with the tape that bound the sheet music. Its paws scratched at the french polish of the piano. The gas leapt and bobbed. The mantle seemed to choke suddenly, giving off greenish licks of fire.

'I didn't even know he was looking for another job.'

'Oh! didn't you? He's been looking for some time. Several weeks.'

'He never told me.'

For the second time Lois Schofield smiled.

'I'm afraid I can't help it if he didn't tell you everything.'

'But you would have thought – '

'Would I? Mitzy, get down there. I don't think I would. After all it was his own private affair.'

'Private?'

For the first time Lois Schofield came down the steps. She crossed to the piano and, standing there, gave the cat a light cuff with one hand.

'You didn't expect him to stay here for ever?' she said. 'Did you? Not with his talent? Not in a town like this?'

'He never talked to me of going away.'

'Well, perhaps not to you.'

The cat made a dart for the tape again, scratching the piano-lid. Lois Schofield cuffed it sharply.

'Haven't you an address?'

'No, we haven't.' Something about the word 'we' seemed more hostile than Lois Schofield's way of standing on the steps, her voice or her scolding hisses to the cat on the piano. 'I don't suppose we will have, either. Not until he gets settled in rooms somewhere.'

'Where is the job?'

'That we're not sure about either. It may be in London. It may be anywhere. It's in one of a chain of dance bands.'

She came forward and, as if interested suddenly only in the practical matter of giving the shop more light, reached up to adjust the gas-mantle. The cat, free again, made spasmodic darts at the tape and somehow pulled it untied. With a flap the rolled music sprang open and the cat made fisticuffs at white uncurling pages.

'This wretched light.'

Lois Schofield tugged at the chains controlling the gas-light. The attempt to give a better light was not successful. Under it her face appeared a metallic yellow-green.

'Would you mind if I – ' Pulling at the fingers of her gloves Constance stood aside while Mrs Schofield fiddled again with the light. For a moment the shop went dark, then sprang harshly into full light again.

'Mind if what?'

'I was going to say would you mind if I – well, one day if I came in perhaps you might have an address?'

'Well, you can come in. Yes.'

The cat complicated itself in futile struggles with the tape, so that half the sheet music slid from the piano. With a sudden dart Lois Schofield went after it, rolling up a sheet or two of music and hitting it fiercely about the ears.

'What with one thing and another! Cats! First one thing and then another – !'

The cat leapt down from the piano. It rubbed along the counter, making noises like grating whispers, unwanted.

'Would you mind if I asked you one more question?'

The fingers of Constance's gloves stuck out again. Nervously she had dragged every one of them into the shape of a thin black bean.

'What question?'

'You know that Frankie and I' – it was so difficult to explain this simple, obvious thing that she could not even look up. Instead she kept her eyes on the cat, rubbing its body along the foot of the counter. 'We've known each other all this time. It was much more than knowing each other. You knew that, didn't you?'

'I knew you were friends of a sort.'

'Oh! More than that. More than friends.' It was growing more and more difficult to explain a fact of such obviousness that she was overcome with a sense of ridicule and pain. 'I would have given – It was like – '

Mrs Schofield began packing up the sheet music on the piano-top. She found the pink tape and neatly, rather snappily, tied the sheets together.

'I think if you want my honest opinion Frankie had stayed in this town quite long enough,' she said. 'He'd stayed so long in this town he was beginning to be like it.'

The gas began to blob again and Constance did not answer.

'After all what could it ever be for a boy like Frankie but a dead-end?' Lois Schofield said. 'He'd got his life to think of.'

Constance did not look up. It was impossible to explain all the long complicated phases of her life since the day when, blown across the churchyard in the summer air, she had been tricked into thinking the church was falling down.

'Good night,' she said. The words were hardly audible above

the blubbing of the gas-mantle and the sudden calling of a child from the back of the shop.

'Good night, Mrs Turner.'

As unconsciously as Constance had dragged at the fingers of her gloves, Mrs Schofield smiled.

Constance lifted the catch of the door. The bell rang and she went out. The street was dry and cold. She walked some distance along the pavement before, behind her, she heard the bell ring a second time. She turned and looked back. Half-hopefully she expected to see Mrs Schofield there, perhaps with some word she had forgotten. But it was only the cat, thrown out, landing on soft feet in the gutter.

She walked on. The fingers of her gloves stuck out emptily and she did not notice them. The cat walked behind her in the gutter. Soon she pulled so hard at one of her gloves that it came off and she dropped it. The moving object falling to the pavement attracted the cat, which sprang forward to play with the glove and then rubbed its body against her legs, soft as air, before she could pick the glove up again.

'What do you want, Mitzy?' she said. 'The glove?' Unthinkingly, still walking, she spoke aloud. Without knowing it she began talking to the cat, and then the air, as her friend. 'The glove? Is that what you wanted?'

She threw the glove forward on to the pavement, so that the cat could run and pounce on it as if it were a scrap of prey.

'Mitzy, Mitzy – not that way,' she said. 'This way if you're going to come with me.'

Alone except for the cat she walked across the town, staring into the darkness, throwing her glove in front of her.

Chapter Six

The afternoon was dry and clear when Melford drove out, a week later, to The George and Crown. It was almost, he thought, like a March day. Occasional whirls of dust went spinning along the roads. In some fields winter corn was high enough to make loose flags that waved in the wind. On distant copses the buds were smoky red. It was the sort of day, he thought, when you might expect to turn a corner and come upon the first naked flowers of coltsfoot, yellow by heaps of roadside stone.

It was time once again to make his arrangements for the meet at Ascott St Mary.

He drove on for a mile or two and then, giving the horse a blow and a drink at Staughton, where a brook ran over the road, he heard behind him the honking of a motor-horn. He reined his horse tight and turned to see Blackman, well muffled in brown ulster, yellow plaid scarf and a cap with ear-flaps, driving an open touring car.

'When are you going to sell that damn thing and get something that goes?' Blackman called. 'Where are you bound for?'

'Ascott. I'm going to fix up my room there. For the meet. I always stay at The George and Crown.'

'Stay with me!' Blackman said.

'No,' Melford said. 'Thanks just the same, Tom. But that's what I always do. It's become a regular thing with me. I wouldn't think of Ascott any other way. They make me very comfortable.'

'You could bring the girl over!' Blackman said.

'Well, now hold on,' Melford said. 'I draw the line –'

Blackman rudely blew the motor-horn. Melford pulled his horse to the side of the road and Blackman, honking again, drove slowly through the water-shoot. Above the noise of the engine and the lap of wheels in water he called:

'How long are you going to be over there?'

'I may stay the night,' Melford said.

'Good,' Blackman said. 'I'm going to Huntingdon to see a man about a bunch of bullocks. I'll call in on my way back.'

'Huntingdon?' In his restriction Melford still measured all distances by the capacities of the horse. He supposed that Huntingdon was all of seventy miles, there and back, and he said incredulously: 'But you'll never do it, man. Not by dark.'

'I'll be back by six. And I'll probably drop in at St Ives as well,' he said, 'to see the man with seven wives. Lucky man. One a day. Save me a treble Black and White!'

Melford drove on into a crisp, March-like afternoon, glad of Blackman. He almost seemed, with Blackman, to break free of himself. With Blackman he felt he might be able to face more serenely, with less embarrassment, men like Rampling and Beety Beeton, if they should happen to be there. He would also be able to show Blackman his trout. He thought of his trout not only with pride but with a certain sense of mild defiance. The trout, he always thought, proved that he could do things.

At The George and Crown, in the garden at the back of the pub, Mrs Corcoran was pegging washing on the line. She seemed to come forward with some haste, he thought, as he tied up his horse in the pub-yard.

'Did you get my message?' she said. 'I've been trying to ring you since two o'clock.'

'Ring me?'

Her face was a curious yellow-grey colour. Her eyes were snail-like objects, bulging and bagged. She was not the Mrs Corcoran, he thought, who had suavely and calmly bullied him on an autumn afternoon.

'Is something wrong?'

'Phoebe's been naughty. She's been very naughty,' she said.

The word naughty, he thought, seemed a curious one.

'I hope nothing's wrong?'

'She was out on her bicycle. Two days ago. No, three. I've had such a packet I can't remember.'

In the face of physical crisis he felt hopeless. His throat went tight and cold.

'She was taking a hill too fast. She lost her head and had a fall. I told her not to go. Now there's been a little trouble.'

All the time her eyes, snail-like, the skin yellowish underneath, did not look at him. And suddenly, he did not know why, he felt that he did not believe a word.

'I didn't even know she rode a bicycle.'

'Oh! sometimes. It's Bertha's really. The girl I got in to help behind the bar.'

'But is it serious? Is she all right? What's the matter?'

Mrs Corcoran licked her lips. They were dry and flaky and she licked them again.

'She's in bed. She's rather poorly.'

'What about a doctor? Did you get the doctor?'

She licked her lips again. Her protuberant yellowish eyes failed to focus him.

'The doctor's with her now.'

He followed her into the pub. The queer stale old-beer smell of the bar, closed for the afternoon, hung about everything as he walked through. Mrs Corcoran went into her parlour-office, reappearing with a cigarette in her hands, blowing smoke-clouds.

'Have one?' She handed him a packet. He had hardly time to refuse before she said: 'Oh! my God, I've run out.' She left him to go to the bar, coming back several moments later with a fresh packet of cigarettes from which she was tearing the wrappings. 'I don't know where I am. I've been on my feet all night.'

He had not time to answer this before the doctor came downstairs. A little man, with a curious brown wooden-like skull, completely hairless except for comb-like fringes of grey above the ears. His manner hard and brusque; his grey eyes darting at Melford.

'I'd like a word with you alone, Mrs Corcoran.'

He spoke with a strong Scottish accent. He stared with hostility at Melford.

'Oh! it's all right, doctor. This is – this' – she hesitated a second time and licked her lips – 'this is Phoebe's friend.'

The doctor looked contemptuously into Melford's face and walked away.

Mrs Corcoran led the way into her office and the doctor

closed the door. Cold and sick, Melford walked up and down the entrance hall. He wished he had taken one of Mrs Corcoran's cigarettes. He walked into the lounge. The fire was almost out in the grate. His trout, lips pouted in its glass case, hung above the fireplace. He stared at it for some minutes and a voice said:

'I'd like a word with you, sir, if you dinna mind.'

He turned to see the doctor. The brown hairless skull was extraordinarily monkey-like. The eyes were scornful, almost hypnotically keen.

'I understand you're responsible for this lassie's condition?'

Melford did not speak. He felt that a man like Blackman would have said: 'And what the hell is that to do with you? What the hell if I am?' but he was incapable of any kind of answer. His mouth fell open; he made a gesture with his hands, palms upward, and the doctor said:

'How long has this girl been ill?'

'I understood – '

'What is this story about a bicycle?'

'Well, I – '

The doctor waited. He kept fixed on Melford a glare of contemptuous respect.

'I just arrived. This is the first – '

'You just arrived? When do you mean – just?'

'This minute. I had no idea – '

The mouth in the brown skull snapped open. The bark that came out was so rough, Melford thought, that it was almost indecent.

'If I thought there was any kind of – '

He broke off. He held Melford for some seconds longer in a glare. Suddenly he gave up. He screwed up his eyes and went to the fireplace. He peered at the case with the fish in it, emitted another bark and said:

'A trout? Where did a trout come from in these parts? Who caught that, I wonder?'

'I did.'

'Oh! ye did?' He turned, fixing Melford with the same monkey-like scornful glare. 'Then it's a pity for your own peace of mind you didn't stick to your fishing.'

He went out. Cold air swept in from an opened door. The

doctor was already in the yard outside before Melford rushed after him.

'How ill is she? Could you tell me how ill she is?'

'I canna say. I'll be back tonight,' the doctor said and walked away.

Back in the parlour-office Melford found Mrs Corcoran. Her eyes, screwed up under cigarette smoke, seemed more baggy, more snail-like than ever. Her cigarette was dying rapidly to its tip. Holding it quivering in her mouth, she lit another from it and then let the first drop on the carpet, crushing it with her shoe.

'Did she fall from the bicycle?' he said. 'Was it the bicycle?'

She said 'Yes' and then 'I told you' and again she would not look at him.

'Is it – ?' He was helpless. Certain words were difficult to frame and he gave it up. 'What is it? Did she – '

'She lost the baby,' Mrs Corcoran said. 'Two days ago.'

The only rational thing he could think of was to walk in the garden. Before he went she said, 'I'm sorry you can't see her. Not yet. She's too ill. Not until the doctor says so.'

He wanted to strike her. He remembered the afternoon when, with chilly calm, she had first frightened him. Now she was frightened. Her eyes were miserable and yellow. She was going to pieces and could not face him. He stood over her and felt himself shaking and said:

'What happened? What have you done to her?'

She gave a dry blubber, then coughed. He actually struck her across the shoulder. She stared and staggered a little, but to his surprise she made no protest. She seemed almost glad. Then he struck her a second time. Her cigarette jolted from her mouth and she did not bother to pick it up and he said:

'What have you done to her? Tell me! – tell me what I can do.' A moment later he had his first practical thought. 'I'll ring the hospital. I'll get Bedford. That's the nearest. I'll ring the hospital.'

'Not the hospital. Not hospital. Please.'

A terror of hospitals set Mrs Corcoran weeping. She wept with ugliness, without restraint, her face buried in her hands. Suddenly he felt sorry for her, then sorry for what he had done. He tried to express it by helping her to a chair. She sat down as if unaware of it and then, after staring at her for a moment, helpless again, he went out to telephone.

The telephone was in the passage. It was fixed to a wall, with a handle that turned and a receiver that required pressure on the grip before transmission could be heard. He forgot the pressure. For a quarter of an hour or more the line was without a sound.

He gave it up and walked in the garden. It was cooler now; the greenish western sky gave signs of frost in the air. When he came back he tried to telephone again. Instinctively he remembered the pressure. The bell tinkled several times and Mrs Corcoran put her head out of the office door and said: 'You shouldn't get the hospital – not without telling the doctor. The right thing is to tell the doctor.'

'You think I can wait about here for doctors?' he said. 'Damn the doctor!'

It was half past five, quite dark, by the time he talked to the hospital. Already, by then, he was sorry for his second outburst. He talked with morose, frightened politeness. The hospital wanted the name of the doctor in charge of the case and he had no notion what it was.

'Hang on a minute,' he said. 'Hang on.'

Mrs Corcoran was not in her office. He heard sounds, however, in the bar, and went in to find a girl with bobbed black hair filing her nails as she sat behind the bar. The sound of the file on her nails made his blood run cold.

'Gillespie,' she told him in answer to his question. 'Dr Gillespie.'

'Gillespie!' he shouted into the receiver and heard no answer. Then he remembered the pressure again. He gripped hard and a voice said, 'Is it an emergency?' and suddenly he found himself saying:

'Of course it's an emergency. Can't you hear? This is Mr Melford Turner speaking.' And when there was no response: 'Melford Turner. The former Mayor of Orlingford.'

Almost punctually at six o'clock Blackman arrived.

'Ah! good. Splendid. Already standing them up,' he said. 'Heads or tails? Winner pays.'

He slapped a coin on the bar, keeping his hand on it.

'Don't losers usually pay?' Melford said.

'Winners this time,' Blackman said. 'Same in the end. It evens up.'

'Tails.'

'Heads it is. I pay. Two double Black-and-Whites, Miss. And what's for yourself?' he said.

'Thank you, sir,' she said. 'I think I need one, now you come to say.'

Before there was any chance of explaining this Blackman said:

'And where's this whale, Melford? The trout you're always talking about?'

Drink in hand, Melford led Blackman into the lounge to contemplate the trout. The fish, he thought, did not seem so large now as he had always imagined.

'Tom,' he said. 'Tom. Listen – there's been a bit of bother here.'

He tried to tell, as simply as possible, and with words that he thought would strike Blackman as being undistracted, what had happened that afternoon.

'You see,' Blackman said, 'what I told you. Never bother about kids. They only lead to trouble. Never hang on where kids are concerned.'

'Tom, she's very ill. They'll let nobody see her.'

'Come back and have dinner with me,' Blackman said. 'There's pheasant tonight.'

'I'll get dinner here. They'll give me dinner,' Melford said.

He remembered the pleasant dinners he had been accustomed to eat there. First the dinners of Mrs Duncan. Then the dinners of Phoebe and her mother. He remembered the excellent apple-tarts, the lamb and red-currant jelly, the potatoes with their flavour of nutmeg.

'You're coming home with me,' Blackman said. 'We'll get half a dozen more stingers down us and you'll feel better.'

'I've got to stay here, Tom. I'd never forgive myself if I didn't stay here.'

They had several more drinks, paying for them by the same process of spinning a coin on the bar, winner paying, and then the telephone rang.

The girl from the bar answered it and then came back from the passage to say:

'It's for you, Mr Turner, sir.'

As he picked up the receiver he forgot again, in the first second or so, to press it with his hand. Then he pressed it and suddenly a voice gave a crackling bark:

'Hello! Gillespie here. If the former Mayor of Orlingford has time to listen I have something of importance to say to him. Is that the former Mayor of Orlingford? Listen, sir, will ye? I must request you not to interfere with the course of my professional duty by ringing hospitals for my patients –'

'I thought it was *my* duty.'

'Duty? Ye have no duty!' the voice barked. 'Your one and only duty is to keep out of the way, mind your own business and make yourself as scarce as possible before I come back there. A course of action you might have done well to adopt six months ago.'

'I thought I was acting for the best.'

The voice barked on for some time, in harsh Scottish accents, about the danger and folly of acting for the best and then added:

'I trust you've not been in to see my patient?'

'I have not. I wish I had.'

'Ye'll wish nothing of the kind!' the voice barked. 'Do you hear? I will tell ye when you can see her. And it'll not be today, I warn you, it'll not be today.'

At the other end of the line the receiver came down with a crash. He felt suddenly cold and ill, with sweating hands.

He was glad to go home with Blackman. At the farm Blackman had a housekeeper, a Mrs Brawne, who cooked almost a good a soufflé, in this case of pineapple, as Agnes Twelvetree ever made. The pheasants, with their accompaniment of brussel sprouts and wafer potatoes, were excellent too, and so were the macaroons that were served with the soufflé. He ate rather fast, out of strain and nervousness, drinking several glasses of claret with the meal, and Blackman said:

'You see, old man, you were hungry. You can face it now. That's if there's anything to face. Which I doubt. Women are tough. And after all there's no kid to worry about now. That's all over. You can put that out of your head.'

That was the one thing, he told himself, he could not put out of his head. Under the influence of another glass or two of claret he might forget it temporarily, but inside himself, far down, he felt there were already the gnawing aching beginnings of a long and desolate woe.

'I tell you what,' Blackman said. 'I've got a solution.' He could not help wishing again that he lived as well and easily as Blackman, with such a flow of careless solutions. 'We'll ring the pub. The doctor will have been by now. You needn't ring. Mrs Brawne will do it for you.'

Still at the dinner table, Blackman rang for Mrs Brawne.

'Mrs Brawne, will you be good enough to ring The George and Crown at Ascott. Give Mrs Corcoran Mr Turner's compliments and ask very kindly how her daughter is. Be sure to speak with Mrs Corcoran. And, Mrs Brawne – Mr Turner says that the soufflé was the best he ever tasted.'

Ten minutes later Mrs Brawne reappeared in the dining-room to say:

'The girl is fairly comfortable, sir. No worse and no better. And Mrs Corcoran's compliments, sir, and will Mr Turner be spending the night there?'

'No,' Blackman said. 'He'll be spending it here. Get a bed ready for him, Mrs Brawne, will you? Thank you.'

When Mrs Brawne had gone Blackman said: 'You see? Never meet trouble half-way. Sleep on it. Have a glass of port. Let's have several glasses of port. We'll both feel better.'

'Tom,' Melford said with deep feeling. 'You've been wonderfully decent and kind to me.'

After playing billiards for an hour or more, always betting on the result and even on things like how long a ball would take to run, he went to bed at midnight.

A three-quarter moon was shining. There was sharp white frost in the air. He drew the curtains but the moon shone through them starkly, keeping him awake. And lying awake he thought of Phoebe Corcoran. At first his thoughts were heavy and congealed. He had never been able to sort out a crisis, especially where women were concerned, with directness or simplicity – just the opposite of Blackman, to whom solutions came as easy as putting a wager on a fly.

As a result he thought of Phoebe Corcoran in a series of pictures. He remembered her as she had been a year before, when snow had bound him to Ascott for a week and she had talked to him at nights, in the rosy light of his bedroom fire; and then the afternoons, the spring, when he had visited her and she lay and looked up at him from the bed, an animal snug in the heart of a nest; and then the summer, in the garden at the back of the pub, along the stream, in the meadows, with his little bits of local history, his fishing and his trout that was such a triumph; and then at last the day when he had first seen a change in her face, his first awakening to the fact that, like a blown flower, she was no longer merely pretty but mature and beautiful, wonderfully transformed.

Lonely and starkly awake and agitated, he realized how he had been happy with her: exactly as he was with Pilfer or Brandy or any other horse. She had never been exacting. They had never had an argument or a cross word or a discussion about anything. He hadn't the brains for it anyway but she had never even teased him, as some people did, into arguments he could not sustain. She had simply been warm and soft and unexacting: an animal to be played with, to grow fond of, to leave alone and then play with another time.

At five o'clock he got up and dressed. He carried his shoes downstairs, putting them on in the big stone porch of the farm-house. It was four miles from the farm to Ascott and the moon was still not down as he started walking there.

It was after six when he arrived at The George and Crown. Every grass and twig and hedge-tip was thick and white, like new candle-wick. In ditches the dead weeds of winter, cow-parsley and dock and strigs of thistle, were skeletons of hoar.

In one of the bedrooms above the pub a light was burning. In the pub yard stood the open Renault the doctor used. He tried the kitchen door, went inside the house and stood on the cold stone flags, listening. There was no sound of voices. Overhead only a board creaked and then, after a long silence, another.

He came out again and stood in the yard. Behind the pub, over the low lip of hill, all white with frost, day was breaking under layers of cloud. He walked about, cold, feeling nothing for about half an hour, until part of the cloud was pink and the frost in half daylight, stark and bristling everywhere.

In exactly a week the hunt would be meeting. He remembered Brandy. It was some comfort to know that Brandy had been taken good care of by Brown. He was cheered to think he had Brandy, that he was not alone after all.

He had just removed the staple of the half-door in the horse-box, the words 'Brandy, are you there, Brandy boy?' actually on his lips, when he heard the kitchen door open and shut again.

Across the yard, in the white frosty air, the monkey skull of Gillespie, in the moment before he put on a thick felt hat, seemed browner and bonier than ever.

'Doctor. Doctor Gillespie.' He actually ran the twenty or thirty yards across the yard. 'I hoped I should catch you.'

The doctor stood by the Renault, drawing on a pair of thick sheep-skin driving gloves, turning up the collar of his coat.

'How are things, doctor? How is she?'

The doctor bent over the driving seat and found the starting handle. Melford thought he looked at him with the same brusque contempt as yesterday.

'Ye can go up to her now,' he said. 'Ye'll not disturb her now.'

The doctor fixed the starting handle into its socket under the bonnet and gave it a preliminary turn.

'I've signed the certificate,' he said. The voice was almost pious; the manner half-ecclesiastical. 'I am quite satisfied.'

'Satisfied? Satisfied with what?'

'That death was from natural causes. At first I thought there had been some' – he paused – 'jiggery-pokery.'

Melford stared. His body seemed to drain itself of blood, leaving a shaking husk.

'But good God, man – '

'I might have been called in earlier, that's all.'

'But good God, man,' he said. 'Good God.'

The doctor leaned over the driving seat again and switched on the ignition. Then he turned the starting handle. It was again a preliminary turn and the engine did not fire. Then he wrenched the handle quickly and sharply on the half-turn and the engine started with a roar.

'But when – how long – ?'

He could not frame his words. Above the shaking noises of the car he uttered what sounded like a few shapeless gasps of protest. His throat was dry. He remembered how the doctor had jibed at him over the telephone: the former Mayor of Orlingford. And he hated the brown, bullet monkey-like head, the pious Scots reproaches.

He found himself seizing the lapels of the doctor's overcoat, his hands shaking.

'Couldn't you have done something? Couldn't you?'

'I think,' the doctor said, 'ye might have thought of that before.'

He suddenly put off the hand-brake, let in the clutch and drove the car away.

'I'll bid ye good day,' he called coldly in the final moment before leaving. 'Good day.'

After the car had gone it was dead silent in the yard. He stood for a moment or two alone, blind and shaking. Daylight was growing fast. Frost on roofs and branches and the palings of the garden fence seemed starker and whiter than ever. His feet were cold. Rooks in straggling black patrols flapped across the sky into a grey-blue sunrise, out towards the bare palisades of oak-woods that, within a week, would be sounding once again with the cries of hunting.

He started to go into the pub. At the kitchen door he heard the first stricken cries of Mrs Corcoran's lamentation. She lay across the table, scratching with her nails at the scrubbed deal board.

He stood as helplessly in front of her as he had stood before the doctor. His feelings were numbed and frozen out. He did not even know if she knew that he was there. Her fingers scratched in agony at the grain of the table. Her voice wailed from under the scraggy fringes of her hair.

He stumbled about the kitchen and she must have thought, hearing him suddenly, that he was about to go upstairs.

'You can't go up there!' she said. 'Not now. Not yet. Not up there. Not until she's ready. She's not ready to be seen.'

He had nothing to say. He did not want to go up. He had not the courage or the wish to go up. He knew that it was no use: that now or later, there would be no one there.

He went out and walked across the yard to the stable.

Inside, at the first touch in his nostrils of the sweet, warmish ammoniac odour of the horse, his feelings broke. He stood in the shadowiness, lacerated. He groped and found the horse, pressing his face against its neck, weeping.

'Pilfer,' he said. 'Pilfer. My God, Pilfer.'

He did not realize, either then or later, that as he stood there he was using over and over again the name of a horse he no longer possessed. He simply shut his eyes and groped against the warm smooth flesh, seeking comfort, blindly, in the dark.

When he recovered it was full daylight. He took the horse collar down from its hook and twisted it over the long chestnut neck. He found the rest of the harness and put it on. Then he led Brandy out of the stable to where, under a cart shed, his trap was housed. He backed the horse into the shafts, fixed the remaining harness-buckles into place and then remembered Blackman.

He felt that he ought to telephone Blackman. But he could not face, for a second time, the idea of going back into the house, where Mrs Corcoran wailed across the table and scratched her nails against the grain of it. He had not the courage to face it again. He could not bear the thought of the dead.

To his relief, as he climbed up into the trap seat, Brown appeared, bow-legged, smoking a pipe and with a sack over his shoulders against the chilly morning air.

'You're up betimes, sir,' Brown said.

He put his hand into his pocket, found five shillings and gave them to Brown.

'Thank you, sir,' Brown began cheerfully. 'It's a sharp 'un this morning – '

'Brown, if Mr Blackman should ring, tell him,' he said, 'that I've gone straight home. And tell Mrs Corcoran, will you, I'll be over some time?'

He drove slowly out of the yard. He knew that he would not be over. He let the horse go forward at walking pace, the reins loose on its back, up the slope and out of the hollow where, among the meadows, the pub lay.

At the top of the rise he halted the horse, sat for a moment and then looked back. The sun was shining everywhere on stiff white frost. The pub was quiet, its chimneys smokeless. Beyond it, in the meadows of which he knew the names so well, the alders and willows by the banks of the stream were like trees of salt, glistening in the sun. And beyond them, on hoar-white slopes, the shadows of oak woods fell in long blue angles down fields of winter corn.

They, he thought for a moment, were the woods he loved. That was where, with such happiness, his trout had been caught.

His tears began to fall again. Blindly he signalled the horse to go on and, driving on through white hedgerows, among frosted fields of corn, knew that he would never hunt again at Ascott St Mary.

Chapter Seven

He had neither the courage nor the wish to tell Constance what had happened. It was impossible for him to explain that, at Ascott St Mary, much more beside a girl had died. And so in his own way, much as Constance had done about the carriages at her wedding, he kept quiet about it. He did not want to make a fuss. It was not really necessary for her to know and in time it would all blow over.

But as she crossed the square, two days later, her face huddled down into the collar of her coat, she heard her name called by Agnes Twelvetree. She was not aware that it was only at the fourth time that she lifted her face and turned and recognized the figure of the solicitor's daughter, who was exercising her Labrador.

They talked for some time under the chestnut trees. Mostly Constance listened with averted face. What little she had to say was in answer to Agnes Twelvetree, who presently said:

'You were bound to hear sooner or later and I didn't want you to hear from any Tom, Dick or Harry. That's why I told you.'

'It's very kind of you, Agnes. I'm glad you told me.'

They stood talking a little longer, until Agnes Twelvetree finally said:

'I'll find out about the time. I'll let you know and then pick you up tomorrow, about an hour beforetime.'

The following afternoon the two women drove out, in Agnes Twelvetree's car, to Ascott St Mary. The day, after a third frost, was soft and squally. The woods had lost their brittle wintry touch and now smouldered with tarnished buds, glowing under spirited gusts of rain.

'No nearer than this,' Constance said. 'This is as near as I want to go.'

She halted with Agnes Twelvetree at the corner of the church-yard. A low stone wall separated the small burial ground, with its head-stones, glass domes of white artificial flowers, old rose-bushes and big English yews, from the road. The yews waved and bowed darkly in the wet wind. The path that led to the porch of the small squat-towered church was damp with rain.

At the last moment before leaving home she had gathered a bunch of snowdrops, which she wore, as always, upside down on her coat collar.

'If you'd like to hear the service, Agnes, please go,' she said. 'I'll be all right here.'

Presently Agnes Twelvetree, who hated men and never missed either a wedding or a funeral if she could help it, went into the church.

After that Constance stood alone in the road, gripping her nails into the palms of her hand. She held her head up, staring straight in front of her. Rain began to fall in quicker gusts, slanting white across the head-stones. She did not move. She had forced herself to come there and she looked strange and taut in the act of waiting.

Presently she heard the sound of singing. The afternoon was so cloudy that inside the church the lights were burning: a thin candle-glow. She stood with eyes fixed on these lights for ten minutes or so before a *cortège* appeared at the church door: a parson in surplice, three choir-boys, six other choristers, a sexton and a line of mourners in black. The coffin, of plain oak with brass handles, was covered with purple cloth. It was being wheeled to the grave on a bier.

She forced herself to watch all this. She did not take away her eyes. She stared at the lowering of the coffin and the dusting of earth on the lid. Like big magpies the parson and the chorist-ers stood above the grave.

As she watched it through drifts of gusty rain she found her emotions rising: greatly magnified, as in the case of Hyde, by the sufferings of other people. Her eyes kept dry, but inside herself a long cold pouring of grief began: at first for Melford, then for the girl who had died.

She wondered about the girl. She had not the remotest idea what the girl had looked like: dark or fair, tall or fat, young or not so young. As she watched she kept thinking of the head-stone with its inscription of Susannah Whitworth. At the same time she remembered Frankie. He had always laughed at her dreamy supposition about Susannah, dead so long ago. Now she wanted him there with her. She knew, somehow, that she could explain everything to Frankie. She could tell him things. She could make him, and no one else, understand why she had brought herself there, forced herself to watch and why she was drowned in her own cold grieving.

Yew boughs beat against each other in the rain. Surplices flapped like flags. Wreaths, mostly of white lilies, shivered about the yellow cave of clay. In a few minutes the parson was hurrying across the churchyard, leaving only a few mourners clustered in the rain.

Agnes Twelvetree came back up the church-path, the wool of her scarf beaded with rain.

'Ready?' she said. 'Shall we go?'

'Just a minute.'

She forced herself to walk up the path to the graveside. She made herself stand there for some moments, looking down at the coffin. The only other person standing there was an old shrunken little woman in a black straw hat and with a black umbrella that she could not open in the wind. She leaned on the umbrella, watching with keen old eyes while Constance un-pinned her snowdrops.

Constance held the snowdrops for a moment and then drop-ped them on the coffin. Distinctly the little woman with the umbrella, with ears as sharp as eyes, heard the word 'Susannah' and then Constance walked away.

'Phoebe,' the little woman hissed. 'Phoebe. Phoebe her name was.'

With squinting amazement she watched the figure of Con-stance as it drifted back to the road.

Agnes Twelvetree too had seen the snowdrops fall. Driving slowly away in the car, out of the village, past The George and Crown with its drawn window blinds, she said:

'I couldn't help seeing what you did, Constance. I'd have thought you loathed and hated her.'

Constance sat staring in silence at the road wet under rain.

'If I were you,' Agnes Twelvetree said, 'I know I'd have loathed and hated her.'

'I don't loath and hate anybody.' Now, inside herself, she felt grief in cold full flow. 'Only myself,' she said.

Back at Orlingford Agnes Twelvetree decided to be as cheerful, candid and brutal as possible. It seemed to her the only way of choking Constance out of a deep cold mood.

'Well, now we've got that lot over come in and have a wet of something and thaw out. And I don't know about you, but I've caught a chill on the kidneys. At least that's what it feels like – excuse me while I run.'

Over tea, preceded by a quick large whisky taken up in her bedroom, Agnes Twelvetree carved about the dining-room like a person with a ruthless and invisible knife, brutishly cutting away, as she felt, some of the nonsense of the afternoon.

'I noticed Melford wasn't there. Couldn't face it, I suppose. Just like a man.' And then went on: 'You'd have thought he might have had the guts to turn up. After all if it hadn't been for him – I suppose you think I'm a bit of a stinkpot for saying that, but I can't help it. That's how I feel. It makes me boil to think of it. Do you mind?'

'You know nobody minds what you say, Agnes. We get used to you.'

More brutally still Agnes went on:

'And there's another thing I wanted to ask you. Have you heard from that Johnson fellow? Where is he now?'

'I've never heard,' Constance said. 'I've never even written.'

'I should think not. There's a limit when it comes to lowering yourself that far. I know he ran out on you. I hear things. Candidly,' she went on, as if no hint of candour had ever encroached until that moment, 'I could never understand what you saw in him. Could never begin to understand.'

'Women always say that about each other.'

'Well, what *do* you see in him? What *was* so marvellous about it all?'

'I could talk to him.'

'You could talk to me, couldn't you?' Agnes Twelvetree said in her blustering way. 'Talk to me until the cows come home.

I've seen what you had to put up with, the way you felt about things. You could talk to me, couldn't you?'

'Not like that,' she said.

Undaunted, Agnes Twelvetree bludgeoned on to the end, until long after tea was over and she was thinking of another whisky, but the mood was never broken. Only once, just before Constance left, was it possible·to see, she thought, the hint of a breakdown, and this was when Constance said:

'I wish I'd known what she was like. Susannah, I mean.'

'Phoebe, dear, Phoebe,' Agnes Twelvetree said, 'if you're talking about the girl. Not Susannah – not unless that dark horse Melford has been keeping another one somewhere.'

'Did I say Susannah? It was a slip of the tongue,' she said.

After Constance had gone Agnes Twelvetree sat in her room for some time, helping herself to occasional whiskies and then castigating herself with growing ferocity, beating her hands:

'You had to go and blab all over the place, didn't you, you poor fool? You might have had the sense to treat her gently. Couldn't you treat her gently? Couldn't you see? Couldn't you tell what she was going through all the time?'

Under a full moon, that night, Constance lay listening to the church clock striking every quarter. She did not play the gramophone. She lay staring starkly at moonlight filtering white through the curtains, her cold grief unbroken.

Some time past midnight she got up, put on her dressing-gown and started to write a letter.

'I told myself I wouldn't write,' she wrote in it. 'I said I was too proud for that. But here I am – here it goes, I'm writing. Oh! Frankie, it isn't simply that I wish you were here. It isn't that. But before you came I had no one to talk to. The days were so empty when I had no one. But with you I could always explain things – I don't know how it was but somehow it was always like that with you – I could always explain. And now I can't explain. There isn't anyone. There's no one I can tell about this afternoon, and how I felt it was my fault about this girl of Melford's and that I felt I'd killed her, I was responsible, do you see? But if you were here I know I could tell you. I know I could. You'd let me get it off my chest and then love me and I should feel better. But now, I don't know how it is, I feel guilty – it's hard to explain on paper, but somehow I'm haunted. I'm guilty. I feel I'll never rest – it's like those days I told you about, the time I first came here.'

'Couldn't you come down?' she wrote. 'Perhaps I love you too much, but I somehow can't get on without you. I don't mean come for always. I know you have your own life and all that, but perhaps for a day? You could catch a train in the morning and then go back at night. I would meet you at the station and we could go somewhere, perhaps for tea or something, or if you didn't like the idea I'd meet you at Nenborough, at the junction, so that you needn't come all the way up here. Would you? Don't think it's silly, will you? If you couldn't spare the time I'd come to London and meet you there. You've only to tell me the day.'

It was a long letter and by the time she had finished it the clock was striking three. She addressed the envelope 'C/o Mr Leo Schofield', marking it 'Please forward'. After that she put on a skirt and jumper, with her winter coat on top, and went out to post it.

The squalls of the afternoon had blown themselves out. The streets were dry and bare. In the empty square, brilliant under moonlight, the market-cross stuck up, as it so often seemed to do, like a small ship on a shore of salty sand.

As she came back from posting her letter at the far corner of the square she stopped at the cross and, after a moment or two, sat down on the stone ledge that ran circularwise round the foot of it. She sat there staring at the moon, the chestnut trees, the little stone town hall with its flagstaff, the pleasant tall stone houses about the square. She felt alone but, for the first time that day, neither lonely nor guilty any more. The mere act of expressing her thoughts on paper to Frankie Johnson had broken through her cold hard grief until at last she felt sane and calm and no longer haunted.

'Oh! Frankie – you see what you do to me. I know I love you too much but there it is – I can't help it. I can't explain. It's one of those idiotic things you can't explain.'

Without knowing it she spoke a few of the words aloud. And from the doorway of a draper's shop a policeman on night duty, who had watched her come out of the house, cross the square and at last sit down, came forward to speak to her.

'Isn't it a bit late for you to be out, Mrs Turner?'

'Is it?' she said. 'I suppose you might say it was early too.'

'You've only got your slippers on.'

'Have I? I'm sorry,' she said.

'It's very chilly,' he said. 'If I were you I'd get back to that nice warm bed.'

She lifted her face, white, very tired, skeleton-sharp in the moonlight.

'How do you know there is a nice warm bed?'

Embarrassed, he coughed once or twice and did not answer. The note of frigid bitterness in her voice was so totally unexpected that he wished he had stayed in the shadow of the draper's door.

'I'm going now. Good night,' she said.

'Good night, madam,' he said.

He watched her cross the square, slow, vague, almost unreal in her quiet slippers, almost like a ghost under the moon.

You saw some queer things on night duty, he thought, you saw some damn queer things.

Quietly, keeping a grip on herself, trying not to fuss, telling herself that letters took time, she waited for the rest of the week for an answer to her letter. When it did not arrive she found, gradually, that her sense of guilt returned. The recollection of the girl began to haunt her again. It was all very well, she thought, to appear at funerals, to drop flowers into graves, but you couldn't escape as easily as that. It was all a deeper, darker, more complex thing.

Then on the following Sunday she sat facing Melford at midday dinner: she at one end of the thick mahogany table, he at the other, the roast-beef, the horse-radish, the mustard between. She did not eat much. Between courses he made, as he always did, little pagodas of biscuit, cheese, and celery, with crowning dabs of mustard. It was getting towards the end of the celery. The end of the celery was the end of winter-time. Between meat and sweet he complimented Mrs Butterworth on the Yorkshire pudding. Then he was silent over the apple-pie. She was silent too and did not take apple-pie. It was all as it had been before: roast-beef and horse-radish, cheese and mustard, apple-pie with cream. It was all as it would be next Sunday, all spring, all summer and for ever, unless something happened to change it all.

She watched him take a clove from his mouth, look at it and put it on the side of his plate. Then she made herself say:

'I am very sorry about the girl at Ascott. I've been wanting to say that.'

He had no idea what to say. He stared at his plate and, with utter inconsequence, thought of Blackman. He had been shooting with Blackman all the previous day. There had been an extraordinary number of birds of all kinds. He had shot a snipe, down near the osier-beds, the first snipe he had ever shot in his life. He had taken half an hour to retrieve it from the marsh and had fallen behind the other guns. Even so he had never shot so well – it had done him good, he thought, the shooting.

'You weren't at the funeral,' she said. 'I was there. I went over.'

'No?' He was shocked. 'No? You? You went? You mean you –'

Appalled, he could not go on. It was as if she had let him down in public, as if she had behaved badly on some occasion that affected his reputation. After all there was a limit, he thought.

'I can't believe it – I can't think why you –'

'I had to go,' she said. She spoke with a taut candour she might have learned from Agnes Twelvetree. 'It was my fault.'

'Your fault?'

'I can't explain. But it was my fault. That's all. It was all because of me.'

He became aware, suddenly, of his apple-pie getting cold. As he ate it he remembered that he had thought of getting the snipe set up. The snipe was a very pretty bird, rather smaller than he thought. He had tried hard for a pair all afternoon but you hardly ever got a second shot at anything so shy.

'How could it be your fault? You didn't even know the girl.'

As if, she thought, you had necessarily to know people in order to do them wrong.

'That makes it worse,' she said. 'I wish I had known her. It might have made it simpler for both of us.'

'I don't want to talk about it,' he said abruptly. 'What made you bring it up anyway? I want to forget it. It's all over. I want to forget it all.'

'Was she very young? I don't even know how old she was.'

'I don't want to talk about it,' he said.

Silently he attacked his cooling apple-pie. The edge had gone from the meal. All his enjoyment of yesterday's sport, which had helped him to forget so much, was tarnished. He finished his pie in silence and then, out of sheer habit, constructed another pagoda of cheese and mustard.

'We talk like strangers,' she said.

'It's a little late to think of that,' he said, 'isn't it?'

'I suppose so. I suppose it is. But I had to say what I've said. I had to tell you what I felt. I'm responsible – I know. I can't explain, but it's all to do with me.'

She got up from the table suddenly and went out, leaving him confused, half thinking of her, half pondering on snipe, the pleasant crisp afternoon by the osier-beds and the way it had ended with a big cold supper at Blackman's. The only way he could possibly forget was to throw himself into things like that – shooting, riding, walking, and working hard – they were his only ways of escape. And suddenly he folded his serviette, went out and found his stick and started to walk to Hardwick Spinneys, a good brisk stretch before tea-time.

In the drawing-room, alone, she sat with her legs curled under her in one of the big leather chairs. The fire had been well made up with coal and oak-logs, making the room fragrant, hot and drowsy.

After ten minutes she fell asleep. She had not slept well for four or five nights. Under the heat of the fire, exhausted, she went into a deep unconsciousness, coming out of it slowly, two hours later, to dream with cruel vividness that she was in a church, kneeling below a niche in a wall.

Before her was a figure of Christ. Its folded marble robe came down to the ankles, leaving the feet bare. She was unaware of its face. It was simply on the feet that her gaze was concentrated. She was prostrated before the feet in futile, speechless supplication. She knew also that she had been prostrated there a long time without an answer. She knew that the feet were simply of marble, dead and cold and unresponsive.

And then in one of those miraculous changes that happen in dreams she was suddenly anointing and washing the feet. They were warm. She could feel their sinewy living texture. The water with which she was washing them was warm too, warm and unctuous with lather, warm and smooth with the soap as she rubbed it in her hands.

As she washed the feet she lost all sense of futility and began to cry with joy. She heard voices and with exultation she found herself repeating what they said to her.

'How beautiful are the feet,' she said. 'How beautiful – '

She woke up. Shuddering, but with the sensation of warm and greasy soap still on her hands, she sat for a long time staring at the fire, dazed, the dream still cruelly vivid. The impact of cruelty arose from her own frustration. One moment the feet had been warm and living. The next she could not grasp them any more. The wonder of the moment when they had sprung to life under her wet hands was a miracle that had gone cold and could not be repeated.

Ten minutes later she was walking across the churchyard. Inside the church it was still quite light; there was no service that afternoon. For a time she walked quietly about the empty pews. The church at Orlingford was remarkable in having two naves of equal width, an architectural curiosity that Melford was fond of pointing out with pride to visitors who noted something unusual about the spaces of the interior without quite knowing why.

Presently she sat down, almost without knowing it, in the pew she always used on Sundays. She stared in front of her for some time and then looked up.

In a niche in the south aisle she saw the figure of Christ she had seen in her dream. She knew then that she must have looked at it scores of times, Sunday after Sunday. The same marble robe ended above the ankles, leaving the feet bare.

She got up, crossed the church and stood in front of the figure. As she stood there she remembered with overwhelming vividness the warmth of the feet in her dream, the soapiness of her hands, her crying exultation at the beauty of the feet as she anointed them in the moment before waking.

She reached up to touch the feet. Her hands remained poised in air. She realized then that she wanted the feet to be warm and living as they had been in her dream and that she was afraid to touch them now. She stood poised in this attitude for several minutes. It grew a little darker in the church and the feet were grey. She shut her eyes for a few moments, hoping to recapture the dream, and then when she opened them again she realized for the first time that there were smears of pink on the feet, giving them the appearance of living flesh.

Suddenly she was no longer afraid of touching them. She prepared to reach up, back in the suppliant attitude of her dream. She felt an exultant certainty of purpose, a return of the joy she had already experienced, and at last she touched the feet with her hands.

The feet were cold and lifeless.

'Oh! God,' she said simply. 'Oh! God. Dear Jesus. Help me. Now. Help me please.'

Some weeks later, towards the end of February, she received a letter: not from Frankie Johnson but from Miss Wilcox, her dressmaker. There had been no reply from Frankie Johnson. 'Could you please call in?' the note from Miss Wilcox said. 'Your dress is ready for the final fitting.'

Miss Wilcox had her premises in a small bow-fronted house where a silvered card hung in the front window. '*Dressmaker and Costumier*' the card said. '*Personal Satisfaction Guaranteed.*' In the room behind the card Miss Wilcox made dresses, did alterations and tailored occasional ladies' costumes, making up customers' own materials if and when required.

Miss Wilcox, in her late thirties, was delicate and spare. Her small face, with a crop of tightly crimped fair hair which she put every night into curling pins, had the pink, china-smooth attraction of a doll's. In tea-shops, on buses, or in church men were often attracted by this face, with its bright grey-violet eyes, its doll-like curls and its air of seeming younger than it was; often Miss Wilcox could feel, in her own words, that she had managed to click again. She had managed to click once with a bank-cashier named Parsons, a very small man who used a three-inch raised platform behind the bank counter so that he could see customers better and keep well up with his work. This had still prevented him from seeing, at first, what every man saw sooner or later: that Miss Wilcox had one foot shorter than another and wore a surgical boot with irons.

The devotion of the bank cashier lasted for six months, when suddenly he asked for a transfer to the south of England. The qualities that had made him a good bank cashier had kept him devoted to Miss Wilcox for longer than he really wanted. The iron foot had created, for a time, a desperate situation and he was very glad head-office had been so nice about the transfer.

For the next fifteen years Miss Wilcox went through the same process of clicking quite often. Men smiled at her, loved her face and left her suddenly abandoned. She lived mostly on bread and lard. She liked bread and lard. It was very good lard, home-made, from pure pork, and she bought it in quarter pounds from a pork-butcher by the station. She drank large quantities of tea with it and in winter it was beautiful on toast, fresh-made where she worked, before the fire.

Peering out of her window, between leaves of berried laurel, sewing and cutting with cleverness and industry, thinking of the times when she had clicked or thought she had done, Miss Wilcox gossiped relentlessly. With genteel and foolish malevolence she picked the world to pieces rather as she picked to pieces the dresses and costumes her customers brought in to be altered into this year's styles. Her voice was refined; she gossiped with nice-ness. In her keen delicate eyes everyone was nice. There was never a person who was not, according to Miss Wilcox, nice in their way.

'Do you ever hear anything of that nice family named Warner these days? They were so nice. Three girls and a boy. The father worked at the electricity. He was a sidesman for a time. Wasn't there some trouble about the eldest boy – money some-where? I thought that's what it was. I felt so sorry for them – such a nice mother and such nice girls.'

Every afternoon a woman named Parker came in to help her. Parker was a big slow cart-horse with a face like putty and dis-tinct coarse moustaches. She sewed on buttons, swept the workroom, answered the front door bell and carried coals for the fire. She brought her own tea in a paper bag, two pieces of bread-and-butter and a piece of plain cake, and she ate it furtively, her big face held close to the bag, so that she should not waste the crumbs. At five o'clock Miss Wilcox gave her the last squeezing of the tea-pot with a little milk but no sugar and Parker made strange noises as she ate her cake and bread-and-butter: pleasurable champing noises, with occasional snorts, like a horse eating oats from a nose-bag.

'See who that is, Parker. Make haste. People don't want to be kept waiting on the step all day.' Miss Wilcox bullied the big ungainly Parker as if she were a terrier yapping at a cart-horse. 'And didn't you bring the buckram? I thought I asked you to bring the buckram? Answer the door and then fetch the buckram and don't stand there gaping.'

Constance arrived on an afternoon in February when the air was like spring.

'I'm glad you called in, Mrs Turner. I was beginning to think you'd forgotten me. You'll soon be wanting to wear the dress, won't you, with the weather picking up now and spring not far away? Another few weeks and we'll begin to think about hearing the cuckoo. Now if you'll just slip off your dress please.'

Constance took off her dress. She stood rather stiffly, not speaking, in the centre of the fitting-room. Miss Wilcox unfolded the new yellow dress, shook it loosely with her hands and let it fall over Constance's head and shoulders.

'Of course the cuffs and collar are not finished. They've still got to be done. Had you made up your mind how many buttons the cuffs were to have?'

Miss Wilcox, with pins in her mouth, kneeling, jumping up, neatly hopping on her ironed-foot, put fresh tacks in the dress where needed, talking all the time.

'I thought you must have been away. I hadn't seen you for so long. But then I'm a bit out of touch with things here. I don't get out much. I daren't risk it when the weather's bad. People are always coming and going and it's months before I hear. Like those nice people who kept the wool-shop in Market Street – the two Miss Smiths. I didn't know they'd gone till yesterday.'

Presently, in her shrewd expert way, she noticed that Constance was thinner than before.

'You've lost an inch or so here, Mrs Turner. I'd better run the tape over you again I think. That's right – you used to be thirty-four there. Now you're barely thirty-two. I think I'd better bring you in a bit there – we can always let you out again later. Just relax a tiny bit – let the hands go. That's right. Just let them go – not stiff, just naturally.'

Again in her sharp quick way Miss Wilcox noticed how stiff the arms were, how quickly Constance renewed the habit of clenching her hands.

'No, altogether I haven't been out much. I used to get to the pictures once or twice a week – but now, I don't know. The last three or four times they weren't up to much. And the orchestra isn't half so good as it used to be. They haven't got the same pianist now. It was worth going for the music alone. But now he's gone and they've got that Mrs Harrison again. I never liked her. She just thumps away.'

Somewhere in the street, on a house-top, a thrush was singing. The sky was a high brilliant blue, clean of cloud and Miss Wilcox said:

'I'm glad you chose yellow. It isn't everybody's colour. It looks awful on the wrong people, but it's right on you. Do you ever go to the cinema at all?'

Arms stiff at her sides, hands clenched again without her knowing it, Constance said in a low flat voice that she never went to the cinema.

'You ought to have heard that pianist they had,' Miss Wilcox said. 'He was brilliant. He could make the piano talk. But now, as I say, he's gone and it's not the same. But from all you hear the pictures are going to be talking ones soon and then I suppose they won't need orchestras – not that they'll come to Orlingford yet awhile.'

Kneeling, hopping, cleverly concealing her ironed foot under the skirt of her dress, prattling in her genteel nice voice, pins in mouth, Miss Wilcox, probed for information and said:

'Of course things went on there, didn't they? Everybody knew that. That Miss James was in it. The girl in the cash-box. I do know that for a fact – that I do know.'

Constance listened in silence, hands clenched, staring at her own big brown eyes in the long oval fitting mirror where the reflection of Miss Wilcox hovered below the yellow dress like a hopping, creeping fly.

'One of my clients is a sister of the man at the telephone exchange – so it didn't have far to come, that I can say. It was because of that he broke it off with Miss James. It seems he found out about her and this other fellow. He put his cards on the table and had it out with her.'

In the street the thrush sang with such piercing solitary brilliance that it punctuated with excruciating sweetness the silence of the fitting-room.

'They said at one time – of course you can't be sure it's right – but they said at one time – anyway I do know she didn't work for a time. She was very poorly for a time – that I do know, but whether it was any more than that I don't know. It doesn't do to say.'

Outside, in the street, the thrush seemed to have flown some distance away, so that when the song began again it was like a thinner, higher echo.

'I know it doesn't do to jump to conclusions,' Miss Wilcox said, 'you know how people are. But you can put two and two together, can't you? You can't be sure of course – but I often wonder if that wasn't why he went away.'

With prinking malevolence Miss Wilcox hopped up from her knees, gave the yellow dress a touch or two and then looked towards the mirror at its reflection and said:

'There now. How will that do? What do you think about that?'

Staring at the reflection of her own brown still eyes, at the dress and somewhere sightlessly beyond them, Constance said:

'I've got to go now. Is that all you want for today? I've got another appointment.'

'Just the cuffs,' Miss Wilcox said. 'If I might show you the buttons for the cuffs. And how many buttons would you think, Mrs Turner? How many do you fancy?'

For some moments Constance stood erect and staring, hands stiff at her sides, bright pins sticking here and there from the hem, the bodice and the sleeves of the dress, before she said at last:

'Didn't we say three?'

'We said three but if I might make a suggestion, Mrs Turner – I think four would be nicer. Four in two pairs – a little gap between, you see – just the touch that makes all the difference. What do you think? Shall we say four?'

'I really don't know –'

'Anyway while you make up your mind I'll fetch the buttons from upstairs. They're very nice ones. I think you'll like them. They're a sort of ivy shade –'

Quick and neat on her feet, cleverly concealing the twist of her body by walking with a certain mincing motion, Miss Wilcox went upstairs. She was so excited that she deliberately spent some minutes looking for the buttons. It had been very exciting to watch the face of Mrs Turner as she talked of Frankie Johnson and Miss James. It had been very thrilling to speak of it all in that casual, off-hand way. It had been very daring to put all those questions and very queer, very baffling, never to receive even the hint of an answer.

'Mrs Turner, these are the buttons. Of course if you'd like something brighter –'

When Miss Wilcox came downstairs again the fitting-room was empty. With astonishment and annoyance she stared at it for a few moments before hopping into the back workroom to begin shouting:

'Parker! Where is Mrs Turner? Has she gone? Didn't you see her go? Didn't you hear the door?'

Parker, unpicking a costume coat, peering heavily through a pair of old steel-rimmed spectacles, had not heard. Miss Wilcox rushed to the front door, opened it and stood for some minutes peering up and down the street where the thrush was still singing in solitary brilliance, under a blue spring sky.

Then she hopped back to the workroom. There, excitedly, she began bullying the big, moustached woman who sat peering through her old steel spectacles at rows of broken stitches.

'Why on earth didn't you keep your ears open!' she said. 'Didn't you hear the door? Don't you know Mrs Turner's gone off in the dress and left her old one on the chair?'

The previous evening Frankie Johnson had come down to

Orlingford on a train that left London at five-fifteen, climbed the long woodland gradient at Black Top two hours later and reached Nenborough junction at half past seven. At the junction there was a twenty-minute wait for the branch-line train: time to get himself a cup of tea, a sandwich, and a bar of chocolate in the station buffet and to wonder, for perhaps the twentieth time that day, what the face of Lois, and afterwards that of Constance, would look like when he suddenly appeared in Orlingford again.

Surprised, he thought, both of them, very naturally surprised. Perhaps not Lois so much, because Lois was half-expecting him. Lois, after all, was more than a little responsible. Lois, in response to his letter, had telegraphed him money. Lois had written: 'I know there were a lot of hasty words on both sides and Leo admits it. And I'm afraid a lot of white lies have had to be told and all that. We all know we were wrong, but the plain fact is, Frankie, that the old job is there if and when you want it back again. I saw Watkins yesterday – in fact he was up here, asking about you and complaining about that Mrs Harrison they've got there now – horse-hoe on the keys he calls her. Another thing is that Leo is a lot better. He's under a new doctor now – Dr Thompson, a youngish man from Aberdeen – who is giving him different treatment. He's on a non-starch diet for one thing and the funny thing is that he's put on weight and hasn't anything like the old gnawing pain. I know that pain of his hardly ever let up and that's what made him so short-tempered and difficult sometimes. Anyway I think I've talked round him – of course he thinks he's talked round *me*, but that's neither here nor there – and I just wanted you to know that your old room is here if you want it. If you need the fare or anything let me know and I'll telegraph it – but come down one day anyway, just to talk about it and see how the land lies. We miss you, Frankie – it doesn't seem the same without you.'

The girl at the station buffet was pretty, wearing her hair in the new style, bobbed and dark. She too had reason for surprise. A bill for the Granada at Orlingford hung on the wall behind the big copper tea-urn and he smiled and said:

'I see you've got a bill for the Granada over at Orlingford. I hope they give you a free ticket too?'

'They do,' she said, 'but I haven't been over for a year or more. My friend goes. I never get off in time.'

'Try one evening,' he said. 'I play the piano there.'

'No?' she said. 'No? You? – never, do you?'

He smiled at the simple, widening surprise that made her eyes moisten and brighten under the clipped fringe of hair. Women, he thought, always looked more attractive, more living, when surprised. It seemed to wake them up.

'Fact,' he said.

'No?' she said. 'Well, I'd never have believed it. I must have heard you play.'

'Come over again one night,' he said. 'How about it?' He smiled and caught her eyes, holding them for a second or two. 'I'd walk back with you to the station.'

'How would you know I was there?'

'Telephone,' he said. It was amazing too how simple women were. 'I'm there at six. All you've got to do is to ring through and ask for Frankie Johnson. Come to the second house. That finishes at half past ten and you'd have plenty of time to catch the last train down.'

He flirted a little longer, leaving the buffet only when the Manchester train came in, full of boot-and-shoe travellers, tired and heavy with sample cases from journeys in the north. A few of them caught the branch-line train and played games of pontoon on outspread evening newspapers for the last seven miles. On that train, on some of the old wooden coaches, the gas-lamps were still of the old-fashioned sort, with a naked flame, and as he sat there in the murky orange light there was a smile of continuous pleasure on his face when he remembered the girl in the buffet, her moist bright eyes and how surprised she had been.

He liked surprising girls. He remembered how surprised Constance had also been, with her big astonished eyes, the evening he had first met her in the shop and played for her the piece of Brahms she could not remember. He remembered too her surprise when he had first kissed her and the still greater, awed, almost frightened surprise when he had appeared on a snowy day in the shop, to find her imprisoned in the cash-desk where Miss Mackness always worked. He had hardly ever lost, he thought, the trick of bringing that particular light to her eyes.

Later, at the Schofield shop, it was exactly as he had expected. Lois herself was so surprised that she cried a little, laughing at the same time. The long changeable winter had been terribly dismal without him. She too, between tears and laughter, had that same trembling, fluttering sort of light in her eyes that made him pleased with himself, amused and flattered because she was glad to see him back again.

'You must go and see Watkins tomorrow,' she said. 'Go and catch him before the matinée begins. That's the best time.'

He agreed that that was the best time. That would give him a chance to push his head into the pigeon-hole at the pay-box and say casually, smiling, before Miss James was aware of it:

'Anything in the balcony, miss? How about one in the back row?'

Miss James too would be surprised. Even under her rather thick powder she could not help blushing. He had even noticed sometimes that she blushed across her chest and arms. 'Tomorrow she'll have something to blush for,' he thought, 'when she sees me back again.'

In the morning he woke late, had bacon and eggs in bed, read the morning paper and came down about eleven. At half past eleven he walked to the end of the street to get a hair-cut. In London, playing at odd evening engagements, occasional dances and once or twice at suburban At Homes, he had found it an advantage to let his hair grow longer. That morning in Orlingford it seemed thick and untidy and out of place and it was refreshing to sit in the chair and let the barber shorten it to normal and afterwards give him a singe, a massage, and a shampoo.

'Anything on the hair, sir?' the barber said. 'What would you prefer?'

'Just a spot of the solid brilliantine,' he said. 'Only a spot.'

When he came out of the barber's the sun was shining. It was warm enough to walk without a coat or hat. His hair felt fresh again. He had been very particular about not having a razor on his neck and his hair now looked exceptionally shining, smart, and well-groomed because he had made the barber go over it twice again with the scissors. Now the brilliantine had solidified the fair brushed waves and he could feel the sun on it and on the fresh-exposed skin about his neck and ears. He was, as he had once told Constance, very particular about his hair.

At a quarter to two he left the Schofield shop, walked to the post office and made a telephone call to Constance. He knew that, whenever she walked in the afternoons, she left the house at two.

At the shop Miss Mackness took the call, switching it over to the house extension when he said:

'May I speak to Mrs Turner please? This is Mr Schofield.'

In the house Mrs Butterworth answered. She called him sir and said:

'Madam has gone to her dressmaker's. She said she would be back by four. Perhaps you'd like to leave a message, sir?'

'No message,' he said, 'thank you. It was only about a record.'

By the time he had finished making the call it was two o'clock. He came out of the post office and stood for a few moments in the sun. Then he remembered Watkins, the job at the cinema, and the surprisable, friendly Miss James.

The matinée began at two-fifteen. He dawdled through the town in the sun, arriving in the foyer of the cinema at twenty minutes past, just as the attendant had pulled the red chenille curtains across the doors and Miss James had begun, with smart deft fingers, to count the takings.

The next few moments were exactly as he had expected. He put his head against the pigeon-hole of the pay-box and said, as he had always meant to say, casually, with a smile:

'Anything in the balcony, miss? How about one in the back row?'

A startled and trembling Miss James went white and then, as he expected, began blushing. After a few bewildered seconds she came out of the pay-box and stood in front of him, touching his sleeves with her fingers. He looked round the foyer quickly, saw that it was empty and then swiftly tried to kiss a face that was so blank and heavy that it had the appearance of being drugged with surprise.

Whether her surprise was the surprise of pain or pleasure he never really knew. She pushed him suddenly away and said:

'Not here. Not now, Frankie. Watkins'll be here any moment and I've got the bank to do before they close. I've got so much to tell you, Frankie – so much has happened. Come back about four. I'll be alone then, Frankie.'

'Come on,' he said. He tried to kiss her again. 'Just one before I go – '

'No,' she said. 'No. Not now, Frankie. Go for a walk somewhere and come back at four. I'll kiss you then, Frankie.'

He smiled, reminding her that he would make her keep her promise, and then went out. The drugged effect of the surprise on Miss James' face was so great that she was still standing open-mouthed outside the pay-box when he came back a few moments later and said:

'Oh! I forgot. I've an errand to do for my sister. Where does that little dressmaker, Miss Wilcox, live?'

'Chichele Street.'

'Where's Chichele Street?'

'You go straight through High Street and past the Baptist Chapel. It's almost the last street before you get to the level crossing.'

He walked slowly through the town. It was not bad, he thought, the little town; it was a pleasant change after London, he thought. No: it was not at all bad: the soft stone walls, the square with the chestnut trees, the church with its slender steeple. He was not, on the whole, sorry to be back again. The sun was warm on his hair. From time to time also he seemed to see himself unexpectedly meeting Constance walking home. She, too, like Lois and Miss James, would be terribly surprised. He actually seemed to see the big dark eyes widening, as they always did, almost flowering from bud-like shyness to full aston-ished bloom.

He reached Chichele Street a little after three. He walked twice past Miss Wilcox's window containing the silver-lettered card and then slowly back again. He stood for some minutes in the sunshine. Then he decided that if after all he was going to be unlucky with Constance there was at least Miss James. He would dawdle back through the town and meet Miss James at four.

Some minutes before this Miss Wilcox saw him standing in the sunshine. In a moment of unsuppressed excitement she found herself hopping into the back workroom, hissing to Parker in a long whisper:

'That Mr Johnson is outside. The young man who plays the piano. The one who was so friendly with Mrs Turner. He must be either waiting for her or he's come back to fetch her dress and coat. Go out and ask him if that's what he wants – go on,' she bullied, 'make haste before he goes.'

When, two minutes later, he came into the front fitting-room she was sitting at a work-table, her feet out of sight. 'Shut the door, Parker,' she said. 'There's a draught through the passage.

When the door was shut she put down the dress on which she was working and looked up at Frankie Johnson. She had never seen him at such close quarters. She had not realized how pleasant, handsome and well-brushed he was. The slight twist in the smile on his face attracted and unnerved her at the same time and she stumbled over her words as she said:

'I don't know what you'll think of me, I'm sure, Mr Johnson – but I had an idea you were waiting for someone out there. It wasn't Mrs Turner, was it? – I just wondered because –'

'It was.'

'I wouldn't have thought another thing about it except that she'd gone and left her coat here. She went off all of a sudden and left it. She went without saying and I couldn't catch her. Then when I saw you – I wouldn't have given it another thought except that when she was here she was talking about you.'

He smiled. The smile was not for Miss Wilcox, nervously gathering pins from her work-table and sticking them into a brown velvet pin-cushion that sat on her desk like a mole, but at the thought that Constance had not forgotten him. He knew, suddenly, that she would be glad, as Lois and Miss James were glad, to see him back again.

But Miss Wilcox, taking the smile as being for herself, smiled back and said:

'I don't know if you will be seeing her, Mr Johnson, but perhaps you'd tell her she left the coat and dress here and that if she doesn't come back for them I'll send my woman with them at half past five.'

'Of course,' he said. 'Glad to do anything I can.'

He smiled again. She fluttered perceptibly, hastily jabbing pins into the mole-like cushion, and said, smiling again herself:

'Are you back in Orlingford for good now, Mr Johnson? Are you going to play at the pictures again?'

'I think so.'

'I'll tell you something,' she said. 'It isn't the same without you down there.'

'No?'

He moved nearer, half-leaning against the table, smoothing one hand across his hair.

'No. I used to think you were wonderful,' she said. 'It was wonderful to hear you play.'

It suddenly struck him that, sitting there, neat, delicate, fresh-looking, still in her thirties, she had something about her that was quite attractive. He smiled again, still with the unconscious disturbing little twist, and said:

'That's a nice dress you've got on if you don't mind my saying so. Did you make it?'

'Oh! I make all my things.'

'It's pretty,' he said. 'It suits you.'

She gave him a little simpering expression of thanks and began blushing a little, searching frantically for fresh pins. The dress was a neat medium blue with a wide scalloped collar in white that was not unlike the collar of a choir-boy. She knew that the collar had the double effect of making her look slightly broader and, as she hoped, much younger than she was.

Unconsciously she smoothed her hands down the front of it. The next moment he was leaning across the table, smiling again, trying to kiss her.

She had not been kissed since the bank cashier had done so several years before. Now she started to tremble convulsively, trying to avoid him by putting her face in her hands.

'Oh! no, oh! no,' she said 'Oh! no, I don't think you should. I don't think so.'

Then suddenly she went completely still. Her whole body became rigidly motionless as he put his hand on her hair, pushed back her face and kissed her without a word.

She had never been kissed like that, by anyone, even by the bank cashier, and as she struggled out of it she began saying, almost with a whimper, almost pleading, but again he could not tell whether with pleasure or pain:

'You shouldn't do that, Mr Johnson – you shouldn't do that to me – '

A moment later, not thinking, getting up quickly, forgetting her foot, she hopped up from the table. And then, before she knew exactly what she was doing, she reached up to him with her face and kissed him quickly.

'There,' she said. 'You'd better go now before – '

In the same moment he became aware of her foot. The surgical boot with its ugly iron looked big and clumsy. He forgot to smile and said:

'I must run. I've got an appointment with someone at four. See you again some day – '

On Miss Wilcox's face there was no surprise. He opened the door quickly, said 'Good afternoon' and hurried out into a street of bright spring sunshine where a thrush was singing madly in a garden elm while Miss Wilcox hopped with biting fury into the back workroom, hissing:

'Parker! Isn't it about tea-time? Haven't you got the kettle on? Do I have to wait all day?'

Chapter Eight

Constance went out of Miss Wilcox's small front fitting-room, turned right and walked through the back streets of the town. It was nearly March. In a few weeks the gardens would be bright with daffodils.

She walked slowly, looking down at her feet. The yellow dress had been pinned at the waist and bodice, on both shoulders and again at the hem. It would need another fitting, perhaps two, before Miss Wilcox would be satisfied. The pins at the edges of the bright yellow fabric shone in the sunshine. The unfinished cuffs and collar still looked as if someone had taken a pair of scissors to them and slashed them away.

In twenty minutes, walking slowly, stopping occasionally to stare at a garden, a tree or merely at the warm blue glint of slates against the sky, she reached the churchyard. She came in by the back gate, beyond the east window, walking slowly along the path and then into the church by the north door. Crocuses, all orange flat open in the sun, were blowing here and there about the grass, and for a few moments she stopped and looked at them, her arms hanging stiff at her sides.

Inside the church she sat in her usual place, staring straight before her. In her customary way she began to focus her eyes, after a few minutes, on the figure of Christ in the wall. She sat for a long time without moving, her fingers spread out stiffly, like forks, on the edge of the pew in front of her.

After a time she got up and, her hands in front of her now, walked over to the niche in the wall. She stood before it for some time, quite motionless. Then her lips began to move. She might have been offering a prayer or she might have been talking to herself, merely musing or remembering, but presently the lips were moving very fast, still without a sound, gabbling noiselessly.

Finally she took a step or two nearer the Christ figure. She lifted her stiffened hands and touched the feet. The feet were stony and cold and for the first time she made an audible thinning cry.

A few minutes later she was walking up the steps of the church tower. At first they were stone steps, on which her feet rang hollow. Later they were wooden steps and her feet were quieter. She had climbed them all with Melford, on a winter afternoon, to see a skein of animals unravelling itself across the fields and to hear him talking excitedly of a day in his boyhood when a prince rode to hounds and his father had said, 'Look, Melford, look – that's something that perhaps in all your life you'll never see again.'

Some time after half past three she had climbed outside, on to the battlements, as far as she wanted to go. For a few minutes she stood looking down on the churchyard, freshening every day with spring grass, at the many crocuses flat like stars in the sun and at the square beyond. At the corner of the square was the shop, with its pleasant well-masoned walls, its advertisements for tea and coffee and the coffee-roaster visible in the side window, and then running back from it the garden wall, with the stables, the apple-trees and the pears beyond. It was quite true, as everyone said, that the distance between the church porch and the door of the house was very short – too short, as so many people had pointed out to her, to make the use of carriages worth while.

Presently she climbed up to the parapet and stood there. For a few seconds longer she stared straight in front of her, across the square. The skirt of her dress lifted in a breath of wind, sweeping softly across her legs, rising gently like a flapping yellow flag. Almost at the same moment the clock began chiming for a quarter to four and in the shop Melford took out his watch, snapped it open and impatiently put it back again.

'Three and a half minutes slow,' he said.

A moment later she fell. From the square no one saw her fall and presently, on the grass, there was no sound except the sound of bees in crocus flowers, hardly enough to break the calm and peaceful air.

'I fail to understand it,' Melford said. 'It was never like this in my father's time.'

MORE ABOUT PENGUINS, PELICANS AND PUFFINS

For further information about books available from Penguins please write to Dept EP, Penguin Books Ltd, Harmondsworth, Middlesex UB7 0DA.

In the U.S.A.: For a complete list of books available from Penguins in the United States write to Dept DG, Penguin Books, 299 Murray Hill Parkway, East Rutherford, New Jersey 07073.

In Canada: For a complete list of books available from Penguins in Canada write to Penguin Books Canada Ltd, 2801 John Street, Markham, Ontario L3R 1B4.

In Australia: For a complete list of books available from Penguins in Australia write to the Marketing Department, Penguin Books Australia Ltd, P.O. Box 257, Ringwood, Victoria 3134.

In New Zealand: For a complete list of books available from Penguins in New Zealand write to the Marketing Department, Penguin Books (N.Z.) Ltd, Private Bag, Takapuna, Auckland 9.

In India: For a complete list of books available from Penguins in India write to Penguin Overseas Ltd, 706 Eros Apartments, 56 Nehru Place, New Delhi 110019.